THE
DREAM
STEALER

Peter Essex

Chapmans

First published in Great Britain in 1994 by Chapmans
An imprint of Orion Books Ltd
Orion House, 5 Upper St Martin's Lane,
London WC2H 9EA

A CIP catalogue record for this book is available
from the British Library

ISBN 1 85592 811 6

Typeset by Deltatype Ltd, Ellesmere Port, Cheshire
Printed in Great Britain by
Butler & Tanner Ltd, Frome and London

For Eric and Coral

Acknowledgements

I would like thank the following good people for their help and hospitality:

Sue Fellows of Ealing, and Elsewhere.

Lydia Waters, a librarian of Johannesburg.

Ros Corby of Spain.

Rowena Essex-Clark, a tireless researcher.

David Hall-Green, an artist and a friend.

Penny Hickenbotham, who typed my manuscript.

Karl Duncan of the Atlantis Bookshop, London

'While many things are too strange to be believed,
nothing is too strange to have happened.'

Thomas Hardy

THROUGH A
DARKSOME
GATE

One

At Ashburton in Devon, Jenny Oxenham broke her journey. At a roadside inn advertising real ale and home-made shepherd's pie, she stopped and lunched on exactly that. Her Citroën 2CV received petrol, pumped in by an old codger in overalls who knew about the weather, or said he did. He warned toothlessly of mists up ahead. Jenny paid him, polished her spectacles and drove on.

Onwards, through tall woodlands of oak, ash and birch, stretching with early summer nakedness into a clothy sky, while littler trees beneath them, nearer to the soil, were already spiked with green. On days like this the blunt hills were absorbed by sky, enmeshed in a backdrop of strong, dead colours that said only that summer could wait its turn. She drove diligently. No mist so far, but bundled clouds were patching her journey with rain.

Dartmoor's roads were narrow, moist black tar, edged with raw stone walls, gates and styles and cottages here and there; warty old stone and whitewash dens with squint little windows and silent-mouthed doors. For Dartmoor sees little and lives in silence.

At a packhorse bridge she drew up to give way to a baker's van, and was glad she'd halted. She switched off the engine and the whop-whop of the wipers died with it. Here there was mist, pale and moist, running with the breeze. She got out; into the west wind, too thinly clad, and with no idea why she should do so, walked several paces down the road, where she stood as though listening intently. Not a house was in sight; not a car besides her own, not a person. She took a few more paces which brought her to the river. She was entranced by the leafy boughs and the peep of birds. Tickled by smooth rock, rippled by fish, the River Dart whispered and sighed beneath the stone bridge. Jenny stood quite still, listening. She did not know when last she'd been so aware of nature's lust for reconciliation . . . And while so absorbed in sound she heard more than the silver-toned stream. She became aware of a voice, old but explicit and crackling with warning.

She ignored it, ignored the psychic instruction, got back into the Citroën and drove on. This she should not have done. To do so was a mistake. She knew it and was agitated. There was nothing clever in such defiance. Sometimes it could be argued that clairvoyance was more of a curse than a blessing; more of a loss than a gift . . . It was up to her, of course, as to whether she obeyed or not. And she would have, had the warning come four hours earlier, in London. She would have stopped then; gone back to Kensington to her maisonette and her cat, stuck her feet into slippers and read the Sunday papers. But not now. Not now that she had come so far. Jenny fumbled in her glove box for the slab of Cadbury's Fruit and Nut that she'd laid in, found it, tore the silver paper with her teeth until a ration of squares became available, then bit them into her mouth, and when that row was dissolved, another. She hardly tasted it, though.

Onwards. Climbing now onto Dartmoor's misty upland. A posted sign stood white and erect with one arm pointing to her destination: Two Bridges. It informed her that one bare mile remained to be travelled. The mist was thickening; she switched her headlights on. The radio, that had been muttering to itself all the while, produced a Beatles' tune that was a favourite of hers, so she turned up the volume. A dense cloud of Lennon and McCartney filled the interior, relaxing her. She liked these guys and the unique aural chaos they could produce. Even the Royal Philharmonic were doing Beatles' melodies these days. She gave the volume control another twirl. The future was with percussion.

> Penny Lane is in my ears
> And in my eyes
> Wet beneath the blue suburban skies

That was when she saw him.

A man in a cape; a blue cape, dark with rain. He was standing in the middle of the road facing her. His arms were raised defensively, his fingers clawed. His face, lit white by her lights, was a gape of horror. His eyes were wide, and before she struck him she thought she heard his scream.

She was screaming. Screaming as the Citröen belatedly swerved, then went on swerving as the braked wheels bit and skidded, slowing but not stopping the vehicle. The car had taken on independent life: wilful, brutal life. It rattled her, throwing her about like a dice in a cup. Pain seized her as brute matter in the form of the steering wheel came up and smacked her somewhere high, and the noise of her terrified throat increased till it rang hideously. Out of control. She. It. Everything. The car steered itself into a row of fence poles. She tried to face the wheel in the opposite direction and suddenly succeeded, banging instead into the hard stone parapet of a bridge. And that was where the Citröen, having run out of perversity and momentum, came to a halt.

Back in Penny Lane: there is a fireman with an hourglass.
And in his pocket is a portrait of the Queen.
He likes to keep his fire engine clean, it's a clean machine . . .

Jenny walked slowly, which was as quickly as she could walk, back to the point where she'd hit the man. She was crying. Unstoppable tears were welling from her eyes, and her throat was choking with sobs. Looking for the shocking evidence of death, she found the place on the tarmac that was marked by the panicked rubber of her tyres. The place where the brakes had first been stamped. No one lay there. Of course, the blow had been terrific. She recalled the moment of impact: the clawing hands, the thud of metal striking flesh. Awful. God awful. He must have been flung for yards, clean off the road. She searched the wet bracken, noticing as she did that only her left foot was shod. On the other, naked white toes squished into sodden bog flowers. A lone raven went by, cawing in the grey invisibility. A grazing animal raised its head, watched her for a moment, then lumbered off. No man was there; no stricken victim, no traumatised corpse.

She walked back along the road, towards the duck-like rear end of the Citröen with its red tail lights glowing like devil's eyes through the mist. Then the mist became rain, hard and cold on the soft warm leak of remorse on her cheeks. In the glow of her car lights a man was standing. *Standing*, thank God! Relief came with a rush; disbelief in its wake, then a residue of minor hope. But this was no accident victim standing there, that was obvious. And apart from that, he had on a grey mac and a tweed trilby.

She said straightaway; 'I hit someone. A man.'

'Good God! Where?'

She gestured: 'Over there.'

He strode off in the indicated direction, shouting over his shoulder as he went, 'I've telephoned for an ambulance. I heard the bang. Thought it best.'

'Yes,' she said, following on, glad of his long stride and tacit promise of guardianship.

'Where?'

'Here,' she said, while describing a full and bewildered circle.

'There's no one here.'

'I know.'

More men appeared; one holding a flashlight, one an umbrella about which the grey rain fussed. He gave the handle to Jenny, and closed her fingers on it. He smelled of cigarettes and booze and perennial kindness. A black Labrador joined the group. All of them, including the black dog, took their orders from the first arrived, and the search was broadened. They tramped up and down the road and in the bracken, stooping and pushing at foliage, muttering. Not a thing. It was no good. Doubting questions arose: 'A man you say?'

'Yes. A man.'

'On the road?'

'Yes . . . Strangely dressed.'

'And you definitely hit him?'

'Yes.'

'There's no one here. Dead or alive.'

'What you need is a drink and some dry clothes,' said the first arrived.

And that was the truth. Jenny nodded miserably, keen to take instructions.

'We'll have to get your car off the bridge,' he said. 'It's a danger where it is. Come on.' He led them all down the road to the desolate red glow of the Citröen, where he made a crouched inspection of the front of the car, frowning seriously as though the property were his. On straightening he said, 'Well, it looks driveable. Might have a bit of a limp. Try and drive it . . . That's if you feel up to it.'

Jenny sensed the pain of a bruise high on her forehead, but was otherwise sound. She got into the driver's seat. Previn was on the radio. An equal favourite but not now. She switched him off, started the engine and manipulated the gear lever. The Citröen reversed amid loud metallic scrapings and a tinkle of glass which suggested the loss of a headlight lens. The man rapped on her side window. She opened its hinged lower section.

'All right?' he said. 'Take her up the road fifty yards then turn sharp left. You'll see my inn straight ahead.'

It was as he said. A signboard informed her that she had arrived at The Saracen's Head, which would be, she hoped, the last, the very last astonishment of the day. For this was the very hotel at which a room was reserved for her. She had arrived without knowing it at a place she knew quite well.

To describe this hotel as 'pretty' was no real exaggeration. On better, clearer days, one might even call it 'quaint'. Then it stood up rather sharply in the valley of the West Dart river; lonely and white like a remnant tooth in an octogenarian's grin. The Saracen's Head had two bridges flanking it: one that Jenny had collided with, and one that she had not, both very old and made of Dartmoor granite. It had a girth of various well-aged trees and a green pond complete with ducks. More feathered creatures patrolled the verge, one of which barely escaped the wheels of Jenny's Citröen as it wobbled into the car park. There was something dramatically wrong with her vehicle; a buckled wheel, she feared. For some inexplicable reason the hooter of the damaged car began to sound. She thrashed the button until the sickly sound stopped. Then, as she opened the door her temporary mentor caught up with her again.

'Look.' He became sympathetically close. 'You've had a rough day. I don't know where you're headed but my guess is that this car won't get you far. You could do worse than to put up here until things are sorted out.' Raindrops were dribbling comically off his earlobes and nose. He added relevantly, 'I'm the proprietor here.'

15

'I'm booked in,' she said.

'Booked? Here? You don't say. What a coincidence.'

'Yes.'

'Of course; Mrs Oxenham.'

'Miss not Mrs,' she pointed out, thinking how trivial, as she did so.

'Well, Miss Oxenham, let's get you inside, for heaven's sake.'

With only one piece of luggage to be carried, this did not take long: a short dash towards a double doorway, then into the interior of a large and curiously olde-worlde lounge, and into a silence overlaid by the patient tick of wooden-cased station clocks hanging on every wall. Clocks of pinpoint accuracy, smugly synchronised. She liked the sound of them.

A gold-framed mirror gave her a picture of her farcically bedraggled hair; a picture further distorted by the wet lenses of her spectacles. She resisted the impulse to shake off like a dog, and noticed she was still only partially shod. They had by now reached the alcove housing the reception desk in which stood a lady with greying black hair which was enviously dry.

'Miss Oxenham has arrived,' said the proprietor. 'The key for twenty-two.'

'The key for twenty-two,' echoed the greying lady, fetching this item from a collection of many keys.

'We'll dispense with the formalities,' said the proprietor, 'until you're dry. What I'd suggest is a hot bath and a stiff drink.'

His treatment of her couldn't be faulted, yet there was something faintly odd in his behaviour. He had a practised smile, switched on or off, according to need. His hair was sandy where it was dry, dark and spiky where it was wet. His eyes were of variable blue. He had broad hands of the kind concert pianists pine for. Extensions of his mood, they now held the keys to twenty-two in a rather mistrustful way. She had paid and he would deliver them, but not willingly.

'You've been here before,' he said, as though recalling some unhappy past event. 'I never forget a name.'

'Two years ago. Same time.'

'Ah yes.' His changeable pupils darkened. 'That's right . . . This way.'

People watched her progress. People behind newspapers in

upright chairs and deep sofas. She felt the touch of their eyes. She sensed disapproval from the havens of upholstery. A portrait of HRH The Prince of Wales pitied the bedraggled new arrival. A painting, of a Georgian naval officer kitted out for sea, cut her dead. Thank God for the staircase that took her out of sight.

Room twenty-two, on the other hand, opened its arms in an attitude of welcome. A giant four-poster bed was at its heart.

'Look,' said the proprietor, 'I shouldn't worry if I were you about what happened on the moor . . . The strangely dressed man.'

'Not *worry*?'

'Let me put it this way. If you hit something it was certainly not a human being.'

'I saw a human being.'

'An owl perhaps, that flew into your windscreen . . . An unlucky badger on his way across the road.'

'I don't think so.'

'In this mist . . . '

'It was a man.'

'I know that you didn't hit a man. If you had then there would have been a dent in the front of your car. A rather large and very obvious dent. Your car has no more than a scraped mudguard, scraped when you ran into the bridge. Also, people struck by motor cars don't tend to wander off under their own steam. They lie around, groaning, or not groaning, depending. Take it from me, you're in the clear.'

'I'd prefer official confirmation of that.'

'Of course you would. What I'll do is I'll phone the police at Exeter, and tell them what you told me. The Chief Super is an old chum of mine. We were in the Met together . . . before I became an inn keeper.'

'You were a bobby?' she said with a stab at friendly sarcasm. 'Now this.'

'Yes, quite a letdown, still . . . '

'You've been very helpful. Thank you.'

'Once a bobby . . .'

'I'm sorry. I don't even know your name.'

'Tremayne. James Tremayne.'

She took his hand and was numbed by a voltage of

antagonism. He hurt her with icy distrust, forcing her to break off and step back. And yet nothing but sincerity was apparent in the tone of his next words: 'I hope I've put your mind at rest.'

The man was a paradox perhaps even to himself, needing to be aware of his own mind where she was concerned. She didn't mind ambiguity just as long as it wasn't directed at her. Then it was an intolerable vice. She mentally manhandled Tremayne from her room, and his suave, professional smile came and went as he departed.

The conflict, if not resolved, diminished temporarily as she reviewed her own condition. While fingering a painful lump at her hairline she walked into the centre of the room. This wasn't the room she'd occupied on her previous visit. She had seen it before – but only in passing while a chambermaid had been servicing it – and had loved it at once, with its great Jacobean four-poster and genteel chintz. The carpet nursed her cold feet in its pile as she went to the window, reached up and drew floral curtains against Dartmoor's grey obscurity. This done, she undressed, then went to the bathroom and opened the taps.

Jenny studied what emerged from the drowned voile of her dress in a cheval mirror. She was on good terms with her body. At the age of thirty-two it looked, and felt, as it had a full decade earlier. It wasn't athletic; it wasn't the sort of shape that won through to the semi-finals at Wimbledon. But it had what it takes to be noticed – by men.

It was, however, to her face that one's gaze was quickly drawn; to lips that were dimpled at the corners, fully budded in the middle and the colour of bottled cherries; to cheeks that were lit to a nice glow, and touched by sorrel-brown hair that fell in twists of uncertain length; to a face that hovered delicately between numerous expressions, all with an aptitude for discovery. Now she raised both arms and pressed back the border of hair at her temples to examine the bruise there. It didn't seem large or likely to be troublesome. She let her hair drop back into place, then turned off the taps.

The bath, big and brass-tapped, was now full. She added to the steaming water a pinch of salt, one drop of essence of cinnamon, of cloves and camphor, two drops of arnica (the first to preserve, the last to heal), then took off her spectacles and lowered herself into the tub. It was wonderfully good. It enclosed her warmly, heightening her senses. She thought about James Tremayne, letting the enigma of him trickle into her mind until there was enough of it to make some sense of. Strange Mr Tremayne. It came to her that his attitude, his unsettling ambiguity was the product of fear. The man was scared of her. He mustrusted her, and every gesture and look he'd offered bore out that diagnosis. She didn't know why that should be so, not exactly, but several possibilities existed, all of which had to do with her reason for being there. And the more she thought about it, the more it connected. It had to have something to do with that – with the haunting. The haunting of Wistman's Wood.

Wistman's Wood wasn't far from there; a mile, if that, over the moor; an easy stroll along a sandy cattle track, and there it was. A wild, weird grove of stunted oaks, so vastly ancient that Bad King John might have patronised their shade. He'd certainly known of their existence and forbade their destruction, for there exists in Whitehall a dusty piece of parchment on which is written that decree . . . John couldn't have known of the ghost of Rory Tremayne, though. Rory Tremayne had come to Wistman's Wood much later, in Georgian times. Rory Tremayne, the ancestor of James, her host, her enigmatic host . . . Yes, that was it: the reason for James Tremayne's strained behaviour. Of course! Suddenly surrounded by truth she wondered how she ever could have missed it. The fear in James Tremayne was the fear that she might disclose what he wanted hidden, for it was not a man that she had struck with her car, but a ghost. The ghost of Wistman's Wood . . . Rory Tremayne. Rory Tremayne, as portrayed in seafaring cape on the wall of the hotel lounge.

She had met the ghost she had intended to meet, and whom she had come all that way for, and she'd blown it, fluffed it. No second opportunity would be granted. In this pursuit they never were. Jenny thrashed her legs in the water, and groaned.

But hold on.

There was a factor here that hadn't been properly considered, and it was this: though the mist had obscured the ghost from her, it certainly would not have hidden her from it, for the state of optics between living and dead was not comparable. This being so, there was room for a bit more optimism. If, as it now seemed, the first encounter, as bruising as it was, had been intended, then a second encounter might well be part of the plan.

Reflecting on this possibility, Jenny took time to soap her body with a tablet of Pears, leaving no part untouched, noticing as she did a lightening of the room as if signalling the re-arrival of sun over the dark splotch of England's south. And this was so. The coverlet of clouds was dragged off the moors to be replaced by butterflies and skimming swallows and the odours and pomp of the flowers of spring.

Cleaned, dressed and re-energised by a sense of things to do, Jenny left her room. She stood for a moment in the small portico before the hotel, then stepped out. She walked past the duck pond and dripping trees towards the bridge that she had clipped with her car fender, then onto the road. The slate roof of a cottage shone wetly like the scales of a fish. Trout Cottage; it was aptly named. It had a cattle gate at its rear that was signposted 'Wistman's Wood'. She walked slowly up the slope towards the gate, opened it and passed onto a sandy track upon which several rough-coated cattle stood waiting with the infinite patience of their breed. She passed them, through the indolent smell of warm dung, and walked on, pensively, uncertain of where she was going. Wistman's Wood was not on her mind at that juncture, nor her intended destination . . . What she desired, although she didn't know it until she had obtained it, was a view of the surrounding moorlands. The route she took was not along any path, but over the rough grass of a hillock. It wasn't the largest hillock thereabouts but from its minor summit she could see down to the road and along it. She could see the hotel, its dual chimneys feathered by trickles of smoke. She was conscious of the feel of the wind. This wind of Devon was unlike the other winds of Britain. It empowered. It blew in a sultry, feminine way, giving, not taking . . . She could also see the owner of the hotel.

James Tremayne, in shirtsleeves and cords was on horseback. The man was seated well on a tall and undoubtably aristocratic chestnut; an arch-necked, flag-tailed beast that looked irrepressibly and impishly loaded with vigour, but was nevertheless walking most obediently beneath its rider. Another horseman was with him, not as well mounted as Tremayne, and a pace or two to his rear. Jenny placed him as a policeman, she did not know why – the Chief Super from Exeter – the old chum who would officially inform her that no charge of manslaughter was being considered.

Neither horseman saw her. They were in truth quite dutifully studying the heather and gorse along the road. She could faintly hear their voices and occasionally a jerk of laughter, and the clip of horseshoes. They came abreast of each other, pausing at the spot where the skid marks showed her moment of panic, then walked unexcitedly on. Jenny squatted and watched. Since girlhood she had loved to spy on people – especially men. They were so different when unaware of being spied on. Their entire metabolisms slowed like bears in a winter landscape, to an amiable, quiescent level. Like the friends in the valley, relaxed and easy. Tremayne looked comfortable, even handsome, with those square strong hands resting nicely on his horse's shoulders, as though he really liked the animal.

It was the horse, the chestnut, that sensed the watcher on the hill. Twitching its ears, it turned its big head curiously towards her and snorted. Tremayne did not immediately follow the gaze of his horse, but when he did he saw her at once. She stood up and waved tentatively.

He caustically tweaked the tip of his cap. Yes, there was something about this man that suggested little tolerance for the guest in twenty-two. She hoped that would change: hope, based on the intuition that he would see the need for change.

Something was going to happen, and soon. Something that would shake James Tremayne to the core. This she was clearly told. What this something was, lay unrevealed. This was the annoying part about clairvoyance – its inrush of radiant incompleteness, its single gasp momentum – there, then gone, in a heartbeat. She knew that some event soon to take place would affect Tremayne profoundly. It would have much to do with her. That was all. She had learned over the years how to make the most of these communications, however; how to judge and interpret these fantastic bursts of vision. She'd had a lot of practice.

In her youth, at the age of seven and a half, while skating with friends on a pond not quite frozen over, young Jenny had broken through, gone under and 'drowned'. Her father, a senior pathologist, had himself confirmed the death. A certificate had been signed, a funeral date set. Telegrams had been sent out to advise the family of their tragic loss . . . Wasted effort. After thirty-six hours of pulseless 'sleep' Jenny had 'awoken' and demanded in a loud voice to be fed. And was fed.

The 'awakening' was not fêted. The family was overjoyed, and equally over-awed. The medical fraternity (other than for those directly involved) was disturbed, shaken and, on the whole, slightly disenchanted with Dr Oxenham. The term 'miraculous' was attached to the event, for miracles need have no medical antecedent. Oxenham gave up his practice. As for Jenny . . .

Had one not known her well before the thirty-six-hour death, one mightn't have noticed the change. She'd always been 'different'. A dreamer; a starer into unoccupied spaces as if at some vast arena of fascinating activity; a compelling enquirer; an effortless winner of school prizes for Grammar and Art . . . The change was subtle, yet to those who were close to her, profound. Something was going on beneath the surface, something quite out of the ordinary.

The new Jenny was less quick to laugh, more prone to concentrated bouts of brooding silence. She had become less overtly quizzical and insistent on explanations from those around her. At least, from those around her who were mutually visible to each other. There were others: Watchers. Invisible Watchers.

This was her secret. This was what had happened. She had returned from the thirty-six-hour death in the company of others. She had always suspected their presence. Now, she knew they were there: the Watchers. Now she could see them, and they her. They were protective. Jenny was advised about many things that were going to happen to her, before they happened, in time to organise a defence, if defence was required. She always knew what to expect; not in every detail, but with sufficient accuracy to permit the remainder of her years of youth to come and go unscathed.

At nineteen, after the death of both parents in a car crash (which she had warned them how to avoid) she left home to study Psychology at Oxford. At twenty-six she was invited to Zürich by the Karl Jung Institute, to assist in the furtherance of the late master's work – a (pseudo-cabalistic) look at Jung's concept of Synchronicity. A tonic period in her life. A period of discovery of self; of exploration of the irrational richness of life and the astonishing facets of soul. Jung as never before. By then she was totally converted to the late professor's work in thought and deed. They'd had a lot in common: friends on the other side, for one thing, and a shared conviction that spirits had an independent existence, and owned a translatable language.

This then was the woman on the hill; the woman smiling pensively, almost wistfully, in the direction of the horsemen below. She felt a twinge of responsibility towards James Tremayne. She felt like calling out: 'Hey! Be careful.' But of course didn't. For dancing on the edges of her smile was a wrinkle of impish expectancy. Poor Mr Tremayne, he wouldn't know what had hit him.

Jenny stretched her arms, indeed her entire torso, skywards in a lingering gesture that might have appeared deliberately worshipful but for the sound of a short, self-gratified giggle, midway. Clairvoyance could be a drag, but this wasn't necessarily the case. It had its lighter side. It could even be downright fun.

Two

Chief Superintendent Walter Hughes sneezed, once, twice, blew into a white handkerchief and said through chronically inflamed sinuses, 'Shit.'

'*Gesundheit!*' said James Tremayne. 'You should have something done about that.'

'I am doing something about it. That's why I'm here. I am allergic to police work, Jim. That is why I have temporarily shed my uniform, and why I'm out riding on the moors with you. For my health.'

'Well, do you think she hit someone before hitting the bridge, or not?'

'The bloody woman fell asleep at the wheel, Jim. That's what I think. Nothing unusual about that. In the split instant of unconsciousness, she imagined it. Dreamed it, then awoke in a panic and stamped on her brakes. It's the commonest cause of accident in the world.'

'That's what I thought too.'

'In the absence of any evidence to the contrary there's no reason to believe otherwise. Now if we could leave it at that, I'm sure that my overall condition will improve.' Wally Hughes passed a final glance over his shoulder towards the watcher on the hill. 'Secretive little wench, isn't she. She wouldn't have shown herself if your chestnut hadn't flushed her out. Nice tits, mind you . . . I've always thought you made a good career move, Jim. All that totty hanging around just begging to be goosed by the boss man.'

'Never screw the paying guests, Hughey. That's rule number two.'

'What is rule number one?'

'Never break rule number two.'

24

'And rule number three?'

'Rule number three is in the event of having broken rule number one, and is never to do it again.'

'Does rule four apply to those who have done it again?'

'Precisely. As does five.'

'Too strict for me, Jimbo. Too stringent a doctrine by far. Still, I can see the point of such a puritanical code. It's a question of financial ethics. Some might think they've done you a favour and expect something off on the bill.'

At the bridge they turned off the road. James's chestnut just loved to be off-road in the thick grass and bracken. She'd once been on the track, a sprinter, and had turned so sour and rough that she'd been ruled off. But the thick grass, and the bursts of speed up to the jumps, and to dirty her white stockings up to the knee, she adored. She'd never needed schooling over the jumps; it was in her blood. She just stood back and flew. And she had the courage to get up after a fall, and go for the next jump and not flinch.

They rode cross-country at a pace that threw up the peat in chunks, then up a steep bridle path, their mounts drawing great heaving breaths for the savage straight gallop to the tors of Tairn Fort and Steven's Grave; cauldrons of Saxon magic, places of genius.

To love a place one must truly see it and know its secrets. James Tremayne knew Dartmoor, and loved it. He loved its Domesday bleakness and dearth of humans, and tor-crested hills and breakneck valleys. Its scowling schisms between sun and mist. It was amity and it was conflict – a maverick territory. The Devil might comfortably have lived there had God not arrived first. The Tremaynes of Devon had also existed there for two centuries and a fraction.

The men on horseback turned around at Steven's Grave and rode home at a walk. James thought about the woman in twenty-two; and the closer he came to her the more he thought. She irritated him. There was something about her that got to him like burr. It wasn't merely the result of the overripe inaccessibility of the woman either. He'd joked about that, but, God knows, the forbidden orchard syndrome was a problem, as Wally Hughes had so truthfully observed. The hotel could at times become quite tensely charged with itinerant women whose very walk was invitational; sweetly cheeky female sales reps from London and Bristol, southward bound without a care or a scruple. He was no monk. But it wasn't that. It wasn't leaking testicular hormones that were bothering him. Bothering him was the question: what did the woman want? Or more to the point, what did she want that she shouldn't be allowed to have, and should be prevented from having?

The fact that he was Devon-born predisposed him to being more than averagely distrustful of the motives of the human race, but genetics alone couldn't account for the niggling suspicions of what she'd brought in with her baggage. It had to be that she had come for the haunting, what else? What other explanation could there be to account for her constant return to The Saracen's Head? Though he had only been there for two years, James had records that told of prior visits, all coinciding with this date.

He considered that remarkable fact. Remarkable in the sense that the haunting of Wistman's Wood was a most significant date on his calendar, too. For the belief (firmly held by the local community) was that it was the terror-stricken ghost of none other than Lieutenant Rory Tremayne, a seafaring ancestor of his, who came to the Woods year after year to re-enact the tableau of his own violent death. There was in the whole of Devon no ghost of greater punctuality. Now it was one thing for the local community to take an interest in the ectoplasm of the area. They were to a man, in any case so piskie-haunted and fey, and so fond of ale and cider that ghost-seeing in the mists was no exceptional event. They saw these things almost every day, blinked and burped, then walked on home, and no harm done.

But this other thing; this persistent investigation, this audit of his family history, ranked as interference, bloody unwelcome interference. He couldn't see the point. Was it necessary to look into these quaint old superstitions in order to debunk them and spoil some old codger's brush with his imagination? What was more, Rory Tremayne had lived and died quite tragically and should now be left to moulder and rest, in peace. Death was all about peace, not spiritual badgering. The woman was a menace, a pain in the butt. He did not want her there. And he did not know what to do about her being there.

And there she was. Kneeling forward at the duck pond,

26

feeding breadcrumbs saved from breakfast to a quacking, feathered armada. Bent forward and showing her ample décolletage to best advantage was the woman from twenty-two. She turned towards the horsemen with a smile that the most callow of men would have had to recognise as friendly.

They rode to the stables. The horse stalls were perhaps the oldest part of the hotel. Fire had taken the main buildings in 1760 but the outbuildings hadn't burned. They were stone with clay floors, and the air smelled of good, green cut hay. By the time the horses were cared for the sky was darkening. Wally Hughes went off to his room, whistling. James went to his suite, in silence, noting as he did that Jenny Oxenham was no longer at the pond.

She had infiltrated the guest lounge by the time he came down and was sipping from a glass that he presumed contained gin and tonic. He dispensed a nod, then passed into the dining room, where he did an inspection of the tables, adjusted the attitude of the wine waiter by threatening to sack him summarily if he took as much as one more sip from the Chablis stock, did a brief pre-emptive tour of the kitchen, pausing as he did to admire the gaping seventeenth-century cooking fireplace that had been discovered during recent plumbing renovations, and which he was slowly refurnishing with authentic utensils, then came back into the lounge.

She was still there, still sipping. It was midweek, so, but for the local regulars who were steadily putting it back in the tap-room, trade was slack. Hughes was still in his room. The only other guests, a party of incredibly fossilised archaeology seniors from London, were elsewhere. So she was alone. He could, by exercising gross impoliteness, have ignored that fact and got on with his work. He hesitated. And that cost him the initiative.

She said, 'Hello, Mr Tremayne.'

'Hello, Miss Oxenham. Everything all right?'

'Fine. Wonderful. That room – ' The unended sentence blossomed into a gesture of pleasure.

'Like it?'

'It's magnificent. That Jacobean four-poster . . . '

'It's as old as the inn. Just say the word if there's anything we can do to make your stay more comfortable.'

One had to admit that she had good breasts, and good hips,

27

too. Essential components in the formation of feminine beauty. She said on a smile, 'In fact there is something . . . Won't you sit down for a moment? Could I buy you a drink? That is, if you have the time.'

While managing to appear indispensably needed elsewhere, he sat. The chair was not a favourite of his, in that the state of its springing was a dreary reminder of things to be done. He sank into it and closed his hands over his knees. 'I won't have one right now,' he said with a glance at his wristwatch.

'I haven't even had the chance to thank you for being so kind this afternoon. Thank you, Mr Tremayne.' She took a small sip from her glass. 'Was that the policeman you were telling me about, the man you were riding with? Is he your friend from Exeter?'

'Good heavens. How perceptive of you. Yes, that was Chief Superintendent Hughes . . . I'm pleased to tell you that he doesn't think you hit anyone, either . . . He thinks you fell asleep.'

'And dreamed it?'

'And dreamed it,' Tremayne confirmed.

'It must look like that I suppose.'

'Oh, absolutely.'

'And is that what you think, too?'

'It's the only explanation.'

'Is it?' She peered at him over the rim of her glass. 'You know, Mr Tremayne, you could be right. But if you are it would be the strangest coincidence.' She said, as though not expecting an answer, 'Do you know why I come here every year?'

'How could I?'

'It must be obvious.'

'I presume you like the place.'

'Oh, I do.'

'There you are then.' He began to rise. 'Don't think me rude, but – '

'Please stay,' she said with such earnestness that he did. He sank back and she went on, 'Look, what I really wanted to say to you was this: you have no cause to be apprehensive about me.'

He implied by expression that this admission was absurd, but said nothing. The tick of many clocks gave a message of passing time.

'Mr Tremayne,' she said as though hurt by the silence, 'I know how bizarre what I told you sounds, but that is what I felt I should say to you, you understand. I felt it was important.'

'Well, thank you for your frankness.' It sounded more caustic than intended. 'Yes indeed. Very good of you.'

'I wanted to be honest with you.'

'Yes. Thanks. And now I'm intrigued. So why don't you admit why you *do* come here year after year?' He sensed he had frustrated her, which didn't displease him. He leaned forward, looking professionally attentive, saying, 'Huh?'

She had small, regular teeth which she raked over her lower lip while at the same time admitting a subliminal sigh. 'All right,' she said, 'I will.' And to her credit she did.

She had come for the haunting at Wistman's Wood. She was, and had been for many years, an active member of the Society for Psychical Research, and had on behalf of the SPR done investigative work at many of the haunted estates in Britain; estates and castles and supernaturally charged mounds and ley lines. Impressive stuff. Good credentials, he supposed. Ghosts, however, were her main line of work. Corby Castle, Widecombe-in-the-Moor (he'd heard of the ghost of Marcy Jay at nearby Widecombe), Daneway House . . . The list went on. But no ghost beckoned to her as did that of Rory Tremayne. Wistman's Wood was her lodestar; her Mecca and towering frustration. It had, she confessed, become more than it should.

'It draws me, Mr Tremayne, in a way that is hard to describe. It's as though there were some buried information in me, hinted at but not disclosed, that brings me back constantly. I'm Devon-born, like yourself, and from the South Hams, so that partially explains my interest, but only partially. I know very little about Rory Tremayne, and yet I sense an affinity towards him that feels almost ancestral.'

'So you come every year?'

'Yes.'

'And have you ever seen or made contact with this ghost?'

'I'm not sure.'

'Not sure? Surely you either see or you don't see? It's there or it's not. It is or it isn't. Existence has rules, Miss Oxenham, which if not fulfilled prove nonexistence.'

'I saw a ghost today.'

The absolute simplicity, the stunning, unequivocal way of it threw him: *I saw a ghost today*. Yes, he believed she had. And the belief of it thrilled him and sent a shiver upwards into the nape of his neck where it lingered. His distrust of her waned. Conversely he was more annoyed with her than ever, and said coldly, 'Describe what you saw.'

'It was brief, Mr Tremayne; over in an instant.'

'Describe that instant, then.'

'It was the cause of my accident . . .'

'Jesus!'

'His face was stark and his eyes looked as terrified as they must have at his moment of death. He wore a sort of cloak. I can't describe what I saw better than that. But I can recall the features of the face. I'd seen them before, you see, so recognition was immediate. The features, Mr Tremayne, were those of the man in the painting you can see from where you sit. The naval officer in the frock-coat and three-corner hat.'

'I don't believe you,' he said flatly.

'It's the truth . . . That painting is of Rory Tremayne, isn't it? Your great-great-grandfather, Rory Tremayne, killed at Wistman's Wood one hundred and thirty years ago today, while trying to escape from Dartmoor Prison? He's the man in the painting, isn't he?'

He was not consciously aware of the effort of confession. 'Yes.' The word simply made itself known.

Funny how a single word can bring down an entire wall of fixed and cemented attitudes. He wanted to rebut his statement the moment it was out. But that would have been pointless. And now the only person he was annoyed with was himself.

She had stood up and walked towards the painting, and he'd followed.

'It was done at the time when he was a lieutenant in the Royal Navy, in command of the brigantine *Penzance*,' he said. 'Yes, that's Rory Tremayne.'

'You have his eyes, you know.'

'The painting was done at his wife's insistence, so that she could have something of him while he was at sea.'

James Tremayne had never stood before or stared as intently at the portrait of his great-great-grandfather as he did then – nor subsequently been so critically inspected in return. He'd never really cared for the painting, but had hung it there out of some latent sense of respect, and because of the mood of salty antiqueness it lent to that sector of wall. Even so, his ancestor had contrived to be the unassimilated piece of decoration; as one who has distaste for his immediate surroundings but can do nothing to alter them and had to stay. But James saw now that what he'd perceived as distaste was not that, but was the tweaked-down-at-the-corners look he sometimes saw reflected in his own small mirror. A grin that was struggling against great odds to make it to the surface.

The sound of a gong shimmered down the hall. A swell of laughter came from somewhere, and the festive pop of a cork.

James took a deep and restorative breath. 'You'll have to excuse me now,' he said. 'Lots of things to do, as you can imagine.' His innkeeper's instinct took over. 'If you're dining in then I thoroughly recommend the table d'hôte. Our chef's a genius with cidered pork.'

She regarded him with the guiltless, silent stare that looks so innocent but penetrates like a spike.

'And may I offer one last bit of advice, Miss Oxenham? Don't go to Wistman's Wood tonight.'

'I don't intend to.'

'It's wet underfoot. It's treacherously slippery along the pathway after rain.'

'I'll bear that in mind. I am eating in.'

'*That*,' he said, 'you won't regret.'

'And I have one last question for you . . . What *is* it that you're so afraid of?'

'That's easy to answer,' he said, for the first time committing himself to freely given truth. 'What I fear is the death of common sense.'

The chef *was* a genius. The cidered pork came in a ceramic dish, piping hot. It was creamy and laden with good chunky bits of meat and all sorts of other succulent stuff. It was, in a word, irresistible. Jenny, the owner of Rubenesque thighs (despite fresh air and team games) since prep school days, saw no purpose in sudden self-denial, and ate the lot. The dining room was low-ceilinged, and despite every window being open, was warm enough to cause thirst. She drank a bottle of mellow

Rhine Riesling while her thoughts wandered freely amongst the events of the day. There was no call to do anything now but at a leisurely pace. In fact there was nothing to be done at all but have dinner and then to surrender to the Jacobean four- poster. She made a foray to the cold table and came back with baked apple and clotted cream. That rounded it off. Then a cup of coffee, a stroll in the grounds, a cigarette. No further reason to stay awake presented, so she went to her room.

The day was still light, but had acquired the torpid appearance that signals its end. A breeze was licking the curtain edges into motion, playing a kittenish game with the fabric. A breeze with healing qualities. It pleased her to undress and nudely to receive its feather touch, and be engaged in its terrestrial doings. She imagined a silent affinity between it and her. And for that reason she declined to clothe or cover herself when she lay down. The four-poster indulged her. It passively accompanied her to the other side of consciousness where she was attracted by a powerful and manipulative dream.

She went to stand before the cheval mirror of her room, where she was met by a reflection, not of herself but an imitator. The woman staring back had the features and caramel beauty of a mulatto, a stunning raven-haired half-caste, copying her every movement. She felt that it was intended that she should be absorbed by this body. It was right that this duality should exist. Incredibly energised and graceful, she began to dance. There was no movement that she was incapable of, no step that she could not instantly master, so that though the dance was foreign, intricate and primitive she did it with ease. There was a throb of hand-beaten drums, a fusion of high and low sounds; a drub and patter and whirr of infective vitality that ran into her, overtook and possessed her in a prolonged, convulsive thrill. It was in her belly and in her hips, in her legs and arms – an entanglement of sound, irresistibly voluptuous. Yet something caused her to stop . . . A noise. A new and different sound had arrived, unrhythmic yet seemingly part of it all; a persistent scratch, scratch, scratch, as though caused by someone on the other side of her door wishing to gain entry. She opened it and saw a creature, scarcely manlike, yet failing to meet any other description. It was masculine, small, yet not lacking in perceived stature. His head was comparatively big – as oversized as a newborn infant's, yet marked by ages of experience. His eyes were slitted, his eyebrows arched, stretched upwards as one who is attempting to awake from disturbed sleep. His legs were stunted and bowed, and upon his chest was carved a design. Carved, yes, for the little fellow was undoubtedly made of wood. He waddled stiffly into the room, noticing her in a cursory way as he did. He stretched his joints, as best wooden joints may be stretched, then seemed to come fully awake. Black, beady eyes took in her fleshy nakedness, discomforting her. His voice was querulous. 'What took you so long?'

She did not know what had taken her so long, yet privately agreed that arrival at this juncture had been slow. It didn't seem wise to admit this though, not at this stage.

He said in an intimidating way, 'You're not what I expected.'

Though she had expected nothing she said, 'And neither are you.'

'Have you danced?'

She had, she said. She would have liked to repeat that amazing experience, but the drumbeat had ceased.

'Come, then,' he said. He stepped off jerkily in the direction of the cheval looking glass, and without meeting any impediment stepped over its rim. It was as though the glass had dissolved into pure water. He melded into it – became part of it – accepted as though in water. There were ripples that obscured him for a moment, then he materialised again as something seen at the bottom of a shallow pond. He indicated that she should follow, and unhesitatingly she did.

She found herself not in a pond, but in a room, an attic, quite alone. The weird homunculus seemed to have vanished, yet she could sense that he was not far away, and that he was watching her intently. The aperture through which she had arrived had converted into a low door, locked and keyless. There was one small dormer window, curtained with cobwebs so copious and cohesive as to ensnare the very moon. The window latch was jammed. She tried to undo it, but couldn't; then tried with greater force as uneasiness grew. It was hopelessly stuck. She searched the room, hoping to discover some other potential way out. None was visible. And the uneasiness became a thudding of her heart not unlike the drums that had recently entranced her. It seemed unreasonable to be so intimidated, for

33

even though she could not escape from the place, it did not seem to contain any objects of danger. In fact the attic was bare but for a single old-fashioned brass-bound sea chest left to moulder in a corner. She approached it. Its top was cambered. Its lock was huge, and a key protruded from it. A voice she recognised as belonging to the wooden man came faintly, yet commandingly, from its interior, 'Open up.'

'No,' she said, surprisingly loudly.

'But why not?'

Because the fear was no longer contained by the walls of her veins, but had engulfed her and was howling about her ears.

'You've always sought proof,' said the voice from the trunk. 'You've cringed around on the out-walls of it like a kicked dog, wanting to be let in yet too cowed to come when called. Now I tell you, "Come in." You won't be harmed . . . You'll never get another chance to discover the amazements I have on offer. If you want it, open up.'

The appeal was strong, the tone reassuring. She reached towards the lock, then recoiled. 'I daren't.'

'What nonsense. What are you afraid of?'

'A force too strong for me to control. A dreadful destination.'

'Yes, that is a worry . . . But don't you want to know what's inside?'

'Very much.'

'There's only one way to find out.'

'Who are you?'

'I don't have a name, only a purpose. Open up. You won't regret it. I'll change your life.'

Tensely, she took hold of the key.

'Turn it!' commanded the voice.

She squeezed and applied pressure. It revolved, issuing several faint squeaks and one conclusive click. It was unlocked.

'Open the lid.'

She almost didn't. The command, though firm, was all but overridden by the return of absolute fear. Arising from the chest were waves of virulent hostility so powerful as to beat the air about her into pandemonium. Something extraordinary and awful was depending on her to proceed. This she should not do, but seemed to lack the ability to prevent. It was as though

34

her fingers had an intelligence of their own and were capable of treachery. The lid was raised, the interior exposed. She had the sensation of looking into a deep and unfilled grave.

There lay the wooden sculpture, unmoving but for the eyes which glinted and slid over her hungrily. There was a half-bound ledger, and an old duelling pistol. These three things lay on naked plank. She saw them all as clearly as if a powerful shaft of light was shining into the interior. Then the wooden man sprang at her. She had the sensation of having been struck a great blow to the temple, and of falling backwards, bleeding, stunned.

She awoke with a gasp, and an echo of demonic laughter in her ears. She was on the floor, trembling with fright.

From midnight to dawn she stayed awake, held from sleep by a turbulence of confusing images and questions. Clearly the dream she had just experienced was no ordinary picture writing by her own subconscious. The form and impact and amplification of imagery was more than her mental equipment was capable of. She had been invaded telepathically, but by whom, or by what? And to what purpose? She could find no starting point from which to begin to explore these questions. A mulatto woman; a sense of primitive dance knowledge; a wooden homunculus with magical ability; a mirror as permeable as water; a sea chest in an attic of terror; a book and a pistol. The struggle to get onto terms with these images went on into the first rays of sun, and was undiminished at breakfast.

There, over coffee, in jolt of intuition, she glanced up to find that she was being studied by her host, and in a receptive way. There was at once that glorious tingle of creative awakening that precedes revelation. That here was the repository of all the required answers seemed suddenly to have become obvious. Before the man could glance away she'd fixed him with a smile that was intended to exert traction, and did. Tremayne came to her table on a waft of grilled bacon and haddock.

'I trust you slept well, Miss Oxenham.'

'Quite well.'

'The room? Satisfactory?'

'Why shouldn't it have been? Is that a stock question for guests in twenty-two?' She laughed flatly, amused by her own bitchiness, nevertheless not liking it. There was no point in sparring with the man. Moreover he looked as though he'd had as bad a night as she. There were lines of strain at the edges of his mouth and eyes that hadn't been there when last she'd seen him. 'Won't you sit down and have a cup of coffee with me?' she asked encouragingly. 'It's quite delicious – which I don't have to tell you.'

After a fractional, indecisive pause he sat. A waiter brought a cup for him, which she filled. He pulled his chair in closer.

'Do you really want to know how well, or otherwise I slept, Mr Tremayne? Yes, I think you actually do. Have you ever slept in twenty-two?'

'As a matter of fact I have.'

'And how did you sleep?'

'Like a baby, if I remember. Why?'

'Oh, nothing . . . Mere curiosity.'

The subject of Rory Tremayne fell by its own precarious weight into the midst of conversation. He said, 'What is it that you really want? So you say you saw Rory Tremayne? *I'm* not convinced. But let's assume that *you are*. What do you intend to make of it?'

'Nothing that would injure you in any way, Mr Tremayne.' She said honestly, 'I verified to myself that the ghost of Rory Tremayne exists. But have no proof of it. No evidence. So what could I possibly make of it? I'm reconciled. A private victory, but nothing to shout about . . . Why, even *you* believe I was deceived by my senses.'

'I didn't say that.'

'A change of heart!'

'I wouldn't go as far as that,' he said flatly, overriding her pleasure. 'Look, I don't know you, but I think you're sincere. Yesterday I didn't think that. I thought you were a sensation seeker.'

'I've come up in your world.'

'Sincerity on the other hand, like good intentions, can be hazardous to those on the receiving end of it.'

'You'd rather I was a sensationalist.'

'I'd rather you were neither. I'd rather not be involved in this . . . and wouldn't want to be left out either.' His voice sank as if confessing to a woefully wrong attitude. 'I don't know what to think.' Then he laughed as though not wishing to be taken too literally.

36

'Well, that's a relief,' she said. 'Confusion: all the good ideas of this world are born from it. We're getting somewhere.'

'We are? Yes, I believe we are. But is it somewhere where I want to be? You intrigue me, Miss Oxenham. So I wish to know more about the things you wish to know about . . . But I don't judge you to be any less dangerous today than yesterday. So if you can live with that, then so can I.'

'I can because I need your help.'

'On condition that I can withdraw it at any time, it's a deal.'

'Yes,' she confirmed. 'At any time you like.'

'All right. Yes, I can live with that.'

'You asked me how I slept. Let me answer that question in this way: I feel as though I'm still where I was while asleep. I need to return from that place to this. To cast off a dream . . . '

'About Rory Tremayne?'

'No. *Listen*,' she said. Then, overwhelmed by the need to be properly heard, she rebuilt the dream as though by living fragments. 'It begins with the sound of drums – throbbing – throbbing, which exhilarates me more than I can tell you . . . Did I say "me"? No. Not as you see me now. A thousand times more voluptuous than what you see here. I am a mulatto beauty with hair like the mane of a horse. The drums lead me into a dance that is at first quite slow, but speeds up and becomes more possessive . . . My God, what a dance . . . A writhing intricacy of steps performed as though done a thousand times before, drive me into a frenzy. Then I hear the impossible, a sound below the level of the drumbeat, that reaches me nevertheless . . . A faint but insistent scratching on the door. I open it, and in comes the ugliest little bow-legged creature you can imagine. He's carved of wood. His head is too big for his body . . . '

James Tremayne's cup met his saucer with a clatter.

'Miss Oxenham – '

'The wooden man speaks to me . . . I won't deal with what he says, but my impression is that he has been waiting, and not very patiently, for me to arrive . . . He leads and I follow, and arrive through strange means at a place that I perceive to be an attic, with but one piece of furniture – an old sea chest – '

'Stop,' Tremayne demanded.

'Mr Tremayne – '

'I'm breaking off. I'm withdrawing . . . '

'Don't. I'll stop. But this is wrong. I need your help.'

'Miss Oxenham, believe me, you need no one's help. Your information is precise.'

'The attic exists; and the sea chest . . . ?'

'Yes. All of it. And the carved figure.'

'But that's wonderful.'

'It's bizarre. Please. I'm convinced. Just stop.'

'Stop? As in some amusing parlour game, a turn or two of magical mind-reading to give you a thrill. No. That isn't the object. If you can account for this dream, or any part of it, then you must tell me so. I'm serious.'

'I can account for it.' His face and lips were pale. His arms hung slackly. 'What you saw in your dream exists. I know because they belong to me. I can show them to you.'

'Are these things in your attic? Here at The Saracen's Head?'

He nodded bleakly. 'Yes! I even know where to find the mulatto woman you described.'

'Is the wooden man in the chest?'

'Yes.'

'Is there a pistol in the chest, and a book?'

'A book,' he said bitterly. 'It's so much more than that. It was, and still is so much more than that. Its author was my great-great-grandfather, He wrote it, secretly, while incarcerated in Dartmoor Prison for a murder that he could not possibly have committed, then bribed a warder to smuggle it out. It's the strangest, most bizarre story I've ever read – too shocking by far for the publishers of his day who branded it as defamatory; supernatural bunkum, outrageous lies and sexual filth. They wouldn't touch it. I think he knew he never had a chance of being believed, and that was why he wrote his story as if it were pure fiction – a novelette. His aim, I'm sure, was to create doubts as to his guilt, but in the event that never happened, because the book was never published. That was more than he could take; the final straw. He broke out of prison but was quickly tracked down by bloodhounds to Wistman's Wood, and killed there in a fight . . . His book was put into the chest with the rest of his belongings, and shoved into the attic. End of story, until today. No one has ever read Rory Tremayne's manuscript but myself and possibly the Tremaynes before me. In fact, until this morning, here and now, I was the only living person who knew of its existence. Now you do, too ... Would you like to read the manuscript, Miss Oxenham?'

'The feeling grows and grows in me that I must.'

'I feel it too, Miss Oxenham. God, yes. And though I know now that it wasn't your intention to enthral me, you have. I'm in awe of you.'

'There's no need to be. I'm a very ordinary person in most respects, with one extraordinary exception. But the exception is not necessarily a gift. There are those who consider clair-voyance to be a forfeit, a spiritual character defect.'

'Mere jealousy. It is a gift.'

'It's a tool, Mr Tremayne. A facility to make possible the impossible.'

'Yes, I can see that, too. An extraordinary facility, like infra-red light in the darkness making all that it touches visible, but only to those provided with the facility.'

'Yet there since the dawn of time.'

'Amazing.'

'A human light with which to penetrate the regions beyond the world of matter; an illumination of the hidden world.'

'And you say I shouldn't be in awe of it!'

'No more than you should be of the world of matter.'

'But I know that so well. I see it and touch it, and smell it. I hear it. Nothing's hidden.'

'And that is how I see the other world.'

'You've increased my awe, not diminished it ... I also feel that I've waited far too long for your arrival, Miss Oxenham. Now it's my turn to ask for help,' his pupils moved in a pained arc of thought, 'and I dare say – forgiveness.'

'Forgiveness?' She knew what he was getting at but wanted to rub it in, to increase his own state of doggy remorse.

He didn't oblige. 'You know what I mean.'

'I suppose so.'

'Good,' he said guiltlessly. 'Now will you help me?'

'To do what?'

'To right an historical injustice.'

'You're convinced that Rory Tremayne was wrongfully accused.'

'Oh yes,' he said passionately. 'And so will you be when you've read the book.'

She waited for him to continue. There seemed to be so much more that he wished to say, but didn't.

The route to the attic was along a passage way of carpeted, lax floor boards that squeaked and murmured. The door was in an alcove, painted white like the surrounding walls, with a padlock to keep it true.

'Mind your head,' said Tremayne as he unlocked.

She thought at first that she'd made a mistake, the attic was not as the dream had portrayed it, but vastly cluttered. A standing lamp, minus shade, a knee-high wall of dusty books, a mounted stag's head with some Christmas tinsel stuck up one nostril, several paintings of sombre hue, and a canvas tailor's dummy. All these things had to be moved in order to reach the sea chest. A good strong sun stood in for her ailing moon, but there the differences ended. The dormer window was robed in cobwebs and stuck fast. The sea chest of Rory Tremayne was the duplicate of its phantom.

'Is this how you saw it?' he asked. 'Is this as it was in the dream?'

'Yes.'

'My God,' he breathed.

They fell into quiet debate as to who should open the chest. They both perceived significance in this action, and that a moment of decision would be required. The key, the rusted keeper of the relics within, protruded temptingly. Yet Jenny knew that to turn it, right then, was not the course of action they should take, and that the event should be postponed. That was what she told James Tremayne, who was either not listening, or had heard her and decided that such shilly-shallying would serve no purpose. In either event he moved decisively to undo the lock. He had knelt and taken hold of the key before she could do more than say, 'Don't!'

'Open it!'

Now the second command had come from neither Tremayne nor herself. It had come from the interior of the antique chest; an impossibility that was repeated moments later, with greater vehemence. 'Open up. Fool!'

It was at that moment that she realised just how deep was the abyss over which she was poised, how endlessly sheer. She was dangerously ill-equipped for this encounter.

40

'Open up!' screamed the voice. A tantrum of commands. 'Open up! Open up!' A turbulence of hate beat the air about her into frenzy: active evil of greater force than she had ever before encountered. She was dealing with an incubus of unrivalled strength. This was no mere imp with impish motives for attack, but a malicious elemental, cunning enough to have lured her into its trap. God, how it was screaming. It seemed inconceivable that James Tremayne couldn't hear it. But he couldn't and yet was acting precisely as instructed.

She tried to prevent this. She caught hold of the sleeve of his jacket then didn't know what more to do or say. And he seemed bewildered by her mute action, and pressed well meaningly forward towards the lock. This had to be prevented. He had to be told that no matter how many times in the past he had delved into the contents of this trunk, he should not do so now. An awakening – a powerful revival of occult life had occured within the brass-hooped chest. A violent incubus had come restlessly to life; a century and a half of incubated hate had just hatched, and was clamouring to be let out. What hunger it must have. And all that stood between it and escape into the world of the living were some planks of worm-eaten oak.

She knew these things. She knew she had to stop Tremayne. Stop him dead. Yet she couldn't. Her limbs weren't functioning. She felt frozen, as though encased in ice. She managed only to say, 'No,' and with an unsustainable effort, 'Violent harm.' The words fell winglessly dead to the floor. The warning didn't carry. The key was turned.

'Snick,' said the lock. 'Snick – trick – quick.'

The lid was opened. She heard Tremayne say smugly, 'There. No harm done. Not that *I* can see.' Which, coming from one as blind as he, was an excusable nonsense. He felt no blame for what happened next.

Jenny felt a jolt reminiscent of the car collision she'd so recently experienced – a resounding bang, then a period of internal confusion, of which those on the periphery of the event showed no perception. She'd become the centre of a dizzily revolving ring of faces, wide-mouthed and silent as though totally aghast. But there was sound – a frenzied throbbing of tribal drums that drove the ring at an ever-increasing rate, multiplying the fantasy. There were instances of clarity; brief, vivid flashes of recognition. She spotted the obscene face of the wooden man, then it was gone. She focused momentarily on the face of Rory Tremayne, and he on her, desolating her. Then James Tremayne wobbled into view, taking root, slowing the vertigo, penetrating the drum thunder with his resolute Britishness.

'Steady on. Goodness me, you took quite a turn . . . That's better. Hold on a tick. I'm going to fetch you a glass of water.'

This he set off to do. She heard the clatter of his feet in the passage then the clank of plumbing.

She used the time to stand up and go over to the open sea chest and observe the contents, and be observed in turn. She knew that it would be disastrous to show fear. She took a deep breath, then exhaled unsteadily, bending forward.

'Got you,' said the wooden man, baring rat-sharp, tiny teeth.

Jenny gave him a depreciative look, then took out the book that was the handwritten testimony of Lieutenant Tremayne. It opened readily at a page of pleasingly penned sentences, faded, yet easily read. At a whim she lied to the wooden man, 'Your death is written here.' She sensed he did not like to hear that, and pressed on; 'You hold no surprises for me. An incubus like you can be destroyed, you know. Exorcised. Zap! Snuffed out like a candle flame. It's quite basic. Thirteen simple words. I could do it now. But I won't. You're out. What's done is done. But don't annoy me. Don't interfere. And *don't* try to make trouble, or I'll change my mind and say the words of the exorcism, and that will be that. I'll have killed you.'

'I'll kill *you*,' said the sharp-toothed mouth.

She leaned over and took the wooden manikin in her hand. It made no objection, no movement at all as it was raised, yet her hand and entire forearm tingled fiercely.

Tremayne came, bearing water, and found her holding the carving. 'Ah,' he said, 'you've found it. Ugly little villain, isn't he. Is he the one? The one you dreamed about?'

'Yes.'

'It had to be. Still it's bizarre . . . It's Nigerian, you know; mid seventeenth century, I'm told. And that's Rory's old horse pistol . . . And *this*,' he lifted the manuscript from its resting place, 'this is the strangest story ever written.' He gave her the tumbler. 'Drink up.'

The water was good. The dreadful chill had left her body and now she was perspiring heavily. She put the wooden man back in the sea chest, and wiped her moist palms on her dress. Tremayne, she noticed, was regarding her with an air of sympathetic curiosity. He said, 'You took quite a turn.'

'You shouldn't have opened the chest,' she said, at the point of anger. 'It was a blunder.'

'But I thought that was the whole idea.' He held up the half-bound book. 'To get this. How else was I supposed to get it out of the trunk? You do still want to read it, I presume?'

'Of course.'

'Well then.' He held out the manuscript closing the subject with the tart comment, 'even you couldn't have got it out any other way.' He let the lid drop back into place with a thud, then turned the key.

A useless action. The incubus was in spirit, not just wood, and it was at large and close at hand. It was in the timbered roof or the dusty shaft of sun, or behind the tailor's dummy or the row of moth-eaten books; somewhere there. An invisible cloven-footed force was stroking her, nuzzling her objection-ably, crawling on her surface, tautening her nipples with necromantic kisses . . . It was daring her in a cowering way. It feared her. Yes. She could sense fear in its tentacled touch. And she could sense something else: that she could dominate this thing if she applied herself to the task. She could make it subservient, and there was nothing wrong with that. Here was a spirit from hell, hanging around like a stray dog, tail down, just waiting for a sign of acceptance. She felt quite flattered, in fact, by its intuitive sense of trust. Moreover, under instruction, its malicious zeal would be curtailed, and it might even be persuaded to perform a useful function. What was unwelcome in heaven could, with care, be used on earth.

With these thoughts in mind, and her host leading the way, Jenny went down to the lounge, to get, as Tremayne put it, something stronger than water to drink.

Having analysed this dark new spirit, and defined her objectives, too, she felt more confident and at ease, and more forgiving towards James (yes, he'd asked her to call him that, while descending to the ground floor), who had, after all, done nothing *intentionally* stupid.

43

They took up seats opposite each other in the lounge, in a small nook, catholicly decorated with bits of old brass and farm implements, within earshot, of course, of a large wall-mounted clock. He personally brought wine and glasses. Perhaps the alcohol was intended to dull her reaction to a confession that he felt compelled to make, there and then. It was that the ghost of Wistman's Wood was a fake, a local conspiracy, inspired by a predecessor – he knew not whom – with the intention, most likely, of gaining a listing in *Haunted Inns of England*, and a consequent improvement in trade.

'I thought you should know that.'

'So there isn't a ghost?'

'Never was.'

'Is Wistman's Wood the place where your great-great-grandfather was killed? Or is that also a local fabrication?'

'No, he died there. The prison records still exist in the archives of the Duchy of Cornwall. I could show you photocopies of them. As for the rest . . .' He gave a prideless grin and a small shrug. 'I'm sorry.'

'Don't be.'

'Well, I'm glad I've told you that.'

'What brought on this urgency to confess?'

' "Urgency" might be the wrong word,' he said. ' "Necessity", might better qualify. Fact is, I did it for your own good.'

'For my own good? I want to be absolutely clear on this. For the sake of my mental health, you're prepared to have this fraud exposed?'

'Look, don't get me wrong. Something very peculiar happened to Rory Tremayne in West Africa all those years back.' He reflected on this statement, as though the words had opened many doors, many emotions. Too many. He hastily said, 'But that was *then* and this is now.'

'Long ago, when things were different? When witches flew, and mirrors spoke?'

'Yeah.'

'But not in this day of Seven-Four-Sevens and tickertape?'

'Hardly likely, is it?' he said passively.

'How do you account for the dream I had, and the realities it contained?'

'There's no denying dreams . . . Or telepathy. The Russians

are into telepathy; brain impulses; Edgar Cayce. I can go along with that.'

'But no spooks.'

'I'm afraid not.'

'Do you still want me to read Rory Tremayne's manuscript then?'

'The one thing has nothing to do with the other. Of course I want that. I'm not totally without belief. I believe in luck. I believe in God and the Methodist Church . . . And I believe in the law of averages, which in this case points out with awful certainty that I'd have to wait for another hundred years before someone else like you came along and asked to read the manuscript of Rory Tremayne. And as I haven't got that sort of time, yes, I want you to read it. It's hard to think of a greater agony than Rory must have had to endure: convicted for a murder that he couldn't have committed. Incarcerated for life. Imagine being in his place. I have – a thousand times. His suffering must have been so awful that the pain of death came over him like a balm, like the touch of a mother. His *pain. That* is his ghost. That is what haunts this house and Wistman's Wood, Jenny. Poor, bloody Rory Tremayne, deprived of freedom and robbed of honour. Give him back his honour. I believe in Honour. And I believe he did, too. You'll see . . . You'll wish you had known him. Rory McKay – that, for the sake of convention, is the name he took in the story. And that is the only fiction . . . but it's not up to me to convince you, is it? It's up to him. Read it and then tell me what it tells you.'

That day was the antithesis of its bleak, glum predecessor. The earth had turned and had rolled onto a cushion of warm harmony with the moors buttoned plumply in the middle. Jenny, the manuscript grasped to her breast, walked into this pleasure-land, with small, thought-laden steps and turned towards the cattle gate marked Wistman's Wood. She passed through then went on, keeping to the cattle-trod, sandy track that would take her to the place where Rory Tremayne had died. There was no other place where his cry of innocence would be more coherent than there.

Wistman's Wood wore a face of prodigious age; age that had exceeded by far the limits of venerable dignity and given in to dotage. Its stunted oaks stooped everywhere, speaking of hard driving winter winds that had turned their promising growth arthritic. Grey, blotched with lichen and knotted, they leaned on granite blocks, resting in the heather, and rustling with secrets. The Wood took her in with suspicious unwillingness. She sat upon a downcast rock and regulated her breath and her mood to that of her surroundings. A hawk swooped by on silent wings – off into a God-filled sky. While here on earth, in Wistman's Wood, an old voice, whispering like the scrape of many leaves on one another, said, 'Read of the past. Read of the past.'

The handwriting was bold, intelligent and honestly spaced. She scanned a few lines, unmethodically yet critically, as one might appraise an approaching stranger who intends to become acquainted. The man was not delicate or subtle.

I believe in God the Father, and I believe in his principal opposer. In the untainted blue of mid-ocean, at the frontiers of heaven, you would think that the Devil would stay scarce. And you'd be wrong. I found him there. His name was Silus Strangeways . . .

That's where I found him. But I won't detain you there. For no matter how demented was his behaviour at sea, what I must tell you about took place on land, south of the Equator, east of Accra – east of the Oil Rivers of the Niger where the true Slave Coast of Africa slinks muddily into the sea – at Calbar. Old Calbar where the River Cross leans out its dirtied arm into the sea.

There, at the height of the tide, close hauled, with a fathom of water to spare, the schooner *Pluto* slipped over the mud bars at the mouth of the Cross River estuary and dropped anchor. We fired the long gun and the great sound wrenched shorewards in a plume of smoke that Africa swallowed with a yawn. It was a summons to the rivermen – the savage black paddlers who would take Strangeways upriver to his trade.

In the meantime there was stillness and heat, a backcloth of haze and walls of dark green jungle close enough to prune. There was the distant thud of surf to remind me from where I'd come – and nothing, but nothing to inform me on what lay ahead . . .

A LONELY
PLACE
TO DIE

Three

God could not, would not even at his most punitive, have invented such a scourge of heat as that trapped at the mouth of the River Cross that day. It bore down with the full weight of the sky. It sucked and breathed and was filled with shimmering misery, half mosquito, half moisture. Gasping mangroves trailed long, green arms down into the river, and clawed the mud with fingerlike roots into banks of spongy grey. Here crocodiles lay as dead as fallen trees, until they saw the oncoming canoe. Then, sprouting legs they belly-crawled into the skin of the river, vanishing.

This was the dry season and the river was as indolent as the air. It was pulseless, rotting in its mud, stinking. Sullenly, it gave passage to the dugout, darkly reflecting the blades of the paddles as they met water. Rory McKay trailed his hand in it and found it tepid and as nasty as it looked. He glanced back towards the anchored, bare-masted schooner, and saw that the tars were rigging awnings on the deck to shield them from the suffocating sky. Some would die. The river fever would take its toll, as it always did. A last glimpse of the river mouth, oozing like a wound into the sea, its piled sandbanks, its clutch of thatched huts, scratched from the earth. This was Calbar, where in the old days, the days of unhampered slaving, a score of tall ships would have been anchored. Now, only the *Pluto*. He could still hear the pounding surf. Then they rounded a bend and the noble sea vanished behind screens of foliage which took the sound of it, too. Here the river narrowed, breaking into reed-clogged channels where long-legged birds waded and the croak of frogs swelled up into an immense arch of noise, not overriding the chant of the Negro paddlers yet making their sound seem less.

Even higher on the scale was a vivid intrusion of bird calls – a trumpeting , warbling, and tweeting, and a whirring of wings of every hue. A water snake of marvellous green wriggled quickly past, momentarily unsettling the rhythm of the Negroes. Now trees closed down upon the channels, marching, thick-trunked up to the water's edge, roped to each other with festoons of vines, their canopies thrown clear across the river in a plan to cut out the entrance of any light not the colour of green; tunnels of green, deep dark green as though lit by a topaz moon and not the bright sun. They slogged into these coiled veins, chanting endlessly, into the stagnant bloodstream of their gigantic host. A zone of sombre quiet that lulled then fatigued – then tore apart its mantle of peace with eerie shrieks that flew out of the foliage from God knows what direction.

Rory saw something that he took to be some sort of smooth-skinned river beast, but which turned out to be a human corpse afloat upon its back. Then he saw in quick succession four more floating cadavers, all staring upwards into the green roof, and one that lay face down, spread-eagled. The paddlers did not lose a stroke, did not spare a glance or stop their chant: 'Voom-a voom-a voom-a – '

A resonant sound, like a large drum being lazily beaten, it seemed to emerge not from their mouths, but from the depths of their very chests. These were strong men, narrow-waisted with shoulder muscle that bunched and slid beneath black skin. These were fierce men.

'Voom-a voom-a voom-a – '

Presently Rory became aware that he was indeed detecting the throb of a slow beating drum. The Negroes had adjusted their strokes to it in such a way that the whole effect was akin to the sound heard when pressing one's ear over a person's breast.

'Voom-a thub. Voom-a thub – '

The river seemed to come to a dead end at a bank of writhing foliage which the canoe headed for at undiminshed speed, only to veer at the last minute from certain collision into a dog leg, which then led into another, and then a whole series of bewilderingly arboreal loops that tied up and disposed of all sense of direction as though it had never existed. Fingered branches swooped and touched him, conveying to him, you are alien, you are feeble, but we are part of the jungle, the towering green jungle. It belittled him. It yawned at him with vast indifference. It summed him up as meaningless, alive or dead, now or in the future. More cadavers lolled by.

Voom-a-thub. Voom-a-thub.

Here was a place where flowers burned like the low flames of lamps, leaping and falling with infallible life amongst the brooding foliage. The impulse to retreat from these viscera of absorbing green came and went like a warning shout, blurred by distance. But even had the choice of direction been his, he couldn't have changed it, for he couldn't speak a word of the language of these savage paddlers, and neither could his companion, a sailor who was seated in the bows, blankly staring as though deserted by all thought. The man was passively stroking the lock of his musket as one might the hand of a wife. Strangeways' canoe, which also contained the overseer who controlled these Negroes, was well ahead, quite out of sight.

Then suddenly it was in sight, for the river had widened and straightened. The cloaking green pavilion drew open, admitting a close sun that crashed upon Rory's face, startling him. He took the straw hat that he'd laid at his feet, divested it of a leaflike insect as big as his thumb, and put it on his head. A jetty walked out on rickety wooden legs, but this was not their destination. The banks shrank further back admitting both canoes into a vast languid lake. A hippopotamus came up blowing like a whale, spied their canoe and yawned apathetically. Rory knew he was seeing things that would bite into his mind and live there for ever, incredible things. The sun had converted the water into bronze. It gleamed, and in places its polished shallows were swathed with flocks of pale birds. He'd absorbed so much now that his brain slumped into lassitude. A lassitude that had interrupted his sense of duty. Quickly, he glanced back to check on the position of the *Pluto*'s longboat with its escort of sailors. It had kept station. Its oars, four a side, were pressing it smartly along, rattling in their locks, and a sailor was leaning over its bow-mounted carronade, gesturing. Laughter – a quiver of white man's gaiety tinkled in the air. It was the gunner who'd laughed. Why? It seemed an important question for a while. Why such a ludicrous response to this strange wilderness? What was the man thinking of? A village of reed and mud huts slipped into view like warts on the skin of the marsh. The drum sound was emanating from this place. Negroes, dressed only in loin cloths, came crawling from the doors of the huts, and more in greater numbers were emerging from the tree line, from no apparent path. The leading boat kept to its course. This was not their destination. Creek Town lay a full mile further north, at the far end of the lake. It arose as from a paste of mud and mangroves – a splendid, true castle with earthen battlements and turrets two storeys high. An amazement. An awesome investment in power.

Though Rory had been expecting it, the salute of the longboat's carronade startled him. It shot into the tranquil face of the lake like a fist. Ten million birds rose, soared, filled the sky with a layer of panic, then resettled just in time to be scattered again by a second gun, this fired from the fort. Rory watched a puff of smoke from its discharge envelope the southern battlement and hang there blowsily. A jetty of better quality came into sight.

The interior of the Creek Town castle was larger than Rory had anticipated, and more filled with confusion and stinks than a chicken coop. Apparently the arrival of the slavers was an event worth celebrating, for Strangeways' party had been met at the jetty by a monkey-skinned praise singer who'd preceded them though the gates, prancing and yelling. Strangeways, as senior man, had strutted ahead of the other Englishmen. Rory had come next, followed by half a dozen sailors, swaggering, but as nervous as rats. The crowd came nudely wriggling, black, sheened with sweat and with nostrils quiveringly flared to sniff the skins of the white men, as though it was they who'd imported the disgusting stink. The party progressed through a straw-roofed bazaar, shifted along by the ragtag mob, all singing and clapping. They swayed, danced, gesticulated and shoved, creating a thick blur of sound and motion so foreign to the Englishmen that they knew not whether to fear or laugh, so did neither, but made their features tight and veiled, and felt grateful for the weight of their weapons. In Rory's case two horse pistols of the most modern design, and a cutlass.

Here and there, Rory noticed, hanging back from the crowd were creatures with skins that were neither sambo black nor hoary albino, but of the blushing creamy sepia of the half-caste

Creoles of New Orleans, and of these mulatto women some were beautiful.

So on this tide of stench and joy they arrived at the town palaver house where awaited their host, the half-caste, Duke Ephraim. Ex-Royal Navy, Lord of the River, head of the House of Duke, war hero, infamous villain, he was a man of extraordinary wealth. He held up both arms and, in a miracle of obedience, all sound ceased. 'Welcome,' said Duke Ephraim to Strangeways.

His real name, that is to say the name his father had bequeathed him, was Ormond; John Ormond. His father had been a noted Liverpool slave dealer; his mother the daughter of a royal chief of the Efik tribe. He'd been born at Calbar and sent to Bristol, England to become fledged as a gentleman. But his father had died, and John Ormond, in trying to get back to Africa, and his roots, was captured by a press gang. Strange-ways had told Rory all this. The captain of the *Pluto* had thought it a huge joke that a Calbar prince of the blood should be pressed into the Royal Navy. Ormond had served out five years as a deck hand with the West Indian Station, and as a gunner in the Mediterranean, and had then come back to Africa, to the River Cross, where he'd reunited himself with his mother, then set up slave factories; one at Calbar, which the British Anti-slave Squadron had shelled and burned, another at Creek Town, too distant and well fortified to be attacked with any hope of success. And that was how things stood. This was the man who stood before them dressed flowingly in Arab style, arms now aloft, now beneficently lowered; silently adored.

The palaver hut was an open-sided affair of poles that supported thatch. The poles bore shelves, and from the shelves stared ranks of human skulls. There was a table of ships' planks, and benches made from the same material, at which Rory was not invited to sit. Strangeways sat, as did Duke Ephraim and his factor, about whom Rory knew little, other than that his name was Jemmy Honesty. He was an English-man. He had but one serviceable arm. The rabble, having lost their momentum, and being required to shut up, lost interest and began to disperse. All went away but a clutch of children whose curiosity was undiminished. Sucking lumps of rocksalt as though it were sugar, and entwined with the roof posts they stared on.

Strangeways, in earnest discussion with Ephraim, showed no outward concern for his officer, or his men. So after an hour of being thoroughly ignored by his superior, and just as thoroughly inspected by the piccaninnies, Rory gave the knot of sailors this message: 'If the captain calls for me, tell him I've gone off to reconnoitre.'

'To reconnoitre, sir?' The British sailor is expert in conveying his opinion at a step below insubordination.

Rory walked away from the palaver hut. One of the little 'black birds' unwound himself from his pole, forsook his companions, and came after him. Rory saw this without taking notice of it. The sun lay centre sky, like a violent weight on his his shoulders. It had stunned the inhabitants of the fortress into postures of submission. He saw through open doorways how many of them had taken the antidote of sleep. The heat had swept clear the alleyways that he'd previously travelled of everyone but for one old hag, already so desiccated that she was impervious to it. And as he passed her he felt the tweak of fingers on his shirt and heard her cackle. He repulsed her from his sleeve as though ridding himself of a noxious spider, but found himself somehow to be still attached to her invisible web. He could feel the filmy touch of her residue on his skin, and it made him lengthen his stride and touch the handle of the horse pistol in his belt. At the gate to Duke Ephraim's fort he paused, wondering whether to return to the palaver. But on looking back, there was the hag preparing to reintercept him.

He walked on along the path towards the landing stage, or the one he assumed to be that, for it was the best worn path of the three that presented themselves, and seemed to lead towards the river. It was only after he'd walked several hundred yards that he realised that he'd misjudged the direction. The pathway had led him into the jungle, which closed down on him with a suddenness that was alarming. For he could no longer see the sky, or the castle, but only greenness on all sides – this, too, affected by the silence of noon. There were vague and fretful twitterings from the curtain of its foliage, but its former energy lay sapped. He retraced his steps, or attempted to, but found that he'd left no trace of his outward progress on the rotted leaf floor. One track led to a dead end, another to a trickling creek where he encountered something long and slithery that wriggled past his feet in a yellow-banded blur. He retreated, finding himself then upon a broader path that he determined to stick to, but which was no more rewarding than the others. It was then that he became aware that for a while he had been in the vicinity of a sound – vague but consistent – that reminded of the swish-crack, swish-crack of a bullwhip being brandished. In the hope that this was indeed a sound made by human endeavour, he followed it.

He found the bullwhip . . . and Father Theo. He walked into a crucible containing truth and falsehood so wonderfully mixed as to be inseparable to him from that moment on.

Four

The mind of the Negro is inferior and rough, and so thoroughly defended by heathen superstition, fetish and juju, that to enter it, other than by cannon fire, is a prodigious task. As for Christianity and the Gospel, he will listen for days on end, bent forward in a posture of deep attention, eyes aglow with the light of comprehension, then in the very next hour go out and commit the most base of sins.

There is but one recourse – to flog him. To tie him, hand and foot, and lash him until the shock of leather scourges the Devil, screaming, from his interior. This is an essential measure. Neglect it and you may work, Bible in hand, for a year without making a single convert.

Indeed, it had taken Father Theophillus twelve bitter months to appreciate this axiom. A year of baffling disappointments during which time he'd led more than a score of Satin-infested souls towards the Cross, only to see them snatched from his grasp by a dark power, a power vast and terrible and frustratingly unopposable. In his thirteenth month he had (in anger, God forgive him) lashed a sinner from one wall of his yard to the other, and in the pattern of blood discovered Africa. For there is no gradual comprehension of this land. One stares at it in bafflement for seasons on end, then suddenly, as from a dark night, it is upon you like a powerful wild animal, dangerous, but less frightening now that it is known.

Theophillus had found in the hiss of plaited leather the means to counter the throb of the juju drums and the whisper of mumbo jumbo that hung like mist, dripping from the green-leafed jungle just beyond the bamboo walls of his compound.

Now, in his thirty-sixth month on the Slave Coast, he could consistently cause to congregate on the mud floor of his mission

56

two rows of squatting, sober men and women to whom the whip was never quite out of sight. He accepted the inevitability of its employment now; its usage as a tool to reach the soul. As the farmer toils with his hoe to improve the heartsoil of his ground so he applied leather to skin. And, lo! The crop improved. To the glory of God.

In this frame of mind he flogged the Nigger, July – a favourite of his. July, the woodcarver, who had been his original convert, whose ebony statue of the Virgin graced his altar, who had gone at night to the fort, got drunk and fornicated with a whore.

Ninety-seven lashes had come upon July's back ribs, reddening the whip end, raising wheals as thick as rope, cutting at the sins of the flesh. Theo's wrist ached; a strain was lurking in his back muscles, and his body was obscenely fountaining sweat. He took a ladle of water and drank it, observing as he did a small but brilliantly hued bird that came to sit in the tamarind tree to which July was roped by his wrists; suspended from a stout low limb in a crucified pose. It seemed to wink at Theo then fluttered into the depth of the foliage. How beautiful it was, how minutely perfect, and enigmatic. A tune filtered through the leaves, a trilling and warbling of complex sweet-ness, that made Theo quite sad. All beauty made him sad since he'd come to Africa, for here all beauty was inseparably wedded to evil. One only had to observe the reddened back of July to be assured of this basic truth. He averted his gaze from it and drove once more at the inhabitant devil.

Theophillus heard the thud of a cannon firing a blank, the short-snouted six pounder that the slavers' longboats carried, and always used to salute the high walls of the nearby fort at Creek Town. He kneeled and his mouth moved silently, 'O Lord! Scourge them. Bring them down. O Lord, in your wisdom, cast them out.'

The prayer did not entirely descend upon the slavers. It was multi-directional, embracing Duke Ephraim in his fort; his freakishly fat mammy, the Queen of the River; Gospel mockers, such as the one before him; devils, jujus, and witch-doctors; fevers, fluxes, worms, dropsies and colics; gin, rum, mimbo; polygamy . . . All these things fell within the scope of his entreaty.

'Damn them.' He stood and squared up to his task. The dual

syllables, when repeated, also provided a useful chant whereby to measure the strokes.

'Damn them. Damn them. Damn them.'

There was not an inch of skin of July's back that was not radically scourged, so Theo refurrowed the welts. A farmer at the soil of the soul.

And that was Rory Tremayne's introduction to African evangelism. That was the fantastic scene into which he wandered in the hope of finding direction. And though Rory had no idea as to the purpose of the punishment, he saw at once that it was effort wasted. The Negro was upright only because he was tied to a tree. His head was lolling. His eyes were blank. The man was dead. In fact, he had that sheenlessness of colour that in the black man arrives long after death.

Swish-crack.

The process was bizarre but Rory had no immediate intention of interrupting it. He cleared his throat merely to make his presence known. The effect however was to startle Theophillus into almost dropping his whip.

'Who are you?'

Theophillus' question might better have been phrased, 'What are you?' as that was the nature of his scrutiny of the intruder.

'I'm Rory McKay, an officer of the schooner *Pluto*.' Rory advanced into the clearing in order to assist the older man's eyes.

'A slaver?'

'Yes.'

'A deplorable trade.'

'Some think it so. Others commend it.'

'An ungodly trade. I see you're very young.' Theophillus had recovered his grip on the whip handle; he looked towards his unfinished work, poised himself for another blow, but instead delivered poetry in Rory's direction.

'Curst be the winds, and curst the tides that bore
These European robbers to our shore.'

Then he struck, and again, until ten more cuts had been registered, after which he paused.

Rory said, 'Sir, this is excessive . . .'

'Excessive! Contemptible man. Who are you to interfere in His work?'

'God's work? This?'

'Yes.'

'May I ask, sir, who you are to assume that?'

'I am Father Theophillus.' He gestured towards some huts of mud and thatch as though seeing domes and arcades: 'My mission.'

'I didn't realise you were a preacher.'

'You didn't ask. You blundered in.'

'Even so, if I may make my point – '

'No, you may not. Do you criticise me? How dare you – you pup. No, I'm unfair to that innocent beast. You heathen.'

'I'm a Christian, sir.'

'A despot then.'

'Have a care, sir. You're an old man and a clergyman too, and I respect that. But an insult is still an insult. I merely wish to make the point . . . '

Swish-crack.

' . . . that it seems to me to be unnecessary, even immoral to flog a dead man.'

Theophillus paused, not because of the impact of Rory's statement, but to unpick a knot that made itself in the whip end. Then he let fly with another stroke.

'He's dead,' said Rory. 'Can't you see it?'

Swish-crack.

Here was insanity, Rory thought. The point was, what, if anything, was to be done about it? A decision was not long in coming. It should be stopped. There was something infectively misanthropic about it, as though if left unchecked, he might be the next to be touched on the shoulder by such terrible passion. Moreover, it was illogical. It should be terminated without violence and with the smallest possible effort.

Having decided this, Rory walked obliquely away from the flogging post, halting when he figured he was beyond the range of the corner vision of the clergyman, then circling to his rear. The flogging went on. The man had an aptitude for it. He'd strike then cast the thong to his rear along the ground, rear up his arm, then curl it forward, and *swish-crack*. The simplest way to intercept this action would be to step forward at the appropriate moment and tread upon the whip end. So that was that he did. When the thong lay behind Theo on the ground

Rory anchored it beneath his shoe. The forward stroke took up the slack – the handle jerked loose from the preacher's hand, which slowly came to sense that it was weaponless. But the loss of the bullwhip did nothing to promote good reason, for a desolate wail came from him. He peered uncertainly at Rory, then lifted his gaze upwards towards the mottled green dome of foliage, frowning, as though Perdition itself lay above in the suffocating leaves. He examined it at length, searching for its hidden face, its diabolical reason.

Then, in a passion of disappointment, he called out, 'Oh, evil! Evil! Oh, evil!'

Rory followed his gaze, and saw only luminous green. Perhaps there was an evil presence visible to the preacher. But if so, it was too vast to be reached and too primitive to be shamed. For this man of God looked defeated and humiliated, and so deeply crushed beneath its exorbitant weight that he was lost, even to himself.

'Can't you see it?' Theo flung up his arms like a drowning man. 'It's on us. It's around us. Here! There!'

'I can only see trees.'

'No. No,' said Theo desperately. 'You must search. For your own sake.'

'What is it?'

'Evil. This is the kingdom of it, and I, by the grace of God, am its single adversary. You must oppose it, too, or become its subject and be irrevocably, spiritually ruined.'

'I see only trees,' Rory said stubbornly. But he knew whence the priest's accusation sprang. He could feel the power of the jungle again, diminishing him, just as it had on the river.

Suddenly Rory felt a scalding pain in his hand, and on examining it saw that it was cut quite deeply in the web between thumb and forefinger. A steady trickle of blood was emerging from the gash, dribbling to his fingertip, spotting the jungle floor with daubs of red. He could not recall having been inflicted with this wound, nor any possible reason for it.

Five

Strangeways was well known as a hard trader, but then, so was Duke Ephraim. For days they sat and haggled in the palaver hut; bickered, ate pulpy fruit and spat out pips, epithets and lies. They drank from a cask of superior brandy as though the contents held mere water, the captain convinced that he had the stronger head, Ephraim believing the flies and heat to be his secret allies. Both were greedy and rabid cheats, though each believed himself to be the superior deceiver. Financial ambuscades were cunningly set. For instance, of the goods in trade brought by the *Pluto* there was not an item that was capable of reduction that had not already been reduced. The gunpowder kegs had false heads fitted; each bolt of linen and calico was cut short. The hogsheads of rum were diluted. Ephraim, in turn, had ordered to be shaved the heads and groins of every of his slaves – not a grey hair among the lot. Every anus with the flux had been plugged with gum. Skin, ulcerated by disease and cut by fetters, had been polished up with palm oil. Nails were trimmed. The surface of Ephraim's merchandise gleamed with health and vitality.

Trading, therefore, was a matter of one person trying to sin more effectively than the other – an adjustment of iniquities. That an outcome was ever reached was an amazement. Strangeways did not succumb to the insect plague. Ephraim's brain was impervious to brandy, and a deal was struck at a rate of one hundred iron bars per prime slave. A bar was considered to be worth half a New England dollar, or else a pound and a half of tobacco. A fathom of calico equalled a bar, as did one pound of gunpowder. A standard Birmingham musket was worth twelve bars, as were two hogsheads of rum.

The arithmetic of the trade thus became straightforward: one slave equalled one hundred and fifty pounds of tobacco, or a fathom of cloth, or a hundred pounds of powder, et cetera. Ephraim, it was agreed, would receive in addition to this, a dash of ten per cent, payable in common soldiers, muskets and brandy. Four hundred and twenty slaves would be supplied. Jemmy Honesty produced a quill of exotic colour and entered these agreements into a book. Strangeways and Duke Ephraim shook hands above the pages. A chicken's throat was cut and the blood let drip on the cover. A solemn and unbreakable oath of good faith now existed. The cheats rested. It was the eleventh day, and the hottest.

The sun was the master of all. It shrank the shade of the palaver hut, agonized the ground, distorted the very air. The mud-walled homes at the edge of the square shimmered gaseously. It sucked all nourishment from human flesh, and came into the brain in the form of an ache which quite replaced all thought, and even the desire for thought. And yet, abroad in the imageless cavern of the mind, were bits of something, probably habit, that passed as volition. Rory, for example, when told that there was to be a celebration replied, 'That's good.' Though he had no idea why he should think it would be good. Nothing else so far had been good. 'Where will it be held?'

'At Mammy's house,' said Jemmy Honesty, while the side of his face contorted into a wink. 'Music. Dancing at Duke Ephraim's mammy's house. There will be play. Oh! You'll like it.'

Rory had difficulty in believing that this would be so. He imagined a bonfire and prancing naked Negroes. And thought he would prefer to sleep.

'You'll have a fine time.'

Jemmy Honesty wore an earring and a small pigtail and was a habitual snuff-taker. One brow and cheek owned a frowning, livid cutlass scar. And as further evidence of dire combat, his right hand was absent from its wrist. He was probably not as uncouth a man as he looked. Still, when he spoke of 'fine times', the words oozed thick with vowed debauchery.

Rory's picture of naked Negroes re-formed into that of naked *female* Negroes, slim-waisted – full-breasted; mulattos perhaps, tossing horse-tailed hair. He'd been moved to stare at creatures such as these in the streets of Creek Town, and some had boldly held his gaze.

Now Jemmy Honesty went away. Rory watched him enter one of the alleyways that riddled the interior of the fort. Then he too forsook the shade of the palaver hut: the last to go, so he thought. But the piccaninny who had previously attached himself to Rory was in reality the last to depart from the hut – eventually feeling the need for sleep.

Rory dreamed of a quadroon-coloured girl who danced invitingly before him to the throb of a drum, with movements exquisite. A rope of seduction bound him to her, and he danced as he had never done before; he in relentless advance, she in reluctant retreat; he trying to grasp, she never quite graspable. But within this dream there was another, too, a formless image of danger, that also danced, that also beckoned him onwards . . . Episodes of blindness prevented him from seeing this thing clearly; an agglutination of his lids that slowly became the greater part of the dream, until he was totally without vision – still dancing, but blindly and with no objective.

He was glad to awake to the lazy shadows of dusk. A large but spindly spider was clinically consuming a cockroach on the bamboo table a few inches from his face. A fly droned fitfully about, invisible beneath his roof of musty thatch, while at the doorless entrance to his hut a piccaninny squatted, regarding him with commanding ovate eyes. Rory was becoming used to finding this boy in his path. He said, 'Hello,' and received mute acknowledgement of this greeting. Rory sat up, and his bed of bamboo creaked. The spider hurriedly dissected its meal, and the fly made circles of noise around his head. The piccaninny threw up his chin, puckered inquisitively and regarded him in this pose while Rory put on his shirt and thrust his feet into his trousers. There was, Rory supposed, little else worthy of surveillance other than he. The hut was secretless – a single, small room, a table and a bed of bamboo, and a wall shelf which held a Dutch looking glass and a calabash filled with water in which many small things lived.

Rory buckled his waistbelt (noticing that he was losing weight) and secured his pistols therein. The piccaninny, now weary of his scrutiny, conjured a big mango into his hands and bit off its tit.

63

'What's your name?' Rory decided to take the association further, practising his trade pidgin in the process. 'Your name be what?'

A mouthful of pulp brought forth two juicy syllables which to the white man's ears were delightfully quaint. 'Run Run. Your name's Run Run?' More of the same sound emerged. 'In any case, that is what I'll call you.'

Run Run seemed content to leave it so.

Rory patted himself. 'My name be Rory.'

'Ror-ry.'

'You're a clever little sod, that's for sure.'

Inevitably a drum began to throb. Creek Town was recovering its pulse, but unhurriedly, as in a yawning awakening of doorways and windows in pleasurable approval of the dusk. Good things were expected at dusk.

Run Run knew about the feast that was to take place at Mammy Yellowbelly's house at the bend in the river. He had helped find dry logs for the bonfires that would burn there. Later he would go back and watch what went on. In the meantime there was no lack of curious things at hand. There was this oddly coloured human to be observed; a creature, nut-brown of face, neck and forearm, yet milk-white everywhere else. Strange. Most strange, and not very pretty when naked. His nose was very pinched like the others of his kind, thin, and with nostrils so small that it was doubtful if they served any purpose at all. To have eyes the colour of sea, and hair that of new thatch was no advantage other than as a curiosity, either. These men were constantly moist, and the slightest effort almost dissolved them in sweat that gave off a stench beyond belief. Moreover, they farted like elephants, as this one did now, with a slight bending of the knees to achieve greater volume. A thing no black man would aspire to do. Run Run was forced to conclude that this multi-coloured tribe of humans must be of less quality than his own. Not that he held this against them or minded them in any way.

This one, for example, was friendly and brave. It was he who had stood on the tip of Pastor Theo's whip in order to bring to an end the merciless flaying of his father. And though this act had not saved July, it had doubtless been intended to. So towards this creature in particular he felt quite warmly. And

64

here was a strange thing: his father, July, though dead and buried, had made it quite clear that he liked Rory, too. For July, in voice, was still very much alive. There were messages that came straight out of the air in his unmistakable tone. 'This is a good man,' he had been told. 'My son, there will be things I will ask you to do for this one.'

With this in mind, Run Run sucked out the last offering of the mango, lifted himself and followed Rory into the darkening street.

A scoop of hot wind passed them on the street, causing Run Run to think of rain, and Rory to clutch at his straw hat. It died, replaced by dusky stagnancy. Rory went to the hut of the Cappy of the sea ship, and entered. The sound of the Cappy's cough rattled like a chain. Then there was talk. Soon both men came out, looked at the sun which was dying in an angry way, agreed on something with a laugh that held no friendship, then walked towards the west wall. Run Run dared follow them no further.

There was a place in the west wall that had crumbled during the previous rainy season, which, for want of lime and oyster shell had never been repaired. Rory had become accustomed to the usage of this convenient gap when going to visit the sailors billeted in the longboat. The men had strung up an awning beneath which they had some private trade going, cleaning muskets for Duke Ephraim's soldiers. They'd shot parrots and some monkeys. But rest beyond a certain point makes men doltish and mischievous, so Strangeways theorised.

The effect of the deal on the captain of the *Pluto* had been to touch off suspicion that all was too good to be true. He was cheerful in a cautious sort of way, energised by distrust. He distrusted the tars, he said they were bound to be up to no good. He did not specify what kind of mischief they might undertake. Having stated his concern, he walked ahead of Rory, whistling tunelessly. The path was broad enough for them to have taken it abreast, but Strangeways' spindly legs were pumped with energy, which was why he almost bowled over Theophillus who was on an opposite tack. They met with exclamation, Strangeways' first: 'Hell's bells, sir!'

'I beg your pardon, sir.'

'Are you drunk? Couldn't you see me?'

65

Theophillus saw Rory and recognised him. 'Ah, it's the slaver. Who is this blasphemous man with you?'

'I'm Captain Strangeways,' said Strangeways with bluster.

'Well, Captain,' said Theophillus, 'I wish to inform you that Hell has no bells. But I'm sure you will discover that of your own account . . . I hear that a deal in human torment has been struck between yourself and Duke Ephraim.'

'Who is this fool?' Strangeways prodded the preacher, seething.

The question was impassively ignored. Theo addressed Rory. 'I must talk to you about matters that concern us.'

'You may speak in front of my captain. I've told him about you.'

'You're the whipping preacher?' Strangeways said on a gust of irritable mirth. 'Why, I should hire you on the spot . . . Lieutenant, enter this man's name in our papers as Beach Captain, and give him the going rate.'

Strangeways, elated by his wit, resumed his stride, and Rory would have followed had Theophillus not placed his arm earnestly on his. The preacher flung a final retort at Strangeways. 'The only sound you will hear at your final destination will be the screams of the damned.' Then he tugged irritably at Rory's sleeve. 'You shouldn't have told him. Why did you?'

'Why did I? you make out as though deep conspiracy exists between us. There is no such thing. I saw you kill a Negro. I agreed to be present at his burial. There's no more to it than that.'

'You saw me kill him?'

'That is what I said.'

'But you did not see that.'

'I saw you whipping a dead man.'

'That's more accurate.'

'It amounts to the same thing.'

'You observed something. You made deductions. You are in a land where nothing is as it seems. July was as nearly a Christian as he was capable of being. That is to say he knew of God and Heaven and Hell, but as something living above a tree, in it, or below it, something unforgivingly indifferent to him. It swallowed his soul. He died.'

66

'Then you applied one hundred lashes.'

'As was my duty to the Almighty. How else was I to reproduce the knowledge of sin in him?'

'Your tuition was a failure.'

'I admit it.'

'You, too, will have to answer to God.'

'I'm willing to. I look forward to the event.'

'I'm unconvinced, Father Theo.'

Rory took a step and once more felt the frustrating traction of the preacher's hand.

'I understand,' said Theo, fervently. 'Oh, yes. I see you doubt me, and I'm pleased by it in a way. You're attuned to falsehood, and intolerant of it. And that's good. You misjudge me, and that is not bad either. You have the mental strength to survive this thing . . . I remarked on that to myself when I first saw you. You're unlike the others. You're quite out of place here, dangerously out of place. You don't belong. And I'm not the only one who's aware of that.'

'Father, what is it that you're trying to tell me? What "thing" am I to survive? Be plain. Is there a plot? A danger from Duke Ephraim's men?'

'Ephraim doesn't love you, to be sure. But the harm I'm warning you of is greater than he or any other living man could do. It is your very soul that is imperilled. But there is so little time . . . There is to be a feast in the Old Town.'

'Yes, I know.'

'You were on your way to it? Yes, I suspected that. I waylaid you to prevent you from going. And just in time.'

'But I am going.'

The preacher's anxiety became intense. He still held Rory's cuff, as though by this purchase he would prevent the slide to degradation. 'No, you mustn't. You of all people. I have expert knowledge. It's Satan's playground, that house. Oh, you mustn't go.'

'I thank you for the advice.' Rory freed his arm.

'Heed it then. You have no idea. This is no feast such as you're used to. There are powers abroad beyond your comprehension . . . But I see I'm failing to convince you.'

'You have no duty to convince me.'

'Ah, wrong! So wrong. Rebuff me totally if you will. But that will not reduce my obligation one jot . . They've interfered with the grave of July. There! I thought that would strike. I went to the grave to sprinkle holy water, and found it burrowed into. The air seethes with bad intentions.'

'Some beast of the jungle dug it up, surely. A hyena perhaps?'

'That can be ruled out. The face was showing, nothing else. And the body had not been fed upon, but mutilated by the removal of the eyes.'

'The eyes? Why the eyes?'

'For witchcraft of the most heinous sort. I think you are in danger.'

'That is pure speculation,' said Rory heatedly. 'I will not be put upon by this mumbo jumbo.'

'This is not England. No ring of protective churches guards you here, but a single priest with his upheld crucifix.'

A shallow ray of sun, surely the last of the day, cut a hole through the green, inflamed a bouquet of scarlet flowers, then failed. It was a moment for decision.

'Trust me,' said Theophillus, praying that the young man would. But Rory walked onwards towards the river.

'So he dies,' said the preacher to the inrushing night. Then he set off along the path that led to his mission. Theo jogged while on the open path, but where the jungle closed and pressed its curtains of foliage onto his legs, he slowed. From there on he walked with the caution of one who suspects ambush. He darted the shadows with sharp eyes and muttered incantations. Also, he did not cease praying for Rory McKay.

Six

To dig in your father's grave, and take the things that were his in life, is an ugly thing to do. But if it was the voice of Father that commanded that it be done, then even if those villagers who could not hear the command scorned you for it most violently, in yourself you need feel no guilt. The wisest course of action then is to obey the spirit voice, and admit what you have done to no living soul.

Yoruba the fetish witch, who spoke to the river spirit, and was spoken to in turn, and knew what the jungle said to the wind, could not be considered a living soul, not in the ordinary sense. That is not to say that she was dead in the ordinary sense, either. As her clients were both the living and the dead it was necessary for her to be able to visit either camp. Let us classify her then as, simply, existent.

So it was in search of this existent thing that Run Run went with the eyes that he had pried from the face of his dead father; and one other important belonging: a necklace of leather upon which hung a single tortoise-coloured cowrie shell. Never before had he gone so deeply into the jungle, and he was afraid, but believed that a heavy trust had been placed upon him, and this sustained him. Luckily he found Yoruba, in her earthly form, in a small hut that was leaking smoke through its thatch. He was not surprised when immediately ordered to surrender his father's things. A skinny forefinger beckoned irritably through the smoke.

Yoruba took the shell, scratched its speckled dome; sniffed at it, tasted it, peered into its mouth for a while in an anticipatory way, then pronounced its inhabitant absent. In this case she was not referring to its original mollusc proprietor, but to the little fetish spirit that she herself had implanted there on Run Run's father's behalf, some years ago. Perhaps it had been killed off by a stronger fetish. Perhaps it had been seduced from this small home to another. Or it might have been pure maliciousness that had caused it to vacate. The point was, that at the time of Run Run's father's death, his cowrie shell fetish had failed for one or other reason to do what it was supposed to do. That is to guard the good man. July was dead. Yoruba was worried.

It was she who had paramount authority over the spirit population for the district and so it was her responsibility to discover where things had gone wrong and, primarily, if the fetish spirit had turned bad and was on the loose. For then there was no knowing what mischief it might get up to. Her reputation was at stake. She must find the thing, or at the very least find out what had become of it.

With this aim in mind, she prepared herself to be not of this earth for as long as it took to locate the truant fetish spirit. And for this difficult task she would need all the visual help she could get. July's excellent eyes would supplement her own. She warned little Run Run not to peep while she made ready, or risk being turned into air, then stoked her small fire into a large one. Run Run could feel its heat and hear its crackle. Also, he could hear the incantations of Yoruba, which continued for so long and in such a monotonous tone of voice that he dozed off for a while; he was not sure for how long. But when he heard her voice again it had adopted the growl of a leopard, which naturally caused him to start, to jerk his eyelids apart and look where he was forbidden to look. And not just to look but to stare in amazement. His expectation was that he would find himself in Yoruba's hut, but this was not the case. He was out in the jungle, following the familiar path that led from Duke Ephraim's walled village to the little Roman Catholic mission of Father Theo. Yoruba, if she was there, was not visible, yet he could hear the leopard sounds she imitated so well. He was moving, he noticed, swiftly but without voluntary effort, as though caught in the flood stream of a river. He had no doubt as to where he would be deposited, for this path ended at the clearing in which stood the house of Theo's god.

More amazement! Though the wonderful river did lose its impetus at the gate of Father Theo's mission, it had, apparently, while sweeping him forwards, transported him backwards, too.

For his view at that moment was not of that moment, but of several yesterdays prior to it. He saw his father, as he'd seen him before, tied wrist and ankle to the tamarind tree. He saw Father Theo, drenched in sweat, rolling up his shirtsleeves while bits of Bible-say came dribbling through his lips. He saw him raise the whip and lash it on the reddened-black back, and again – *crack*, and again – *crack*. He could hear exhalations – one of effort – one of agony. He watched the punished flesh jerk, noticing that the small cowrie shell fetish was where it had been for so many years, dangling in a groove of chest muscle. And it, too, jerked in sympathy with the pain.

Run Run tried to close his eyes, to rid them of the view, and did succeed after an intense struggle to shut out some things. But there was little relief in this, for the whipping sounds were as terrible as ever. And Yoruba's leopard growl in the blindness was too awful to endure. So he looked again, at the very second when his father gave up life. He saw the shadow of the soul separate itself from the body. In human form, yet able to fly, it trickled, here and there, then lifted and disappeared. And Father Theo saw nothing of this, but lashed on, and on.

Now something else attracted Run Run's gaze. A small light, similar to a candle flame, had made an appearance at the mouth of the cowrie shell. It lingered there, as though attached by a wick to the cowrie's mouth. It was marvellously yellow and alive. Then almost as quickly as his eyes could follow it, the flame darted away. At first it hung in the air before the preacher's face, then it dived completely into one nostril, then shot into his mouth, then out again, then onto the roof of the church, dancing, frightening a small bird into startled flight. For a while it vanished in the thick foliage of the tamarind, then it swooped down with a hiss like flame meeting water, into the mouth of a new arrival. Then out again. What a thing!

Run Run observed the arrival of the white man from the jungle path; a tall man with two pistols dug into his belt. The little flame, with crazy intensity, was circling in a blur of light about the man's head, flinging itself at him, spluttering on his sweat, leaving scorch marks, apparently unfelt. For all the while the man showed no discomfort. In fact, the expression on his face on observing Father Theo with his whip was firstly of relief. Astonishment came later, then repugnance. Then by means of standing on the tip of the whip, he put an end to the harrowing of July.

And it was at that instant that the inhabitant spirit of the cowrie discovered an entrance into its newly selected home – a minute scratch upon the hand of the seaman. It enlarged it with a single swift strike and wriggled in. The lieutenant, with a puckered frown, looked at his bleeding wound, then sucked it.

He could suck all day and not drag the spirit out. Run Run knew that. Yoruba knew that. He could hear her cackling with mirth from somewhere nearby. Father Theo trumpeted vastly at the tree tops, but his craft, like mist, changed nothing that it touched.

Seven

Bathed liquidly in the fire glow, Mammy Yellowbelly looked as fat as a cotton sack. She wore a bright red dress of no defined structure, and was decorated with more gold than Rory had ever seen outside of a Spanish treasure haul – chains of it and chunks of it, some crafted, some raw, glinting on her neck and wrists. The sheer weight of it was such that all bodily movement needed assistance. She was flanked by slaves whose function was to prop her as she walked and to manipulate her arms in the event of her wishing to gesticulate. Her chair was made partially of gold, and it was orbed with human skulls. It had been placed at the top of a case of stairs that ran up to an imposing verandah. Here sat the mother of Duke Ephraim, ruler of the River Cross and all its people, some of whom had lit several rousing bonfires on her lawn.

Rory, too, had a place upon the high verandah, at its extremity, at the side (the amputated side) of Jemmy Honesty. Before them in the gay light of the bonfires cavorted a crowd dressed mainly in cast-offs and tatters of European clothing of which they seemed inordinately proud. There was music; drums and other wooden contraptions that were being robustly thumped; and a twanging of native harps, more drowned than heard. Stilt-walkers marched precariously on high, plodding stiffly this way and that as though about to fall, yet never falling. Extraordinary entertainment by any standards. Jemmy Honesty took it upon himself to explain the significance of the ceremony that was about to begin. 'Make doctor,' was how he expressed it. Jemmy, when so inclined, quaintified his vocabulary with bits of pidgin talk, the trade lingo of the Slave Coast: 'Makey de ship come up out de sea. Makey de slave-cappy do palaver.'

What did he mean by 'Make doctor'? The explanation was demonstrated. A boy appeared; an albino dressed up in imitation sailor's rig. Here was something curious, a touch of local humour – a clown? Apparently not, for wound around the child's neck was a rope, a sort of steering device by which means several minders were controlling his direction. The sailor-boy came through the middle of the agglutinous dance, walking, if one could call it that. His legs were moving, one foot was being placed before the other. Thus he was advancing towards the house with his face upwards-turned and his pale eyes reverently fixed on the person of Mammy Yellowbelly, as though in a trance. A dream, not of his own, but of those surrounding him, in which, nevertheless he was inextricably implanted. Rory felt a deep shiver in his spine. The crowd grew still. The music diminished. The albino kid kneeled.

'What now?' said Rory, *sotto voce.*

'Make doctor.'

'They won't harm him?'

'Not much.'

'How much?'

The answer to that of course, depended largely upon one's point of view. What was great harm to one might be no harm, or even of benefit, to another. What happened was that a man dressed in a sleeveless surcoat of chain-mail, his features obscured by the mask of a snarling beast, came stalking out of the trees. Both of this creature's hands clasped the handle of a long crusader's sword as it flashed and cut bright circles in the gloom. The swordsman slashed the air near the neck of the albino boy, then turned away. Rory breathed an audible sigh of relief – premature in the event, for the movement was calculated merely to add to his momentum. The sword flashed in an overhead arc, met the boy's neck and severed it clean off the body. A jet of red fountained upwards. Football! The severed head became an object of sport. Ululating and baying the crowd surged forward, revived, dancing, booting the bloody trophy about from one end of the lawn to the other.

There was an instant of illusion – a trick of light perhaps – that, had Rory blinked, he might have missed. It was of the little albino, his body intact, as though aglow with pale fire, as pale as the skin of the moon, standing where he had knelt in a lacuna of silence. Then he shimmered and vanished, and the howling insanity condensed in his space. The pitiable residue of the child lay where it had fallen, slowly bleeding.

'A sacrifice,' said Jemmy Honesty flatly. 'A necessary component of business hereabouts. Trade hasn't been that brisk since the Royal Navy took a hand . . . Look at Mammy smiling now, will you. Things are sure to improve.'

'It was barbaric.'

'I wouldn't let her hear you say that,' hissed Jemmy, waving his stump. 'Oh, that would be a bad mistake.'

Mammy Yellowbelly preceded her guests into the interior of her mansion, to a dining room with a long and fantastically decorated teak table. A French clock, minus its pendulum, was the centrepiece. There were pewter mugs, some with broken handles, china ornaments, including a large spotted dog, and a ship's tureen with something bony and decaying lying in it. There was a coming and going of partially naked black girls laden with food and drink, mighty bosomed and small, sweating freely from their labour. The floor creaked with their tread. As before, Rory's place was adjacent to Jemmy Honesty's. He noticed all these things as one sheathed by the abstraction of his senses. A layer of numbness had come between him and all else. So when he asked Jemmy Honesty how he, an Englishman, could serve a family as barbarous as the house of Duke, the reply only vaguely impinged.

'No word such as barbarous exists in the vocabulary of these people. Its closest description lies in a word meaning "insatiable power". I serve a man of insatiable power. His people, dear Lieutenant, have no will, no expectations other than to somehow be used up by his house in any way Ephraim chooses. As you saw.'

'Have they a word, then, for stupidity? How can the murder of a child dressed up in sailor's rig cause trade to improve? It's plain stupid. And you, a man of education by my guess, you weren't always like this, I'll warrant.'

'Lieutenant,' Jemmy kept his voice below the burble of conversation, 'I don't give a tuppenny damn for what you think. That's a fact. So please don't wank in my ear. I've seen the inside of a debtor's goal, and don't intend to revisit. I'm well off here. Don't fuck up paradise, McKay . . . My good advice to you is to sit down, look pleased with life, eat a lot and get as tight as you like. There are no limits as far as that goes. Mammy loves happy drunkards. Don't bite the hand . . . Have a drink, Lieutenant, and for your own good, take that fusty look off your face.'

'But we, as Englishmen . . .'

Honesty looked as though he might gag on this information. 'What the hell,' he said, 'has who *we* are got to do with it? You're new at this game, aren't you, Lieutenant? Yes, I thought so. A slaver by necessity. They make the worst sort. Why the hell didn't you find other employment?'

'Who'd have me?'

'Were you in the Navy?'

'Yes.'

'Disciplined for some offence?'

'I was on watch when we ran aground.'

'A scapegoat.'

'I'd rather not go into it, other than to say that I wasn't without blame.'

'Your trouble, Lieutenant, is that you take too much upon yourself.' He confided in a raucous undertone, 'I was once like you. Now I'm like me . . . When I'm grey and old I'll be moral.'

'You're confusing morality with sheer stupidity.'

'No I'm not. I'm equating them. You're the one what's confused.'

Rory studied his advisor exactly, and at the end of his scrutiny knew that Honesty was right. He had no argument and was bitterly confused about many things, including the subject in hand. Insanity was in the air, as infective as the plague, and as lethal. With a shake of his head he said, 'Anyhow, I want no part of it.'

'Lieutenant, I'll be blunt with you.' Honesty turned to face him. 'You are making it impossible for me to be cordial. You are endangering yourself, and tainting me in the process. You have both food and drink before you. Attend to it.' Jemmy took a copious pinch of snuff.

'I couldn't eat,' said Rory.

'Then drink. Just stop clanking, will you. Drink.'

'I will.'

He thought the alcohol might somewhat haze the present. It did, illuminating instead concern for his future. How could he carry on like this? One day he would be judged by God for his earthly deeds. Would the record show that he had done what he could to leave this place in a better state than he'd found it? Would it be said that he'd lived by the Commandments? These troublesome ethics set up a hard impasse which was equally in need of dilution. He drank apologetically, but fully.

'It's called mimbo,' said Jemmy Honesty of the substance they were swallowing. 'It's made from the sap of the mimbo palm. You can drink it all night without shitting through your teeth, and still be fond of it in the morning.' With this recommendation, he filled Rory's tumbler from a pewter pitcher, giving the glass a friendly chink, and producing in this sound a vein of camaraderie.

Rory shot some more of the mimbo. He wasn't a stranger to its taste, he'd drunk it before, downriver at Old Efik Landing prior to his ruinous run-in with the Navy. He liked it less than he remembered, though the flavour seemed basically the same. Of course, he'd been drinking it then for the sake of enjoyment, whereas now it was to obliterate his conscience, and to get the stink of the river out of his nostrils. This skulking about in evil-smelling creeks was getting him down. Slaving was not what it used to be. No, sir. When one had to murder little kids to ensure good trade, then it was time to pack it in. The game, if ever it could have been thought upon as such, was no longer worth the candle.

Holding to this chain of thought, Rory drank two more tumblers of mimbo in quick succession. Then on a wave of disgust that simply overflowed he said loudly, 'It was a foul thing to do,' then immediately looked towards Mammy Yellowbelly to see if the criticism had reached her. Possibly it had. She was looking at him, chewing and watching with the indifferent placidity of the very fat. He did not feel threatened, nor was he cowed into looking away. In fact the very benignity of the exchange encouraged him. He raised up his glass towards her as he would have were he toasting her health, whereas quite the opposite was true. 'May you rot,' said his mind to hers. She broke off her gaze and said something sharpish to the slave who was feeding her.

Rory felt that in a small way he'd done well. He looked down at the contents of his own dinner plate: a stew of sorts; a peppery, thick swamp, into which a large insect had just mortally flopped. He drank more mimbo, feeling its slothful stir in his mind. Around, above, and on all sides a blur of conversation passed, unheard but for short, disconnected passages.

'A good day's work.' Strangeways' voice.

'Why, Captain, we'll have you slaved in a week.' This, Ephraim's bold promise.

Mammy Yellowbelly flung a shriek of laughter down the length of the table, mingling it with the words, 'You wait – tomorrow.'

What was to be tomorrow? Tomorrow he would accompany Strangeways and some sailors down to Duke Ephraim's slave barracoon, there to begin the process of human selection; to peer into mouths for rotten teeth, and into female genitalia for whatever rot might lurk there; to prod and pull and pry apart, and cause to jump energetically up and down every slave in this place, so that none who was unwholesome would be taken up. Then they would brand the skin of those selected with the motto of the *Pluto* and send them downriver to the ship. And that, more or less, was how he would be occupied for that entire day, and the next, and for however long it took to fill up the main deck of the *Pluto* with slaves – four hundred and twenty, hip to hip, head to foot, ankle-chained and groaning.

Suddenly, into this appalling prospect walked the most sensual woman he had ever seen. She was mulatto, but uncontaminated by Africa; not over-seasoned with negroid looks, but sulky and dusky enough to torch his groin. Her skin was as pale as cream, her lips full and red. Her hair was Spanish sepia – *abundante*, flowing into the base of her spine. Her breasts were ovate, full and taut, slightly asway as she walked. He found her eyes, then couldn't leave them. He tried. He could not. So he stared. As though they were alone he and she, and lovers at that, he stared, feeling the inner forces that lovers feel, and the speeding pulse, and the urgent need to touch. All she gave were eyes of laughter, ridicule and contempt. She did not carry trays like the black women, nor did she do any form of work. She came and she went, leaving him incredibly stirred. It was the stab of Jemmy Honesty's arm-stub in his ribs that made Rory realise that his mind was wide open to the world. Honesty, muttering, dug into him with furtive warnings. 'His wife, you fool. His favourite wife.'

'Duke Ephraim's wife? You don't say? How was I to know?'

'They're all his wives, the whole rubber-buttery.'

'What, all of these women?'

'He has over a hundred. You mustn't stare at 'em.'

'It wasn't intentional. I imagined I'd seen her before.' Yes, upon reflection, that seemed true. He was nagged by some previous intimate knowledge of this astonishing mulatto.

'Don't think of shagging any of them,' said Honesty, hoarsely severe. 'He'd personally cut your ballocks off.'

'Thanks for warning me.'

'I don't want trouble. Trouble is like dog shit. It gets up everyone's nostrils, and it's hell to get rid of.'

'You would know about that.'

'I know a thing or two,' said Honesty, unscathed. 'I've survived here. I tell you there's rules that may not be broken, and they concern the mind as much as the body. In England, where it's cold, it's different. Here the climate reaches into your mind and germinates the crazy-seed.' He peered intently into the amber liquid of his tumbler for a while as though in search for the remainder of his analogy, then said, 'Your thoughts just take you over in the jungle. They're bigger and stronger than in England. The rule is throw out the crazy-seed – before it gets a chance to grow.'

Rory mulled over this not uninteresting philosophy, then disregarded it. Jemmy Honesty was just too damned uncouth to be taken seriously.

'There's rum if you want it,' said Honesty, gesturing generously towards an adjacent flagon. 'And gin . . . Are you drunk, McKay?'

'A little,' Rory admitted.

'I think I am. Do you think I am?'

Rory felt obliged to forego the truth. 'Not a bit.'

'I think I am,' said Honesty again, and then, as though he'd been severely criticised, became belligerent. 'What of it!'

'I think you are quite sober. You make an interesting point . . .'

'You make an interesting point.' Honesty aped him be-littlingly. 'Don't piss down my back, McKay.' He muttered something to himself, then took a great swig of mimbo. 'I dare say I do.' He said more passively, 'But what I've told you is the truth. You must get that wench out of your mind. It's the crazy-seed.'

'I have.'

'I saw the way you looked at her. So did Mammy Yellow-belly. Watch out for Mammy Yellowbelly, she's full of magic and mischief. If she don't like you, you could be witched.'

Rory saw no reason why the freakish woman should wish to harm him, yet turned towards her to assess the danger. He saw none. Mammy was watching him, masticating with the slow deliberation of a cow, producing an impression of bloated complacency – no more than that.

He drank some brandy and thought depressingly of the day that lay ahead. He drank until his hostess, with one sturdy slave underpinning each blubbery armpit, arose, muttered some incantations (apparently blessing all at the table) then waddled goldenly off.

Strangeways, too, decided that he had had enough. He called his lieutenant to him. They bade Duke Ephraim a good night then left together.

The bonfires were down. The patch of blood that marked the albino's life's end lay blackly like a hole in their path. Both body and head had been removed.

The good citizens of Creek Town, having drunk themselves to a stupor, lay fallen as though mowed down by grape-shot. Some survivors had bottles still plugged into their mouths; some were crawling; some were fornicating exhaustedly amongst the shrubs. Amongst the latter category were sailors. Strangeways payed these transgressors no heed. A drum was giving off little cushions of rhythm of minor but ceaseless influence.

They walked towards the gap in the fort wall, pricked by the fire of mosquitoes, aided by the pallid hand of the moon, glad that they were soon to lie down and sleep. 'Sleep,' said Captain Strangeways, 'is nature's fondest gesture . . . It was a polite affair tonight. But we'll make up for it.'

Before entering his hut Strangeways paused. 'You did not

please me today.' He tapped Rory's chest with his forefinger. 'If that fool of a priest comes close to me again, I'll cut his nose off. Do you hear me well, Lieutenant?'

'Quite well.'

'I mean it literally, Lieutenant.'

'I believe you do, sir.'

'I'm tired. Good night to you.'

Yet sleep served Rory unsympathetically. He passively expected it. Instead, all the day's events rearrived, sometimes several at a time, marching about, fully aware as to where to kick in order to agitate him. For instance, there was the discomfort of the meeting on the river path with the whipping priest, Theophillus. The preacher had placed him badly with Strangeways with his insinuation of mutually held deep secrets. Strangeways hadn't liked it, and would undoubtedly make hay of the incident. The loutish Jemmy Honesty was accusingly active, too, digging away with the stump of his arm into some unconscionable areas of thought. No sleep while Honesty was about. No sleep while the crazy-seed set down roots. Here was the real problem. The mulatto woman. He couldn't get her out of his mind. Nor could he forget the albino kid. It was illogical. Two such diverse images and emotions should have been easy to separate, but this was not so. They solidified into one. Beauty and horror, so intermixed and entangled that he couldn't tell one from the other. They were attracted by some force of argument that he couldn't fathom.

The moon discovered his discontent and made it greater by lighting the miserable place that contained him. It came to the window, reached in and sat boldly in his eyes. It whitely streaked the mud walls, making visible more squalidness than he could stand. It cast a shadow – a foreshortened human shadow in the silver patch at his door. Someone was at his door.

Rory's skin crawled. He expected an attack, an animal-like prance that would bring the intruder upon him. He tensed. No attack. The moon poured down its eternal silver. The shadow did not budge, neither came or went. If it came he would deal with it with pistol-fire. This decided, what remained to be done was to get the weapon into his hand. His arm glided with the quietness of a snake towards the table top where his pistol lay, and even as it did the horrible doubt occurred as to whether he'd primed it. He could not recall having done so. It was his habit, as was prayer, neither act leaving much of a mark, whether done or omitted. In any case, the hand en route to the pistol had met a snag, a splinter of bamboo perhaps that had hooked into the fabric of his shirt; a small entrapment that nevertheless caused a largish sound. He panicked, recoiled, jerked outwards, ripping his sleeve, upsetting the dubious equilibrium of the cot which spilled him helter-skelter onto the floor, into the table legs. There was a crash of falling objects.

All that remained at the threshold of his hut was the emptied silver shaft of the moon. He dashed into the lane, unarmed, dressed only in his shirt. There he stood for a while, searching the shadows, seeing no one, hearing nothing, smelling the rot of the fort and hating it.

Eight

The pistol had not been primed. Rory discovered that in the morning. The weapon, one of a pair of modern cavalry design, did not use a flint and lock, but was detonated by means of a hammer falling upon a cap or pill which instantaneously ignited the powder; a very effective advance over the old system, providing the owner did not neglect to insert one of the little copper caps. Having but recently purchased this pair of pistols from a smith in Birmingham, he had not as yet really become acquainted with them. A negligence he proposed to rectify at once.

With the sun still low, he stuck both pistols into his belt then went to the lake and potted at anything that presented – frogs as big as plates, several crocodiles, parrots, an empty rum firkin that he tossed into the water, then holed four times out of five at thirty paces. The pistols sat well in his hand, they were handsomely austere and true.

Duke Ephraim's slave barracoons were blemished stockades of timber poles driven into the ground with about a hand's width between them. There were two high gates, likewise made of rough pole. Inside was a compound and some open-sided thatched huts, but not a tree, and not a single corner where privacy could be had. This structure possessed the south end of the fort: the marshy end. Jemmy Honesty had his house near at hand, which made Rory wonder if the man had been born lacking, or whether snuff had rendered his nostrils senseless. For the air in that part of the fort was so rampantly vile and fly-infested that the mere act of walking there was an ordeal. Rory's stomach kicked sickly as he approached the stockade entrance. Strangeways was already there, as were some of his sailors. The captain had come prepared. He'd brought a pouch of camphor, which, when fastened between his teeth, theoretically banished the stink, yet didn't deter the flies in any noticeable way. They came down on the Englishmen in a rapacious thrum of wings and with variant methods of torture – some sucked, some stung, some merely crawled. The Negro guards bore the insect plague without seeming to be inconvenienced. Two of them loosened the heavy crossbar then shoved the gates open, and when that was done, Jemmy Honesty cracked the stock whip he had brought. Perhaps this was to advertise his terrible presence to those in the interior, for a droning began: a sound of human origin, much louder than the flies.

'It's funny,' said Jemmy Honesty. 'No matter how many times we tell 'em it's not true, we can't get the idea out of their thick woolly skulls . . .'

As he did not proceed, Rory asked him, 'What are you talking about? What idea?'

Strangeways took out his anti-stink device in order to say, 'They think that white men are a race of cannibal sea-demons. 'Ain't that so, Mr Honesty?'

'So they drone,' said Honesty. 'And they howl . . . And you can't tell 'em different, and you can't bribe 'em different. And the whip makes them even more sure of it. They're a queer bunch, Captain . . . And by the way, the camphor bag is a first-rate idea if I may say so.'

Both smell and noise grew more acute as they came upon its main source: a hundred or so prisoners, chained in pairs, neck to neck, conversing in a language of whispers and groans, and some not at all, for they were beyond doubt, dead. Now Jemmy Honesty complained substantially about the black man's weird ability to will himself to death. For they had all been in prime health at yesterday's inspection: 'Sleek as lizards.' And now dead. How did they do it? No atmosphere of sorcery surrounded them. No demon energy stared forth. There was fear. It was detectable in every gesture and in the rolling whites of their eyes. Fear could tangle a man's viscera – but surely not stop his heart.

The dead were dragged away to some place beyond the walls of the barracoon. A batch of the living had their neck chains unlocked, and were prodded at musket point towards the white men. The work of the slavers began. Strangeways had chosen the responsible task of examining teeth for signs of unacceptable age. This he accomplished by squatting on the candidates' chests, leaning on their jawbones, then peering into the gap. Those who made the grade were passed on to Rory, whose job were to get them to jump up and down, while flapping their arms. Any who showed signs of premature fatigue were rejected. This wasn't as simple a task as it sounded. There were many who did not want to look good. For in looking good what else were they doing but sealing their fate? Vigour and stamina were thus in little evidence, and Rory was confronted with a shambling, stumbling sequence of men and women who seemed incapable of any sustained effort and whose only energy was fear. They could or would not clear more than three inches, perhaps for half a dozen skips, before arriving at the point of collapse. The whip didn't improve matters much. But Jemmy Honesty said with good humour that it was always the same. They were as full of tricks as a bagful of monkeys, but he had a cure. He took out his pistol and shot one non-jumper through the head. 'Now they'll jump, by God.'

The sun leapt forward in the sky. The grading proceeded with efficiency. From Rory's station the slaves were taken by sailors for branding with the motto of the *Pluto*. An important step, for from the moment that name was burned into their flesh, they were the property of Captain Strangeways. Now Strangeways had to pay for their keep, and if any died, the loss stood in his books. Time was of the essence. Yet at dusk of that day, out of a hundred and three examined, only thirty-seven had made the grade. As for the remainder, some were fed and some were killed. Those whose energy was irreversibly drained were led down to the jetty where they were clubbed to death, or near enough to that state for the river effortlessly to drown them.

A fresh, new head had been given space amongst the rows of skulls in the palaver hut. It was that of the albino boy last seen intact at Mammy Yellowbelly's celebration. Now, drained to the colour of parchment, slack jawed, and unhappy, its pallid eyes took in the white men who had come to complain to Duke Ephraim about the quality of the merchandise down in the barracoons.

'It'll take us months to get slaved at this rate,' Strangeways grumbled. 'Months. The rains are due at the month's end.' He said emphatically, 'We must be away before the rains.'

'Things will improve.' Ephraim stabbed positively at the air with a lit cigar. 'There is a war between my neighbouring tribes, which they must somehow finance. And in any case, my overseers will be bringing new merchandise down to the barracoons tomorrow. There are, I'm told, some prime gentlemen amongst that lot.'

Strangeways tapped from a keg of rum, muttering. Boneless fingers of night came to touch the palaver hut, enveloping all within. Good nature flowed out of the rum keg and there was laughter. As for the countenance of the albino boy: that ceased to look melancholy and vacant, and became intensely spiteful. Of course, this change of attitude was mere shadow conjuring. Its actual animation was not visible. Rory watched the face dissolve into darkness, then return in lamplight, but scarcely paid it attention. He was amongst memories of the day – the perpetual groaning, the crack of the whip-end and the clank of chain, and his soul felt dirty. He did not blame himself for a single death, yet they weighed on him terribly, bent him at the neck.

The heat drew back ever so slightly and cicadas, crickets and frogs came out, shrieking and bellowing at the sky, 'Give us rain.' But the sky stayed cloudless, and the moon claimed it fully. It pressed its silver cheek upon Rory as he slept, waking him from a dismal restless dream, disclosing as it did his even more dismal real circumstances. All seemed as it had been on the previous night. He turned his eyes sufficiently to observe the door of his hut, torpidly wondering whether the shadow visitor had returned. It had. In a second Rory's pistol was up and pointed. What kept him from firing he didn't know. For the shadow had become more than that. It had become its owner – a human; a stealthily advancing human – a person, anonymous but for outline, carriage and scent. And these were of woman.

She was mulatto. With a gesture of tolerance, almost of endearment, she brushed aside his pistol hand. A haze of darkness that was her hair swept the moon from his eyes, and in its midst was a face that was intensely beautiful. He recognised her. She was the woman he had ogled at Mammy Yellowbelly's house – the wife – the favourite wife of Duke Ephraim. A groan that was intended as protestation shrank amicably in his throat, and even that minor sound she stopped with the pressure of a finger. There was to be no noise. When he was clear on that point the finger was lifted away and replaced by lips so softly applied that it was as if a butterfly had alighted, trembling. It was as he had never before been kissed; a butterfly, yes, but only for as long as it took to take his breath away. Then a bolder attitude took charge. Her tongue curled smoothly into the cavity of his mouth, searching, it seemed, arousing little groans impossible to mute fully. He begged her to undress and she did. Her bare breasts touched him, spreading puddles of warm pleasure. He touched them, pressed them, kneaded them, wishing for no more than to be allowed, for ever, to do that. But more, much more was to come. Brazen woman, she mounted him, tossing back her mane of hair. Then she rode him in the dark, in a black velvet night with belly and breast agleam and streaming sweat. Rode him, demon-eyed, until his manhood cringed from contact. The moon, having seen this wild dance of love, gasped, and drew a veil of cloud across its face. Rory thought he heard thunder, but it could have been in his mind. It could have been the crazy-seed bursting frantically into growth.

He was sure that it rained, because he awoke to the sound of splashing water, and with a steady dribble of it on his forehead. Dawn pissed greyly down upon Creek Town. The mulatto woman was gone. He felt as though he'd had no sleep at all, and lapsed into vague disquiet.

Nine

Run Run, having had a taste of being turned into air, then remade in his prior likeness, became keen on such stunts. And Yoruba, who was weary of this sort of basic chore, and was keen to advance much more deeply into the underground spirit world of Srahmandazi, saw in the lad a potential that very few possessed. She needed an apprentice, someone who could take over the task of producing the less complicated spells and fetish objects that the villagers were so keen on. She needed just such a willing and talented youngster to train up as a fetish witch. So she called on Egbo the Executioner, who owed her many favours, and had him kidnap the boy in broad daylight from the mud fortress of Creek Town. Run Run put up a token struggle. He knew what the citizens of the fort did not know – that he was not being taken to be sacrificially killed, but to a new home, and a new, improved life. Why should he wriggle? Why should he resist?

He entered into apprenticeship with Yoruba on the same day; at first as a mere fetcher and carrier of anything she called for – bones, seeds, feathers, bits of skin, tufts of human hair, stones, bark. The items required in the practice of charm making were numerous. Being quick and observant, he learned at the same time some elementary magic, and of the nature of spirits. All things possessed spirits. Trees had spirits, herbs had spirits of medicinal value, spears had brave spirits, and cooking pots dull ones. But these were all lesser souls, and of no real consequence. The souls that a witch such as his teacher had most to do with were of a much higher order – human souls. She became very serious and stern when giving instruction on the subject of souls, sometimes pressing home the importance of the matter by means of a rap of her knuckle on his skull. He was expected to answer questions.

'How many classes of souls are there?'

'Each person has four.'

'Yes, four. And what are they?'

Unhesitatingly he gave them. 'There is one that survives, and three that die.'

'Tell me about the three mortal souls.'

'The first lives outside the body of its owner, in some wild beast deep in the forest. The second is the shadow cast by the body, which dies in the grave. The last is our dream soul.'

'A monkey of a soul, a giddy-headed thing, this dream soul. Off it goes when its owner takes a nap, to wander about and act the fool with others of its kind. It gets so tied up in silliness and gossip that it sometimes forgets to come back in time. Its owner wakes up without it. And *there's* trouble . . . It was sickness caused by the lost dream soul of your father that first brought him to me.' She applied her knuckles to Run Run's skull as though vexed by the very memory. 'Did you know that, boy?'

He had not known that. He said so, wincing.

'Your father had the most troublesome of souls. He lost his shadow once, and I had to find that, too. He was a difficult man from first to last. Always drunk. Always fighting. Always coming groaning to me – begging for new spirit charms to be hung on him – love charms. Hate charms. Charms to make him invisible to elephants. He was careless and lost them all.'

'I saw the little fire that lived in the cowrie.'

'So you did. It had been weakened and confused by disrespect for it by your father. It could have saved him had he heeded it in time. But your father threw its warnings away as he threw away all things that served him well.'

'Is it in the Englishman, Rory, now?'

Yoruba gave a sigh of annoyance which ended in a most python-like hiss. She scuffed her heel at the edge of the fire which gave a dance of fascinating sparks. Presently, when she'd thought the matter through, she said, 'I want it back.'

'But how. . . ?' Inquisitiveness was aborted by means of a hard knock to the skull.

'How many classes of souls are there?'

'There are four, Teacher.'

'And that is all that I require you to know. You're a meddlesome little boy; more like your father than pleases me. I

89

should turn you into a lizard to teach you some manners. I did that to your father once.'

'I'll try harder, Teacher.' The lesson had taken a nasty turn. Run Run tensed for flight.

It was a joke. Beneath its stingy drape of breasts Yoruba's rib cage quaked. 'Seeing you asked the question, boy, answer it. Show me how clever you are. Go on. How will it be done? How will I get it back?'

'I don't know, Teacher . . . You'll trap it?'

'That's right. I'll trap it. I'll lure it out and back into its home. The white man must be made to wear the empty cowrie shell, though, that's essential. Clever boy. We'll snag it with a powerful spell, we'll suck it out of him and back into the shell. That's what we'll do.'

Emboldened, Run Run asked, 'Would that harm Rory, Teacher?'

'Harm him?' Yoruba stared distantly at that prospect. 'He looked strong of body. They came from the sea, these white men; out of the sea. They look strong, but so does a shark look strong until it's on the beach. They shouldn't come here but they do. And then they die. Harm him? . . . Well, that depends on how long he lasts of his own account. He'd certainly be more use dead than alive, wouldn't he? I could trap his immortal soul if he were dead, seal it in a basket and keep it till the end of time. It would be a very valuable thing to have, but tricky and troublesome, and in need of education, too . . . No, I haven't the patience for that. All I want back is the cowrie shell spirit. It took a lot of time and energy to bring to birth, and to give it a good attitude. Why should I just let it go? It's mine. I want no more than is mine.'

Yoruba, it seemed, had come to the end of the subject. She stood up, and began her nightly beauty ritual which entailed smearing her entire surface with vegetable-butter. When thoroughly polished, she came back to the fire and lay upon her mat. Run Run, too, prepared to open the gate of his dream soul. He was nearly alseep when she quoted a proverb, 'Sand sinks in water; water sinks in sand.'

Even the most innocent of things, when in the wrong place, will disappear – that is to say, die. Was she referring to the unfortunate accident that had befallen Rory at Pater Theo's mission? Run Run doubted if it was Yoruba's intention deliberately to harm Rory. Her craft was one of opposition to harm . . . The riddle lacked the urgency to keep him from slumber.

That's not to say that in the avid jungle thereabouts, and in the sleeping town, there was an absence of practitioners of magic who loved to do harm. For Creek Town was thick with wicked people, people who did nothing else, aspired to no other achievement than successfully to cause wretchedness and premature death amongst the population. There were poisoners and curse merchants, stealers of men's shadows and men's dream souls and fetish guardians; and dispensers of incurable insanity. There was Egbo who went around with his great Crusader's sword depriving people of their heads. But of all these wizards and night-mates there was none more skilled in human destruction than the creature–god Sassabonsum. Here is something bestial, so horrifically vile that even those who have survived his touch cannot adequately describe it. It is as though the shock of contact numbs one's memory for a while. Which might be considered a blessing, but with time a picture stirs. It is remembered that they were out walking on a path in moonlight when they became aware of someone else ahead of them, approaching, perhaps, or standing at the path's edge to allow them room to pass. And so they passed, and in doing so inevitably brushed against their fellow traveller. This is the moment of horror. They become aware of a stench so violent that they reel from it. They look into a face, one side of which is wholesome, even handsome, the other, rotten with putrefaction. This thing, half corpse, half man, then embraces them. Soon they fall ill, desperately so, fortunately, one might say, with no recollection of the cause of the disease until at the last minute. Death is merciful. There is no antidote.

Why then, surely one should not go abroad at night, and if such a course of action is unavoidable, then evade all strangers on the path. Quite so. But Sassabonsum is not quite so easily thwarted as that. For the element of evasion of this or that course of action scarcely matters. Neither is good or bad luck much of a factor. Sassabonsum's selection is premeditated, his act well planned. He has collaborators – queens and overseers; malcontents and wizards; anyone, in fact, with an axe to grind.

Mammy Yellowbelly had taken a sharp dislike to Rory McKay from the word go. His digs and overt insults, his loud objections to the trade-charm ceremony, worked at her dinner party. None of these things went down well. When the charm failed to produce the sort of upsurge in fortunes that was expected of it, what other conclusion could be arrived at than that the Englishman was actively working against her and her son. She decided on strong action, and sent a message to Sassabonsum to call at once, which he did. He was given a mandate to sort out the problem caused by the perverse Englishman: 'Go find that white man and turn him off. Better do it soon before more mischief. He's got power, that one. He can make things bad.'

It was true. There was something about that tall white man, some indefinable inner stance of strength and purity that in other circumstances she might have found most attractive, and wished to corrupt to the full, but which in the present trade climate amounted to serious trouble. No time for fun. The man needed to be exterminated, and not in a nice way . . . These were Mammy's thoughts after having got rid of her evil-smelling executioner. Sassabonsum would do the job. Of that there was no doubt in her mind. He never failed. Still she felt unsettled, as though she had not done all she should do to expedite the removal of McKay. Time, after all, *was* a factor. And Sassabonsum was not necessarily the quickest of actors. Moreover, he naturally had a constant backlog of work.

This was the predicament that gnawed at Mammy Yellowbelly long into the night. She needed to find some quicker form of extinction. Yet something that couldn't be laid at her door. Then she hit on it. Suddenly, compressed by her genius into an audible announcement: 'Jemmy Honesty!' Yes! One white man killing another, if the circumstances were appropriate, would kick up not even a ripple of bad feeling between her and her customers. Mammy's distress melted, her melancholy vanished, she sent for the second elected executioner.

Jemmy Honesty had lived close to Mammy Yellowbelly for too long to be caught by surprise by this her latest request. Kill McKay. Provoke a duel and shoot the pestilent man between the eyes. Of course, he could not openly refuse her, though privately he presumed more difficulty in this course of action than he was willing to let on. McKay looked like a level-headed sort of fellow, not at all the sort who might be provoked into rash arguments and deadly insults. Moreover, he didn't fancy his chances against that modern pair of horse pistols that McKay always wore. Naturally, he did not voice his misgivings to Mammy Yellowbelly, he feared her far more than McKay. He did, however, set about reorganising her plan in a way that would substantially improve his chances of survival.

He went straight away to his house and dug into a trunk which contained many things – mostly junk. A pair of perished indiarubber sea boots, a brass sextant with its eyepiece astray, a telescope of ancient design and several other useless nautical bits and pieces such as a seaman gone to shore might hold on to. What he removed from the trunk was a leather pistol case which on being opened presented a single, long, Spanish, naval pistol, obsolete but sound. He tested the mechanism. The cock fell with a crisp 'snick' and a burst of sparks. Excellent. He loaded it with fresh powder, rammed in a lead ball, opened the priming pan and fed it with powder.

There was no reason to disbelieve that if this pistol was fired at Rory McKay, that it would not drill him good and solid. All that remained was to enlist some desperado to do precisely that.

Ten

She came again, and in exactly the same circumstances as before – as a shadow on a carpet of moon. Becoming a woman, then a lover. Nourishing him and draining him both at once; forming that perpetual, painful, calamitous agitation of the soul that is unwisely known as Love. She was marvellous. She was moisture for his thirst, a soft wind for his heat. She was his glimpse of paradise eternal. He praised her with every lovely name he could invent while she bore him on wings of ecstasy beyond mountains, beyond clouds, over horizons previously unknown, to their sacred, sexual feast. Then sleep, inevitable sleep into which she vanished like vapour.

The dawn was miserable for a hundred reasons, all of them centring on her.

That night she had told him that she was not only the wife of Duke Ephraim, but his half-sister as well, and that she lived in the house of her mother – the atrocious Mammy Yellowbelly. This new revelation upset and disorganised him. Though why it should have was unclear. What was worse: sleeping with the wife of the man one most loathed, or the daughter of the woman one most loathed? He wished her address could have remained unknown: the Night from whence she had first come. But even had he not known these things, the reality would have been the same, it would merely have been hidden. And ignorance is nobody's friend . . . There was, in any case, nothing he would do about it. No course of action other than to expend the day for the sake of the return of night – and her . . .

He groaned and sat up. A young and serious voice said 'Hello.' It was the boy, Run Run. His head was cocked contemplatively to one side.

'Hello to you.' Rory swung his legs off the bed and faced his visitor in a friendly way. Run Run, as was his custom, had independently made himself at home on Rory's reed mat.

'Well,' Rory said, 'I haven't seen you for a while.'

Run Run nodded with great intent, pleased with his understanding of this man's language. Pater Theo's Bible classes had, if nothing else, achieved that much. He gestured in the direction of the jungle.

'So that's where you were.' Rory took a ripe mango from a pile of fruit and offered one to his guest.

Run Run took it but did not eat. He was not there to breakfast and socialise. He was there, at Yoruba's bidding, to do something important, and time was limited. From his own neck he took the cowrie shell necklace that had once belonged to his father. He dangled it for as long as it took for the white man to show a clear interest in it, then gave it to him.

'Hello,' said Rory. 'What's this, then? A cowrie shell on a leather thong?' He inspected it approvingly, then made to return it.

Run Run had anticipated this move. He had, in fact, rehearsed by gesture and word his next actions. He refused it avidly while pointing to Rory's neck. 'For you. I bring.'

'For me? Why, thank you.' It would have been churlish to refuse the gift. Rory looped the fine leather thong over his neck. The cowrie dropped into semi-concealment amid the whiskers of his chest. He examined the effect in his Dutch looking glass. 'Thank you,' he said again. But by then there was no one but himself in the room. 'How odd,' he said to himself.

That morning the stench near the barracoons seemed to have diminished. Strangeways showed relief in this. Instead of clamping his camphor bag in his teeth he wore it about his neck, which unfortunately allowed him to be more talkative. Sleep had, to a small extent, recharged him with optimism and he was of the opinion that they might yet weigh anchor and be off before the rains. As they were currently in the process of being soaked by a squall this seemed unlikely to Rory, and he said so. 'This,' Strangeways gesticulated knowledgeably, 'you can't call this rain. When it rains here, when it truly rains, it's all you can do to breathe without drowning. This is mere cat's piss!'

Thus degraded, the clouds withdrew and the rain dried up, leaving mist and a brilliant arc of colour to bridge the battlements of the town. Green parrots screeched unmusically. Rory fancied he could hear the dirge of the slaves while still some way off, but it must have been some other sound, for they were quiet that morning: a new batch, he was informed by Jemmy Honesty, at the stockade gate.

'The new ones ain't so sad. They've still got hope of a warrior's death and that keeps 'em perked up.' He chuckled at some unrevealed thought.

But if a quick death was the food of hope, then it was the elixir of hate. The eyes that watched the white men enter were filled with hate; fired and flashing with hate. Unsubmissive hate. Jemmy Honesty felt bound to offer an explanation: 'These gentlemen are from the Guinea coast; Coromantee Niggers. War prisoners, they are, and aggrieved by it . . . But what do you think? Are they not prime?'

'Coromantees don't sell in the West Indies,' Strangeways grumbled. 'They're troublemakers, the most treacherous villains on the coast. Do you take us for fools, Mr Honesty?' Strangeways spat. 'It was Coromantees who started the Jamaica Rebellion, sir.'

'They're good articles. Ay. As good as any.'

'No one wants Coromantee Niggers any more.' Strangeways sounded angry, but it was play. It did not matter a damn if they were Coromantees, and if Coromantees were thought of as dangerous merchandise. For Strangeways could pass them off down Cuba way as Alampos, or Ashantis, or Angolans, and who would know the difference? This sort of churlish dispraise could be more or less expected of a slave-trader about his work. An essential component. Cloth for the tailor, tin for the tinker . . . so why was Jemmy Honesty so awriggle with discomfort? His eyes were everywhere but on the man he was dealing with, and when he spoke it was not in his usual bantering tone, but with a timorous ring.

'Well, if you don't want 'em – ' Jemmy cut himself short by way of delivering a reprehensory kick to an adjacent black behind.

'Who said I don't want 'em?' Strangeways countered. 'But they ain't prime. They've got reputations, sir.'

Rory observed this spurless cockfight, thinking how out of balance the thing was; such a purposeless strutting about. The whole performance was too large, too protracted and over-stressed. By now they should all have been agreed; but no.

'See Duke Ephraim, then,' snapped Honesty. 'Those goods were brought in special for you. He won't like it.'

' "Like", sir, cuts both ways. I don't *like* being asked to pay good money for bad merchandise. I will see him, sir, and I will see him *now*.' So saying, Strangeways marched towards the gate, pausing only to snap at Rory, 'No need for you to come.'

Honesty took it upon himself to accompany the captain, muttering something sourly inaudible, and pinching snuff into his nostrils as he left. As the sailors from the longboat had not as yet turned up, Rory found himself without white company. Seventy or so Coromantee war prisoners stared at him, fixed him in their minds, and assassinated him there in seventy different ways. It was disconcerting to be so vastly and silently detested. He shuddered beneath the force of the scrutiny. There was no warding it off. It simply leapt the barrier of contempt which he tried to erect, and came for him. Came for his heart, his spine. He became quite troubled, agitated and edgy, and his breathing quickened as it does before a fight, with that strange tingle of hair on the neck and forearm. A soundless warning voice descended on him hard. He heard advice. And it was to beware, watch out, for there was more to this than the pelting stares of the Coromantee prisoners. There was a deadly threat . . . Of what? The prisoners were manacled, laden with chains. The trees that surrounded the stockade were filled with sounds of small life; a harmless tweeting and cooing. Beware of what? Watch out for what?

Of a Coromantee wishing to die as a warrior and supplied with the means to do so. The man sprang out of the seated crush of slaves not three paces from Rory. A moan of sound swelled like a slow-growing wave, gathering volume, propelling the Coromantee on a crest of shouted fury. Up he rose. Up came a pistol, aimed with bulged eyes straight at the heart of the devil from the sea. It was an old naval pistol, thick barrelled and weighty, and with every chance of success. Rory saw all this as a series of events, each one brilliantly impressed before it crystallised into the next. He observed the fall of the hammer and its shower of sparks, he heard the detonation of powder in the priming pan as a distinct 'poof!'. With a half second of life remaining, he thought how wickedly unfair it was to die like a dog in this awful place. But all these visions and expectations were as workings of a mind that was wholly split into separate centres. There was a part of him that was not at all awed by the attack and was not caught up in abstract observation, but had been at work from the outset in pursuit of survival. It made him lithe and quick. So by the time the Negro had aimed, he had to aim again. The sea devil was a yard from the spot where first he'd stood, and gathering speed. And even as the primer ignited there was more aiming to be done. The white man danced like a gazelle over his gun sight. The explosion shocked the birds from the foliage, but further than that did no injury. The Coromantee did not really mind. He had acted with valour, and now he would be quickly killed and his surviving soul would go home, to a place of shelter and honour. It happened as promised. There was a thrash of musket fire from the barracoon warders, and his soul burst free.

Rory took up the naval pistol from the ground. A warder came up and haughtily demanded it, but he would not give it up. He shoved the man aside and walked out of the stockade and into a rain wind that blew volumes of good sense down on him. As he walked, the litter of perplexities lifted away and what was left was a clear view of treachery. When he entered Jemmy Honesty's home it was with the intention of killing him straight off, of shooting him right between the eyes. And the idea seemed passionately just. But on finding him and confronting him it occurred that a whole lot more could be done to rectify the wrong. For there is nothing more satisfying than educating a bad man in the consequence of his sins. There is beauty in violence if violence is just.

Honesty began to lie bleakly while backing away: 'I heard a shot . . . My God! Don't look at me like that, McKay. I had nothing to do with it . . . Is that the pistol that was used? Is that the weapon?'

'It is.'

Rory held up the pistol as though to hand it to the man, then whipped it towards Honesty, clubbing his cheek with the long heavy barrel, opening a furrow of red. 'This is the weapon.' He hit him again, feeling bone break like shingle. 'Was this your idea, Jemmy?'

'No. I swear.'

So sweet to strike again, this time across the ear. With his good hand Jemmy Honesty shielded his face. His little eyes bobbed and yelped in their pouches, but no sound of pain came from him until he fell with a groan.

'Was it Strangeways' idea?'

Honesty's jaw worked, opening and closing as though wishing to produce speech, managing only to mutter and spit blood. More blood was trickling from his ears, and more still from his destroyed cheek. Rory drew his pistol. To finish him off seemed the proper thing to do, and though he wasn't fully committed to the act, he was closer to that than charity. Then Honesty's eyes glazed over and he fell onto his face. And that saved him. Rory threw the assassin's weapon down, then left, feeling savagely triumphant, in search of Captain Strangeways.

Silus Strangeways went into hiding for a week behind the malicious tin walls of the house of Mammy Yellowbelly, guarded by the queen's musketmen, not even trusting his own tars. The conspiracy was obvious.

As for that loathsome lady, she summoned Sassabonsum once again and told him that it was established beyond doubt that the English lieutenant had juju that could stop bullets at three paces. She warned that this white man was shielded by some extraordinary power.

That was true.

Eleven

Contrary to optimism the schooner *Pluto* was not slaved and away before the skies thickened and the rains came. In fact, the purchases were scarcely halfway done before the onset of the wet season, or, as the white men trapped there described it, the Season of Sickness. Beneath the tarpaulin canopy that the sailors had rigged near the jetty, three of their number died in the first week of rain. It happened with astonishing suddenness: from fever to coma to death in a day and a night. More men rowed upriver to take their places. More died, one by his own hand. For now, imprisoned by ceaseless rain, there were no pretty abstractions and exotic views, no place to turn but inwards, and there were those who could not stand what they saw in their interiors. Strong drink made things more tolerable.

The slaving went on. It had to. For this was what they had come to do, and no man gave serious thought to its abandonment. The rains pressed down, roaring. The river rose, sluggishly sending out tentacles of water to find spaces for its progeny – new pools, pimpled with rain, poisoned with drowned animals, steaming. The barracon floor degenerated to stinking mud in which Duke Ephraim's sullen merchandise floundered, while their buyers slipped and cursed. Purchasing continued, but sluggishly, for the tribal battles that caused good supply had more or less been washed out. They made up for the lack of war prisoners by taking up more women and children. Slaves died. And the forest grew salubriously, almost unseen.

It was impossible to live there and not be affected by such adverse conditions. The groping sogginess of air and heat drove Rory towards a state of defensive moroseness. Constant mistrust of Strangeways and Jemmy Honesty enervated him, too. His clothes, always damp, became weak with rot at the seams. A chronic rash came out in his groin. The earth beneath him, the puddles he walked in, the air around him, swarmed, swam, shimmered with insects with no other object in life than to single him out for devourment. He pinched them, squeezed and crushed them in bloody warfare, but they came on. The days were blurred by such torments as these.

But, ah! The nights!

She came to him every night to lift him from the afflictions of Creek Town; her soft hand touching, her sweet breath touching, they flew. They soared. He fervently wished this state would never change, and refused to think of its inevitable end. It would end. One way or the other, it *would* end. But in the meantime – madness. The crazy-seed had grown, towered out of sight, sent down roots into the substance of his will. Once, after having come to him from out of a storm, as wet and lithe as seaweed, she dragged him out to copulate beneath a lightning-lashed sky. Once, on a rare rainless night, he pursued her along jungle pathways, catching her at the entrance of a cave that echoed their gasps like a lusty onlooker. They lay in the voyeur cave until dawn. And in the dawn, as always, he awoke to find her gone.

Yoruba, who was really exerting herself on Rory's behalf, almost washed her hands of the affair on that particular occasion. To be dashing about all night on the trail of this randy sailorman was not her idea of fun. She could hardly keep up with him, and in general it all seemed like more trouble than it was worth. The cowrie shell spirit was a valuable article, but, as things were turning out, a tricky one, too. It had refused every incentive to come home, and she had no idea why this should be so. While the cowrie shell dangled receptively upon the white man's hairy chest, the cursed thing was dashing about inside him, refusing every inducement to return. The situation was trying her. She might have abandoned the project had she not been aware that powers besides hers were intensely interested in the foreigner. Sassabonsum was stalking the man, and that could only mean one thing. Someone – it hadn't taken her long to work out who – wished the man mortal harm. And the daughter of Mammy Yellowbelly was obviously involved in the plot.

Yoruba loathed Sassabonsum and had done so for all her long

life. She was a healer. He was sickness. She was a charm maker; he, a charm breaker. She gave; he took. She was as implacably opposed to him as it is possible to be, and turned her hand against him whenever the opportunity presented; as it did now.

That night at the Devil Cave she had woven a blanket of invisibility and dropped it over the sleeping foreigner. Sassabonsum had come into the cave, stinking, as usual, like a corpse and had almost stepped on the slumbering man without seeing him. He had awoken the daughter of Mammy Yellow-belly with a whisper, but even she had not been able to find her lover. They had groped about in the gloom, fumbling on the floor of the cave; finding only a rockadder and a nest of scorpions. Yoruba, who had dissolved herself to mere eyeballs, dodged the would-be murderers with agitated amusement. This Sassabonsum was not a thing to be trifled with. He was as terrible as he looked, and quite capable of doing her drastic harm. She could, however, not resist the temptation of a few mocking bursts of laughter that rang about in the cave long after she'd fled.

She went home and rested, but not for long. She needed the counsel of her own spirit guardians in order to discover what was really going on. The risks in confronting Sassabonsum were huge. She urgently needed to divine a strategy. So when Run Run came in she instructed him to build up a fire of certain magic twigs, and when this was well and truly alive, she travelled on its smoke to a place where all secrets were laid bare like an ant-cleaned carcass . . .

Rory, on awakening in the Devil Cave, wrinkled his nose – gave a catlike sniff then a jolt. An intolerable stench was wedged solidly in his nostrils. A dozen men, dead for a week. But not a corpse to be seen in the sallow light. No evidence at all that he had inadvertently slept in a grave. He thought he must be imagining it, stood up and stretched, and felt a shiver of dread as though tweaked by a cold hand. This sensation required an effort to disregard; a contrived, loud yawn. The walls repeated the false sound – *awn* – *awn* – *awn*, until they were swallowed up. The stench remained as pungent as before. He took a step towards daylight, that is to say, in the direction of the cave mouth, and at that juncture his foot met something that did not resist, but fell over with a small but well-echoed thud. The toppled object was a little man, a wooden statuette no larger in size than an extended splay of fingers. It was carved in the fashion of the art of that district, with dwarfishly bowed little legs and a potbelly with a protruding bellybutton. Its chest was lightly burned and carved with some geometric design that made no sense to him, and it wore a carved necklace. To each elbow was tied a leather purse from which brown feathers protruded. Its chin was rather angular with lips extended as though about to bestow a kiss, and its eyes were squeezed into tight slits. It seemed to be intended to depict a rather lecherous-minded sleepwalker, and made him chuckle. He was sure that she had left it for him to find, and keep. A lover's gift. On emerging from the cave he noticed that the statuette had not been recently carved, though its feathers were new. He dropped the little fellow into his jacket pocket.

The plateau on which he found himself was quite some distance from Creek Town, and the ground was sufficiently elevated to enable him to see the mud-walled fort and parts of the sinuous river, also deep brown. He could hear the river, too, in its rush towards the sea – towards a horizon made invisible by brightness. The earth was dewy, and every available space was hosting groups of fantastic flowers. Gay, wide-mouthed flowers, sad, hanging blooms, frivolous sprays, were dancing concertedly before the morning sun. Friends of his. He felt as though he was being intensely observed, and as though his depth of vision, too, was wonderfully magnified.

Then, as fast as this good feeling had come, it went. A gust of effluvial air passed by. The sunburst blanched before a rumble of lightning-slashed cumuli, and the jungle stiffened with tension, and grew quiet.

Sharp premonitions of danger contested for Rory's attention all of that day; coming and going, as between one breath and the next in pangs of unexpected anxiety, or bursts of information of the utmost clarity. He might be warned, for instance, that his enemy had taken on the form of a particular small rock, or of a shrub, or the monotonous *tunk-tunk* of a certain bird. Whatever it was, this thing would then loom into his senses with such massive signals of enmity as to overpower him momentarily. Then the fright would pass, leaving him trembling inside, yet somehow strangely energised. He felt the need to walk, to walk constantly. During periods when he was required to work, he paced the barracoon from one stockade wall to the next. And when not at his employment, he would walk to the river, then back again with no need in mind besides the imperative driving of his limbs. On these marches he frequently got soaked, but on the whole, the sky was less weighted with cloud than it had been for a long time. There was a period during that afternoon of absolute sun.

Rory found himself, without quite knowing to what purpose, at the mission of Father Theo. Theo was teaching the alphabet beneath the shade of the whipping tree, with a school of piccaninnies in a half circle squatting about him. Rory would have turned and gone had the clergyman not spotted him, and invited him over.

'Come, I'm nearly done here. Sit down. Sit down.' He gestured towards a buttock-worn log. 'I made a fresh fruit pulp we can drink . . . Children, off you go.'

His scholars escaped in a rush. Rory's limbs accepted the rest, feeling inexplicably more calm. Theo disappeared into the interior of his chapel for a while, emerging bare from the waist up, bearing a pitcher and two earthen tumblers. A large brass cross on a mat of grey chest hair threw a beam of power, then dangled, swaying, as its owner bent forward in order to pour. A tongue of thick pulp curled into the offered tumbler. 'There,' said Theo, 'drink.'

Tangy-sweet goo nested in Rory's palate.

'Do you want to pray with me?' Theo asked.

'I don't know why I came,' Rory said. 'But thank you, no . . . And, anyway, who or what is there for me to pray for in particular?'

Theo seemed set to argue, but sat instead with a plump sigh on the log. Side by side they drank the heavy warm juice.

'The fruit,' Theo said. 'There is nothing to compare with it in Europe. Is that not so? For your health's sake eat plenty of it while you're here. The pulp contains the antidote to many ailments . . . Are you well, my son?'

'Don't I look well?'

'Frankly, no. You look unnaturally drawn.'

'It's the rain. It never ends.'

'You must not let yourself get ill. Don't take the night air under any circumstances, the night dew is just as liable to bring on fever. The smell of rotting fish causes sleep-disease. The Guinea worm . . .'

'I really am quite well,' Rory said.

'You haven't been with the women, have you?' He hung his mouth in expectation of learning the worst.

Rory said, 'No.'

Theo exhaled. 'The *women* . . .' He was lost for words to describe this aspect of insalubrity.

'I merely felt irritated. Can you blame me? Things seemed a little difficult, so I went for a walk, and quite inadvertently came here. Now that the sun's out, I feel better.'

'Indeed. Well, you don't look it. But primarily my business is with your soul, not your flesh. You must guard it here with double vigilance. Read from the Book morning and night – the Twenty-Seventh Psalm. It is the best cure for melancholy in the world; Psalm Twenty-Nine to realise His omnipotence: "The voice of the Lord divideth the flames of fire. It breaketh cedars. The God of Glory thundereth . . ." Ah, Rory, there's power enough in those words to squash Satan like a bug . . . If only I had a bell.'

'A church bell, Theo?'

'Yes. To defeat the sound of the drums. To cut a swathe of pure sound into the jungle, like the Sword of Gabriel. I'd build a tower for it . . . But I'm rambling. My concern is for you.'

'My health is fine. As I said, things seemed a bit difficult for a while. No longer.'

'Dif-ficult.' Theo mulled on the twice-uttered word as though a search through its syllables might reveal Rory's deficiency. 'Tell me what you mean by "difficult".' Sensing reluctance he urged, 'Go on, my son. I can help you.'

Rory looked warily at this proposer of spiritual aid – the rotund, stubbled face beneath the black shovel hat, the pale, layered flab where the brass cross lay asthmatically lifting and falling. He perceived strength in the cross, but not in its bearer. But as allies were thin on the ground he did not write off this one. He asked for more pulped fruit and received it. Then, with no particular intention of steering the conversation one way or the other, said, 'Are you Run Run's teacher?'

105

Theo's eyes flickered over him in a troubled way. 'And what do you know about that particular child?' he asked. 'What are you driving at?'

'He speaks English. I was merely interested in learning who his tutor was . . . Are you offended, Theo?'

'Offended? Of course not. Did I seem so? It wasn't intentional . . . A bit of a shock that you should bring up his name, that's all. Did you know that he was kidnapped by a vile witch called Yoruba and taken off into the forest?'

'But when?'

'A full month ago, I'm told. At first we feared him to be dead . . .'

'He's certainly not dead. I saw him a week ago. I awoke, and there he was. He gave me this.' Rory tweaked the necklace thong and out hopped the mottled brown cowrie.

Theo reacted as though stabbed in the heart. His hand flew defensively to his cross. His tumbler slipped from his hand. He blanched, and his mouth wobbled open and closed making unintelligible sounds that resolved with effort into the horrified gasp: 'That was his father's.'

This disclosure meant nothing to Rory. Clearly, in exhibiting his little gift he'd caused ferocious shock, though he couldn't understand why. He dropped the cowrie shell back into hiding, but Theo's alarm still swelled. His eyes bulged. His features reddened. His slackened jaw closed with a snap.

'It's from the grave,' he jumped up, yelling. 'Know ye not that? Fool! Take it off. Oh! Messenger of Satan sent to buffet me . . . Lord help me shatter this evil.'

So saying, his hands flew at Rory's neck, clawing into a stranglehold. His fingers gouged into Rory's windpipe, squeezing like tongs. But the grip was not intended to hurt. It was intended to deprive. The thong snapped, and Theo, with a triumphant howl, gained the cowrie and held it at arm's length. Rory beat off the grip on his throat and pumped his deprived lungs. He was too surprised to prevent Theo from doing what he did next, which was to hurtle the broken necklace towards the forest. Both thought that that would be the end of it – the cowrie would fall like a seed in the gullet of the jungle, gulped, gone. It did not happen that way.

With its broken thong whizzing, it rose erratically,

zigzagging like a cumbersome bug not quite in mastery of flight but winged, nevertheless. Theo shouted, 'Go, you creature of Satan,' and that was the measure of time it took to acquire its maximum altitude. And that was where it vanished: in mid-flight. It was as though for an instant it was trailing a brilliant tongue of flame. Then it was gone; gone without evidence of ever having been more than a hallucination. But when Rory blinked, he discovered a mote of light imprinted in his vision.

'Pray!' roared Theo. 'Pray for all you're worth.'

When Rory did not drop to his knees, Theo dragged him down; gathered his arms about the reluctant Christian and fell with him, anchoring them knee to knee, chest to chest. Enveloped in Theo's protective embrace, preserved by his munition of holy utterings, Rory made no move to get away. Small thoughts of escaping from this spitting madman came and went, delivering no energy. He could hardly remember when last he'd felt so weak . . . It had been years ago . . . He had been standing on the deck of a frigate, closing on a French privateer when a musket ball had struck him in the chest, kicking him onto his back. It was as then: a sudden emptying of power and spirit and a careless giving up to what must be. No musket ball today. Today he'd been bloodlessly struck down from the instant that the cowrie had been torn from him. He did not know why or how.

A hiss of wind came by. The whipping tree shrugged its million wet leaves and sent down a shower on the sheltering men. The larger of the pair ended his embrace and stood, the other made no greater movement than to slowly sag his head. He had that look about him that, in the tropics, inevitably precedes serious illness. And considering the hardships he'd been put through – both in physical form, and ether – who could wonder at that.

Twelve

It took a mighty effort for Yoruba to launch herself into midair in pursuit of the hurtling cowrie shell. She would not have tried such a problematic thing had the shell stayed empty, for to jump up is one thing, to land safely is quite another. A badly-judged spring, such as the one she'd made, could cause one to end up miles off course. But that is beside the point. For, in the event, the cowrie spirit made a last second decision not to abandon its proper home. It shot from the Englishman at the speed of thought and dived into its shell. And she sprang after it, caught and bagged it, and came down rather well amid the branches of the tamarind tree, thus ending that difficult episode.

But Yoruba knew that in capturing the spirit of the cowrie shell she'd caused more damage than she'd cured. For without the well-intentioned spirit in his interior to guide him through the maze of curses and spells into which he had inadvertently stepped, Rory would die, and unpleasantly, too. The powers ranged against him were quite too wicked for him to withstand on his own.

On the other hand, her own spirit guardians had counselled her not to attempt to frustrate Sassabonsum, whose reprisal would be inevitable, and terrible. They cited instances when she'd opposed him in the past and had been badly mauled. She cited cases where Sassabonsum had been the loser. They berated her for her stubborn intolerance of the half-decayed creature, and called her a lover of vengeance. Of one voice they said, 'Let him be. What does it matter if one more sea devil dies? His life has no worth to us. Let Mammy Yellowbelly have her way.' Reluctantly, she decided to follow that advice. She went home and extinguished the fire of invisibility, returning into her earthly shape in good time for a dinner of stewed yams.

It was little Run Run who subsequently caused a change of heart, and persuaded her to defend the sickening Englishman. He told Yoruba that a juju doll now had Rory under nightly observation from a shelf above his bed.

'Describe the thing,' Yoruba said.

'It is small.' He demonstrated how small. 'Its eyes are slitted, its legs bowed.' He imitated its bow-legged stance. 'And it has leather purses tied to its elbows from which feathers grow.'

'I know it,' Yoruba hissed.

'Its mouth is puckered.' He puckered.

'It has been put there to steal his dream soul,' she said. 'It is because of me. It is because of the protection I gave him that they have had to go to such lengths . . . I'm weary of this affair, Run Run . . . I've recaptured the cowrie shell spirit. Did I tell you that?'

'Will you rest now, Teacher?'

'That's the question, isn't it. I can, but should I? I should, but can I? Answer me this, Run Run: do you think the sea devil is worthy of saving from Sassabonsum?'

Without the slightest quibble: 'Yes.'

'You must be sure of it. Think hard before you answer. For if he is a worthy man then we, you and I, Run Run, will fight them . . . Yes, *you* too. And the dangers will be immense. *Immense*. You will see things as you have never seen them before; the evil and ugly in extreme. Have you the stomach for it? Eh? You could die of fright, or lose your way and wander forever in the out-world. And supposing you did survive it, would you wish to have Sassabonsum as *your* enemy, too? And Mammy Yellowbelly? An axe in the neck would be preferable to that. Is the man's life worth the gamble? Answer "no", that would be sensible. Think of your own immortal soul, for that will be risked on the battleground of the out-world where this war will be fought. Think before you reply.'

He thought he was doing that, whereas his answer was already formulated and lying in a corner of his mind. Yoruba's words of danger had merely stimulated the decision, transformed it into a challenge no adventurous lad could resist. 'Let Sassabonsum try!'

Yoruba rapped his skull so hard that his eyes swam. 'Just like your stupid father; never answering a straight question with a straight answer. You're a hazard not a help. I'll ask you again. Is the Englishman worthy?'

'Yes,' said Run Run. 'Yes . . . And I'm *not* afraid of Sassabonsum. Why should I fear him?'

Yoruba's face soured like a sucked-out lemon. 'You will see – you pup. Now shut your impudent lips and open your ears. Listen to me – do *all* that I say, and *nothing* that I forbid. We are going on a journey that can't be measured by the laws of time and distance accorded to this world . . . Oh, and I must warn you, Run Run, what we are about to do is in opposition to the will of my guardians. No spirit hand will help us . . . Lay the fire of invisibility, then. Come on. Be quick, boy. Every moment we delay increases our disadvantage . . . Put on the twigs and logs, boy, place every one perfectly. Yes, that one facing the rising sun, that one, the river, and that one pointing upwards towards the out-world. Light it with the tallow of the Great Helmsman . . . Ah! . . . It comes.'

With a splutter and jump a small flame sprang from grass to twig to the belly of a log. Yoruba, bent forward like a drinking leopard, nourished it with her breath. She needed help. 'Come over here and blow, boy. My breath is frail. Blow on it. That's right. Look how it grows. It must be strong and lasting in order to carry us there, and back.' She cackled. 'That's *if* we come back . . . *Blow*.'

It took his breath and spoke back with a roar. It grew by leaps, throwing pain at his face, dancing to its own crackling tune. Now it was ready. The magical logs were combined in bright power.

'It's time.' Yoruba beckoned. 'Come kneel here with me, Run Run, breathe in the smoke, breathe out your human form. That's how it's done. Come, Run Run. Come to the gate. Don't let go of my hand. *Don't* – Run Run.'

The thought had struck him that if the perils of the out-world were anywhere near as stringent as Yoruba had warned, then it would be folly to proceed unarmed. Hanging on a thong on the doorpost was an old battle-axe; a stout-handled thing with a chopping blade set into its bulbous head, and protruding into a long, deadly spike. It was in order to fetch this instrument of war that Run Run broke contact with Yoruba. Within three strides he'd grasped it and had turned. Three more and he was

110

back at the side of his mentor, or at least, where he expected her to be. She was no longer there.

Undaunted and feeling more or less as heroic as any youngster might with such a potent weapon at hand, Run Run placed his knees exactly on the marks left by his vanished teacher. He leaned towards the flame as he had been instructed to do and breathed its smoky chemistry to the limit of his lungs. A massive coughing spell occurred – nothing else. He did it again. His head reeled, otherwise no bodily change was noticeable. He swooped down for a third attempt, and this time had scarcely taken a sniff before astonishing things began to happen. As a bubble floats on a river, frailly made of its mother substance, so he became precariously buoyant on a tide of inexorable power – part of the fluid into which he was bound, yet liable to vanish without trace at any second – unimportant, transparent, bodiless and without self-direction, yet fully aware.

He floated for a measureless time like this, observing the awesome scenery past which he was swept, while a great tired moon climbed wearily into a black sky, converting substance into shadow and shadow into reality, and soundlessly instructing the bubble that was Run Run: 'Go on – go on.' What option had he but to go on? He passed through plains so barren that no tree or grass existed; no soil or sand, but rock, endless and unhappy, scoured with yawning fissures, perilously sharp, that split the stream into vicious torrents. He survived a row of rapids, bobbing and dodging, speeding past knife-edge rocks, and onwards – onwards towards what he feared at first must be his death plunge – a thundering, tumbling waterfall that dunked him so deep that he thought he would never surface. But surface he did, and just in time to observe the fate of the river. Unwillingly roaring and writhing it was being swallowed whole, gulped up by a gape-jawed cavern and sucked into the belly of the earth. He knew he had to escape it now or be received into everlasting nothingness. But how? He was part of this thing; a sphere of panic with no more impetus than that provided by the imprisoning current.

Who knows where the power that rescued him came from. At the very edge of the abyss, at the point of eternal extinction, lashed and distorted by the plunging body of energy, he shot free.

Ah! The relief of it. Deliverance, no matter how short-lived, is a delicious thing. He floated. A bubble in the breeze, however, is a most flimsy and perishable item. The membrane encompassing him gave up with the faintest 'pop', and he plunged, tumbling head over heels towards inevitable death. He struck bottom with a jolt that was by no means fatal, and when at last he dared to open his eyes he discovered himself to be in a room that he vaguely recognised.

The voice of Yoruba growled in his ears. 'So you arrived, and with the Despatcher.' She gave the battle-axe a disapproving glance. 'It can't do you any good here. Better give it to me.'

Run Run felt disinclined to obey. He improved his grip on the handle and glanced belligerently around the room. It was Rory's hut. He thought she should know how he felt: 'I nearly died on the river. I didn't like it. Why did you make me go all that way, just to come here?'

'Come where?'

'Here.' He gestured impatiently towards the sleeping occupant to settle the argument, 'It's *his* hut.'

'Well, it is,' said Yoruba, 'and it isn't.'

Run Run gestured petulantly about. 'It's all exactly as I remember it.'

'No it's not. It's as *he* remembers it. It's as your worthy friend, Rory, remembers it. You're in his dream world now, can't you see?'

'There is a difference in the size of things. Things seem much smaller.'

'Of course that's so. But there's much more to it than that. This is the out-world, Run Run. This is the world of your friend's dream soul. Did you expect simply to amble over here, foolish boy?'

'It's nice. It's pleasant here.'

'It can quickly change.'

'Is he sleeping?' Run Run went over to the bed and peered tentatively into Rory's face. 'Can he see me?'

'Not him, but his dream soul will, when it emerges that is. We'll wait for it.'

'Can he hear me? If I touched him, would he feel it?' Run Run experimented, cupping Rory's forehead with his palm. 'He's so hot. Is he sick? See how he sweats.'

'It doesn't surprise me that he's sick.' She dipped her finger into the little well of water that had accumulated in the nape of Rory's neck, then sniffed the moisture. 'Very sick. Perhaps he'll die, anyway. These foreigners have no real strength.'

The sleeping man gave a groan. Yoruba started back like a cat, then stole forward again, stooping until her face was very close to his. His eyelids began to tremble and flutter. It wasn't until that moment that Run Run noticed the little carved wood figurine of the dream soul stealer. For it was then that it, too, showed signs of animation. It blinked its eyelids distinctly – once – twice, then peered about maliciously. Run Run didn't like the way it regarded him.

Yoruba was contemptuous of the ugly, bow-legged dwarf. 'You,' she spat. 'I know your game, you toad. Stay out of my way, or I'll chop you into firewood. Run Run, show this nasty creature the Despatcher.'

Run Run held up the battle-axe. He made it whistle through the air. The dream soul stealer looked unimpressed. It gave an insolently loud yawn.

Yoruba hissed, 'Quiet.' Again she leaned over the sleeping man's face, sniffing. 'It's near,' she said in an excited whisper. 'It's very near.'

'What's near?' Run Run suppressed his voice, too. 'What's very near?'

'His dream soul.'

'What will it see? What will it do?'

'How should I know?' Yoruba said tiredly. 'It's a leaf on the current; a feather in the wind. Our only concern is to guard it, and ourselves, from extinction.'

'And what will we see?'

'We will see all and everything. We'll see the evil genius of this juju doll at work. And we'll fight it . . .'

'Be quiet.' The wooden gnome cocked its head as though listening intently. 'It comes . . . It's here.'

Fever. It strikes inside the skull like heated poison, melting the chains and rivets we have loaded upon the phantoms of madness, and out they crawl. Like figures in a mist they form then vanish, then re-form in altered shapes and disguises. They talk.

113

'Hello.' The greeting was directed at Rory. Its sponsor, though unpromisingly ugly, exuded good fellowship when saying, 'Remember me?'

'I don't know. Were you in the Navy?'

His friend laughed jerkily, showing fierce, little yellow teeth. 'No. Try again.'

'It's no good,' said Rory. 'I can't recollect . . .'

'But you do recall having seen me?'

'I think I do.'

'My face is hard to forget. You once described me as a dirty-minded sleepwalker . . . Ah! I see you remember now.'

'The wooden dwarf? I didn't know you could talk.'

The figure did a carefree little dance: a stiff-legged jig that seemed intended to convey pleasure at having been recognised. He suddenly stopped, and again gave his yellow-toothed grimace. 'She isn't coming tonight,' said the dwarf. 'I'm her messenger . . . Well, I'm a lot more than a mere messenger. But anyway, I was sent to tell you that.'

Rory felt a pang of remorse. He was sure that he must have done something, behaved in some reprehensible way to have caused her to take this course of action.

Confirming his guilt, the wooden man said accusingly, 'It's your fault completely.'

Rory beseeched, 'Tell me what I did?'

'It would be simpler to explain to you what you didn't do,' said the wooden man. '*You* didn't *ever* go to *her* . . . Tell me how many times did she brave the night to come here to be humped?'

'I prefer to call it "making love".'

'You're dodging the question.' The dwarf's teeth flashed in anger. 'Answer up or I'll hurt you.'

'I'm not certain.'

This reply did not please the inquisitor who gave a stiff but belligerent spring towards Rory. 'It was more than a thousand times,' snapped the sharp row of teeth.

The exaggeration was left unchallenged. Perhaps some uniquely local form of accounting was practised here. Rory merely said, 'I'm sure you're right.'

'And you haven't been to her once, have you?'

'No.'

'There you are,' said the dwarf, appeased. 'If you want to see her, you'll have to go down to Mammy Yellowbelly's. It's as simple as that . . . You do want to hump her – pardon me – make *love* to her, don't you?'

'More than words can tell.'

The dwarf leered, wagged his tongue about and made some lewd thrusts with his pelvis. He was obscene; vile. He kept up this revolting dance for his amusement, gyrating his hips, jerking his tongue in and out. It was while following this repugnant performance that Rory noticed that he and the dwarf were not alone in the room. The boy, Run Run, and an old, droop-breasted crone were present. They stood flanking the posts of a staircase that had become a feature of his room, one on each side of the balustrades, frowning so intensely that their eyes had vanished amongst angry shadows. He assumed that they were guarding the stairs; they seemed to be occupied in that way. Run Run held a battle-axe with a long, spiked tang, which he raised, as though to display his potent ability while pointing sternly towards the dancing dwarf.

'Do not go with him.'

A surprising thing to say as no such thought had entered Rory's mind until this warning had been said. What he'd intended to do, and still meant to do, was to go to the house of Mammy Yellowbelly, to his lover. And he needed no guide to show him how to get there. Why, he had no more to do than to ascend the stairs and he would be there. On the other hand, he was bound by a debt of gratitude to the little wooden man, who despite tawdry behaviour had advised him well. So he addressed the dwarf civilly, 'You have been of great help.'

The dwarf ceased to dance. Rory went on in the same tone. 'I'm going up the staircase now. I know what it means to do so. I will be alone . . .'

'You have no idea what it means,' interjected the old woman, 'or how much you will pay. Do not go.'

Rory examined her face properly for the first time, and saw that it showed compassion and an abundance of worldly wisdom. He called her mother: 'Mother, I must rise.'

He felt as light as a ghost, and knew that the dwarf was responsible for this facility. He could travel with no effort, and with no contact with the ground. He knew that there was a risk that this gift might be abruptly withdrawn, so took immediate advantage of it to ascend the staircase that led to Mammy Yellowbelly's.

The house was not as he remembered it. It was much bigger, with many more rooms through which he passed in search of his love. The rooms, though filled with the sounds of revellers, were nevertheless unoccupied. Empty rooms. There was disorder. Chairs were overturned, smashed glass littered the floor. Two hermaphrodite beasts were mating on the dining-room table, grunting and powerfully thrusting. Another flight of stairs gave hope that he would find her still higher, and he did.

The door was locked. He banged on it hard until it was opened. It was the dwarf who admitted him. Now his form was more human and he wore a cloak. He handed Rory a large key – which at the same time might have been a pistol – and instructed him to open a further door with it. Again he became aware of the presence of Run Run and the wise woman – guardians, once more – tenaciously standing at the further door, opposing entrance. Scowling, they warned him not to open it. He advanced. They pleaded. He brushed them aside and worked the lock.

Theo sprang from the interior, raging against his enemy, the rain forest. He bore in his arms the limp body of a child, a headless child which nevertheless wore a halo of brilliant light.

'Take up thy burden,' roared the preacher. 'Take it. Go from here.' He held out the angelic corpse.

Rory was unwilling to be so burdened. He shoved Theo abruptly out of his path, feeling ashamed by his rough treatment of the man of God. But the dwarf swirled his cloak like a matador and Theo and the angelic corpse dissolved.

'This way,' said the wooden dwarf, lecherously gesturing towards a bed, a four-poster, screened by satin drapes, where Rory knew he would find her. Now pure lust drove him towards the bed – a consuming need to couple with her, drive into her, spray her with his seed. So interference was met with anger.

Run Run and the wise woman were no match for Rory. Nor did they do well in their campaign against the dwarf. In short, sharp exchanges they were being flung about, helter-skelter, like paper caught in a gale. Still the two unasked-for guardians came on, invading him with warnings, clogging his path with impediments of time and space, tiring and exasperating him. What appeared to be an arm's reach away stayed an arm's reach away. Despite a huge struggle, he could make no headway. Finally, he could stand it no longer. He took the old woman by the throat and threw her. And discovered that she *was* as frail as paper. His fingers dug through her; she tore; she vanished in an impetus of sound, an echoing scream that swirled and crushed her to oblivion and sped her into nothingness.

The wooden man applauded, grinning: 'She's gone forever,' he said. 'Gone. Eternally gone. You did it.'

One more step.

He reached the bed and touched the satin drapes – and stopped – suddenly aware of the presence of malevolence; hatred beyond anything he'd previously encountered, an ingenious cruelty that came down on him like a curse.

'What are you waiting for?' said the dwarf, smiling amicably. 'Go on. You've got this far. Are you going to stop now?'

'Never!'

He jerked the drapes apart.

She was there, naked.

Strangeways was there, naked.

Strangeways was humping her.

There was no better word to describe the actions of the captain of the *Pluto*. She was bent forward on hands and knees, and he was banging at her rear end, rutting like a dog. From her breasts to her buttocks she was atremble from the battering. Her eyes took in Rory unastonishedly. No change occurred in them but for a perceptible increase in pleasure. As for Strangeways – his head was thrown back like the howling cur he'd always been. His eyes were slitted. His lips were drawn. His teeth were grinding on ecstasy.

A throng of emotions seized Rory: pain, humiliation, jealousy, rage. They gathered into one compact paroxysm of unholdable violence.

'Kill him,' spat the dwarf.

The instrument in Rory's hand had firmed beyond doubt into his own pistol. He raised it, pointed it, took it to within an inch of Strangeways' temple, then pulled the trigger.

The sound was as a boom of cannon fire.

It shocked the dream out of his mind. He awoke on a gasp with upflung arms and frenzied heart. His mat was as wet as though floated though a river. It was pouring with rain. Mosquitoes were sucking him. He could hear their whine on the rotten smelling air. He felt so weak he could hardly draw breath, and he was burning with fever.

HOTEL METROPOLE

Thirteen

On the last few pages of Rory Tremayne's handwritten manuscript were some illustrations done in Indian ink, which though unsigned, bore the hallmark of the author; the same ardent, quick-wristed strokes with which he'd carried the story from start to finish. There was a drawing of a tall ship at anchor in a tropical estuary: a sharp-prowed schooner with its sails furled. Some black men stood leaning on sticks in the foreground, placidly staring at it; the *Pluto*, Jenny presumed. Another sketch was of the head and shoulders of a narrow-featured man with a frowning scar and a sharklike grin, who could only have been Jemmy Honesty. In the background was a stockade where several naked, chained men stood. Other, lesser drawings, divided this from his final and most painfully done work – the mulatto woman. She was as exquisite as his words had described her; her eyes were flashing, her lips drawn as though caught at a moment of ecstasy. Her hair was flying like a black flag in a gale.

Jenny Oxenham found herself intently drawn to this picture. So poignantly did it reach out and enthral her that an observer of the woman seated there with the open book before her might have sensed an act of recognition, as one who has found in an old, family album her features mirrored in the sepia print of an ancestor long gone . . . And perhaps our observer wouldn't have been that far off the mark.

For Jenny's experience in life was not average, and fantastic possibilities were her meat. So the antique records of Rory Tremayne held enchantments for her that couldn't normally be extracted from paper and ink. But there was more to it than that. There was an inherent provocation in this document, a call to arms that was irresistible to any seeker of Truth. And if nothing else, she was that. Jenny Oxenham was a challenger of the dogmas of science where science was arrogant, and it was arrogant in its scorn of psychic events.

The empowering west wind had come alive to tug at the pages of the manuscript. She closed it; the book that had taken her from morning to noon to enter and exit, and still held her in its outreach.

There was a quick movement above her that was the hawk, returned from its hunt, and when it had passed she was left staring at a sky puffed up with wildly dyed clouds. Her back was aching and rigid and her eyes felt strained, but these discomforts were minor. She felt she was part of a more intense pain.

On the same night that Captain Strangeways had been killed, the Royal Navy had made an upriver raid on the fortress at Creek Town – had blown up the fort and its barracoons, freed the slaves and driven Duke Ephraim and his ragtag army into the hinterland. They'd taken the *Pluto* as a prize, and also arrested Rory on charges of slaving *and* murder. The evidence on the latter charge had been slim (a pistol ball that had undoubtedly come from the barrel of Rory's distinctive weapon). Then Jemmy Honesty had testified as to the virulent hate that had come between Rory Tremayne and his captain after Tremayne had been shot at while in the slave barracoons. That had weighed heavily against the defendant. Even so, the judges at Exeter had declined to hang him, but had sentenced him to life imprisonment, which had had the same effect. An awful and violent end to life. And dishonour.

Rory Tremayne had not killed Silus Strangeways. A man who murders another, and then sets out passionately to prove that he didn't, is hardly likely to try to gain support for his lie by admitting that he had done exactly what he was accused of – if only in a dream. Neither does he owe it to his accusers to show a motive for the crazed deed – if only in a dream. No, he does not commit these follies. He writes quite another sort of tale in which the grime of guilt is carbolically erased from his skin, and deposited elsewhere. The innocent, on the other hand, like children, expect the truth – no matter how bizarre – to be believed, simply because it is the truth.

Rory had written the truth. The book shouted to be believed

122

and she was solidly on the side of the believers. 'Not guilty.' she said audibly, then having pronounced that, stood.

Wistman's Wood, besieged by glorious summer on all sides, had relinquished some of its early morning ill-humour. Feeling good, feeling sure, she began the walk back down the sandy cattle track that led to the inn, to James Tremayne. And she thought about the man as she walked, and wondered how much of the ancestor was in the descendant. At first glance they were recognisable as kin. The eyes were the same, down to the quizzical hook in the centre of the brows, and the jaw was as obstinate. These features showed a promise of strength, but had he the temperament for adventure of Rory? Would he have acted in the same way Rory had in the same circumstances, with the same determination and zest? Now the answers to these questions were critical to her future course of action . . . Yes, there was to be that. For what had begun as an act of compulsion had converted, midway, into an act of awe. This book was fantastic. Merely to put it back in its box was unthinkable. There was so much that could be done with it. It was an entire parcel of hidden truths; and hidden truths were her reason for being.

Clearly, James Tremayne was a factor. He was the owner of Rory's articles, and therefore had to be won over to her cause. His participation was essential, but by no means guaranteed. Still, she felt nicely optimistic. If he was anything like the Rory she'd come to know, then nothing would stop him.

There *was* danger. She knew that. *That*, the Watchers had already warned of, even as they were warning her now, in their usual assertive way. The premonition was oppressing her. And it was savage and deadly. But does the true explorer, standing on the threshold of the virgin wilderness, turn back because the guides have warned of attack? No way! The territory was vast and inwards beckoning, and her sense of mission was over-powering. She would take precautions, but she would go on.

In muddied shoes she ended her walk. The path had brought her back to the stone wall at the boundary of the hotel. A small gate opened at a shove, then needed to be shoved again over grass that had built up at its base. Now she was in the grounds. She could see Tremayne, talking to his friend, the cop from Exeter, at the river where several guests were flicking at the stream with their trout rods. She hadn't yet worked out her strategy. She didn't want to be seen by Tremayne, but submitted to this necessity, and walked in his direction, towards the river's edge to stand watching the current break, bubbling and swirling, over water-smoothed rock. Inevitably he saw her. He tapped his friend on the shoulder, then came towards her.

'I got on well with Rory,' she ventured. 'You were right. It rang true. As you knew it would.'

'As I'd *hoped* it would,' he said with pleasure, holding out his hand as though impatient to take back the manuscript.

She didn't give it over, but said, 'He wasn't guilty of killing Silus Strangeways. But can't you see there's much more to this thing; more that Rory intended to give?'

'No. Is there?'

'Mr Tremayne – '

'James, remember?'

'James . . . You've let me into your secrets, your book, and your longing to restore your ancestor's honour. That must have taken a lot of trust. More than I would have had were I in your position.'

'Are you thanking me?'

'In a way. Yes, I'm grateful. It was an experience. It's shown me a lot.'

'Shown you what?' He smiled unexpectedly. 'Why don't we go and have some tea?'

'Why don't we just sit here?'

'All right.' He took her arm, steering her into the shade of a tree. 'Shown you what?' He sat, patting the grass near his side.

Dewy grass flexed under her buttocks; dampness licked her warm skin. It would leave twin clinging patches when she stood. She got comfortable, and lit a cigarette.

'God, it's peaceful here,' she said, wishing for a moment that there was no more to do or say than that. But there was. 'Don't you think that if Rory wasn't guilty then it should be made more generally known. Huh? I mean, is it enough for you and I to sit here chewing grass stalks, pleasantly agreed?'

'You'd like to make more noise about it?'

'I'm converted. You're converted. Is it enough?'

'It doesn't satisfy me as much as I thought it would, I must admit. What you and I believe seems scarcely important.'

'No,' she said emphatically. 'That's where you're wrong. It's important all right. Hell, it's vital. It's the first effect, without which there could be no other. The essential first turn of the wheel. We've started. Where will it stop? It's momentum.'

He laughed at her in a teasing way.

'It *is*,' she said adamantly.

'Yes it is, I suppose. Where would you like it to stop?'

'God, I'd love to knock over a few sacred cows. That would give me a kick . . . Where would I like it to stop? . . . I don't know yet. But I'll tell you this: proving Rory's innocence on a worthwhile scale would prove much more than that. It would cause a stir. Cause some scientific demolitions.'

'They're the sacred cows? The dictates of the sceptics?'

'The blind and the blinkered. They piss me off.'

'God, it's tempting. I like the way your mind works, lady. But you've got precious little to aid you. Proof transmits belief. That's what it boils down to: proof. Are you saying that you can actually come up with proof?'

'I honestly think it's all written here.'

'It's just one man's book.'

'Don't ever underestimate the power of one man's book. The world is receptive to honesty. And then there's the wooden man. It too has power. You ought to know that that figurine isn't the quaint little curio that you take it to be. It's full of energy, and it's restless and unpredictable.'

Once more he was the arch sceptic: 'Are you trying to tell me it's alive?'

'In a psycho-dynamic sense, it *is* alive. And for some reason it's chosen me as its medium; its transmitter. I don't know why it happened, just that it has. And it is dangerous. The thing *is* dangerous. I'm its hold on life, so it may not wish to harm me. On the other hand it might. Opposition is its food. Destruction is its joy.'

'As it destroyed Rory.'

'Mmm . . .' She limited her agreement. 'But Rory lacked the defences that I've got. He wasn't capable of opposing such a strong psychic force as that. I am – I've studied this kind of phenomenon for the better part of my life. I think its power is exploitable. I'd certainly like to find out.'

'Would you?' he said tentatively. 'Sounds slightly hair-raising if you ask me. What's to be gained if you get hurt?'

'It's a risk.'

'Jenny, I'm getting the hint that you've already made up your mind. I don't know if it's such a good idea. In fact, I'm almost sure it's a bad idea. But if you'll take me by the hand, lady, I'll go along.' He took her hand, opened the fingers and fused his fingers between them. It felt good. Then he raised the joined hands to his lips, blurring his words on her skin: 'I would hate anything to happen to you, Jenny. I mean it.'

The honesty of it sank into her. She didn't care why he had changed his mind about her, only that he had. She closed her eyes to hold on to the flow, closed off the beauty of the afternoon to enhance the greater beauty of touch, and instead was struck by a jagged flash of insight that made her whole body stiffen.

She saw the death of James Tremayne. She was in another place and in another body – not hers – not here. The sun was hot upon her back. Violence had come and gone in a blur, and a leopard was licking at a puddle of thick blood. It was Africa. It was beckoning. Then it shimmered and vanished and the present re-emerged. James Tremayne had let go of her hand and was regarding her in a surprised way. She was almost unable to talk.

'God . . .'

'God – what? What's going on?'

She shivered in the aftermath like a dog in a draught; was about to tell him, then changed her mind. He wouldn't believe her, and that would cause an argument. The man, she realised sadly, was still immersed in scepticism. She was going to try to reason with him, but he was rapid with anxiety.

'For heaven's sake, Jenny . . .'

'I'm sorry.'

'Well, what was that all about?'

'Nothing.'

'I wish you wouldn't lie to me.'

She wished she didn't have to. 'I came to the realisation that it wouldn't be a good thing for you to get too close to this research.'

'Why?'

126

'You'd be out of your depth.'

'Nonsense,' he said severely. 'We were practically agreed . . .'

'I've changed my mind. You mustn't become involved.' She said with finality, 'I know that now.'

'But I am already involved.'

'Then that's far enough.'

'Stop trying to organise my life, Jenny. This is my show, therefore my terms apply.'

'James, listen to me. It's too dangerous. Please.'

'You are asking me to believe what is beyond belief.'

'Yes. Beyond belief, as truth often is.'

'We spoke about danger.'

'More than we spoke about. Much more.' She stood. She made herself tall, straight and adamant, and while he was still getting to his feet, said, 'You wouldn't survive it, that's all.'

'Hell! I've survived being hit on the head with a bottle. I've survived several nasty race riots and I don't know how many pub brawls . . . Oh, and an IRA bomb. So I hardly think that one little wooden man . . .'

'You have no idea.'

'Haven't I?' He conveyed vast distaste for this unreasonable statement. 'Then *give* me an idea.'

Reluctantly she did: 'Have you heard of the concept of obeah?'

'Voodoo?'

'Black voodoo,' she said, 'as was commonly practised on the Slave Coast of old, then exported to the Caribbean by the slaves brought there. Its basic use is to commit murder by magic, or to gain any perverted desire. It's never used other than to do harm. It's what Rory had to contend with . . . And I believe that the vitality of that curse has revived and found a genetically matched target: you.'

'Oh, come off it.' He disposed of her warning with a curt flick of the wrist. 'I'm not in the least concerned about that. That sort of mumbo jumbo leaves me cold.'

'There's little reason for you to be concerned while you remain here in Devon. It would be a simple matter to see to your safety in Devon. I'm talking about Africa: Calbar and Creek Town; the fort on the River Cross.'

'I think I'm hearing you wrong.'

'No, you're not. To resolve this, to close the book of Rory Tremayne properly, there's no alternative but to relive its vital episodes. So that's where I must go.'

'To *Africa*?'

'Yes.'

'That's crazy. I can't go.'

That suited her well.

But by that evening he had changed his mind. He could go. He came softly tapping on her door, wearing a suit and tie, and a face of utmost determination, to tell her that. 'I feel that you're my responsibility,' he said. 'Don't try and argue with me. I've thought the thing through. I can go. I want to go. I've heard all that you've said, and I believe you. But I'm not put off. Africa, after all, isn't the faraway place of Rory's time. It's a jet-hop from Heathrow – no sweat. I'm in.'

She listened. She watched him. Objection formed, then dissolved. He was both formidable and vulnerable; a composition she thought she might grow to love.

'Come in,' she said.

Fourteen

Run Run, caster of spells, maker of fetish charms, exorcist supreme, though not absolutely averse to the infliction of pain, could remember with unhappiness Yoruba's method of instruction: the bare-knuckle ramming of facts past the skull bone, as if raw ache was an essential ingredient of memory. He was far easier on his own young apprentices. He had two – a boy and a girl, acquired on consecutive days and therefore respectively called Monday and Tuesday. He questioned the boy, 'Now tell me, Monday, how many classes of souls sustain man and woman?'

Monday put down the load of sticks he was carrying, from which the evening cooking fire would presently be built, then came to sit attentively before his teacher. 'There are four,' he said.

As quick as a lizard was this little fellow. 'And what are they?'

'There is one that survives and three that die.'

'Tell me about the three mortal souls.'

'The first,' said Monday, 'lives outside the body of its owner, in a wild beast deep in the forest. The second is the shadow cast by the body, endangered at night, strong in the morning, dying in the grave. The last is our dream soul.'

'Very good,' said Run Run, massaging the protruding bones of his old knees. 'Light the fire now.'

Tuesday, who was deverminising Run Run's woolly, grey scalp, said, 'Tell us about the soul that lives in the wild beast, Teacher.'

What this precocious little lady was referring to was not animal souls in general, but one specific soul. The leopard that visited him and spoke in pitiful coughs and growlings, like an old and complaining hag. He was not in the mood for that story, nor did he consider it appropriate. Nevertheless, Tuesday was doing such a fine job cracking lice that he felt obliged to come across with the condensed version of the tragic tale: 'It all began so long ago that only the shreds of memory remain . . .'

'Eeeh,' they said, leaning on their ears.

'There was a huge fort at the fork in the river. Believe me when I say huge.' He expanded his arms to their full reach. 'I mean *huge*. A thousand people lived inside its walls in comfort. There were kings and overseers and the Queen of the River who was so fat that she needed four strong slaves to manipulate her limbs.'

'Sshh,' they hissed in encouragement of more detail.

'There came a white man – one good one from the many bad. Good but proud. Proud enough to oppose the God-Queen, fat Mammy Yellowbelly, and sneer at her spells and refuse her food. Well, you can imagine what she thought of that. But he was so arrogant he hardly noticed the problems he was causing. Or if he noticed he didn't care. What does a white man know? So they blew magic at him, but he just stood like a tree in a storm, bending but not falling, which made Mammy's rage all the greater. She laid all sorts of badness on him – her own wicked daughter; Sassabonsum; death-wished war prisoners. In the end they stole his dream soul, and that did it . . .'

The story unravelled into the night. The fire was lit and they sat in the cocoon of light, the listeners quite enchanted, but not to the extent that the entertainment ever outweighed the lesson. This listening was a serious business, an inheritance of history that they in turn would be expected to pass on in fine detail to their successors. In that way nothing that should be remembered would not be remembered. Take the mistake that Yoruba the witch doctor had made in the out-world for instance; she'd assumed that she had power enough to take on the Dream Stealer on his own ground, and that in the event of serious trouble her own spirit guardians would step in and help her. But they did not. They'd warned her not to attempt to frustrate the half-decayed god, Sassabonsum. She didn't obey.

'I know. I was there. Yes, I saw the whole thing, from start to finish. It was a disaster. Never disobey the spirit guardians. If they tell you, "Do this", then do it. If they say, "Don't", then don't. Theirs is the government of the mind ... Though I must tell you that I only learned that rule much later, for I was as keen as Yoruba to give Sassabonsum a hard time. So we went into the dream world of that sick half-bedeviled white man who was taken away, half dead, by his own people to We-Know-Not-Where ... But that is another story ... Poor Yoruba – abandoned by her spirit guardians, her mortal soul at the mercy of Sassabonsum's black-hearted little dream stealer, had one chance only. In order to survive the ordeal she needed the white man; needed to convince his crazy spirit that she was on his side. Does grass extinguish fire? The man was burning. She stood in his way. What do you think happened? ... Of course, she burned up – burned up like a straw and vanished in the wind. An ash lost in time. Yes, I saw this with my own eyes; saw my mother vanish – just like that. How I came back is another story. But when I did, I went in search of her one remaining soul – the soul that lives in the beast in the forest: the leopard. And I found her.' There were tears in Run Run's eyes when he said, 'Treat her with respect, my children. With deep respect.'

'It is Yoruba?'

'It is all that is left of her.'

Run Run would have ended the story then, had Monday, the more enquiring of the children, not come up with his usual batch of unanswerable questions, concluding with: 'So what will become of her? Will the beast live on until the end of time?'

Run Run was too embarrassed to admit that he honestly didn't know. But what does the skilful purveyor of knowledge do when knowledge isn't there? He invents it. He draws on theory. 'To assume that time will one day end is a mistake. Time, as you have already been taught, is a river; a circular river that feeds on its own source, and is therefore never-ending. Whatever it has taken will one day wash up again at the place where it was lost. That is the everlasting truth.'

'Yoruba will return, then, once the circle is complete?'

'She will find a way.' He said sincerely, 'If you knew her as I did, you, too, would be sure of that. Respect the Spotted One, my children, and do as she bids. Stroke her and love her. For she was my teacher, as I am yours. Look into her candle-flame eyes and you will know she is there in soul, waiting. Yes, have no doubt, her every thought is devoted to the task of coming home. Now let us eat.'

Fifteen

It was but a jet-hop from Heathrow to Africa's drowned coast; to the lagoon port of Lagos. A silver-winged short cut to the Slave Coast of old which wasn't producing slaves any more but high-grade oil. Otherwise nothing that affected man had greatly changed. From the moment James Tremayne and Jenny Oxenham emerged from their miracle transport and became pedestrian, like frogs in a swamp but not nearly as happy, they became very wet. They saw little of Lagos, seeing instead the interior of several taxis, that of a boozy hotel foyer, and of a local shipping agent's office with posters curled and half descended from damp. Lagos might have been handsome, straight and proud, or it might have been cringing and decayed. Rain prevented judgement. Rain such as no English sky could have produced: a swishing, solid cataract that took the place of air and had to be breathed. A driving grey mass that compressed sky and earth into a single emphatic and inescapable flood.

A jet-hop to Lagos perhaps, but from there onwards Rory Tremayne would have known more or less where he was at. The only route, not rained out, from there to Calbar lay seawards. Coastal traders did the trip, taking anything to Calbar, bringing anything back. The *Benin Queen* was such a ship, so its agent said.

The *Benin Queen* was old and straight funnelled and chronically acned with rust. That was the only major impression that James Tremayne gained as he and Jenny Oxenham came up the boarding ladder and rushed for cover. Their cabins were aft, and it was there that they learned that any atmosphere not filled by water, is occupied by mosquitoes. No matter. They would soon be at sea. Mosquitoes did not put to sea.

Not so. The mosquito swarms went where the *Queen* went.

Moreover they had allies: cockroaches of the most sociable kind that packed the ledge above James's bunk, twirling their antennae as they watched him at his ablutions before his dented steel handbasin; brushing his hair; dressing and undressing. There were scorpions, too. It could have been worse. James demarcated no go areas with Keating's powder, slept beneath the mosquito net which was hooked to the roof, and on the whole was left alone.

It rained for a further day. Then came the sun, languidly reaching from a morning horizon, then seizing the sky. The *Queen* pushed stolidly at a new blue sea, unaware of change, like a thick-ribbed beast of burden.

They discovered fellow passengers. They came out with the sun: assorted money-diggers in the African dirt, bagmen, oilmen, and traders, gaunt, jaded old codgers, the lot. Like choleric patients of some fashionable sanatorium they combined to fill the static, straight rows of deck chairs, stretched out, feet first towards a mesmeric shore. What was to be seen from this perspective was this: ship's rails, pocked with rust; a line of spraying surf; a whitish beach; a solid wall of green forest. All this was lifting and falling as to the humour of the ship, but otherwise giving no indication that it would ever change. Occasionally a river spread muddy fingers out to sea. And so it was for that day and the next.

They discovered, too, that Jenny was the only woman on board. Women – more specifically, white women – were apparently a species seldom encountered west of the Niger. It was not recommended practice to take white women into the tropics. The Foreign Office had once published something to that effect, and no one but the captain had heard of white females turning up at Old Calbar. The exceptions were an anthropologist who'd published a book, and a Dutch harlot who'd slipped in disguised in soldier's uniform, and had caused a lapse of discipline amongst the garrison of the time.

'Old Calbar, my dear,' said the captain, dispensing his opinion to all at the table, 'Old Calbar is indeed old . . . It's . . . It's . . .'

'It's a hole,' put in a bearded man. 'There is only one single ramshackle hotel – run by a *Greek*. It has no pavements, no gutters, and its only means of sanitation is by rain. In its favour,' he added, 'it rains there a lot.'

'We are prepared for rain,' said Jenny.

Indeed they were prepared for many eventualities. They had each brought several antproof trunks, packed with such things as Dettol and antifungal creme, Elastoplast, binoculars, Bic lighters, torches and spare batteries. Jenny had packed her Underwood portable typewriter. From an adventurous friend James had borrowed a rifle, a John Wilkes .470 double, in case of substantial opposition.

'I cannot imagine anyone, who does not *have* to go to Old Calbar, wanting to go there.' This from the bearded man again. 'I, unfortunately, am sometimes obliged to visit on business. Dare I ask what you intend to do there?'

Now, this unwanted enquiry had been posed in many guises, at every evening meal, but never so bluntly. It had been answered as many times by Jenny, thus: 'I'm an ethnologist.' Which she did again.

'But, my dear,' said the man, gesturing dramatically, 'what could one possibly wish to know about these savages, that is not already known. They are cunning and they're liars. They're riddled with heinous superstitions, make human sacrifices, and even in this day and age eat human remains. Yes, they do . . . A missionary told me he'd found evidence of that. Ghastly. Their chiefs are tyrants, heartless, arrogant and immoral, and every-thing, but *everything* you wish to do must have their say-so. They criminally exploit their own people and get fabulously rich on palm oil revenues.' He rewarded himself with a spoon of soup and a sip of wine, then concluded, 'And they are the most disease-ravaged nation on earth. Have I forgotten anything?' he asked of his compatriots.

The general view was that there were a few other local character traits worth mentioning.

'They distrust outsiders.'

'They loathe outsiders.'

'They have been known to kill outsiders.'

Disconcertingly, most of them were able to name someone who had died there, though not necessarily by violence. Allowing for exaggeration, it did seem to James that Old Calbar might produce some diverting experiences. They would soon know. He went to his bunk that night disturbed by a sense of unreality.

At dawn a change had come upon the coast. The land was meshed to the sea in a haze of swamps and tawny-coloured rivers. The sea, tinged brown by the oozing lakes, lay flat and passionless. The air was still, and grey with drizzle. Old Calbar lay somewhere ahead, forebodingly masked in mist. James's sense of unreality increased. He and Jenny went to the bows in order to gain their first glimpse of the place, and fancied they saw it a dozen times before at last they did. As the captain had described, it was old. It crawled good-naturedly out of the mist, a town of low buildings and warehouses indiscriminately strewn about between belts of palms and other trees, and hibiscus shrubs that bled right down to the river's edge. Native dhows slid by, their lateen sails patched, and slackly sodden. A coaster of similar proportions to the *Queen* was moored in the estuary, and more of her pitted kin were docked along the shore, wedded to dilatory and geriatric cranes, one of which was lethargically lifting cargo. Other signs of life were minimal.

An eroded cement wharf was occupied by small boys who squatted or hopped about at some game, who noticed the arrival of the *Queen* but paid her scant attention until she scattered the morning air with a saxophone-like burp of her siren. Then they collectively stared. A donkey also looked up. In general, it seemed, that this little port's preference was for leisure.

A passenger called Dodds came to James at that point. He proffered a book, the title of which was *Hygiene in the Tropics*. 'Here,' he said. 'I dug this up for you. It's well worth reading.'

'You're very kind,' said Jenny in acceptance.

Dodds had frequently lectured on this subject during the course of the voyage, passing on disquieting information regarding dysentery, sleeping sickness and malaria. Dodds, a burned-up little crisp of a man, was a veteran trader from Luanda. 'Have you brought insect powder?' he said.

'Yes.'

'Useless against driver ants. Have I warned you about driver ants?'

'No.'

'Too late now, then. Just remember . . .'

Crash! went the anchor chain, disintegrating the better part of the trader's last-minute advice.

'. . . Never know when they're going to strike.'

136

'Thank you,' said James. 'We'll be careful.'

'Look.' Dodds gave a rueful grin. 'We've pulled your leg a bit during the voyage, and no harm done. But the truth of the matter is that though this part of the map was once coloured red, you'd never know it. The Crown Colony system used to offer an Englishman a measure of protection, but that's all history. No one's really in charge any more. Treat every petty official as though no greater man existed than he, and when in doubt, bribe. And when not in doubt, bribe. Mostly you will be in doubt. It's a shambles. We traders are holding on by our teeth. What I'm saying is that if you get into trouble, don't expect any help from the embassy. It's a ridiculous situation, but there it is. Forewarned is forearmed, that's what I say.

'As for Old Calbar, well, it's not the most congenial little town on earth, and the locals will take you for a huge ride if they think you're green. My advice to you is not to tell 'em what you're up to, or what you want. Sit back for a few days. Get the feel of it. Let them come to you. They will, soon enough. Find yourself a good interpreter. I know a man here who might be willing to help you . . . Can't promise anything, but he might. It depends on whether he takes to you. I'll let you have my card if you like, by way of introduction.'

'That would be more than kind,' said James.

Dodds said, 'Nonsense, old man.' He gave James his card. 'The fellow's name is Logan. He has an office in the main square, if you could call it that. It's up on the heights. You can't miss it. There is only one road. Well, that's about it. Good luck.'

'Logan,' James confirmed. 'I'll look him up.'

'Tell him that you're friends of mine. He's quite a good sort. Knows the ropes . . . Look, they've sent a launch to take you off.'

'It's really very good of you,' said Jenny.

'In these parts we do what we can for each other.' He gave her an avuncular pat on the shoulder.

'I wish there was something we could do for you,' Jenny said.

'Well, there isn't . . . Mind you, there is. Come back in one piece. And if you ever find yourself in Luanda, look me up.'

'Luanda – count on it.'

'I hope you find what you're looking for.'

'So do I,' said James.

'We will,' said Jenny on a more positive note.

Several black men appeared on deck. One took their passports and disappeared in the direction of the bridge. Another, a man of uncommon proportions, took charge of their luggage. His hands and feet were huge, as were his lips, but his remaining physique was horribly scrawny. He told them with a fierce thump to the chest that his name was Antera Duke. Duke wore a tunic of the kind hotel porters usually wear, from which all but two brass buttons had gone astray, and, beneath that, an ankle-length cotton gown of many colours. No shoes. A turban (or was it an untidy bandage concealing some ferocious injury?) cocooned his scalp.

Jenny and James went about the ship, shaking hands with their erstwhile companions.

'You look extraordinarily well organised, old chap,' said one.

This false impression could be credited to the actions of the hotel porter, who had dutifully decided to station himself immediately to Jenny's rear, holding aloft a partially collapsed parasol. Where the Englishwoman went, so did the umbrella. No such dignification was provided for James, who made his farewell rounds in a state of bemusement. Jenny had the uncomfortable feeling that this was a case of mistaken identity; that she had unintentionally usurped some potentate's official welcome to Old Calbar, but as no one else was going ashore this could not be so.

The umbrella kept station as they descended the accommodation ladder and boarded the launch – a matter of a short downwards step onto the stern sheets. She sat on the thwart with the parasol above her and some dead and dissected crabs at her feet. James took up the space adjacent to her. The porter said something to the tillerman, who laughed, and worked the controls of his small engine. Put-put-put became thub-thub-thub, and the craft a moving thing. Greasy sluggish water came to divide them from the *Queen*, and the rusty plated hull grew distant by degrees of regret. An Englishman finds difficulty in being a foreigner. He vehemently detests all languages he cannot participate in, and is affronted by strange surroundings. He is a nervous export. He and she watched the coaster diminish with a sense of isolation, then simultaneously turned to face the shore. The Smell (while aboard the *Queen* it had assumed proper noun status) drifted over the water in its perfection. A vivid sun came out.

Old Calbar, or what they could see of it, did not seem much interested in their approach. A jetty of river-grimed concrete became the largest thing in sight. Jenny got onto it first. Checking carefully for predators, she crossed the narrow divide, surviving her first footfall on the muddy shore of old Calbar with a satisfied noise, part sigh, part grunt.

'I can't believe it,' she said. 'We're actually here.'

James's sense of unreality was also at its height.

Sixteen

There is no silence as absolute as that supplied by the jungle just prior to the dawn. The beasts of the night have hunted by then, and have either fed or gone off hungry. Those of the day are still dozing. The wind is on the turn, sluggishly wondering which way to blow next. Even those incessant serenaders, the frogs, rest their lungs at this time. Man is but a dream soul, off somewhere adventuring, fighting, sky-larking, making tempestuous love to the wife of another . . . But listen, even so. Cup your hands to your ears, and behold, there is sound. A scrape of snake's scales, as it coils into its dry nest. The whine of a fly.

There is the barely perceptible *tuk tuk* of the gecko on the wall, and no louder than that, a tremor of messenger drums. Who the drummers are and from whence they drum is a mystery to most. As to how they obtain the information they pass on is also a close secret. That the network is vast, and that it is the witch doctors of the area who maintain this system of occult telegraph, is all that is generally known.

Run Run sat with his back against his listening tree, his eyes directed at the death-glow of last night's fire, his jaws slightly parted as though slackened by wonder. Also within the small glow of the embers, with its ears pricked and its yellow eyes attentively blinking, lay a leopard. A lucid message for Run Run arrived from the mind of the cat.

'Listen! Listen to the drum talk.'

'I'm listening, Old Mother.'

'Did you hear that?'

'I heard it, Mother.'

'It's come. I knew it would.'

'It's at Old Calbar, downriver.'

'I've waited so long, Run Run. And worked so hard. Night and day.'

'It *has* been long.'

'But I never doubted, and neither did you. The circle is almost complete. It is good news.'

'It *is*, Old Mother.' He stroked the spotted head with deep affection. 'It is.'

'Now look, Run Run,' she pulled away and began to prowl restlessly, 'you know this is my only chance; my only chance to be remade, to become whole.'

'I know it, Old Mother.'

'The Dream Stealer has to be captured and brought to me. It won't come willingly, Run Run.'

'Have no fear, Old Mother.'

'But I do have fear. Sassabonsum will also know that it's back. And you know what that means . . .'

'I do.'

'Without the Dream Stealer, without its albeit unwilling help, I might just as well be dead.'

'I'll get it.'

'Yes. You get it. Get it at whatever cost. Go down to Old Calbar and find the stealer of my soul . . . And, Run Run, *don't* come back without it.'

'I won't, Mother. I'll take the magic battle-axe.'

'Yes. Take the Despatcher. Go.'

'I'll bring you that little wooden thief.'

'That's good. Now go.'

'I will kill if I have to kill.'

'Yes. Yes. Go.'

'Mother, I will go.'

'But you don't go!' The tail of the cat flicked frustratedly, her mouth showing canines more like daggers than teeth. A warning hissed from leopard to man: 'Be gone!'

'But it will be dangerous, Mother. What if these white people are difficult? What if they're hostile? It's not such a good idea to kill white people. It's formidable, Mother. I must plan carefully. And besides, I have a patient waiting to see me, who has come from a long way off for a charm to ward off thieves, and another, a fisherman, who fears drowning . . .'

The yellow eyes changed radically, glowed with thoughts of

immediate violence. 'Get on with it, or I'll break your coward neck.'

There Run Run's procrastination ended. On that warm and interesting morning he departed for Old Calbar. He went in a slim canoe, hired for the purpose, with four strong paddlers chanting up front, and he and his apprentice, Monday, in the bows, chewing breakfast. The current was favourable, the river spirits friendly. Without accident they reached the estuary port that afternoon. In fact, they passed the *Benin Queen* at her anchorage, and watched the curious derricks as they dipped like long-legged insects into the bowels of the hull, coming up with laden nets of cargo; silver tins of paraffin and wooden crates of machine parts. A barge, tied to the side of the ship, was taking on this load. The canoe curved then towards the shore.

'There,' said Run Run, pointing to a spot on the shore, 'land there.'

He'd chosen a place where several other canoes, like basking crocodiles, lay drawn up on a mild, grassy slope. He'd elected to land there for no other reason than that it looked like an agreeable place to come ashore. Like most infrequent visitors to the river port of Old Calbar, he was not aware that this section of grass comprised the eastern boundary of the Hotel Metropole. Nor did he realise as he stood on dry land, how close he was to his objective. His only immediate sense was one of pain as he gashed his instep on a broken bottle hidden in the mud. It was an inauspicious start.

When the bleeding was staunched he took stock of his surroundings. They had landed beneath a row of high palm trees of the kind that are tapped for mimbo wine. Ahead stood a building made of dilapidated wooden slats, rising two storeys with a sweeping staircase leading to its lower balcony. A faded and peeling, painted signboard identified the building to the literate as the Hotel Metropole. As Run Run could barely read, an opportunity was lost. He took a trusty-looking axe from the bottom of the canoe, concealed it in cloth that he'd brought for that exact purpose, then walked off towards the jetty. The jetty was the natural starting point for his search. All immigrants to Old Calbar, of necessity, had to pass that way.

The Customs shed with its corrugated iron roof, was throwing waves of heat back at the sky. Its door, though still being utilised as such, was rotted off its hinges, so there was nothing to prevent Run Run from walking straight in. Faithful Monday was at his heels. Grimy windows gave shafts of grey light, one of which poorly illuminated Old Calbar's Chief of Customs and Excise, at work. He had a piece of paper in one hand and the stub of a pencil in the other. Before him were many crates of squawking parrots, and some that were silent and contained ivory. There was money in silence. Silence was wealth. As was cordiality. His visitor was invited to sit while the counting of the merchandise was done. Then he made himself available to Run Run who came straight to the point: had any foreign visitors recently passed that way?

Now as far as the Chief of Customs was concerned this was odd. This was very strange indeed. For it was the second time within the hour that that precise question had been put to him. In the first instance the person seeking this information had arrived on a waft of rot; a smell so sharp as to stick like a chicken bone in the throat. This terrible enquirer had stood deep in the shadows of the Customs shed, and his voice had come as though leaking from a corpse. The Chief had felt quite ill, and not a little disturbed by the visit. He sensed that for a little while he'd been in the presence of a fiercely evil and dangerous thing, and had been compelled by fear to answer truthfully. The man who stood before him now was just as formidable but in a different way, and the awe he felt for him was engendered by deep respect. And out of respect he fully answered the man's questions.

'They came from the big boat you can see there in the river. There were two of them. A man. A woman. Both had too much luggage. Rich people. Yes, they came by here.' He didn't mention that in the process he also had become somewhat richer. An illegal rifle had been made legal *en passant*. A good day's work.

'Where have they gone?'

'Where else would they go but to the bed-sleep-house down at the river: the Hotel Metropole. So much luggage.' He said with a wistful sigh, 'They must be *very* rich . . . But here we are, you and I, trusting each other enough to be friends. I wish I knew what to call you. What respectful name do you use?'

'Tell me about the bed-sleep-house first. How will I find it? What does it look like?'

When all was told, all questions answered, the man and his boy servant went away. The Chief went back to his counting, intrigued by his encounters, and worried as well. He was disturbed by his omission to inform Run Run of the presence of his smelly and undoubtedly venomous competitor. He ought to have done that. This conviction grew unendurably; grew to the point where it drove him to the door and out into the sunlight. But, alas, by then Run Run and his boy servant had become distant figures, too distant to be politely recalled.

But Run Run was not entirely unconscious of the dangers or lacking in countermeasures. The battle-axe, though still shrouded, was determinedly grasped. And his eyes were alive and probing. And though he wasn't aware of it, little Monday also had hidden on his person a well-sharpened spearhead.

Seventeen

The Hotel Metropole was, as described by the Chief of Customs, 'A shattered chicken coop, two storeys high, that one good fart might finally disintegrate'. Yet, undeterred by this prediction, it stood now, as it had since steam had first driven ships into this part of the world. It could be said of the Metropole that it had sympathy for man, and that it could adapt to any attitude required of it. It smiled forgivingly on its population of whores. It hugged its drunkards to its breast and suckled them on mimbo and gin. And for those who used it merely as a place of honest residence it provided decently. A measure of Christian charity was discernible in this outlook.

The owner of this remarkable establishment (an energetic, portly Greek) emphasised that his new visitors were to look upon his house as theirs, and were to do there whatever they'd ever wanted to do, any way they liked. His name was Athos. He welcomed his new guests with aperitifs, and in Jenny's case, a fervent hug. The best room – the very best room had been reserved for them; the closest possible room to the WC. He stared in disbelief, mainly at James, when told they would not be sharing. Was this possible? Of course it was. To show just how possible it was he embraced Jenny again, then sprang into action. Orders were shouted up the stairwell.

'There,' he beamed. 'It is done.'

Jenny's room had wooden walls, much flecked with swatted bugs. A brass bed shrouded in mosquito netting, a rocking chair, a chest of drawers; these were the furnishings. It gave onto a balcony against which rested the limb of a huge and richly foliaged sycamore tree. Birds of every colour were active in its branches. She opened some cases, then was overtaken by such a combination of loneliness and lethargy that she did not unpack a thing, but sat in the rocker with her face in her hands. She was intensely glad to hear James's knock.

'I didn't feel like unpacking,' he came in.

'Neither did I.'

'They weren't wrong, were they, Jenny, our fellow travellers on the old *Queen*.' He sat upon the bed. 'It really is a dump, isn't it? But quaint in its own way, too, don't you think? I mean, once you've got used to hoards of little black kids following you wherever you go, and taxis without any floorboards.'

'And scarcely any brakes.'

'Yes . . . Well, here we are.' The unasked question was, 'What next?' He said tentatively, 'Shouldn't we unpack a few things? The wee wooden chappie, for instance? We could start by showing him to Athos and a few other old hands. You never know . . .'

'No.' She was adamant. 'The "wee, wooden chappie", as you're fond of calling it, is, from our point of view, far better off under lock and key.'

'I just thought,' he said incompletely. The heat reduced the desire for completion. He yawned. 'Which one is he in?'

She gestured towards the brass-furnished cabin trunk that held the Dream Stealer, and Rory's old horse pistol, too; both tightly wrapped and wedged into a biscuit tin.

He gave the wall of the trunk a sharp kick.

'Please don't do that, James.'

He said without conviction, 'I just feel that we should be getting down to something.'

'In fact, the opposite is true. We should be doing exactly nothing at this stage; nothing but being discreet and patient, that is. We must let things come to us; that was Dodd's advice. And it's my advice, too. Things *will* happen soon enough.' The latter bit of clairvoyance was not more than a minute old, and might have been more lucid had she not been so irritably sleepy. She said in a vexed way, 'I don't think we should push it.'

'Well,' he stood briskly enough, 'I don't know about you, but I'm going for a walk.'

'I don't feel up to a walk in this heat, James. You go on.'

This he did, dressed in white sun helmet and drill shorts. She saw these segments of him through the gaps in the foliage of the sycamore tree, then all of him, at the river bank, looking curiously at some dugouts. After he had walked out of sight, she took off her outer clothing, then lay down on her bed and almost at once fell soundly asleep. Once she was disturbed by the creaking of a floorboard, and opened her eyes. Through the mist of the mosquito net she observed her room and found nothing to account for the sound. She took the noise to have been made by James on his return, and drugged by irresistible heat, slept again.

It was not James who had caused the board to creak, though. It was the grotesquely proportioned porter, Antera Duke, who had also observed the departure of James Tremayne, then swiftly changed his role to that of calculating thief. But Antera was not after the sort of loot that would ordinarily be considered as profitable. For instance, Tremayne's folding alarm clock was left to tick untouched on his chest of drawers. His expensive fountain pen, likewise was regarded unaquisitively. His eyes glided quickly over such trifles as these while strong black hands began a dextrous search through the interior of James's open cabin trunk, sifting through the layers of clothing until his fingertips made contact with an item of importance. A pair of unlaundered socks. These he extracted and turned attentively inside out. They did not give up anything worth taking. A crumpled voile shirt was the next item to be scrutinised. Nothing there either. Antera's most expressive face assumed a disappointed frown, then almost at once smoothed delightedly out as there came into his possession a pair of unwashed Y-fronts. And, yes, adhered to them was exactly what he was looking for. Spatulate fingers pinched at a brown, anus smear. A speck of faeces was retrieved. A valuable commodity in trade if one only knew where to find takers; and he knew. Encouraged, Antera went on with his amazing search. From a set of embossed hair brushes a veritable nest of sandy hair was extracted. A toenail paring and an eyelash. The scrapings of a mucus-encrusted handkerchief. These were the items of booty that Antera gained that afternoon. When the clothing had been put back in place, and the cases closed, he left the room. It was quite impossible to avoid every creaky board, so he didn't even try.

Jenny, asleep, was as admirable a sight as any *aficionado* of

147

the full female form could hope to see. A sheen of sweat lit her forehead, and her clothing, damp and clingy, seemed hard pressed to contain her abundance. Antera Duke opened her door a fraction, then stopped dead in his tracks. He was no Titian, no Rembrandt, but he knew artistic perfection when he saw it. He had remarked on it to himself earlier but now it hit him like a hammer; a sweetly swung hammer that drove a spike of heat right into his groin. He advanced into the room on tiptoe. A cat could not have moved with greater stealth. He pressed his face against the mosquito net to improve his vision, and went quite dizzy with lust. Faint female smells entered his widely flared nostrils. He drew in deeply. Antera went out of his mind. He ducked his head under the mosquito net at the base of the big brass bed, and there, kneeling before the altar of parted white thighs did things to himself that would have thoroughly disgusted any decent observer.

Jenny slumbered on, quite unaware of the abuse she was suffering in the mind of Antera Duke.

James, on his excursion into the town, was equally oblivious to what was happening in the room of the woman he loved – yes, *loved*. Though he had been slow in coming to this belief, and had only in recent days firmly arrived at it, the conviction was now solid. No more vacillation. He loved Jenny Oxenham, and it mattered not a bit that this deep and joyous feeling seemed at present to be completely one-sided. In the fullness of time he would persuade her to love him, too. There was place in his life for a woman such as she.

Old Calbar, he discovered, was a larger, more sprawled-out sort of settlement than he'd assumed it to be. Beyond the deep water anchorage in the estuary, the town went on in sporadic clusters of palm-thatched huts and minute open-fronted shops, attached more or less to a winding, red dirt track. Where man had not attacked it and driven it back there was forest – thick and fathomless, coiled with vines and chattering with sound. It stood on both sides as though poised to engulf man's feeble efforts; held back by a Moses-like miracle that had almost run out. The heat sapped James but did not appear to be noticed by the barefooted brigade of piccaninnies who'd chosen to string along. There was grinning and larking about. All of them wanted to touch him, so he held their collective hands and walked on. He might not have gone as far as he did had it not been for their presence.

As it was, he passed through the belt of jungle and came up to the scrubby plateau of a small mountain. Here, at a languidly noisy market square where the statue of a woman missionary stood nobly above the throng, half a hundred women vendors had laid their stock out on the ground to waylay trade. And here the dirt track ran to an end. There were several buildings; one that appeared to be a church, or a school, for coming from it was a drone of angelic recitation. At the entrance to another lounged a bare-kneed policeman, smoking, observing the antics of a dog-faced baboon which, thank God, was tethered to a stake. James negotiated his way past it, feeling the pleasure of unexpected discovery. This was certainly the town centre; the place where Logan did business. And if that was the case, then he would take the opportunity to call on the man, and, if possible, enlist his aid. There was nothing to be gained by procrastination. Jenny would soon learn that.

James had assessed the position correctly. Logan's polished brass nameplate was fastened to the lime-washed wall of a two-storey structure overlooking the square. Once in the hall, further direction was supplied by means of an upwards sloping arrow, which James followed, ascending a flight of clean, mahogany stairs, to find himself then before a frosted glass door upon which the name Logan featured again, black upon opaque: *J.J. Logan and Co. Inland Traders*. Typewriter keys were clattering beyond the frosted entrance. James knocked and entered.

Logan (presumably it was he) rose out of his chair with his lips slackened slightly in surprise. He was a large man, rotund, but with the stiff back of an infantryman and with a fierce, grey moustache. Horn-rimmed spectacles saddled the tip of his nose, over which he aimed a glance at his visitor.

'An Englishman!' he said, gesturing affably. 'Come in. Sit.' He glanced back at the paper in the machine, seemed poised to resume typing, then stopped. 'Do you mind if I just finish this?'

'Not at all,' said James. 'I came here on the off chance . . .'

'As you can see, there's no qualified help to be had. If you want something done in Old Calbar, you do it yourself. Have a drink while I finish.' He attacked the keys once more, with vigour.

To reach Logan's liquor required courage. The cabinet was defended by a beady-eyed, grey parrot. Its perch was a protruding branch of wood, partially demolished by its owner's incredible beak. James was permitted access to a bottle of Johnnie Walker and soda from a wire-bound siphon while the bird scratched its head.

'Cheers!' said Logan without ceasing his activity. 'If this letter's to catch the *Queen* then I must finish it now.'

'Oh, quite so.' James drank, then sat in silence for a while, observing the industrious Logan, his office furniture, his feathered companion, a slowly revolving ceiling fan; pleased with all he saw. Here was the kind of enterprise and serious intention that made the tropics pay.

'Palm oil,' said Logan with more vehemence than seemed necessary. 'I've cornered the market at this end, you know . . . Oh, there are bigger traders further west, but I'm the only independent on the coast. Who are you, by the way?'

'Tremayne.' James stuck out his hand.

'Logan,' said the trader. 'Are you the fellow who came off the *Queen*? Yes, I thought so. Well, Tremayne, what can I do for you?'

James proffered the card and was pleased to see Logan smile as he read the name on it. 'Dodds. I thought the man was dead – didn't you? Last I heard of him he was down with fever so bad they could have lit a bonfire with him. It happens out here all the time. White man's grave, the oil rivers. Anyhow, you haven't told me how I can help you.'

'I was hoping that you would be able to recommend a translator.'

'Going upriver are you? Don't recommend it. Damn poorly policed. No good thing happens there. Still . . . Translator, you say . . . Now let me think.' To aid in this process, he, too, took whisky and ran it tentatively around his mouth. 'Translator – interesting . . . Quite honestly, I can't think of anyone reliable. You'll learn quite soon that reliability, as we know it, is a commodity that's in extremely short supply on the River Cross.' Logan curled one bushy eyebrow down. 'Tell me, Tremayne, what's your line?'

'In normal circumstances I'm an innkeeper.'

'An innkeeper, you don't say. May I ask if the current circumstances are normal?' The eyebrow stayed inflexibly curved. 'Are you setting up in opposition to the Metropole?'

'Hardly.' James had known that the time would come when some sort of an explanation as to his presence there would be required. He hoped that Logan would accept something short of the truth. 'Well, it's a long story. My great-great-grandfather was here, you know. On this very river.'

'An adventurer? A missionary?'

'A slaver.'

'A slaver. There's a thing! Those were the days.'

'A reluctant slaver. He wrote a novel on his experiences. You could say I've returned here because of him, as a consequence of the things he wrote.'

'Fascinating. Fascinating.'

The sincerity of the remark encouraged James to go on. 'It wasn't your ordinary run-of-the-mill novel of the times. I can tell you that.'

'May I say – and no offence intended – that I've heard of better reasons for sailing a thousand miles or so to such a shitty place as this. Still, every man to his own. My excuse for being here is money. I make packets of it here without trying too hard. Palm oil. Liquid gold, Tremayne, and the supply is endless. Bloody endless.' Logan was at an open window overlooking the market when he said this. A resonant hubbub of human voices had access to the room through it, as well as a monotonous tinkling of a small, stringed, musical instrument, birdlike in its insistence. He beckoned to James with a jerk of his neck. 'I'll give you an example,' he said.

The example was of extreme unreliability. It comprised the porter Antera Duke, who could be seen from the window, engaged, presumably in shopping. The gangly Negro was lounging about the market square, sauntering between the mushrooms of thatch, chatting to the women stall-owners, flirting hard, yet buying nothing from their baskets. He paused to perform a rhythmic little dance where a marimba was being played, then vanished into the interior of a stall that unlike its neighbours was enclosed by reed walling.

Logan gave a derisive snort. 'Now, there goes our friend

Athos's most trustworthy servant, Antera Duke. A descendant, I might add, of the Dukes of Old Calbar who were the greatest slavers on the coast. But, as I was saying, there goes the mainstay of the Metropole; having a good time, as usual, whereas he should be hard at work at the hotel ... He'll probably spend an hour or two with his chums, getting totally pissed, while poor old Athos tears his hair out down the hill. What a raw deal. Do you see what we're up against, old man?'

'Why doesn't Athos fire him?'

'Fire him? Heaven's sake! He's tried that a dozen times – a hundred times, I dare say. It doesn't work that way out here. Terms of employment here depend on issues quite different from those you're accustomed to, dear fellow. It's up to the head of the tribe as to who works where, and when. Only Chief Amakari – otherwise known as Grandy King Sam, can fire him, and he'd never do that. Duke is his nephew. Come to think of it, though, Antera Duke speaks reasonable mission English. He might – I say *might* – be the ideal man for you. Well, as ideal as you could possibly hope to get in this bloody place. I could have a word with King Sam, if you like. Look! What a stroke of luck.'

And whether one believed in divine favour or not, there was no denying that Grandy King Sam's arrival at that instant in the market square caused an impact that would be remembered in a variety of ways. Onwards came the king – a fat man with a gold trimmed hat and gold weighted limbs – onwards, born on a high bobbing throne of black, carried by black bearers, fifty strong and chanting. And rising from the head of the dark centipede of men was the royal standard, a pole crowned by a bone-white orb that was an irrationally grinning but mournful human skull; right then the only grin in town.

James would remember this moment as fascinating and full of malice, ludicrous yet so bloody malignant that it pained him. He would remember the soulless eyes of the monarch as they glanced towards the window where he stood with Logan – and Logan's deferential tip of his head. He would remember the trader saying from the corner of his mouth, 'He's seen you, Tremayne.'

Eighteen

Antera Duke, for all his horrid aberrations, could not be entirely condemned for what he had done. For he, despite his mission schooling, was steeped in the ethics of Fetish, and where he lived Fetish ruled.

He did not believe, as he had been urged by mission priests to believe, that to know of witchcraft was to know of evil, but rather that witchcraft was a means of protection from evil. He had, on a daily basis, to deal with any number of spirits, some of whom held little affection for him, most of whom, if wrongly treated, could become downright vicious. Sin, to Antera, was not so much a transgression or treason against a loving but distant father, but an ill-advised act against potent, foul-tempered spirits, all very close at hand. Anything that could be done by way of gaining protection, had to be done.

In fact his presence, then, in the market had to do with that purpose. Antera felt uneasy about what had occurred in the room of Jenny Oxenham. Not the petty theft, that wasn't giving him grief. But the sniffing and drooling and the thing-with-the-hand, done like a dog, right there. *Oosh!* He had never done anything as soul-besmirching as *that* before, nor even been mildly tempted to do so. He felt weakened by it, as though something good had been taken from him and replaced by something less. He wasn't sure what. He would leave that to Boogi, the apothecary, to discover and deal with. Boogi, though not the most powerful witch doctor of those parts, was at least the most accessible. And in support of her herbal knowledge she could work a few nice spells as well. Antera ducked into the interior of her hut, then stood there, waiting. The noise of the market place seemed unnaturally diminished by her thin reed walls. As always, a small fire was going, and the air smelled potently of her wares: severed monkeys' paws; a pile of desiccated animal heads; horns and skins; carved figurines into which could be conjured all kinds of fetish spirits; barks and dried leaves strung up in every usable space. Boogi herself seemed not to be present, but Antera knew that she was, and that he should respectfully present his case in the direction of a row of squat, clay juju statuettes in which resided her power. This, after some polite digression, he did.

He put it this way: 'She has put something in me. I don't know how she did it. She has power. She witched me into spilling male fluid all over the floor. What if she finds it? She could use it against me. I feel weak.'

'You are weak.' A voice confirmed Antera's worst fears. 'She has found it. What do you expect me to do now? This is most unfortunate for you.'

'Help me, Mother.'

'That would be helping a fool who would do the same thing again tomorrow. I hate fools.'

'Never again.'

'That's just words, Antera Duke. You never learn. You're like an animal. I see inside you.'

'What do you see?'

She made a sound that suggested considerable pessimism, otherwise gave no answer. The fired danced and Boogi emerged as though materialised out of smoke. She was no beauty.

'What do you see?' Antera asked again.

'Antera,' she said. 'What have you brought me this time?'

From the pockets of Antera's porter's jacket came forth the items with which he'd hoped to do a bit of trade; two small twists of newspaper. Two little pouches that held the various organic discards of the latest two guests to arrive at the Hotel Metropole. He knew which belonged to whom, and was not surprised by the fact that she did too. She opened them, wrinkled her nostrils above each in turn, then declared, 'Of man.'

He acknowledged that this was the case.

'Of woman. This is of she who bewitched you. Yes, she has secrets, Antera. This one knows more than is written on her face. She serves strange powers. Yes. This one could tear you apart. Even I fear her.'

He gave a plaintive moan, then enquired, 'What's to be done to rescue me, Mother?'

A charm would be needed, but not the ordinary charm such as the majority of Whites in the district had (unwittingly) fixed on them; the kind that was used to influence these ignorant foreigners to do this or that, or to keep them from inflicting too much damage as they blundered about Old Calbar. No, a far more potent form of juju was required in this case – a juju strong enough to dominate a witch of proven power.

'Antera, this is a serious matter.'

'I know it, Mother.'

'As I see it, you were trapped. You were helpless. You kneeled at her feet.'

'I did,' he admitted shamefully.

'You did the thing-with-the-hand, jerking like a dog. Yes, like a dog!'

'I confess.'

'This will cost you plenty-plenty to put right.'

'I will pay, Mother.'

She named an exorbitant price. He agreed to meet it. She, with an air of taking on an immense part of Antera's woes, thoroughly explained how she would go about saving him.

'Antera, for some reason, I suspect because of your royal blood, the woman has coiled on you like a python –'

'I think –'

'Don't interrupt me. I cannot get her off you. That would be impossible. She is too strong; too strong to be simply pulled off. All I can hope to do is calm her, and make her see your face.'

'Make her love me?'

'That is the wisest course of action. As you know I am an expert in love charms. I could make an irresistible charm from the things that you've brought. It would strike her like an axe in the neck. She would be harmless. You could do with her what you like.'

'As I like?' he said incredulously.

'Exactly as you like.'

'I would not have to come up to her like a snivelling dog?'

'Not a dog, but a Rainbow Prince.'

'Can you really do that?'

The fire raged up as though whipped by an angry wind.

He bleated an apology, 'Forgive for doubting, Mother!'
'Do you want it or not?'
'Like a bee wants honey.'

Nineteen

A none too steady source of electric power held every window of the Metropole goldenly aglow, nicely complimenting the lingering purple dusk. As if in the employ of the night, a musician was playing a purple tune; a languorous, sad tune on a wood-keyed marimba, while congregated frogs burped and croaked in worship of the hotel's wavering light.

The interior of Athos's establishment was humming with the trade and activities of the widely divergent needs of its patrons. In the ground-floor pub a crush of men were determinedly rehydrating themselves after a day of tropical heat. Not that the dusk had brought relief. The air was stagnant, and they were sweating so copiously that it splashed like rain water from their jowls. Silent mosquitoes, injecting fire, were driving them into desultory spasms of activity that was making the matter worse. In one corner a game of dice was being played, in another, two drunks were swaying to a monotonous quarrel, apparently concerning an injustice that had occurred several years previously. No one seemed in the least bit put out by a gust of revolting air that came through the open windows, lingered vaporously, then drained away. No one in the pub, that was.

In the much nicer surroundings of the saloon reserved for residents, Jenny, James and Logan all noticed the smell. They were seated in easy chairs, more or less arranged in a circle with an embossed brass table as its centre. James felt obliged to comment, 'My God! That was savage.'

'The drains,' said Logan tentatively.

Jenny pressed two fingers into the nape of her neck and went quietly pale, perplexed. It was more than a mere nauseating smell. It had other abilities. It was injuriously penetrative. It was hate.

'Africa,' said Logan putting down his vermouth, 'is a land of unexplicable noises and stinks.'

'That it is,' James earnestly concurred.

It was left at that.

In the gloom beyond the walls of the hotel the stench was noticed at once by Run Run and his apprentice, who were halted dead in their tracks. They had no doubts as to its source.

'Sassabonsum!' gasped Run Run.

Monday gave a little shiver and his right hand stole towards the spearhead in the pouch at his side.

'He's near,' whispered Run Run. 'He's somewhere in the dark. This is bad. This is *extremely* bad.'

'Perhaps he doesn't know we're here.'

'It doesn't matter whether he knows or not. He's after the Dream Stealer, just as we are. We'll have to be quicker than him, that's all.'

'I can be very quick, Teacher.'

'That's why I brought you, boy. Now, up the tree while I stand guard. That's it – on my back and away. Be careful, boy. Remember the warning whistle.' He pursed his lips and produced an owl-like hoot. 'You hear that and you just run. You just drop everything and run.' The latter part of this advice was said to the rustling foliage where Monday had been but was no longer.

Monday swarmed up the sycamore tree, arm over arm, a blur of youthful self-confidence. No one could catch him when he was on the move, not Sassabonsum, not anyone. He scattered a startled mamba that was thinking of sleep while draped on a thick branch, was struck at and missed. So quick was the boy, so squirrel-footed, that the jump from tree to balcony was mere instinct. He laughed as he landed. Sheet lightning chased his shadow on the wall, and before its parent thunder had rumbled, he was in. It was the room that had been rented to James Tremayne. He could see at a glance by the fashion of the clothing that it was a man's room. A twin-barrelled rifle lay on the bed, glaring indecisively at the intruder. He was startled by a movement – his own reflection, which held him in awe for a while. Then for the second time that day, the belongings of James Tremayne were gone through with burglary in mind. The search was diligent and quick. There was no space of sufficient size to hide the wooden Dream Stealer that was not peered into, or into which his little fingers did not pry. The thing was not in that room.

Monday went via the balcony into the sweet-smelling room of the woman. How different it was, how soft the garments and nice to touch. Upon a table beneath a mirror some small urns of powder had been set out, as well as a bottle with thousands of brilliant edges and a taselled testicle-like bulb attached to its head. He gave the bulb a squeeze and it hissed and overcame him with scent. A field of blossoming flowers. He did it again, and it repeated its amazing duplication. He wrinkled his nose and giggled, then went on with the search, becoming more frantic as time wore on. Finally, only one more place remained to be searched, this a stout-looking trunk with a skin of steel and flush-fitted locks that wouldn't open no matter how he rattled them. A kick of desperation brought a muffled shout as though from the contents of the thing. Monday gave a startled jump, then cocked his head attentively and rapped it again. There it was: 'Use the blade, fool.'

The advice from the interior was apt. He'd quite forgotten about the fire-hardened spear blade he'd brought along. 'I will,' he said.

'Get on with it.'

He did. He forced the blade into the thin gap between the lock hinge and its slot, and began to prise. It gave a small click but stayed. He gritted his teeth and leaned his weight on it. Sheer determination made up for stature. Something had to give. It was the lock that yielded. With a dismayed, metallic yelp it broke out of its mortice. Hardly pausing for breath, Monday tackled its twin.

He had a vindictive message for the inmate of the trunk: 'You're a bad little thing, I'm told. But like it or not, you're going to do some good. You see, you're going to fetch Yoruba back from the out-world where you helped to put her. Then, maybe we'll chop you up.'

A malcontented grunt greeted this, and another sound: the warning, hoot-twoot signal from the base of the sycamore tree. He did not do then as he ought to have done. He did not abandon his search and run for it. No matter that he was suddenly as scared as ever he'd been in his young life – no matter that the stench of Sassabonsum had begun to leak so strongly into the room that the good smell of perfume was poisonously drowned out. He was too close to success to quit. He doubled his effort. He called on every muscle in his small body to give something to the cause. The lock stood firm. He closed his eyes and clenched his jaws and wrenched. The lock stayed dedicatedly locked.

Then Sassabonsum was at the balcony door. Half formed, half putrefied, half flesh, half melted with bloody puss that slid like dripping candle wax from his frame, he lurched into the room.

Still Monday stood his ground. He'd always been a determined boy, a resolute fighter, even in the face of serious danger. Lack of prudence also came into it. At any rate, he did not run then even though it was certainly his last chance to make a clean getaway, but remained at the cabin trunk, spear tip in hand, now gauging how best to inflict some damage on this fearful creature. He had no real idea as to what he was up against, nor did Sassabonsum.

Naturally, when confronted by mortals like this small one, who did not turn tail and flee on sighting him, Sassabonsum assumed the cause to be an onset of paralysis: a state of fear-induced immobility, which made his deadly work that much easier. For then he had merely to amble up to the prospective victim, reach out and touch him with his dead side, and that was it. Slow, unremitting disease and premature death would follow. These things he keenly wished for little Monday, as he approached. Savouring his destructive power he stood poised before the boy for a moment.

When Monday struck, it was with the speed and intent of a defensive snake. His little arm, though lacking brawn, had the weight of the spearhead to give it momentum. And all the hours spent in sharpening and honing that instrument paid off in that instant. It was a heroic blow. It sliced between Sassabonsum's ribs at the level of his heart, and would have put a mortal man in his grave. But Monday's enemy was half god, and couldn't be killed as easily as that. He could be badly hurt, though, and he was. He gave a monstrous bellow – shattering window panes, bringing down a snow shower of flaked paint from the ceiling.

In the dining room of the Metropole a waiter with a red sash failed to hold a stack of plates. At a table set for three, James Tremayne retracted what was en route to his mouth, and said loudly, 'My God! What was that?'

Jenny stood suddenly. Her face was ashen as she paced towards the door.

Run Run, who had gone up the tree to find out why little Monday hadn't made his escape, observed the whole thing. Great was his consternation: to flee and leave his over-zealous apprentice to his fate, or join in with his own magically charged battle-axe? That was the question. The whole thing had got out of hand, and no one but Monday was to blame for that. So, should he leave the little idiot to his fate? No.

It was as well that the decision was that quick, for, from his perch at the end of the branch, Run Run could see that Sassabonsum, despite the impediment of the spearhead wedged in his rib cage, and not withstanding the inconvenience of being pelted by jars of cosmetics and other such missiles, had cornered Monday and was about to render the deadly touch.

Run Run, roaring with blood lust, launched himself clean through the window, the Despatcher swinging in a deadly arc. Deadly, even for Sassabonsum, who had faced both axe and man before and knew the combination to be extraordinary.

'Face a *man*, Sassabonsum!' shouted Run Run, 'not a child.' Swish went the axe. 'Let's see what you can do against an equal.'

'Run Run,' breathed Sassabonsum. 'I do not fear you. You are no equal.'

'You fear Yoruba, though. You fear her mighty axe. Here, taste steel!' He swung the Despatcher, driving Sassabonsum back with a blow that would have separated him from his head had it struck where aimed. It connected with the demon-creature's wrist – his putrefied wrist, shearing it clean off. Up reared the severed body part, hitting the roof with a thud, then flopping onto the pillow of the bed like a giant jumping spider come to rest. Sassabonsum could take no more of this. With an agonised roar he bounded onto the balcony, and from the balcony to the tree.

And that was also the route of departure of Run Run, with Monday held by the ear, protesting: 'It's in the box, Teacher. Don't go. The Dream Stealer's in the box. With one swipe of the Despatcher you could open it.'

Had there only been time to do it. As it was they'd barely ducked behind the curtaining foliage before the owner of the cabin trunk reached her room. They heard the slam of a door flung back. There was a suspension of sound that even the frogs, crickets and cicadas seemed willing to observe, and then a scream; a woman's scream of absolute horror that shot from the window and chased the runners in the dark all the way to the silver river.

THE
HAT TRICK

Twenty

Every detail of her entry into the room was kept fresh in her mind by recurrent nightmares. She dreamed of opening the door and seeing the obscene hand in its spreading pool of gore. Then, as if amputation was no handicap at all, it would levitate, and fly at her, and smear her with liquid putrefaction. She would wake, gibbering. She tried everything she knew to forbid its entry into her unconscious mind, and failed. The shock waves of those moments of memory had scourged her too deeply to be erased. The dream was out of control, and it was ruining her nights. Jenny was becoming chronically tired.

Logan considerately invited them to be his guests in his rambling old house on the plateau above the town. She would not agree to go there, but shifted to another room. She sensed that the vileness of the experience had to do with her proximity to the Dream Stealer: it had attracted this evil, perhaps out of sheer maliciousness, or to test its growing power. For the fetish doll had gained in strength since its return to its own shores. She was sure of that. It had not, since landing, verbally accosted her. But its attraction was there, and palpably so. She could feel its magnetic draw, especially when she lay down; a trembling, tingling grip on the skin of her ankles that was trying bodily to move her. This, too, had to be resisted.

She knew that it was only a matter of time before it became fully active and aware of where it was and what capabilities it possessed. She anticipated a severe struggle; a psychic challenge far more formidable than any she'd previously faced. And even though the Dream Stealer was not yet verbally active, it was conveying its will to her; jostling her thoughts in such a way that occasionally an idea would occur to her that seemed quite foreign and illogical, and yet at the same time so insistently and oppressively fixed in her mind that to oppose it was an effort. For instance, that morning, while strolling with James at the river front she had felt compelled to stop; mulishly to come to a halt. The notion that she should immediately return to the hotel had then overcome her. Quite irrational. She'd refused to give in to it and had gone on. They were on their way to the jetty to secure places on the River Cross ferry. For that was the only mode of transport, besides canoe, that called at Creek Town.

James, while walking, was in full praise of his new-found friend. 'Logan has been most helpful. We really owe him a lot. He was as good as his word, you know. He said he'd speak to King Sam about the possibility of his nephew working for us. And he did. He gained permission for Antera Duke – you know, the sensationally ugly porter – to be our translator and guide. I wish there was some way in which we could repay the man – Logan, that is . . .'

'I beg your pardon. I missed that.'

'I said that we ought to find a way to repay Logan for his kindness.'

'No – before that.'

'Antera Duke – '

'He's going to work for us, you say?'

'Yes. Logan arranged it. Decent of him.'

'But Antera works at the hotel.'

'Well, he gives that impression. I think Athos is secretly delighted to be rid of him, though.'

'Why should he be? . . . James, would you mind if I went back to the hotel?'

'But you said you wanted to walk with me to the ferry agent's office.'

She halted. 'I've changed my mind.'

'Are you quite well? You look pale, Jen. I'll go back with you.'

'I've forgotten something.'

'I'll walk back with you, then.'

'But the tickets . . .'

'We'll come back later,' he said leniently.

'I'll be quite all right on my own.'

'That's as maybe, but I'm coming back with you.'

And despite further protestations, that was what he did. She would not allow him to come into her room, though. So he stood at the door purposefully, with his arms crossed over his chest, while she went in. She rapped lightly on the chest. Nothing. Not a murmur from within. Nothing but the certain knowledge that an awakening was occurring; that a marvellously strong elemental was yawning towards life.

She passed a mirror, stopped and examined her reflection. There were lines of strain on her face. She noisily opened and closed a drawer for the benefit of James's sharp ears, then left the room. 'Come,' she said. 'Let's get the tickets.'

'Did I tell you that Logan will be travelling with us as far as Creek Town. No? I thought I had. Fact is, he must visit one of his inland stations beyond it, and so we'll have the pleasure of his company to our destination. I must say I'm relieved about that. Logan knows the ropes. He's respected. He's made a fortune from palm oil, you know. Built up his business practically single-handed. Well, I, for one, take my hat off to him for that.'

Clearly James wished her to join him in praise of the esteemed white trader, so she did. 'How nice that he'll be coming. He seems a decent sort of chap. Knows the ropes.'

'Absolutely. Have you got what you want?'

'Yes. My camera.' She held it up.

'It is a good day for photography, isn't it?'

Truthfully, it was.

'Lock your door,' he said. 'You never know.'

A sensible precaution.

Antera Duke was on the stairwell. He bowed obsequiously, comically low, yet while thus contorted held Jenny unwaveringly in his eyes. Like two small, lurid spiders they wandered over her dress, paused at her breasts then wiggled into the cleavage. She could hear his breathing. For all his gawkiness the man was intensely sensual. Jenny shuddered as she passed him.

Antera shuddered too, and then also walked downstairs and into the street. He watched the white couple until they'd disappeared, then threw a glance towards the dazzling sky. He had a theory about the relationship between ground and sky. It was a case of looking up, or looking down. On looking up one became aware of nothing really, just emptiness. On looking down one saw one's feet. Feet were uglier than emptiness, and less mysterious. So it was preferable to look up . . .

An ignorant man, he didn't realise how romantic were his aspirations, or how similar to those of Jenny's: victory over the commonplace. What was there to oppose it?

Twenty-one

The River Cross ferry seemed as unlikely to endure as an old wood shack taken up by flood water. Yet, according to Logan, it was all of seventy years old. From each side of it protruded giant paddle wheels, gaily painted in orange and green, that churned and clanked with enough vigour, one would have thought, to have sent it upriver at a far greater speed than its actual two and a half miles per hour. From a spire-like funnel – a totem pole of flaking paint – belched sparks and tempestuous, black wood-smoke that miraculously set nothing on fire, while in its bowels thumped a side lever engine as old as steam propulsion. It was affectionately named the *Darling*.

This then was the remarkable form of transport to which they had assigned themselves, in order to reach Creek Town. The forecastle and waist of the *Darling* were heaped with freight of various sorts: tins of Caltex paraffin and lumpy, unmarked canvas sacks, boxes and kegs over which sprawled and scurried, in noisy concord, goats, chickens and piccaninnies, women in brilliant, flowing robes, some suckling infants, some stirring pots, all in amplified chatter as if separated by at least a hundred yards from each other. There were native farmers in singlets and grubby shorts, and warriors with tribal scars on chest and cheek, holding wickedly long spears. The gentlest sound was the inevitable monotonous jingle of small stringed instruments, as mild as doves, almost lost in the clank and squeal of ancient machinery and splash of water from the wheels.

And so, heaving with effort and confined by jungle, they waddled upriver, nudging at swampy water, green-brown and streaked with mist. Where jungle and river met, the smooth water took the trees and inverted them by reflection and spread this upside-down green verge into an upside-down blue sky where lived a plump, copper-coloured copy of the sun. It was as if each tree on the river was joined in battle with its neighbour, pushing, nudging, stretching – all desperate to be tall. The losers were stripped of life, upended and drowned by the press from behind. It was an interminable parade of green with a powerful glory that transcended vision; that shouldered its way into the mind of the watcher because it was inescapable.

It fed Logan with strange religion. 'It is,' he said, gesturing from the saloon door, 'a land of a different god.'

'How so?' James asked.

Logan, outfitted in military style down to bandolier and heavy pistol, looked eminently in command. He considered the question, taking a swig from a hip flask then grimacing pleasurably. 'I tell you, here you can't count on the God of our fathers. No, sir.' He stared disparagingly outside for a while longer, then came and sat at the rough, stained bench on which first-class passengers were expected to mess. 'It is a case,' he said, 'of when in Rome . . .' Another swig, another elaborate gesture. 'You, James, know only of Jehovah, and a place called Heaven. Creation and Preservation. Here, the Almighty and His home go by different names. Here, in this vegetable-soup world, we have Mpungu and Srahmandazi.'

James said, 'Hold on a minute. You're not suggesting . . .'

'Yes, I am. It's absurd to assume that because you're here, your God is in attendance; that because you have exported yourself, you have exported an entire extraneous religion. Jenny knows what I'm talking about, don't you, Jenny?'

Jenny, too, had been gazing at the eternal sombre green, seeing it as through the eyes of the young Rory Tremayne, while a distant part of her mind had been listening to Logan's radical theory. In the steaming heat it took effort to consider another's views. She said, 'I prefer to believe we carry our God within us, and when praying we should pray to the Within. The strength derived is infinite, enough to achieve anything.'

'Inner strength,' said Logan. 'Quite so. But I'm more concerned with your exterior surface: your epithelium. To see that that stays intact is my concern – my deep concern. Here you are surrounded, inundated, overwhelmed by the beliefs of tribes of heathens whose spiritual kingdom is incompatible with ours.'

'But there's no geographic boundary on our God,' James insisted. 'The limits we impose on ourselves can't be imposed on Him.'

'Nevertheless, unless the Christian missionaries had exported *our* God into this territory, he would never have been heard of in this dismal place,' Logan said. 'But Mpungu was always here, as was the place of souls – Srahmandazi. That is the reality of it. Sassabonsum is reality, as are the Orisha and Buruku, and the village fetish tree. I'm telling you this because I believe you're in urgent need of local education. I'd hate you to die of inner strength.'

'Thank you,' said Jenny sweetly. 'We'll try not to.'

Logan, who had been sipping from his flask for hours, finally drained it. The contents had made him morbid. 'Ah,' he said darkly. 'Argue with me if you like, but I see it as my duty to warn you of the pitfalls of arrogance. A scornful eye – a chuckle of derision. It'll rebound; come down like a thunderclap on your head. For instance, James, you think King Sam is a clown, don't you?'

'Well, he is. He's ludicrous.'

'Ludicrous, James? You see, that's your mistake. That is what I'm getting at. You're seeing things in civilised terms, as a European. That's wrong. In fact, it's deadly. Here he is far from ludicrous. Re-evaluate or become a casualty of blindness. Imagine that you have just walked from brilliant sunlight into a darkened, unfamiliar room. What do you do? You stand still. You wait until the obstacles you must negotiate are revealed. That's what you do.'

'Yes,' said Jenny for the sake of agreement. 'Yes, that is so.'

'Believe me, Africa punishes the blunderers. It can break you like an egg on a rock.'

'I believe you,' she said.

Logan wiped his moustache with the back of his hand. Regarding her thoughtfully he said, 'It is necessary that you should both do so. I was telling you about my discussion with King Sam. Well, of course, he'd heard about the mayhem that took place at the hotel. And so he took a great interest in you – especially *you*, Jenny. He questioned me at length as to the purpose of your visit, and he wanted to know exactly what equipment you had brought and where you would be travelling. But his special interest, as I've said, was in you, my dear. He wanted to know if you were a priestess, or whether you were regarded by your own people as one who owns powers beyond the normal. I told him as much as you've told me; that you're an ethnologist – a student of the human race. "Is that all she does?" he said. I told him that it was. He was annoyed with me. I could see it. He thinks we whites are as thick as thieves, and a pretty noxious bunch of thieves at that. He kept on questioning me about you, Jenny. Can you blame him? Something pretty spooky occurred in your room. That's undeniable. I mean that severed hand! And the place was in an uproar and spattered with blood. Why should your room have been turned into a battleground, and by whom? That's the question on King Sam's mind. Naturally he regards what happened as directly to do with you, Jenny, your juju.'

'My juju! What a thing to say. I have no juju.'

'Perhaps not in England – here you do,' Logan said. 'That is the only reasonable African explanation: your juju – your devil brought all of it about. So our monarch's interest in you is keen. Which, in so far as my primary request was concerned, was an advantage, for he agreed on the spot to release Antera Duke from his duties at the hotel so that he could be your guide, and of course his spy.'

'For the moment we must be grateful,' said James. 'For whatever else he might be, Antera has become indispensable.'

And as though drawn to them by the mere mention of his name, the faultless retainer appeared bearing plates of yam stew which he set before them.

'Cook good,' Antera said. 'Taste yummy.' He made a circular motion with his hand over his belly.

Logan spoke to Antera in the vowel-rich language of the river, then in English to his companions, 'I've told him to make sure we have been allocated cabins. Antera will see to it.'

'I thought,' said Jenny, 'that our accommodation was reserved.'

'My dear,' said Logan, 'take nothing for granted other than heat rash and insect stings. They comprise the only inevitable.'

They ate the yam stew slowly because it was awful, even when washed down with beer. There was a party of Roman

Catholic priests who drank water, which Logan said would make them all very ill in less than a day.

The meal was cut short by a single, sharp crack of gunfire. An excited ululation and buzzing of voices arose from those on deck, and the *Darling* listed menacingly to starboard. That they were under attack was the first thought to come to James's mind; the second was for his John Wilkes .470 stowed in his baggage. Should he dash off and fetch it? Too late for that. Thank God for Logan's automatic. On the other hand, no one else seemed in the least bit concerned. 'What *was* that?' James said tentatively.

'It's time,' said Logan, 'that you met our intrepid captain. He takes pot shots at hippos, crocs, anything in fact that when punctured, leaks blood and is incautious enough to show itself above the waterline. Whenever he does it, of course, all the passengers rush to the side to see if he's hit something.'

'And does he ever?'

'Oh, yes. He's a crack shot.'

This said as they were in progress towards a flying bridge – a canvas and teak affair upon which stood two men: a Negro helmsman, holding a huge, spoked wheel, and he who was undoubtably captain of the *Darling*, holding the rifle, a smoking Martini-Henry.

Captain Crow looked anything but a crack shot. In fact, he looked anything but a captain. He was tall, and as yellow-tinged and gaunt as an El Greco saint. He was clothed in a washed-out suit of striped pyjamas and a sun helmet. His unshaven chin was mostly obscured by a drooping moustache. His bloodshot eyes took in the advancing party of three as they might have looked at a particularly obliging and bleedable set of targets. 'Oh, it's you,' Crow said to Logan in a voice tinged with disappointment.

Logan took Crow in his stride. James and Jenny were cordially introduced.

'Did you see the brute?' Crow waved towards the river bank. 'Biggest damn hippo on the river. There.' He thrust the rifle towards James, 'You take a crack at the next one.'

James found himself holding a heavy, bolt action rifle, the barrel of which was uncomfortably hot. He did not aspire to reduce by gunfire the aquatic life of the River Cross, and wondered how Crow would receive that news. 'I really don't think –'

Crow, who was squinting fiercely towards the western bank, cut short the objection with a whack to James's spine. 'There, man!'

'Where?'

'To the right, more to the right – there.'

'Where?'

'My God, it's sticking out like a sore thumb. Go for the spine shot!'

James took aim in the general direction of what looked like a half-submerged rock, closed his eyes and jerked the trigger. A thumping recoil, a deafening bang, sky loomed above the foresight of the weapon.

'Well done, sir!' Crow enthused.

'Well done?'

'You were close.' Crow demonstrated how close with finger and thumb. There was whooping and yelling from the deck and Crow leaned over the side of the wheelhouse to yell abuse-laden warnings at his passengers. The paddle steamer righted itself. James returned the rifle to its owner who reloaded it at once then stood it in a corner of the bridge.

'It shoots to the right,' Crow said. 'Had I warned you you'd have nailed the beast. Have another go by all means.'

By way of refusal James said, 'Thanks a lot. I have my own John Wilkes double.'

But the pyjama'd captain had turned his mind to the less important matter of navigation, and the unpromising conversation died.

Ahead were several humpbacked islands with narrow channels separating them, through which they would have to pass. There were ripples in the water between the green islands, warning of shallows. The Negro helmsman stood straddle-legged at his wheel. The captain had his mouth buried in the brass funnel of a voice-pipe, giving orders that caused the engines to slow and the paddles to bat the water at a more leisurely pace – like a swimmer doing a slow, choppy crawl.

James looked around for Jenny and found her gone.

Antera Duke had shown her to a cabin, one of the half a

174

dozen or so that were available to first-class passengers on Captain Crow's steam vessel. Its floor and walls were of plank, and a single porthole gave a view of the hotchpotch of humans, animals and freight agglutinated to the main deck. The cabin was no bigger than a horse-box, but it did contain a bunk and a mattress, which was more than most would receive on the twenty-mile voyage. Half filling the room were her cases. She sat tiredly on one of them – the one with the broken hasp in which the Dream Stealer was accommodated, and from this position she reached out and locked the door. A flimsy metal hook and eye served where once a sturdy rim lock had held. The wall at her back vibrated uncomfortably, but the bunk looked equally as disagreeable and was occupied by some muscular-looking cockroaches. So she endured her present position. A droplet of sweat, suspended from the tip of her nose, plopped silently onto her bosom. More sweat, following natural contours, was disagreeably gliding down belly and spine, and despite the copious soaping she'd given herself that morning at the hotel, body odour was rising. Worst of all heat rash had set up an intolerable itch in a most inconvenient and delicate spot. Boric acid and cold cream was the recommended treatment. Lethargically, she went about the business of applying it.

Had Antera Duke been peeping through the keyhole of the ruined lock during the minutes that followed, he would have been convinced that the charm that he'd paid so dearly for, was in full swing.

Its exterior constituent was beeswax stained with red ochre, and it was no bigger than a sparrow's egg. Enclosed in it was the waste material of Jenny's body and that of Antera's elaborately mixed. And though its presence had gone unnoticed by her, she had nevertheless seen it, and it was at work. That was how the best charms worked, silently, unobserved, yet exerting constant influence. Thus would its effect melt slowly, but inevitably into her mind. Thus would she become a servant of its will – servant to the loins of Antera Duke.

Antera, in the meantime, was on deck, tucking into yam stew with the appetite of the contented. There was no more to be done but to wait. And he was a patient man; as patient as a crocodile, and as stealthy; and sometimes (as then), he bore a spiky, white grin not unlike that of a crocodile. It signified an up-feeling in his testicles.

Twenty-two

Yoruba the leopard had, over the last one hundred and fifty years, understandably run short of patience. After Run Run's departure, downriver to Old Calbar, she had scraped together what was left of her willingness to wait, and had gone to lie down in Run Run's secret hut in the forest, where the girl apprentice, Tuesday, had attended unstintingly to her needs. There, whatever Yoruba had asked for had been brought. Whatever she had required to be done had been done. Irritability had been soothed; her chin tickled gently, her spotted fur stroked and her long nails sharpened up. Of course, Tuesday could do nothing to help the real Yoruba: the imprisoned mortal soul that glimmered nostalgically in the yellow of her eyes. But in all other respects she tried so devotedly to ease the pain of the leopard-woman, that Yoruba could not help but grow in affection towards the girl. It wasn't surprising that a bond grew between them in that period of waiting; that Yoruba began to experience strange feelings of tenderness towards this caring creature. And the girl was gifted; there was no doubt in Yoruba's mind about that. Monday was the favoured one, but Tuesday had the genuine talent. Yoruba spent time tutoring the girl in the art of mind communication, and found her pupil to be marvellously adept at it. So she went on and taught her some uncomplicated magic that delighted Tuesday's young mind. How to change a leaf into a butterfly; and the oldest of tricks – the transformation of a stick of wood into a writhing snake, then back again to wood. A handy thing to do on some occasions.

They passed the time in such harmless pursuits, but Yoruba never forgot for an instant the cause of the wait – the mission to capture the Dream Stealer, the little wooden demon whose power she would utilise to bring back her lost soul; to re-emerge in human form. It could be done. Anticipation of success had tied her gut into a knot. So on the fourth day, the day on which she had forecast that Run Run would return, she went down to the river bank to await him. With tail twitching and burning eyes she watched the brown river, and listened to its hiss and purr and general conversation with forest and sky. And presently she detected a distant clank of machinery. Tuesday, who was squatting patiently at her side, described it thus: 'The thing that makes the sky black and swims with two arms. It's coming.'

As it did so twice a month. This was no surprise. It was an annoyance, however, for the object of having gone to the river was to become aware in advance of Run Run's return; to listen with her super-sensitive ears for the sound of canoe paddles drawing through water, and not for this noisy contraption. Yet, behold, *there* was the distinctive canoe, yes, with its entire crew of four at full paddle, no more than ten desperate strokes ahead of the smoke-belching river monster.

But look at Run Run's expression! Was triumph written there? Was celebration evident in the bearing of Monday's shoulders? No, on both counts. The speed of return was derived from the effort to keep a safe distance between themselves and the thrashing paddle wheels to their rear, that was all. Yoruba half wished that they'd lose the race – capsize and be seized by the crocodiles. Her heart was cold towards Run Run. She knew that he'd returned empty-handed. The Dream Stealer was not in the canoe. She blew a curse at him that would have stopped an elephant in its tracks. The river-boat gave a piercing shriek from a whistle on its smoke stack, then turned towards the jetty.

Run Run survived the ordeal. His canoe grounded at speed on a mudbank, then he waded to shore, as Yoruba had forecast, empty-handed. Yoruba watched on from her place of conceal-ment. Monday came after his master bearing a sack, but this, Yoruba knew, merely contained the Despatcher. She sensed that it had been used in anger, and was intrigued by that fact, but her disappointment was too great to be dispelled by tales of bravery. 'They haven't brought it,' she told Tuesday bitterly.

'What shall we do, Great One?'

It was not what she said, but how it was said, that caused Yoruba to glance speculatively at the child. There was a hint in the air, if she was not mistaken, of an offer of help beyond the debt of friendship. What was about to hatch?

Yoruba tested: 'Yes, *we*, that is you and I, have come some way, have we not?'

'As you say, Great One.'

There it was! The cunning little imp. Tuesday, the apprentice, was in a hurry to grow up. She'd had a taste of magic that was beyond her usual syllabus, and wanted more. Well, Yoruba could supply more with the greatest of ease. She said with the mind, 'I could show you things; things you would otherwise never learn.'

'You are my mother.'

'Would you do things for me in return?'

'As a daughter; an obedient daughter.'

'They failed me, those two.'

'I would never fail you, Mother.'

'I know that.'

'You can trust me, Great One.'

'I do.'

'I'm cleverer than Monday.'

'I realised that long ago. We will go far, you and I.' So saying, she began to lick her paws and purr.

Twenty-three

'Creek Town,' said Captain Crow with a wide sweep of his arm; a gesture of vast sarcasm that nevertheless had impact. Jenny felt a twinge of awe. She stared down at this rather dilapidated-looking sprawl of huts, saying to herself, So this is it. Creek Town. My God, this is *it*.

The ship's steam whistle gave out a startling shriek. A dugout that had for the past hour or so suicidally kept station beneath the bows of the *Darling*, set in to shore. As did the river steamer, bumping her blunt bows on a rickety wooden jetty. Ropes were cast between shore and ship, and forward motion ceased. Smoke expelled from the stack crept over the roofs of Creek Town until there was no part of it unsoiled. That was how minute it was. It was quite unlike the picture she'd built of it in her mind. Gone was the battlemented fort of brown mud Rory Tremayne had described; melted by the passage of time, perhaps, into a muddy street or two where chickens scratched. Its place had been taken by rows of stunted shacks of no appeal. Still, if it was Creek Town, then it deserved respect. Logan implied as much as he bade them farewell. 'Remember what I've told you.' He added: 'Be careful – damn careful.'

'We will,' said Jenny, taking his extended hand. 'And thank you.'

James thanked him too.

'I will be returning this way when I've visited my station at Old Ikot Offiong,' Logan said. 'Though I can't say exactly when that will be.' Then, with apologetic haste, as though he should have instructed them better while he'd had the chance, he unravelled further advice: 'Stand your boots upright at night. Shake them out every morning. Carry your own gun. Wear a hat at all times. Never, but *never* look a leopard in the eye. And for heaven's sake watch out for driver ants.' There was more to it than that, but those were the bits that stayed snagged in Jenny's memory, like stray lengths of string of dubious utility. She would have to find her own way, she realised; keep her eyes open; follow her own instincts. She could do it: she crossed the swaying gangplank to the jetty thinking that. Also she was giving thought to driver ants.

Their cases were already ashore, guarded by Antera and a relative who wore brass earrings and a loin cloth and nothing else, and carried a six-foot spear; a tall and finely muscled black whose genes Antera could only have remotely shared. It was he who led them into the settlement. It had no love for newcomers, this place. Antagonistic little statues watched them pass, wishing them ill; little monsters of clay or wood, squatting in corners and suspended from trees; and glowering, empty-eyed, horned animal skulls. These misanthropic things glared penetratively at the strangers, daring them to doubt that fetishism could destroy them.

There was evidence of better days: broken, rusting bits of machinery brought there by white men for projects long since abandoned; gear-wheels, pipes, girders, chains, all closed upon and swaddled with creepers and thick-bunched grass. That Creek Town was inhabited might have been in doubt had people not come to the windows to stare silently. Lowly, dispirited and blatantly poor, the people were dressed to match their surroundings, in tattered cast-off European clothing. Some of their women had babies hitched onto their hips, groping at the breast hopefully. When they grew they'd forget the taste of hope. It seemed as though Creek Town's population expected nothing from tomorrow.

The ground underfoot was damp and smelly and slick with puddles. And looming over everything were the leaves – the countless shapes, sizes and shades of leaves that collectively formed the skin of the jungle. Just a layer of vegetable pigment, but it looked impenetrable. To Jenny it looked that way. She summed it up as a barrier, impermeable, and therefore was surprised and gratified with the ease with which she penetrated it and became a molecule in its green veins. A leaf-disguised pathway came up, and into it slipped the spearman, then Antera, then James and Jenny, temporarily holding hands in an

unspoken pact. The bearers of their luggage followed closely –
so closely, in fact, that the happy shout of the encased Dream
Stealer chased straight into her ear: *'Home!'*

Jenny had expected it – the coming of awareness. And yet the
announcement, its spontaneity, its polite exhilaration, came as a
shock. She hadn't anticipated such easy, unadorned joy from
this sombre incubus. Caught off guard, her response was
reflexive: 'Be quiet.' An unnecessary caution as things stood,
for no one could hear the wooden man but her.

'Home!' it said again, quite out of character.

She was wary. 'Don't try any tricks,' she warned.

'Tricks?'

'I warn you. I'll deal roughly with you if you do. And I'm
quite capable of punishing you.'

There was no further conversation for a while. She was
concerned that she had been too abrupt, too hostile, that she
had done damage. As a general rule, in cases of telepathy, it paid
to be dominant; to state one's case, unequivocally. But it was a
complex matter: a balance had to be reached between asserting
one's will and being too submissive. One tended to over-
dominate, with inhibitive results. Possibly she had made a bad
start, but who could blame her. The heat was intolerable. She
was itching. She was damp. Her mind was not functioning at
peak level.

'I don't think you can harm me,' said the Dream Stealer
abruptly.

'There you are,' said Jenny, relieved. 'I wondered what had
happened to you.'

'It's more likely that I'll harm you. I could think of a lot of
ways to do that.'

'A misunderstanding! I was a bit edgy.'

'You should behave yourself. You're nothing here, a fly in a
web.'

'That's a matter of opinion. I chose to come.'

'You didn't choose. You were chosen, and set on course. You
are, I might add, ideal for the job: nosy, ambitious, arrogant;
intelligent, but not sufficiently so to have seen the trap. The
web. And now that you're in it you won't survive it: you
haven't the strength to survive it.'

'So what is the point of my behaving myself, then, as you put it? I can't see any advantage of that. On the other hand I can see definite advantages in being hard on you. You're very primitive, that's obvious. You have a vicious side that needs to be controlled, and I'm ready to control it. Why do you threaten me? That won't work. Your attitude needs correction, and I'm just the one to see to it.'

This was greeted by peels of laughter from the Dream Stealer, as if she'd related an excellent joke. Once the mirth had subsided Jenny said calmly, 'Perhaps you think I can't control you.'

'I think you think you can. What you need to know is that your personality would get in the way. You want to know more, and I can tell you more. You can subdue me only by subduing your own inquisitiveness, and I can't see that happening.'

'You're in for a terrible shock.'

'I'm in your mind. You let me in. You ought to be more careful whom you invite in.'

'I'm aware of where you are, and what you are. My mind has divisions. Your influence is locked into a small, isolated place,' she said.

'It's all connected. I'm growing. I'm growing stronger, and you're growing weaker. That's what happens when I'm let in.'

'You're in as far as I want you to be in.'

'Which is quite far enough. Oh, I can see many things that you'd prefer I didn't see. I can see things that you don't even know are here. There's dirt in here, and darkness. It's darker than you think.'

'You're vile.'

'In a vile little corner of your mind. But I'm not complaining. Things are going well. I've wonderful plans for us . . . you and I. You've a huge role to play. Oh, you'll love it. You'll just love it. It's all so vile – as you put it – so obscenely primitive. The out-world awaits!'

'Many things await. Some you seem to know about, and others that you don't. Which puts a damper on your theory that my entire mind is open to you. And even those things you know about, you don't know what to do about. So I feel pretty much in control.'

'You do?'

'I do.'

'I shouldn't. I'm not your only problem. There's Antera Duke. He wants to hump you. He's had a love charm fixed on you; can you believe it? What a dull ambition. Now *there's* a vile man. Mind you, you might think otherwise.'

'Shut up!'

'God, it's hot,' said James Tremayne. The white cotton of his shirt was stuck pinkly to his flesh. He mopped his brow with a handkerchief, then took the piece of cloth and knotted it into a neck scarf. He said to Jenny, 'Are you all right?'

'Yes,' she said.

'You look a bit washed out.'

'I'm fine; honestly.'

'There,' said the Dream Stealer. 'Caught you out in a lie. You're not all right at all – and you know it. You're struggling.'

'Shut up!'

'Is that all you can say? How unintelligent. I expected more from you. The heat must be really taking it out of you. Why don't you try some magic to make me shut up? I'm really feeling very good at the moment; very strong. Why don't you take me on?'

'When the time suits me I will. In the meantime you're where I want you. I'm very much in control of you, both here and now – and "in the out-world". I'm aware of every trick you're capable of playing, you and your master, Sassabonsum. And I've a counter for each one of them. I have on my side great forces – ancient forces. I know the Names of Power. Don't try my patience.'

Again there was laughter, rising to a derisory shriek then shattering into giggles. And the truth of the matter was that she couldn't break the communication as she'd said she could, not without risk of permanently rupturing it. And she didn't want that. Yet something was going to have to be done to cut down on the sheer loquacity of the little incubus . . .

'Are you a virgin?'

This impious, most uncalled-for query was the final straw. What was needed here was a good dose of psychic torture. The incubus should be made to eat humble pie. She was about to organise this, regardless of cost, when the initiative was taken from her in a marvellous way.

A bell tolled – a brassy vowel of innate strength that fell upon the obscene voice and silenced it. Like the Sword of Gabriel it cut at the night creature, once, twice, thrice, then paused. Then on and on it pealed in a volley of golden sound, dispensing goodness where previously there had been none.

'It's the Catholics,' said James. 'What an unexpected sound.'

Unexpected and wonderful, and relentlessly Christian. But it didn't last. And after the bells, the quiet was stolen by drums, a muffled antagonistic throb, as though beaten from the very earth. Here, at a place where great trees rose like columns, rose until they vanished into canopies of sun-shafted green, Jenny thought she saw a leopard on a branch. A trick of the light perhaps, or of the mind.

Of course, the woman, Jenny Oxenham, was not the only one who was attuned to the mind of the Dream Stealer; not the only one who could pick up and translate its extrasensory vibrations into speech. Yoruba the leopard could do so, too. Thus, from the concealment of a thick branch in a river fig tree she was able to overhear the entire exchange between the white witch from Who-Knows-Where, and the Dream Stealer. It was a moment of acute excitement, which, in her cat form caused a tremble that began at her whiskers and ended at her tail tip which gave an involuntary whisk. Enough of a movement to disturb the foliage and draw upwards the inquisitive gaze of the white woman. And though Yoruba froze then, as only a leopard can, until the party had moved out of sight, she knew she had been spotted. 'She saw me,' hissed Yoruba to Tuesday.

'Does it matter, Mother?'

'It matters. The woman has hidden power. She sends cold shivers down my spine. Did you feel her power?'

'In honesty, no.'

'I did. She's like us. She could be a danger. She has some daring mission on her mind. What can it be? Why has she come? This is not good. Did you hear the mind-talk?'

'Yes. Some of it.'

'A novice might not hear clearly. But I heard it all. I'd know that voice anywhere – *anywhere*. It's *he*!'

'The Dream Stealer?'

'Yes.'

'You've done what you set out to do, then, Mother. You've brought him back.'

Yoruba the leopard glanced pensively at her sickle-sharp claws, opening, then retracting them. Yes, it was true, she had substantially succeeded in an extremely complicated and exhaustive task. The Dream Stealer, the key to the out-world, was, despite Run Run's non-contribution, now almost within grasping distance. And her entombed existence in this spotted, claw-fitted body might well be close to an end. But this was no foregone conclusion. Boding ill was the choice of transport of the little wooden traveller – the baggage train of a rival witch; a witch who had plans of her own as to the Dream Stealer's future employment.

This new impediment – this troublemaker – would have to be dealt with, effectively and quickly, for the thought of a further hundred or so years of disconnection was too much to bear. So the woman would have to be disposed of. The only unresolved question was how. A draught of poison? A spear through the throat? A devasting spell?

'How would you do it?' she asked of her little pupil.

'How would I do what, Great One?'

Perhaps the child wasn't so bright after all. 'How would you get rid of her, the white witch?'

'I would stun her with a spell.'

'I'd thought of a spell.'

'A Fangaree charm, Teacher . . . '

'A Fangaree charm, eh. And what do you suppose you know about Fangaree charms?'

'Nothing, Teacher . . . Nothing other than that they're quite dreadful.'

Dreadful. Yes. That wasn't overstating it. A Fangaree spell would give the woman something to think about. On the other hand, it would take more time than she'd care to spend on the matter. But what was time if not to be spent. Yes. The more she thought about it, the more she felt persuaded to do it. And the woman would learn some lessons on the way to the grave; such as not to meddle in affairs that weren't of her concern. Yoruba was keen to teach her that.

186

Yes, such a charm would be ideal. 'Well done, Tuesday. You're a clever little grub. I shall reward you. Do you want to know how? Of course you do. Well, I'm going to show you how it's done.'

'*Great* One!'

'I'm going to teach you how to make a Fangaree spell. That's a big reward, perhaps too big. Nevertheless that's what I've decided. Take your arms away, stupid girl. Gratitude pains me. I promised I'd teach you things, and I'm keeping my word. That's all.'

'And I shall keep mine, never to fail you.'

'Of course you will. Which brings us to basics – the requirements for the charm. I shall need some things that you will have to get. Some of her hair would do well, and let me see . . . some body fluid . . . um . . . a small insect, a gecko or a mantis. I will need to know her name . . . '

'Teacher!'

'Don't interrupt!'

'But, Teacher – '

'If you don't stop wriggling about you'll fall off the branch and break your neck. What is it, child?'

'It's what I overheard. Just now, when the white woman and the Dream Stealer were going by. This bit about the love charm, remember. Well, it occurred to me –'

'I know what occurred to you. It was that some of my requirements could be got that way.'

'Yes, Teacher.'

The child was right – absolutely right. Any charm that hadn't run its full course could be refashioned and in some instances turned completely on its head. What was good for love was excellent for hate. The act of conversion was simple – a matter of basic ritual. 'Clever girl,' said Yoruba, thinking, 'perhaps, too clever.' She gave the child a wary glance, detecting nothing but optimistic devotion. 'Yes. Well, it seems that you're a quick learner, so now let's see what sort of thief you'd make. Well, what are you waiting for? Get the stuff. Time flies, but *you* don't have wings. Off you go.' Yoruba's leopard paw lent literal substance to her remarks. Little Tuesday was swiped clean off the branch. The fall to ground brought about no injury, but wide-eyed awareness of the need for speed.

Tuesday scuttled off down the track in the wake of the trespassing witch.

Twenty-four

The fort, Duke Ephraim's abandoned fort, still stood. Rory had described it as being made entirely of mud, but this was not so. There were cut-stone ramparts, and these had survived where the mud had not. Blotched with moss, dressed with white bird faeces, networked and gouged by powerful tree roots, and singing with insect life, it stood. It would stand for another hundred years. Some cannon muzzles still poked from one tower; the rest had fallen and lay like expired cigar stubs, jabbed into the earth.

Jenny, who had halted, stopping dead at first sight of the ancient structure, came forward, camera in hand. She walked into its centre, pausing to take snaps. She waded through a carpet of creepers, so thoroughly intertwined as to hide the ground. Something rustled sharply. She started. James, secure in snake-proof boots, arrived at her side. Both were staggered by the same emotions.

As he put it, 'My God. Where we're walking – I mean this exact spot – is where Rory must have walked with Captain Strangeways. I can almost hear the sound of the musicians, can't you? It's incredible. "Filled with confusion and stinks", that was how he described it. "A tide of stench and joy that washed him into the palaver hut".'

'The palaver hut must have stood just about here.' They went to the indicated spot for the sake of photography. 'It's very big,' she said. 'It's bigger than I imagined it would be.'

Antera, as was inevitable, came with his dilapidated umbrella to shade Jenny from the sun. 'There really is no need, Antera,' she protested futilely. 'Oh, what's the difference.'

The difference was that Antera at ten feet from her was an unhappy man, at ten inches he was more or less in heaven. With nostrils flared in olfactory endeavour he was close to swooning. Moreover he was in position then to check up on the juju that he had secreted into the air vent in the crown of her sun helmet. Yes, it was still in place, and undoubtably hard at work. He had great faith.

'Antera,' she said. 'How much further?'

'Maybe walk not far,' he said.

James said, 'I've just had a thought – a rather horrific thought in fact. What if they intend to put us up in Mammy Yellowbelly's old home? Of course, the place couldn't possibly still be standing, could it? But, anyway, that was what flashed through my mind.'

'It would be the ideal place to stay,' Jenny contradicted irritably. 'Let's move on.'

Several monkeys appeared. Weightlessly they ascended to the top of a heap of rubble where they sat, bearded and intent like a row of rabbis. Bobbing their heads they watched the visitors from Who-Knows-Where until they were gone.

Mammy Yellowbelly's house – it could be none other – ravaged but unrepentant, unlovingly treated by fifty-six thousand hard tropical days, still endured. Lopsided, rusted, dented and holed, it remained the best proposition in town. And, yes, as James had feared, this was to be their place of abode. Antera led them to it, but it was James who entered first, instantly falling not into space but a trap of bottomless confusion. He tingled. A mêlée of sounds buzzed dizzily in his mind. Then came brilliant clarity. And it was as if by some miracle of penmanship he had become part of the manuscript of Rory Tremayne; as though he had been dissolved into ink and written on to the pages. He was not alone. There was Jemmy Honesty, beckoning with the stump of an arm towards a banquet table where sat Mammy Yellowbelly in a red, printed toga; as fat as a cotton sack. It was as real, and as unreal as that. A place was set for James or an identikit of James: an empty chair among the many that were filled. Voices came to him. Everyone shouting – no one listening. Servants came and went, black girls, burdened with food and drink, with dugs atremble and bushy genitalia. He saw. He heard. Then neither saw nor heard. There was a sense of directionless movement, of subtraction of present state without future state being disclosed. A place of vacuum penetrated only by a single voice that he recognised as his own, saying, 'I'm quite all right. Quite all right.'

An unusual feature of the sound was an echo that was immense, and of wavering volume. It seemed to him that he needed to gain better control of his speech and all would be well. 'I'm quite all right.' That was more like it. And, sure enough, reality. He was flat on his back. Jenny Oxenham, down on her knees with water bottle poised, said, 'Goodness, you gave us a turn.' Her slightly magnified, very concerned, blue eyes came down to inspect him. He felt an overpowering urge to hug her.

'I'm quite all right.'

'So you've been telling us.'

What else he could see from where he lay was the edge of a large table, the bottom of some dining room chairs, and the interesting knees and knuckles, but not the face of Antera Duke.

'Antera caught you,' said Jenny, 'or you would have come a cropper.'

'What happened?'

'You fainted.'

'Don't remember fainting.'

'Nothing to be ashamed of in this heat.'

'Jenny, I had an amazing hallucination.' He sat up, then stood up, supported by a chair. 'It was as though . . . as though it wasn't me who was coming into the house, but another person: my great-great-grandfather, perhaps. I can't describe it more fully than that it was as if my senses were in place in someone else's body; my vision, my hearing, but in the brain of a stranger. A place was set for me. I moved without intending to move. I was an observer, you might say. It was as if I'd been absorbed into the reality of Rory's writing – not as I had pictured it when reading his story before, but as if I was truly *in* it. Picture Mammy Yellowbelly's banquet in full swing. Jemmy Honesty sitting right in this chair: *here!* God, it was so *real* . . . Could I trouble you for another sip of water . . . Thank you . . . So real, Jenny. I was immersed in sounds and colours of stunning clarity and depth. Jemmy Honesty gave me a wink. He was different: older, leaner, more haggard. A visible rascal, though. Mammy Yellowbelly sort of leered at me.'

'What else do you remember?'

'Naked black girls were serving food and drink – *stark* naked . . . They were tattooed with tribal scars. That's where it ended.'

'Think carefully. Try to recall every last detail.' As she spoke she wrote into a wire-bound notebook. 'It may be important.'

'I'm a bit shaken, I can tell you. Nothing like that has ever happened to me before. I could do with a stiff drink.'

'You came here to discover what had truly happened. You know a fraction more now than you did.'

'Do you really think so, Jen? I mean, was it authentic, not just an incredible flair of imagination?'

'It was authentic. Yes, I sincerely believe that. Be pleased about it. I am. Now let your mind go back. Look at the whole thing again from start to finish. Was there anything else?'

'I don't think so.'

'Emotions? Were you frightened?'

'No.

'Was there a sense of impending danger?'

'None at all.'

'Was it a pleasant experience?'

'It was neither pleasurable, nor unpleasant. I was there, fully plunged into it, yet drawing nothing from it but colour and sound. And, my God, there was plenty of that. It was overpowering, thundering. I could see the minutest things – a bug in the soup; the bloodshot mess of Jemmy Honesty's eyes. Glasses were clinking; floorboards squeaking. Voices tumbled in my ears.'

'Yet no one addressed you directly?'

'I was acknowledged as I moved towards my chair, but by gesture alone. It was uncanny. *They saw me*, observed me – as you do now. How did it happen, Jen?'

She shut her notebook with a slightly exasperated snap, then turned her gaze fully on him. An academic gaze, it toured his features for a while, then fell. She said, 'I don't know what agency was involved. I'm sure, however, that it was exterior to you and that what you went through was no mere memory lucky dip. The images you observed were created especially for the occasion of your arrival.'

'A sort of psychic welcoming committee. Why?'

'I don't know, James. I'm going to find that out.'

'Will it happen again.'

'We can assume that it will. Whatever field or dimension of time you were in, you will find yourself in again . . . I'm guessing. But I think, sooner or later, you'll find I'm right.'

'Dunked in and out like a biscuit in a teacup.' He laughed without enthusiasm. 'Jenny, you asked if there was anything more – well, there was. That is to say, there was at the time, it's gone now. But I know I saw something more . . . It was just a glimpse down a passageway – that passageway, there, in fact.' He indicated and she followed the direction of his gesture towards a narrow corridor of rotted panelling and flaked-off colour that seemed devoid of utility. The passage was empty; dead. There was no point in staring at it. 'There were serving girls using it,' he said firmly. 'Why should I have forgotten who else?'

'Think hard.'

'I have been. It's gone. It was just a glimpse.'

'Perhaps it will come back to you.'

'Perhaps . . . What does it matter? Let's get on with things. Do you know what I was thinking as we were walking here, Jen? I was thinking about Theophillus and his whipping tree, and the murder of his disciple. It all began for Rory at that moment in time, didn't it? He wandered up to it and it closed on him and damned him – and he didn't even know it. How the hell does it happen that a man can be standing on the top step of life, then get such a shove from the rear that he can't halt the plunge, and not even know he's fallen until he's down in a heap and can't get up again. That's what happened to Rory. And it began at the whipping tree. Anyway, those were my thoughts as we were walking . . .

'Then that bell began to ring and it was as if a personal message was being conveyed on each peal. It was that *that* is where *we* should begin: at the mission. At the whipping tree, that's where the search should start. All the way here I've been nagged by doubts as to whether we'd achieve anything; whether we'd find any element of substantial truth that hadn't been wiped out by time. Rory's words, that's all we had – and those seemed to me to be a damned slender thread. Then the bell rang out, like a friend, like a clap on the shoulder. Trees live for centuries. Tamarind trees do. I read that. So it should still be there. A bit taller. A bit older but still the same tree. The only living witness . . . That's where we ought to begin.'

'It would be more luck than either of us deserve if we found the tree.'

'We must. Hell, we know where it is – more or less. It's where the mission is.'

'Where the mission *was*. But that was a building of bamboo and palm fronds; hardly built to last . . . You're right, though. Of course we must look for it. The bell ringer will have something to tell us.' This she was positive of.

Theo's simple, home-grown church was no longer. That much was clear at first glance. The building Antera led them to bore no resemblance to the little bamboo structure described by Rory. It was a product of hammer and saw. Its roof was mossy, and its walls were whitewashed plank with the windows thrown open wide. It had a runt of a spire: an upthrust of timber at its west end that terminated in an open-sided belfry. Father Peter turned his pious, expectant gaze on the newcomers at his door. He showed surprise in the spread of his hands. Like two white pigeons they rose, then settled ecclesiastically at his throat.

A heavenly sound of children singing died. Excited murmuring supplanted it. The strangers came in, genuflected, then sat. The white pigeons fluttered again, this time to dismiss the children, who exited in a silent, speculative clot. When the last had gone, Father Peter came forward. Black shiny shoes poked from the hem of his black cassock as he advanced, sliding like a chess piece. He stopped and regarded them intricately.

'The children,' said Jenny, 'sing like angels.'

'They are angels. Wingless, but nevertheless . . . What can I do for you?'

'I've come to enquire,' said James, 'after a relative. A deceased relative.'

Peter made a noise that was intended to comfort, and his white hands formed into a steeple. He said, 'Few white people die here any more. White folk choose more congenial latitudes in which to expire than these. The blacks . . . *they* die here. There are few fatal diseases that don't thrive wonderfully at Creek Town. Who did you say you were?'

194

'Jenny Oxenham,' said James of Jenny, then holding forth his hand, 'James Tremayne.' Frail and tentative, Peter's five fingers wriggled in the trap of James's grip, then fled.

'We have a book,' said Peter, 'a record of baptisms and deaths. No white person has died in my time here, thus it's to the book that we'll have to refer.'

The book was a rotted, leather-bound ledger, prematurely aged as it turned out. Its paper, damp-stained and blemished into a state of illegibility, held, nevertheless, a mere fifteen years' worth of entries. An older, a *much* older book was required.

'How much older?' said Peter while carefully returning the ledger to a shelf adjacent to the baptismal font.

'The person in question was captain of a slave ship. He died at Creek Town in eighteen twenty-nine.'

The priest gave stunted apologies. 'A slaver, you say. Our records, unfortunately . . . The climate you know – it rots the clothes off your back. And yet the name, Tremayne . . . I feel as though I've seen it, yet can't recall where.'

'Rory Tremayne. But it was not he who died here. Rory died in England some years later. It was his captain, a man by the name of Strangeways, who died at Creek Town.'

'Strangeways?' Peter said. 'I have no recollection at all of that name. Strangeways – no. How did he die?'

'He was murdered.'

Peter gave a small, unsurprised nod. 'Murdered,' he said, as though mentioning a most common form of tropical death. 'May I ask, by whom?'

'That is the crux of the matter,' James said. He glanced towards the ever present Antera and remembered Logan's warning to be guarded in his presence. Still, he went on, 'That is why I'm here. Rory – my great-great-grandfather – was tried and convicted for the murder. An iniquitous judgement in my opinion.'

'Rory Tremayne.' Hands that had grown inactive began to agitate again. 'The names rings a bell. Heavens! Yes! That's it: "rings a bell". That's what it does. That's where I've seen it. That is the name inscribed on our church bell – I'm sure of it. Was he the donor?' This question thrown over his shoulder, for the priest was, by then, at full stride towards the door.

Whether Peter wished to be followed or not, he was. They

came up behind him, halting when he did, which was below the stubby, wooden belfry.

'There,' said the priest, pointing up. 'That's it. I stumbled across the bell – literally stumbled across it – while exploring the jungle nearby. I brought it here, polished it up, and there it hangs. Our pride and joy. Your great-great-grandfather's name, God rest his soul, is inscribed on it.'

And it was so.

Antera was sent to fetch a ladder, but James took to an overhanging tree limb and had gained the mossy roof long before the servant's return. There it was. Tears stung his eyes and his throat pained with wonderful fervour. In a daze of joy he read aloud: 'To the Glory of God. Given by His servant – Rory Tremayne.'

Jenny was dabbing at the corners of her eyes, too. She said, simply, 'Oh, James.'

Father Peter confined himself to a warning that James should watch his step as the moss was slippery. But James felt as though upon opening his arms he could have flown. He rang the bell with the knuckle of his forefinger and it mutely celebrated with him. 'To the Glory of God. Given by His servant – Rory Tremayne.'

'Did he not record his act of charity?' Peter asked. 'Didn't you know that he'd donated the bell?'

Antera had brought the ladder – some sapling staves tied together with bark strips. It was by means of this that James descended, then answered Peter's twice-given question.

'No, he didn't mention that he had. He must have requested that it be made and sent out to Africa while he was in prison. His story ends before that time . . . I forgot to mention that he'd written about his experiences here – fact described as fiction.'

'I gathered that he'd written.'

'Well, in the story he describes a priest, a predecessor of yours, who bore the fictional name of Theo.'

'Theo. He was real enough.'

'I wondered if that might be the case. Well, Theo pleaded for a bell. A bell to "defeat the drums".'

'A bell,' added Jenny, ' "to cut a swathe of pure sound into the jungle – like the Sword of Gabriel".'

'And that it does,' Peter exclaimed. 'Praise God! You must

196

show me this amazing manuscript some time. I'll admit, you've stunned me with your story. And if there was something I could do to help you, I would, for it seems obvious to me that Rory Tremayne was a sorely misjudged man. Still, he's with God now, so be comforted. Rory will have been taken to His bosom. But I'll not sermonise now. The evidence you came to find no longer exists. I hope your long trip was not entirely in vain.'

'Not in vain at all,' said James with a smile. 'And, as for evidence, our expectations don't amount to much. The case was closed a hundred years ago, so whatever I discover now won't have any material effect. I just want to be clear in my mind that Rory Tremayne wasn't a mutineer and murderer. That'll do. I'll be the sole judge.'

'A trial by instinct,' said Peter. 'How magnificently *un*-scientific, and imperfectly apt. I'll pray that your verdict is correct.'

'I've one more request.'

'If I can help . . .'

'You can. Show me the spot where you found the bell. I think Theo's mission must have stood thereabouts.'

'That's what I assumed when I found it. But there's no sign of man-made structures. There was a period of merciless persecution of Christianity in the Delta. Burnings, lootings. Theo's mission must have borne the brunt of it, God forgive them. But come and see for yourself.' Having said that, Peter turned and strode towards the tree line, and was absorbed in foliage. James followed on, amazed by the rapidity of progress of the thin, black-sheathed figure, and his powers of navigation in this insoluble green. It took him little time to discover the spot.

'It was here . . . No. I'm mistaken. It was there.' He shifted a few paces. 'Yes.' Peter's heel crushed into the mulch-matted floor. 'Precisely here.'

One could imagine that once upon a time the jungle had been cleared in this vicinity. The trees seemed younger than their neighbours. Ducts of dramatic sunlight shafted the dome of foliage. It was in such a pool of brilliance that Father Peter stood. He said, 'Do you get the feeling that this is where the mission stood? Don't think about it. Let that famous instinct of yours give an answer.'

'Yes.'

'You know, I think you could be right.'

Perspiring, Jenny burst upon them, then Antera Duke, clutching his folded umbrella in one hand, Jenny's sun helmet in the other. She became aware of a twig that was lodged in her glasses.

'Is this the place?' she asked, while removing the impediment.

From his pillar of uncanny radiance, Peter said, 'It's very possible. Instinct and prayer.'

'Yes, we think so,' said James. He truly did. But which tree of the surrounding ring had been the whipping tree?

'I must leave you here,' said the priest. 'I have duties to attend to. Your man will see you back without difficulty. If you ever need me again . . .' He stepped out of the light. 'If there is anything I can do . . .' These abbreviated promises served as his farewell.

So, where to begin? How to begin? James would have liked to have consulted further with Peter. The priest had inexplicable strength – an incorporeal authority that was truly amazing. James looked up, and up, lost in a complexity of green, awed by the depth of it, quite uncertain how to proceed. He welcomed Jenny's suggestion.

'We must be methodical, and not just lump around in the hope that something will turn up. We must refer to Rory's manuscript again; his descriptions. It would be best if we came here again at the same time of day, as best we can judge it, that he arrived on the spot.'

'But do you think this is where it was, Jenny?'

'If that was Rory's bell and this was where it was found . . .' The rest was left unsaid. For at that moment there was a hiss of foliage, as of leaves struck by a moving object, a fast-moving object, and a little black girl scurried into their field of vision. She did not hesitate or swerve. She didn't look left or right. She bounded at full speed between Jenny and James, in the direction of Antera Duke.

Antera, who had just found a good seat on some thigh-thick exposed tree roots, saw from the corner of his eye what he took to be an ape of some sort in rapid advance. He gaped. That was how long it took for the little girl to reach him. He reacted with the speed of mud. A small, sharp knife left a line of fire on his cheek. Both hands opened in shock, and Jenny's sun helmet changed ownership in the blink of an eye. Antera gave a bellow – a sound toned by anguish more than pain. By the time he'd got to his feet the thief of the sun helmet had disappeared, vanished like a bird in a tree.

The loss – the hidden loss – was a bewildering shock for Antera; the deprival of a dream. He did not care a bit about his wound, or about the hat. The charm. The incredible love charm. Its loss was a stunning blow. For a while he sat with his face in his hands in a posture of despair, but that emotion made way for another. Confusion subsided, and when he stood it was in a quiet and objective way. He knew what he was dealing with. He knew what he would do if he ever saw the little thief again. He would kill her; slit her open from gizzard to groin. That was exactly what he would do.

NIGHT
VISITORS

Twenty-five

They sat together at the river side, the spotted cat and her apprentice. It was a tranquil site, dappled with shade, wearing a smile of green. The river slurped and gurgled like an endlessly suckling, ever hungry infant, while above the water, on slender, bowed branches hung the upside-down straw dwellings of a million weaver birds, all constantly twittering. Fish plopped. Hippos grunted. It was the friendliest of days and the wickedest of days. Dire plots were being contrived. Sorcery.

What had once been a love charm was in the process of being reversed. What had intended to bring pleasure was being reworked into pain. Little Tuesday's dexterous fingers had dissected the beeswax pill, had separated the various constituents and laid them individually on a buckskin drum head. There were some hairs from various human locations, a fragment of impregnated, silky cloth, a termite's egg, the eye of a lizard and the sexual organs of a male and female frog. All in all a very amateur concoction, unlikely to have worked. An inferior spell put together by low-class practitioner. That was Yoruba's judgement. What *she* would make from it, however, would be something entirely more potent and worthy of awe. She sniffed at the items on the drum head, instructing Tuesday as she did: 'This one, this lizard's eye, is quite useless, throw it out. Throw out the termite's egg. Throw away the bits and pieces of wax and the pubic hairs of the man. Good girl. You have the perfect touch, like the tongue of a butterfly. You remind me of myself as a child. Yes, I was hungry for knowledge, too. Now what do we have left over with which to work?'

'The dried body fluid on the cloth. Hair from the rim

of her eyes, and that of her love purse . . .'

'Yes. Those we need.'

'The organs of the frog?'

'Well, those can either stay or go.'

'Shall I throw them out, Teacher?'

'It makes no difference – one way or the other . . . Leave them in.'

'Then that is what we have.'

'Good. Good. Now we can move on . . . What other ingredients? What have I told you? Come on. Come on.'

'Powder of dead-man's bone.'

'Put it in.'

'The mixture of smoked herbs – '

'Ah, but which herbs, little cat?'

Little Cat? Tuesday found the analogy pleasantly apt. She liked the name, and to show it stretched elegantly like a cat. She named the herbs: 'Spike bean to open her eyes. Red pod to open up the ears. Snake root – '

'Yes. Yes. Well, put them in,' Yoruba hissed. 'And don't act smart. I hate a smart banana. Go on! Go on! Dust from a termite's nest – a pinch, no more . . .'

Keeping smartness to a minimum, Tuesday followed these instructions until there lay a minute hillock of ingredients in the centre of the drum head. Then with a touch so tender that hardly a sound emerged, she played her delicate fingers on the Fangaree drum. And though the sound was barely audible, its effect upon the precious mixture was wonderful. It danced. It worked its way into concentric, separate circles, then frolicked together again, then redivided; springing, falling, cartwheeling, perfectly obeying the trembling instruction of the drum head.

At a signal from Yoruba, Tuesday stopped. What was in the middle at that point was taken, every grain and sliver of it, and drained into a pouch made from the scrotum of an infant vervet monkey. Thus was the dreadful Fangaree charm put together. But little Tuesday's deadly tuition was still far from complete. The charm then was an arrow without a bow. It needed direction and needed impulse. So Yoruba spoke on, and little Tuesday soaked up the words explaining the vital steps.

She was told where to locate it: a pathway would have to be selected; a path that the victim was known to use habitually. At a strategic spot somewhere along it, where a line of concealing shrubs bordered it, the trap should be set.

And how to set it up: a frame of bamboo sticks was the requirement, a little bed no larger than would hold the shrivelled scrotum. The final ingredient, a sacrificial life – a gecko or mantis or some small insect – would have to be captured, then tied by means of cotton thread to the top of the charm.

And that she should be still and patient: for she might have to sit for hours crouched over the magical trap, vigilantly watching and waiting for the arrival of the white witch.

And the final, crucial act: to spring the trap; to speed the magic on its way with the accuracy of an arrow, it was essential to gain the victim's attention, to get her to face the magical device if only for an instant. The sound of a snapping twig invariably achieved this objective. All that remained to be done then was to call out the victim's name at the same time as crushing the insect's head with a flick of the finger. Simple. The Fangaree charm was on; working independently night and day to accomplish its mission.

Yoruba went over the entire procedure again; then, to be on the safe side, once more. She quizzed little Tuesday on various aspects. Nothing was left to chance.

'Did you find out what her name is?'

'Yes, Teacher.'

'Say it.'

'Jen.'

' "Jen." Is that all?'

'He called her that, and she answered.'

'Say it again.'

'Jen.'

'Again.'

'Jen.'

'We are ready, little cat.'

'Teacher, will you always call me that?'

'Do you like it, child?'

'Yes, very much.'

'Then let that be your name.'

Little Cat emitted a sigh that had for too long been restrained in her chest. It was a sound of vibrant excitement. Her soul danced with intense anticipation.

Twenty-six

Down on their hands and knees, up to their elbows in dank earth and roots, leaves and colonies of insects, they grubbed and dug for two full days in the silent, listening forest. Word got out about the fantastic undertaking – the strange and exertive ritual of the strangers to the river village. People came to stare at them; to stare and wonder, and with bated breath to speculate as to the form of magic that was being worked. They knew it had something to do with Father Peter's god – He of Sunday, because the priest was a frequent visitor to the site. They knew that the white woman was in charge of the ceremony, because it was she who had marked the site with stakes and patterned it with lengths of string. No one could recollect any such rite having been performed before, or had ever heard of such lengthy devotions. They, the white people, were searching for something from the past. Antera was instructed to tell them that.

Yes, they could understand that. What was magic worth if it was not tied to the search for ancestral knowledge? They were pleased to have been informed about this, they replied. They desired that any beneficial juju so derived might touch them, even in a small way. They were a small people, as thin and frail as burned-out matches, anything that could be spared would do.

Antera was told to tell them that they were welcome to watch. He did so, scornfully.

These were not really free men, James was informed. These rib-thin, tattered creatures lived well below that level. They were the progeny of slaves and outcasts; the very slaves, perhaps, that Rory Tremayne had branded and chained. The Royal Navy had unchained them, but the padlock of ancestry still weighed them low.

On the third day of nothing new happening, the ranks of onlookers was peopled by only the most perseveringly optimistic. And, late that afternoon, their faith was rewarded.

A cross was dug up; a hand-sized, greenly corroded brass crucifix, identical to that described as having been worn by Theo. It was the stoic Antera who found it. Picking about, stork-like over a heap of earth recently excavated by James, he suddenly swooped. 'What this?'

A broken root? A twig? James could have been forgiven for mistaking it for either. Antera drew a knife with a spearlike blade and chopped at the crust. And it gave a glint of yellow. Jenny snatched it. She lowered her lenses to the tip of her nose and inspected the metallic wound.

'Brass!' she whispered to James.

'A cross.'

'Theo's cross?'

It could be none other. James held it up and his audience gave an indrawn moan of awe. He passed the object to Jenny, who was grinning broadly. They were both grinning broadly.

'What a find!' James said. 'That's it then, as far as I'm concerned. I know Rory was telling the entire truth. The bell. Theo's pectoral cross. It's enough.'

She was still smiling as she disagreed: 'I don't think so. We've more to do here, much more. For me there is, anyway . . . Don't you want to find the whipping tree? You said you did.'

Of course he wanted to. 'What I was saying . . .'

'There's so much more to be done. I've hardly begun my task.' She turned away.

'I wasn't suggesting that we stop searching. What I meant was, that if no further proof was found, then I'd be satisfied.'

'I wouldn't.' She succeeded in looking disappointedly at him even while turned away.

'Of course we must search on,' he said.

No more was found that day.

Grandy King Sam had come to Creek Town, and had enquired after them. He was at the house on the river. This was the surprising news that Peter conveyed to them when they met at his church later that day. They, in turn, amazed Peter.

'Antera found a cross. We think it was Theo's. Who else could it have belonged to?' James gave over the relic.

208

Peter inspected it anxiously in the dying sun, holding it cupped in his hands as though in charge of some precious fluid that was in danger of draining away. When he returned it to James it was with the utmost reluctance, saying, 'It certainly was his.'

'Theo's?'

'It must have been. *Must* have been. It is exactly the sort of cross our early missionaries wore. Theo must have died on that spot. Brutally slain for his devotion to God . . . A martyr. The spot will be consecrated – set apart as sacred.' Peter's eyes burned. 'May I hold it again?'

'Of course,' said James. 'We will give it into your keeping, if you like.'

'Would you?' Peter beseeched.

'Of course.'

Jenny felt it necessary to say, 'But we'd like to hang on to it until we leave.'

'Of course.' Peter sounded disappointed. 'Quite naturally you would want to do that. It's a magnificent find. It belongs to you, of course, but . . .'

To James fell the role of beneficiary. 'It belongs to the Church,' he said.

Peter kissed the relic which left a small blotch of earth on his lips. Then he gave it to Jenny. Before they departed he embraced them all. But his voice pursued them: 'You must remember the spot; the *exact* spot. We will all go there tomorrow.'

After a while the church bell began to toll softly, softly, like the dropping of tears.

Dusk swooped. They had misjudged its awful speed of approach. Antera led them in a hurried knot along the pathway that led to the house of Mammy Yellowbelly. The King was at home; a spearman stood guard at the front door, a tall and unmoving silhouette. Sound trickled from the house's glowing windows and from its open door – violins – yes, *yes*, unquestionably violins, and violas and a piano in pursuit of one of Beethoven's exquisite melodies – then a screech as the needle of the gramophone ran awry. There was a cessation of all noise, then a great walloping thud. A noise James, as the proprietor of a pub, recognised at once. Someone had hit someone else squarely in the mouth . . . Beethoven floated out again.

Apparently it was Grandy King Sam who had perpetrated the violence; an efficient hitter of men, quite clearly. His victim, a much slimmer, dark human being, lay twitching on the floorboards of the dining room, wiser than before. The lesson acquired was not to bump into His Majesty's wind-up gramophone, especially when it was playing.

The king beamed at the new arrivals, and with marvellously hospitable gestures bade them enter. He hugged Antera, then fetched him a clout across the side of his head that resulted in some concussive eye-rolling. Antera took no offence, or didn't seem to, for an animatedly cordial conversation ensued, of which, naturally, the visitors understood not a word. What was clear by the frequency of gestures given towards them, however, was that they – the visitors – were under discussion. On conclusion, King Sam came towards them with arms outstretched. His voice hit the bottom notes of solemnity: 'Our fash to hold big cel'bration now 'cos you come make de good thing happen here.'

Antera took over: 'King Sam make big honour to you. Hab come all good pusson to make party. Long lib de King!'

'A party?' Forgiveness for previous poor manners was not begrudged. 'Antera, tell His Majesty that we wouldn't miss it for the world. When is it to be, and where?'

It was to be that very night, at that very table.

Jenny watched the monarch and his nephew walk away in intimate but loud conversation. The gramophone minder raised his head from the floor at this juncture and with oscillating eyes checked to see if it was safe to raise the rest of himself. It was. He stood, cranked the instrument into life, then, as Beethoven's Ninth gathered speed, rapidly escaped from the room.

'Weird buggers,' James said of the departed royals.

This was true. An aura of bizarre unreality was at large. 'A party,' he mused, incredulously. 'Do you suppose our Sam's up to something?'

'Yes,' she said emphatically, then with even more emphasis, 'Yes, he is.' But what? She stood, evaluating the shock that King Sam had caused to her. As one who has been struck a wincing blow to the funnybone, that was how the fat monarch had pained her. She was fascinated and stunned. Here was an extremely dangerous man. King Sam craved to be feared, but being small minded, knew only how to instil small fear. He wanted to be grandly feared, but didn't have the formula quite right, yet. But he was working on it. Let it not be while they were there that he discovered his full potential.

James took her arm and they walked together to the staircase, then went up. As they were ascending she gave her opinion of Grandy King Sam: 'He wants to amaze us, and to impress us with his power.'

'We should look overawed? It's an interesting challenge.'

'It's necessary,' she said seriously. 'He's capable of much worse.'

'He's just an overgrown bully.'

'He's undergrown at this stage, but he's got a fierce potential. We must be very cautious.'

'I'll be cautious.'

'Handle him like a stick of nitro. Be outrageously polite . . .'

A change of direction at the top of the stairwell allowed him to curl his arm lightly into her waist to assist her in navigating the bend. She liked the feel of it. It was a nice forearm: thin-wristed but strong and not coarsely haired. She had no objection to such a forearm playing a role in her seduction. It was worthy of her. It was a major criterion that a lover should be worthy of her. What the forearm was also saying was, 'I need you badly.' The combination was almost impossible to resist. Recently, she had thought a lot about the possibility of this man coming to her bed; tingling thoughts of the tight white buttocks that clung to his shorts when he dug, and the thin line of fuzz climbing from his belt-line up his belly, that somehow promised beautiful sex . . . If he attempted to kiss her, she would let it happen. In fact she might let him go further, much further, it depended on whether their juices mingled harmoniously. She certainly wished he would try. In fact, she didn't leave it at that. She allowed the lamp glow artfully to bathe her features, while gazing into his face.

And he did it. He firmly prevented her from entering her door, saying almost apologetically, 'Jen, I just can't help myself.' Then went ahead and kissed her with his mouth and

and the tip of his tongue. He was shaking, and there was a hint of male pressure in the region of her hips.

There was a radical effect. This sensitive searching heat caused change. Her eyes groped with his, telling him more than words could of this; of her need; telling him that whereas she had thought herself to be the master of this situation, she was not. She was drowning in a cataract of emotion previously unknown. The sensational power of love came thudding into her heart, crushing her with pleasure. What she had thought she could do without emotion, superficially, as if for its therapeutic value, had become a greater force than she could reckon with. New to herself, consumed but triumphant, she said, 'I love you, James.'

'And I love *you*,' he breathed.

She softened her lips – softened and parted them at once so that for a moment they quite surrounded his, then tightened her arms and curved into him, saying into his chest, 'I really love you.' Engulfed in the pathos of this truth; joined strongly and perfectly, they moved into his room.

Smouldering twilight was tracing a purple vein in his window. It enhanced the tawdry furnishings. It lit the way for his hand as it closed over her breast, the breast that hung above her heart, as they lay. He came down on her with his lips slightly parted in a groan; an 'O'-shaped groan that was both lust and tenderness, and was used to bully her mouth until it gave in to gasps as vocal as his. And so they made love. Joined marvellously at mouth and hip; jubilant, but simultaneously aware of perilous change.

As she lay in the still aftermath a cricket chirped its way into her mind, and as though on the shrill of that sound, a stratum of noise developed into a voice. The sound of the Dream Stealer.

'Oh, that was something. That was more like it.'

'What do you want?' she demanded.

'More of the same, of course.'

'More of what?'

'Don't be stupid. Grasp the fact that I see everything, and do everything through you, with you, for you. What's nice for you is nice for me, so of course I set into motion all sorts of exciting games.'

'You had nothing to do with that; with what just happened.'

'Didn't I?'

'No, you didn't.'

'Well, that's gratefulness for you. I went to a lot of trouble with him.'

'With James?' She sat up, suddenly very angry. 'I'll *kill* you for that!'

There was a startled silence, re-infiltrated by the wire-thin chirp of the cricket. Her sharp words had closed the thing down, at least for the time being. She realised that she was sweating heavily, and it was the sweat of fear.

It was too early to talk of supremacy for any side. That the Dream Stealer had enlarged his territory in her mind was unquestionable. He had left his dirty footprints all over the place, and distinctly muddied those hazy and distant reaches of the realms of sex, where previously even she had scarcely trod. Well, she could cope with that. She had neither abandoned her principles nor assumed any new ones.

These were Jenny's thoughts as she showered prior to dressing for King Sam's dinner party. The shower comprised a bucket loaded with water, balanced on a beam. A rope was cunningly attached to it so that when tugged a slop of water descended. A room with a slippery cement floor had been set aside to house this device. Jenny soaped and tugged, soaped and tugged; there was an art to it. Care had been taken not to exhaust the bucket before all the soaping had been done . . . Her rash, she noticed, had subsided. In fact, she felt quite good.

The thing to be borne in mind was that nothing had slipped her guard – *nothing*. She had on purpose provided access to the Dream Stealer into the recesses of her mind, but on a very short and analytical leash. That the incubus had succeeded in modifying her behaviour somewhat was to be expected. She had deliberately laid herself open to its culture in order to better understand it. Everything was under control.

She pulled the remaining water down onto her neck. It sluished over her frugally then disappeared through a hole in the floor, gurgling. She towelled herself, enjoying the fresh smell of Pears on her skin, noticing frustratedly that as fast as she dried one part, sweat moistened another. Still, she felt relaxed; juiced-out, contented and lazy. And into this hedonistic languor crept a rude voice: 'Are you going to be all night, slut?'

'I want a word with you,' said Jenny sharply.

'I also have a few important things to say.'

She pressed her glasses onto her nose, dressed, then went to her room. Someone had lit her lamp. She sniffed. The musky scent of sex was still trapped in the air. She could hear the tap of James's footsteps in the adjacent room; the creaking of his floor. Now here was her real worry: James. The man was a sitting duck – a lamb to the slaughter. There was no doubt that he was being infiltrated by the will of the Dream Stealer . . . Mind you, was this necessarily a bad thing? She doubted if she could do much to deliver him from the sort of hallucinatory experience he'd suffered – if suffered was the right word, for she would have rejoiced in such an enlightening experience. But here was the dilemma: should she succeed in raising a psychic defence for James? For by this very action she might also block out a valuable source of material. And *that* would be most undesirable.

She dressed, moving slowly so as not to gush with sweat. It was while she was applying make-up that communication was re-established. The tone of it was reasonable, tending towards wheedling: 'You and I have known each other for a while, now. I'd say we understood each other's positions.'

'I wouldn't go as far as that,' she replied. 'There's a distinct lack of trust on my behalf.'

'We shouldn't let that divide us. We should try to get on. I didn't say we have to like each other; but simply make things a bit easier.'

With her powder puff poised, she said, 'What did you have in mind?'

'Well, for a start, to keep me locked up in here is an unnecessary restriction, an ingratitude.'

'I wouldn't say that.' Jenny blotted her lips, then peered towards the locked cabin trunk. 'I really would like to take you out, but look at the havoc you work even from in there. I'd have to think – '

'Come on!' he said, 'You like me. I'm just your average base instinct. No more. No less. Give me air!'

'Oh, no. Don't try to hoodwink me into believing that you're my own involuntary creation; my private insanity. You forget whom you're talking to. I may not as yet know exactly what you are – but I know exactly what you aren't. And you aren't that . . . Now I must warn you against harmful interference. James Tremayne is to be left alone. I wouldn't consider letting you out without first getting that undertaking.'

'Done. But why?'

'Because he has no defence. Because he is a good man. Because that is the way I want it. *No* more hallucinations.'

'Why should you care?'

'It's a matter of conscience. He is my responsibility.'

'What a load of crap. Give us the real reason, like how he blows fire up your hole. Lickety spit! He certainly thumped your arse into the floor.'

'You're treading on dangerous ground, little man.'

'I see a compromise . . . Is he allowed to dream?'

'What sort of dream?'

'The sort no man minds.'

'It's not that I want to restrict you. Not at all. But if I let you out anything could happen. Nasty tricks: you love 'em. I'm here to learn what you have to teach, but not to be strung along; and not at someone else's cost. Leave him out.'

'Trust me.'

She didn't have much choice. 'All right then, dreams.'

'I'm out?'

'Yes.'

There was a clickety-clack of small wooden feet, dancing. She said, 'You'll have to wait, though. I haven't got the key.'

The dancing halted as if in midstep. There was the beginning of rage. 'Where is the fucking key?'

'James has it on his chain.'

'I'll count to twenty. If I'm not out by then then the deal's off. Then I'll show you some tricks. Tricks, you *want* tricks . . . *One*.'

'Now who's being stupid?'

'*Two!*'

'I can't just barge into his room.'

'*Six.*'

'What about three, four and five?'

'*Ten.*'

'I'll burn you.'

'Then where would you be? *Seventeen!*'

215

James's familiar knock sounded on the door. She rushed to admit him. Resplendent in clean shirt and strictly knotted club tie he came into the room. Dangling from an extended finger was a ring of small keys: cabin trunk keys. He seemed to expect her to take them.

He stood slightly crouched over the cabin trunk, not saying a word but in an attitude of anticipation, keeping silence until she'd opened the lid. Then, with the brief comment, 'Sorry I took so long,' he lifted the biscuit tin that contained the wooden man and carried it to a table in the centre of the room.

'*Twenty!*' shouted the voice from within. '*Give me air.*'

She did not open the lid at once though. She had, she realised, lost the initiative somewhere down the line. She sensed she'd done a bad deal, but wasn't quite sure who to blame. 'Trust me' is not a good line on which to conclude a bargain with an incubus. She felt slightly demoralised and more than slightly vexed, and was keen not to suffer alone. James was included in her hassle: 'James, why did you bring the keys? When I opened my door, there you were with the keys. Why?'

'Why at that particular time?'

'Why at all?'

He looked at her curiously. 'Have you forgotten? You asked me to bring them.'

'When?'

'When? Well, I know this sounds daft, but I can't remember when. But I know that you did. I remember distinctly that you did.'

'Then you would remember my exact words.'

'Forgive me, Jen. But where is this leading to? Are exact words that important? You *asked* me to bring the keys. Here they are.'

She had asked no such thing. *She* hadn't, but something had. James Tremayne had a look of baffled honesty that was impossible to falsify. He pointed to the biscuit tin. 'Well, aren't you going to open it?'

'Do you think we should?'

'Why not?'

'You do it.'

Wads of paper cocooned the contents. An old copy of the *Guardian* sheathed the pistol. The Dream Stealer's wrapping was less bulky, more literate – some illustrated pages from Roy of the Rovers. Rory Tremayne's manuscript was unwrapped but cruciately tied with pink string.

James took out the pistol, held it up and admired it. 'Handsomely austere.' That was how its original owner had described it, and so it was. James thumbed back the boot-shaped hammer until it bedded with a substantial click: 'Cocked,' he informed.

'Does it still work?'

'It wouldn't be so hard to make it work. There's some spare caps in the kit of the .470 that might fit this thing perfectly, and a cartridge could be emptied to supply gun powder . . . That's all it would take. It's a beautiful piece of work.'

He took aim at the flickering oil lamp, pulled the trigger producing another robust click. Then he lowered the weapon.

'You shouldn't play with guns. Even I know that.'

'Do you know what I was thinking, Jen? Well, it was more a feeling than a thought. As I pulled the trigger I felt almost as though my hands could be Rory's. A glove of warm kinship, if you can conceive that. Weird! And before you ask me, the answer is no, there was no sudden in-rush of noise and colour and movement. All it amounted to was an amazing sense of closeness to Rory Tremayne. More than I've ever previously felt . . . I don't suppose it was worth mentioning, but for what it's worth, there it is.' Holding the pistol slackly he walked to the open window and stared into the denseness of the night. 'I can hear the river,' he said, 'just as Rory must have heard it from here. Did he mention anywhere in his manuscript that he hated the river, Jen? Can you recall him having written that?'

'He didn't have many good things to say about it.' She went to his side. Their fingers brushed, then intertwined.

'Jen,' he said tentatively, 'I came to tell you how I see things now: how I see things between you and me, that is . . .' He spoke quietly, but with the terse, bright-eyed passion of one reaching deep down into himself in an act of confession. He told her that whereas before he'd thought himself to be in love, he had now discovered the true meaning of the experience, and was shaken by it. 'As never before, Jen.'

'Me too,' she said simply.

'Surely there should be only pleasure in such a discovery? Pleasure and joy.'

'Yes?' She framed the word almost as a question, for clearly here was a man in love who felt in addition to those perfect emotions something else. She waited, watching his eyes with growing caution.

He said, 'I think it's this whole bloody set-up that's the root of the problem.'

'What problem?'

'Surely you can sense it, too, Jen: fear. A horribly large and almost animate dread. Dread that something is about to go wrong; or has already gone wrong, only we don't know it. Something that has everything to do with you and me. I walk around with this hollow space in my gut that should be occupied by good old-fashioned happiness.' He said with sudden vehemence, 'Listen.'

She felt compelled to obey.

There were many sounds. She heard the peep of a bat beneath the eaves, and a noise like water gurgling from a bottle, that was not water but came from small green frogs; and a seesawing croaking that was undoubtedly large frogs; and the chirrup of crickets; and a scream from the jungle as of utmost agony, as of a knife in the breast, which was nevertheless just the mating call of a small furry monkey. She heard a cough made by someone in a room below.

'Do you hear it?' he said.

'I can hear all sorts of things.'

'No. No,' he said restlessly. 'The river. Can't you hear the river?'

She listened. 'Yes, I can hear it.'

'It's the carrier of fear. I hate it, Jen. At The Saracen's Head on a still night you can hear the rushing water. It's a friend. But this river, this rotten thing, doesn't flow like water should. It slithers on its belly, loathing everything in its path. How can it be so powerful?'

'You're making it powerful,' she said. 'Stop listening to it if it makes you feel so uneasy.'

'But don't you feel it too? Don't you sense its animosity? Doesn't its very sound coil on you like a snake?'

'No,' she said.

He bent towards her as though drained, and tilted until his forehead touched hers. Then he pressed his lips into her hair.

The gramophone was being played again. The exquisite melancholy of Bach became part of the night. While in amongst the trees a flickering of fireflies transformed into a procession of humans, torch-bearing humans coming on through the forest. Grandy King Sam's guests were beginning to arrive.

'We must go down,' James said reluctantly. He kissed her again, then walked to her door.

'James,' she observed, 'you still have the pistol.'

'So I do.' He looked at the weapon briefly. 'I think I'll keep it.'

'But why?'

'I feel attached to it.'

'But James . . .' She could find no words to work into an objection.

His silhouette wavered in the gap of the opened door. 'Are you coming?' he said palely.

'In a minute. Go on down.'

The sound of him retreated to the stairs and she heard him descend. Amid tendrils of doubt she went over to the centre table.

'Well,' said the Dream Stealer. 'Now, that was very interesting. James has the pistol; you have me. What a perfect design for mischief.'

'You gave a solemn promise.'

'And so did you.'

'Yet you broke it. You influenced his actions again, with the keys, and if I'm not mistaken, the pistol.'

'So what if I did?'

'You're untrustworthy.'

'I'm impatient. There's things to be done.'

'I'm locking you up again.' She reached for the Dream Stealer with every intention of doing that, then paused. 'What things to be done?'

'Your experiment, what else.' The incubus said persuasively, 'Your reason for coming here. Look, you've got to be less concerned with James, and more with me. I'm the one who will give you what you want. We've got things to do, you and I. We need to be closer . . . We need to be friends. Agreed?'

'I've never denied that.'

'Good. Then dig me out of this trash and give me the place I deserve.'

'What of the pistol?'

'It's of no consequence to you and me.'

'I have one vital question. Why is it such a strain for you to be confined in the trunk? What does it matter whether you're in or out? The sides of the case didn't obstruct your view.'

'I see what you're driving at.'

'Then give me an honest answer.'

'I will. It is this: as you've discovered, my vision is not obscured by tin or leather or paper, or any other material. But *yours* is.'

'Then what difference . . . ?'

'Shut up for a moment and I'll tell you. My need is not to see, but to *be seen*. And why? I'll tell you why, in a word: vanity.'

'Vanity? Ridiculous. Why you're quite the ugliest thing I've ever laid eyes on.'

'That's it! My vile appearance. That is the recognition that strengthens. That is my entire pride. Now lift me up and put me somewhere where I can be seen, where I can propagate ugliness on a grand scale. I'm yours. Your most despicable guide and servant, your indulgence in sin. *That's* it!'

The table was laid for twenty, but twice that number of guests had arrived. There were no preliminaries; no aperitif or introductions. The objective seemed to be to get fed, and in the quickest possible time; to grab a chair, then guzzle down as much food and drink as could be fitted down the gullet before some other rapacious diner came along and shoved one off one's seat. This to a gossamer of flutes and violins. To be fair, the white folk weren't treated in this fashion, nor was Grandy King Sam. But the remainder of the diners were in a constant, energetic state of flux.

The serving girls were not naked. That is to say they were not as naked as described by Rory Tremayne. James was not disappointed by this variance from script. This was no hall of treasures.

He drank mimbo, for it was that or rum, and he detested rum. He judged the liquor not to be wildly intoxicating, which had been Rory's mistake too so, like Great-great-grandad, he became drunk rather early on in the evening, and similarly didn't give a damn. There was really not much else to do. He ate some yam chop, expecting to discover spectacular impurities in his food. He conversed disjointedly with King Sam, not forgetting to commend him on his taste in music and the admiral's cocked hat, tunic and gold braid epaulettes which he'd chosen to wear. The king approved of James's outfit, too. But the highlight of the festivity was the appearance, mid-table (he had not seen it arrive) of a full-grown monitor lizard, which seemed to derive enjoyment from massive destruction of crockery. It would swish its colossal tail to the left, and half a dozen assorted pieces of china would crash to the floor; then to the right, with a similar result. No one seemed the least bit put out at having their hot dish so arbitrarily removed. No one but Jenny that is. In the nick of time she elevated her plate. Jen hated waste.

What made James glance away from the table at that moment, he did not know. But that was his next action – and there she stood in the passageway with her dark eyes filling his mind – the mulatto girl. Her skin was as pale as cream, her hair was Spanish sepia and shone like the mane of a horse. Her breasts were ovate, full and taut and slightly asway as she walked. She was exquisite. *She* was exactly as her author had described her. He caught his breath.

Absorbed so fully in amazement that he was scarcely aware of his own actions, James shot from his chair which fell with a clatter. Then he stood there motionless, enchanted.

She too had come to a halt, similarly to regard him. She held one eyebrow raised, one lowered, as though paging through memories long past. Then she gave a little jolt of surprise, almost of fright and turned quickly away. A cape of fluid black hair jetted down her spine. A backwards glance, this with fully developed fright, then she fled.

James sat, fully expecting to be jolted in the ribs by Jemmy Honesty's stump of an arm; or assailed by Mammy Yellowbelly's shrieked laughter. But it was Jenny who drew near. Her hand touched his forearm. 'I saw her, too.' He felt her breath touch his neck as she said, 'James, I saw her too. She was beautiful.'

He shook his head to erase any doubts. 'It wasn't her – not *her*. Was it?'

'No. How could it have been? Are you all right?'

'I'm okay.'

'She was flesh and blood.'

'Is that so? Jen, I've gone through this before. I've seen her before, and in exactly that spot, looking exactly as she looked a moment ago, and doing the same things. The bits that I couldn't remember, well, I remember them all now. She's the missing factor. She's the one who was standing in the passage. Jen, I'm telling you, what I saw just now was a frame-by-frame rerun of the missing section. I'm *telling* you . . .'

'This missing section of the hallucination you had?'

'Yes. Now you've seen it too.' He scowled at her, sensing duplicity, almost snarling. 'What the hell is going on?'

'I don't know.'

'Let's get the hell out of here.'

'And go where?'

'Anywhere.' He propelled her towards the stairs. Grandy King Sam wagged a tooth-shagged chicken thigh admonishingly at them, but otherwise raised no objection to their retirement.

That night it stormed.

Jenny awoke, gathered her gown about her shoulders and closed her window. Fierce gusts beat the panes. A frenzied fork of lightning lit the forest, then was gone. So loud was the drumming of the rain that she seriously feared that at any moment the roof would cave in, or blow off, or something. Bed, therefore, was not a sensible option. She drew her mackintosh over her body and curled into the lap of an armchair. Lightning was almost constant; white flares of shocking brilliance, then utter darkness. Her world became a cask, expanding and contracting with each hammer blow of light.

From where she sat she could see her door, her cabin trunks and the centre table on which stood the solitary figure of the little wooden fetish. She watched it, watched it keenly in the war of colours. Black-white. Black-white; life and death. The contest was formidable.

'Are you there?' she asked. She called the words out loudly but they were absorbed by greater noise. There was no reply; no sign of awakening.

Tiredness crept upon her. The boom of thunder intruded; drove it back. So it was until the sky took its frightful antagonists elsewhere. Then her periods of rest lengthened. When the only sound was the drubbing of the rain, her head sagged and she fell into a deep sleep, where the other side of consciousness came to greet her.

Like a seagull blown from afar, she came to Wistman's Wood, where the stream runs gentle amongst the moist sweet breath of heather. To the room in the inn; the room with the great four-poster bed and oval cheval mirror, and the view of Dartmoor's desolate heart, she came.

She knew precisely what was expected of her. She should become naked, entirely so. She took off her dress and dropped it, then uncased her perfect breasts, and stepped from her panties. Then she went to stand before the mirror. She was pregnant, she observed, grotesquely pregnant. She glided her hands over the hump of her belly, massaging the inflated skin. The feeling was bad, very bad. She lay on the bed and drew up her legs and felt a savage movement in her abdomen, then another, then a pounding of cruel inner blows that was a prelude to birth.

From the deep, red cave of her womb wormed the Dream Stealer. It stood in the bloody gap of her thighs and surveyed from whence it had come, then climbed out altogether.

She said, 'Last time you came through the door. Why couldn't you have just come through the door?' She sat up.

'Last time,' said the Dream Stealer, 'I was not of you, now I am . . . Wash me.'

She did so with a measure of tenderness, but could not get rid of the feeling that she was more child than mother; more offspring than progenitress, and was bemused by this anomaly. She was, in any case, ready to obey her strange offshoot.

'Dance!'

Of course. She remembered now. She had been through this procedure before. Drums would beat, and she would dance. And so it was. But whereas before she had been easily able to adopt the rhythm, and spectacularly light on her feet, now she felt glued to the floor. Drums throbbed, chattered and boomed. The wooden man danced; spiralled and leapt, stumped and jerked, darting his long tongue at her, gyrating obscenely.

She tried to keep up. As the dance went on, so she became more expert at it, more thrilled and excited and lithe, more able to match her partner's intricate steps. Gradually she became master of the drums. They roared in her ears and twitched her limbs. She was music – she was lust. They came together, she and he, touched then parted; unable to stop, unwilling to try. This was pleasure every side up, a hog-wallowing in a dunghill of sound. As a wooden dildo he buried his head in her fur.

She saw herself then; rather she saw a reflected image that was both her and not her. She, the fornicator, the writhing masturbator on the floor, was many times more beautiful than the woman who'd begun the dance. Her limbs were long and goldenly formed; her hair was a tossed black mane. Her mouth was shaped into an oval of groaning want. She was mulatto.

'Is this me?' she asked.

'Yes,' said the oval mouth. 'This is truly you. Your dream soul. Your perfect new beginning – your most marvellous life's end.'

'Am I to die then?'

'Die? In a way. Yet to live as you've never lived before.'

'What now?'

'I think you know.'

James awoke with a start.

It was as though a full-scale river had been diverted in order to empty itself directly onto Mammy Yellowbelly's tin roof – as if God had reneged on his million-year-old promise to Noah. Solid water was coming from the sky to the ground, amid thunder and lightning that convulsed the old house – tore at it with jagged white teeth, threatening to strip it off the face of the earth.

He lit a candle, the flame of which bent like a flag. It showed the roof to be admitting water, not just in steady drips, but with the slanting, vicious spray more usually encountered by yachtsmen during Cowes Week. He saw no purpose in moving the bed to a drier spot as no such place was visible. However, the window was worth shutting. He pulled his jacket over his shoulder and walked over the puddled floor. The upper section of the sash window had been stuck, now it gave way and closed with a slam. There was a tinkling of glass, then a bolt of lightning ripped the night sky into segments – blinding and deafening him. He reeled backwards.

Lithe arms. Delicious shock.

It was she, the mulatto.

Her body was warm, and smelled of the musk of woman. His face was guided to the source of this heavenly aroma. It filled his mind. His tongue lathered the burrow of her sex.

'Am I dreaming?' he asked himself.

A hair caught in his teeth suggested that he was not.

Twenty-seven

Never was there present on Earth a better or more stainfree man of the cloth than Peter. He was Goodness. He was made of moral fibre. Children followed him. Birds nesting in the eaves of his office shat on his table top without fear of retribution. But on that morning, that sultry sodden morning that was the sequel to the storm, as they stood with bowed heads at the probable site of Theo *in articulo mortis*, there appeared to the visitors to be something terrible in this inflexible radiation of virtue.

James felt oppressed by the good man's preaching. He had, after all, just arisen from a night knee-deep in lust and debauchery, and was sizzling with guilt. He felt marked by guilt. Thoroughly stigmatised for all to see. And yet . . . And yet . . . *un*repentant. Worse than that; in his lack of contrition was the germ of hope that more of the same might come his way. He was exhausted, dog tired and dog tempered.

Powerfully good words were enriching the patch of soil that had surrendered Theo's cross. Though James wasn't really attending, a little of Peter's sermon was getting through:

'Infinite passion and pain . . . One amongst a thousand . . . He went out to meet armed men . . . Life perfected by death . . .'

The dream had been vividly real. But if Jenny was to be believed, dreaming *was* reality and merely a different point along the same road. A creative place of realisation. Had he touched the mulatto then, truly realised her as provided for by the ingenuity of his Maker?

'*Dominus illuminatio mea.*'

'Amen.'

'Amen.'

Ex umbris et imaginibus in veritatum. It was done. The ground consecrated, and Theo, the whipping priest, remade in more saintly form than before.

'It would be well,' said Peter, 'if you were to hurry your, er, investigation, your seeking out of the truth in the matter of Rory Tremayne. The rains have begun in earnest, as you couldn't have helped but notice. Last night was an aperitif as it were. It can go on like that for weeks on end when it has set in.' For no given reason he took one of Jenny's hands and held it before walking away.

'He was rather taciturn,' James said of the departed man. 'Not as friendly as usual. I got the distinct impression that he would prefer us to go. Surrender the cross, and leave him in peace.'

Jenny did not agree. 'I really don't think that that was his intention . . . There are, I've read, places along this coast where rainfall is measured not in inches, but in feet. He was merely trying to point out how little time we've got.'

With that in mind, they redoubled their efforts to claim back the past. The rain had softened the soil. Their spades cut it easily, but the sods that were lifted oozed and dripped, and the search deteriorated into a gripping and kneading of black slop that gave nothing but roots and stinks and multi-legged things that emerged at reckless speed. Jenny was bitten savagely on the thumb by some unseen adversary. A long green snake arched up near James's face, then shot past him in a blur.

Digging was suspended.

Peter brought a thermos of hot tea. He had an explanation for the antagonism of the lowly: 'It is the rain,' said he. 'Every insect and reptile in the jungle awaits the rain. It brings them out of the ground in excited plagues. They crawl, they fly, they swim. You'll see. They're inescapable . . . It seems sensible to me to call a halt. You have, after all, found the cross, praise God. That you were guided by Him to it is certain. But what else of Theo's could possibly have outlasted the years? Nothing I can think of.'

But there *was* something else. The whipping tree. Jenny's passion to discover it was undiminished. And when Peter had gone they tried to calculate which of the surrounding tamarinds it could be. There were three good prospects east of the site

227

where the cross had been dug up, all of equal size. They pondered on the problem. If Theo had died in close defence of his church, as was most likely, then it was also most likely that the nearest of the trio of tamarinds would be the one. But the intervening brush was too thick to be paced through in a straight line, and so some other method of calculation needed to be devised. Twine, perhaps, run out, tied to the trunks, then made taut. Yes, this might supply the answer.

Without warning, without a rumble of thunder or a puff of breeze, it began to pour with rain. Grey, green water roared down through the foliage, bending it under, spurting off it in liquid fingers that sunk themselves into the undergrowth. The water was warm and uncleansing – warm and sickly like fever on the skin.

Then as suddenly as it had started, it stopped. The trees unburdened themselves.in drips that plopped onto the broad-leafed shrub, and the miserably drenched humans. Frogs swelled their chests and called, and out of the sodden earth came insects, fungi, and an enigmatic, saturating steaming mist that clung to the ground so that to walk was to float through it, disconnected, phantom limbed.

Beneath the fevered brow of the sky they walked slowly back to the house of Mammy Yellowbelly – mosquito-stung and wilted.

James towelled off then threw himself onto his bed. He felt depressed and restless. But in that climate to be prone is to relinquish any hope of staying conscious, so he was soon fast asleep.

Jenny, damp, but no longer soaked, knocked softly on his door, and was glad in a way when there was no reply. James was no longer showing determination, so rest might be the answer. He was, after all, a vital player in the game, a component that she couldn't do without. She needed to question him in detail as to his awareness of his dream. This was central to her purpose. Yet she hadn't quite worked out how to broach the subject. It would have to be done in such a clinical way that no suspicion of involvement fell on her, or the experiment would be compromised; yet still done sympathetically. Done in such a way as to elevate him across any obstructive guilt complexes and neuroses. These factors were imperative. Her new liaison with the Dream Stealer and her marvellous dream identity would have to be kept strictly secret, for this persona, if revealed, would assume undue importance to him. His response to the memories of the dream would alter. The information would be useless.

She opened the door a fraction and peeped in. He was spread-eagled and lightly snoring, naked but for the towel he'd knotted to his waist.

She, on the other hand, had never felt more awake, more steadfast, invigorated and alert. She decided to go back to the digging, alone if she had to, to discover which tamarind of the three was the whipping tree. It was vital that every passage that Rory had written should be probed and all fiction eliminated.

She did not have to go alone. She found Antera Duke sitting on the bottom step of the exterior flight, whittling at a piece of soft wood. A fairly large pile of white chips lay at his feet. The monitor lizard (she assumed it to be her previous acquaintance) lay close by, one front paw raised as if lengthily considering locomotion. Without having to be asked to do so, Antera stood, sheathed his knife and walked with her, behind her to be more exact. One step beyond her shadow. The reptile watched, flicking its forked blue tongue.

It was midday. Overcast. Hot. A bad time to walk, for the human shadow was a weak thing now, small and easily destroyed. It could slip into a crack in the earth and vanish with catastrophic results for its loser, or be stolen by a doer of evil. Antera knew this. He took care not to step on her shadow. He kept his big feet well clear of it. He knew also that within the patches of mist at the forest edge lurked doers of evil, and so it was a doubly bad time to be abroad. Love, however, emboldens the most timorous of hearts. He was in love, and therefore prepared to take risks such as these. The theft of his love charm had been a grievous blow, but sheer devotion might compensate and bring rewards. So sheer devotion it was, one vigilant step to the rear.

As they walked along the track he noticed a child, a girl, playing in the grass alongside, and thought little of it. Children played, that's what they did. They built little thatch huts which they inhabited with little bamboo people, whom they spoke to and who spoke to them in turn, as this one seemed to be doing.

He hardly spared her a glance, and when he did, it was as an afterthought. They were several paces beyond the child when it occurred to Antera that he had seen this little'un before, and recently. Something jarred, a small movement in the mind of Antera that was really the whole cogged wheel of memory coming to an efficient halt at exactly the correct spot. Here was the thief of his most precious love spell.

The sound that little Tuesday made was loud. She snapped a dry twig, holding it up to do so.

Snap.

'*Stop!*' Antera's word, intended as a thunderclap, a mighty warning to prevent Jenny from facing the Fangaree charm, imploded in his throat, coming out instead as, 'Op'. 'Op', such as the sound made when a diving frog meets water. It was minuscule. It had no effect. Jenny turned with natural curiosity to see what had caused the sharp snap of breaking wood. Antera might still have neutralised the bewitchment had he reacted boldly in the remaining instant of safe time; had he caught Jenny by the shoulder and restrained her by force from looking at the spell-caster. But he did not. Something beyond him prevented this rough action, or perhaps he'd never been called upon to react with such decisiveness in his entire life. At any rate Jenny turned fully and gazed interestedly at the little grinning black girl who it seemed knew her by name, for she called out: '*Jen!*'

The bewitchment shot like an arrow to its target. Its immediate effect on Jenny was not great. She felt as though a moth was hovering at her forehead. She brushed it. It stayed. She brushed more vigorously. It stayed.

Antera Duke felt helplessly horrified, stunned. He knew what the girl had done, and that he was dealing with the agent of a witch. He did not know what to do about the situation. This tinder of frustration did not take long to ignite. Raw fury; bright bellowing fury was the natural consequence. He became quick. Two bounding paces brought him to the place where the witch-child had crouched, but was crouching no longer. There he saw the apparatus of the spell – the minute bamboo trestle – the decapitated gecko – the remnants of his love charm. He picked them up, then drew his blade and sprinted in the direction the spell-caster had taken.

It was a narrow game trail that favoured the small and nimble more than the large and furious. Nevertheless, Antera's long legs and disregard for safety gave him wonderful speed. The jungle closed, vines caught him, roots tripped him, violent weeds stung his legs. He kept on. He broke into a clearing and saw her. And she saw him with round frightened eyes. She looked at him for a moment, then darted away in a different direction. Her advantage diminished. His increased. Her new direction was towards the reed beds of the river where her smallness would not benefit her a bit. And to add to her problems he screamed in her direction: 'Witch!'

The word went out like a swarm of wasps into the jungle. It was an accusation that when flung into the air transformed the peaceful woodsman into a madman with spear in hand and murder in his eyes – and brought him out on the run. For every wrong and every disaster that has ever befallen him has been witch-wrought; that's common knowledge. And so stung into remembering every moment of anger in his life, he's ready instantly to annihilate, without question, whoever has been called that name.

Antera knew this as he shrieked again: 'Witch!' He saw her hesitate, as though struck and wounded. She looked back for an instant, then plunged on. He pounded over an old, broken dugout, now serving as a bridge across a creek. Yes, he recognised this place. A village of fishermen lay on this route. In fact, his quarry had almost come in a full circle. The house of Mammy Yellowbelly was not far. He filled his lungs and screamed his accusation and prayed that his breath would carry to the village.

And it did.

It sent the womenfolk scuttling in search of their children and brought out the menfolk with their long barbed fishing spears. They stood in a row and barred the path to the river. And Tuesday ran smack into their midst.

Antera arrived. With pointed finger he made the accusation formal. He only had to open his palm and display the debris of the Fangaree charm – the mutilated gecko – the bewitching pill – for them to agree: here was a witch. If not fully fledged, a learner. The penalty was the same. Antera took charge of proceedings. He had her nostrils stopped with mud and her arms tied to her sides. Then one of her ankles was bound, and she was hoisted off the ground, dangling head first like a sack. This alone would have sufficed to kill her in due course, but Antera was a man with a mission. He was keen to see blood; quite a lot in fact. He borrowed one of the fishermen's long, barbed spears and darted the prisoner with its tip, and sure enough there was blood. He dragged the sharp spear tip down the length of her spine – more blood. A steady trickle of red that began at her buttocks, ran into the fuzz of her scalp then dribbled to the ground. Nice, but not enough. Antera did a brief, unenergetic dance, and also sang, then made a few more superficial slashes – this time over the belly and into the unhaired genitalia, now poignantly exposed. The captive bundle wriggled, thus setting itself into motion.

The watchers murmured with advice as to what torture next to apply. One, a very old and wizened man, came forward stiffly, bent over and cocked his head until his face was parallel with Tuesday's. He stared questioningly into her bulging, terrified eyes as though searching the writings of her entire life, as though keen to find some compensatory circumstance, some deed of kindness, some hope of redemption. Then as slowly as he had arrived at this posture, he straightened. He looked at the gathered men and shook his sage head, saying, 'Take away her spirit. She is young but very bad.'

Truly there was no need to consider the matter further. The bundle at the end of the rope was given a shove, becoming by this action an unevenly swinging pendulum. The route to death was obvious. Antera had merely to stand firmly with his borrowed spear pointing horizontally towards the swinging target, and momentum would see to the rest. By her very substance the witch would contribute to her own execution. The aptness of this method did not go uncommented on.

On came the bundle. In went the spear. Of course it was not the same spear that he'd begun the job with. These were barbed devices, designed so that once embedded they stayed embedded. Thus, after a while, the many protruding spear shafts complicated Antera's task, to the extent that he decided to finish off the still faintly wriggling bundle by some other means.

Strangulation?

Yes, they all agreed that a dose of neck squeezing would be

highly appropriate. Upside-down strangulation? No. That would not be ideal. The way to strangle, the only way, was to be above the victim, so that downwards thumb pressure could be applied. They cut her down.

Antera's big hands were made for the job. His thumbs were twice as thick and spatulate as the average man's: perfect tools. He examined them. He applied them. They sunk effortlessly into the windpipe in Tuesday's frail neck and stayed there until not a jerk was left in her body. Then the fishermen prodded their blood-red spears right through her body and drew them out point first.

It was not until that moment that Tuesday's spirit departed its host. They did not see this happen. They hadn't the eyes to see it, but others had. As Little Cat went away a leopard roared. And everyone agreed that it was a strangely subdued sound, an anguished sound. Not the usual belligerent growl of that most feared of all beasts . . . And there it was again.

They took the small carcass to the river and tossed it in. Then everyone cleansed themselves, for they truly were spattered with gore. Then they returned to the village, hauled some drums out and danced. It was really too hot to dance, but they were wild with energy.

Yoruba watched on through her yellow leopard eyes, aching with grief; dying with grief.

Sassabonsum, on the other hand, was as pleased as it is possible for half a corpse to be. He howled and whooped and giggled and sniggered, perfectly faking the prowling hyena.

He kept it up until the moon came out.

AN EXPERIMENT
IN DEPTH

Twenty-eight

Jenny loved James. A state of affairs that in other circumstances she would have delighted in. He was a wonderful guy: resourceful, intelligent, sensitive, and very, very sexy. And so, as far as his destiny concerned her, she cared. And that was the trouble. Love sensitises the heart and strangulates the brain. Whereas care increases all difficulties. She was losing her capacity for objective thought; losing credibility. She needed to rid herself of these unhelpful emotions. Unfortunately, once the heart is sensitised, that's it. Like metal, once magnetised, it works. It's obligated to attract opposites.

The very nature of her experiment was at the root of the difficulty. It had caused her to fudge the borders between certain polarities. She had, as it were, confused the purity of direction of science, the essential north and south of subject and object. She cared. She jealously cared for James. How could one be so attracted and not care? How could one do what she had done and not care? She was as attracted sexually to this man as she was clinically. This was unscientific. A mess.

She'd frequently tried to clean up her act, and failed. The situation was weighted against her. The facility provided by the wooden, dream merchant, to rearrange her identity, then migrate into the deep unconsciousness of her lover, had drawbacks. For the vehicle of transport was the body of the mulatto girl; that perpetually crotch-wetted, most exquisitely proportioned creature. There was no optional form, there was no optional mood. Jenny, on arrival, was inevitably over-sexed, and under-moraled.

She sincerely wished it could be otherwise, and in the same mental breath was glad that her wishes had no bearing on the matter. But something had to be done, and quickly, too, for her inability to deal with this crisis was contaminating the all important dream state experiment. And there was something else that it was doing. It was giving her headaches – serious pains in the head.

At least she assumed that it was this unsettling contest of values that was causing what she (with her limited medical knowledge) termed 'pulsations'. She could recall the exact moment of their first arrival. It was when Antera had unaccountably gone off his head while accompanying her to the digging. She hadn't a clue as to what had possessed him and sent him screaming off in pursuit of the terrified little girl. He had refused to explain it. But that instant of aberration had coincided with the arrival of her pulsations. A flickering of vision as if the interior of her eyeballs was occupied by moths; emperor moths; frustrated emperor moths. Sequential to the moths came pain; head-crushing pain, which, thank God, climaxed quite quickly. Then there was a remission of all symptoms and a revival of clear-headedness that allowed her to function; to function in such a way that another attack was an inevitability. Something had to be done. Some form of divorce had to be arranged between the experimenter and the experimentee; between scientist and subject. Something not too emotionally traumatic. But what?

The solution, strangely enough, came amidst a severe attack of the pulsations. A pain-induced look at her inner self: a stab of utmost clarity.

How obvious. How obvious are the errors of self-deception once detected, and how monumentally gross. She had been withholding from her report a part of it that was intrinsic to its substance, and essential to its constitution: *her participation in the events*. Oh, Jenny the clinician was there all right. She was there. It was the other Jenny who was absent. It was Jenny the honey-skinned mulatto wanton who'd been omitted from the text. How very unintelligent of her to have let this occur. How very obtuse; how cringing. If Jenny had no option but to be the mulatto whore, then it was *that* version of her that was worthy of discussion. She would no longer conceal the events that were incompatible with her conscious attitude. Out with concealment!

The pain had dwindled. Her mind shone like a dawn after rain. She read then, at random, from a page of her report.

Dreamer 'A' dreamed against last night. The sequence was repeated. He made love to the mulatto woman. This morning he seemed more coy than usual. Vigorous questioning was needed in order to pry information from him. I could detect no lies. 'A' never exaggerates intentionally, but has a tendency towards factual carelessness, which I persistently contest. What follows is a typical example of dialogue.

'So you say she came again? Now I want you to think back. I want you, in your own words, to relate the entire event. Do not omit any detail, however insignificant it may seem.'

He looked uncomfortable. He does at this stage of an interview.

A: 'Well, Jen . . . well . . . '

'Well, what?'

A: 'Why are you writing this down?'

'I've told you a dozen times. It's my work.'

A: 'Look – I made love to her, or she to me. I'm not sure.'

'There is no need to be embarrassed about this. We're talking about the behaviour of your deep subconscious; a different universe to that in which you stand at this moment; a different language, one of symbols. Take her as a symbol. How did you see her?'

A: 'She was woman.'

'Warm?'

A: 'Yes. Very.'

'Enticing?'

A: 'I'd say so.'

'Sensual?'

A: 'That, too.'

'What did you do?'

A: 'I told you. We made love.'

'How did you make love?'

A: 'You mean "how", as in "*how*"?'

'Precisely, as in "*how*".'

A: 'We did it . . . as you might say . . . sort of . . . I don't quite know what you're getting at.'

'Did you mount her?'

A: 'Good gracious!'

'Well, someone must have mounted someone.'

A: 'Yes. That is, we mounted each other in turns. A lot of mounting went on.'

'Who mounted who first?'

A: 'Is that important?'

'Very. It shows motivation.'

A: 'She did. I awoke, or seemed to awake, slipping from one dream to another; from an obvious dream to what felt like total consciousness, but was not. And there she was.'

'The mulatto?'

A: 'Yes.'

'Naked?'

A: 'Absolutely starkers.'

'Mounted on you?'

A: 'Well, yes, sort of mounted . . . I believe that in numerals the comparative figures are 69.'

'What was she doing?'

A: 'Sort of sucking . . . I really don't think . . . '

'Sucking what?'

A: 'My sexual organ. For goodness sake . . . '

'Was it erect?'

A: 'Sort of.'

'I take that as "yes".'

A: 'You said I should use my own words – I'd prefer to say that I was sexually aroused.'

'Were you sexually aroused at once, or did it take time?'

A: 'I don't see the relevance.'

'There is relevance.'

A: 'Perhaps there is. Yes. I can see what you're driving at . . . Yes. I could feel her lips sliding on me. In fact it was that sensation that awoke me. You can understand that no man could sleep through that . . . And *that's* the relevance, isn't it? That one dream can be obliterated by another in that way; that one dream could be invaded by sensations from another . . . That's weird. That's *more* than weird, I'm telling you. And there's something else that's just as bizarre, Jenny. She enjoyed it. Write that down. She *enjoyed* it. You tell me when last you were in a dream that someone else was enjoying as much as you. She participated in my dream. She loved it. No, I'm telling you. She was the instigator of some crazy stuff . . . *Whew!* She was there. I can't describe it better than to tell you that she was *there*, enjoying it. Lapping it up!'

How close poor James had come to stumbling on the truth he would never know. Jenny pinched the edge of the page in preparation to tearing it, then changed her mind and put it back in her file, there to serve as an example of how not to conduct this investigative experiment, a lesson in inadvisable concealment and deception.

The removal of a roadblock. Now she could see the way

ahead, and it was beautiful. This was no mere analogy. It was truly beautiful. She would tell James everything. They would walk onwards together. Dreamer 'A' and Dreamer 'O'. Alpha and Omega. The beginning and the end. Wonderful.

Now she began to write and her fingers skipped on the keyboard, and the heart was light. A cleansing. A catharsis. Full disclosure, and nothing less. He would read her notes – past and present. She would allow him to do that. No, she would *insist* that he did that. And he would partner her in this amazing intellectual adventure.

Jenny typed for hours; typed at the speed of love. One page was hardly pulled before the next was done. Nor did she spare herself in her reporting. She laid herself bare. Oh yes, she'd participated all right. She'd mounted. She'd guzzled. She'd ridden him every way up, in every numerical configuration conceivable and some that weren't. She set it down. Let the truth be told; let it be out. She had reached orgasm – marvellous orgasm – then thundered on towards the next, and the next, and written about it. Scientific eyebrows would rise; other even more expressive sections of anatomy, might rise. So what! Let them gather what they were equipped to gather. She, the mulatto, had done these things, and would do them again.

Science as Art!

Sensualistic Realities in Cross-Dreaming. That was the title that her publication would bear. She liked it. As a door opener it held just the right message: a tactile exploration of the deep subconscious. Jung would have approved. T. S. Eliot would have been in ecstasy. The doyens of the Society, on the other hand, might be less receptive. It was not meant for them, though. It was meant for the courageous band of psychic investigators who had yet to come. Future torch carriers of the psychic light. Those who would intelligently appreciate her work and build on it. Those yet to come.

She was ahead of her time. Well, perhaps that statement should be enlarged on . . . She was ahead of her time, yet simultaneously somewhat behind. Happily behind, indulging in forgotten science, tapping into veins of golden knowledge that the Moderns hadn't found because they hadn't looked. *For there is nothing new except what has been forgotten.* She was a pioneer in that sense, a new miner in an old mine. As for those who didn't approve of such unorthodoxy and candour, they didn't matter. She had thought that they mattered, and now saw her error. Her priority was to provide a platform, however small, upon which future researchers could stand – to break the rocks for the road builders still to come. And *that* was what she was trying to do.

She typed until it became too dark to see the print on the page, then for no accountable reason leaned forward and began to quake with tears. It could have had to do with the thought of her progeny's survival and acceptance into future academic compounds; or maybe it was just the usual emotional havoc wrought by her periods.

The moth was at her forehead again, tapping, tapping and fluttering, as though caught on a pane of glass, the glass of her vision. A vast disappointment. She'd hoped to have rid herself of this pain-bearing lepidopteran; to have killed it with honesty. But it lived. It had come. It would find a way in as it always did.

Darkness grew bolder. It ran its fluid fingers over her body. She'd always loved the dark. It was sensible to love it; to love the inevitable.

She waited for the pain.

Antera Duke, likewise, was entombed in morbid thought. He, too, was down with cranial pains. In fact, if he and Jenny had taken the trouble to compare symptoms, they would have found some remarkable similarities. But whereas Jenny had made an erroneous assessment as to the cause of her malady, he had not.

He'd been witched, and he knew it. After the murder of the witchlet, he had gone back to the footpath where he and Jenny had earlier walked. There he had searched around until he had found the remaining debris of the Fangaree charm; slivers of bamboo and bits of straw and gecko blood. He'd taken it all back to his room and entirely reassembled it. Then, bit by bit, he'd minutely examined it. He'd broken into the crust of the earthen pill, tweezered it into tiny segments and inspected these with growing terror. He merely found what he'd expected to find, but this in no way diminished the horror of discovery. The Fangaree was concocted, in part, of components that had been taken from his original love charm. Not all of his beautiful charm had been used, just the body slough, some of which was Jenny's – and some of which was *his*.

Jenny had borne the brunt of the evil, as no doubt intended by its manufacturer. Her name had been called. But he too had been tied into that charm, and he too had been hit by it. A glancing blow, but a blow nevertheless. He'd felt its effect immediately. It would, he knew, eventually put him in his grave: kill him, and not in a nice way. Something to do with his head. That was how he would die. The tiny gecko in the trap had had its head squashed, and so that was the part of his body that would eventually suffer. Of course, this counted for Jenny as well. It counted for her to a far greater degree.

Antera was unaccustomed to the feeling called 'guilt'. It was not part of his sense of identity, not one of his accepted guiding stresses. He was a man of consideration and sympathy – not a crook, not a prejudiced man. What was this nameless thing then, this sombre, heavy drowning of the heart? It was a puzzlement to him as to why he had been singled out to be a player in such a tragedy. He was tortured by the ageless and seldom-answered question: 'Why me?' Also: 'Why her?'

He felt dreadful. It was a hard and heavy load this guilt without a name; this depressing knowledge of the mutilation of beauty. A love charm had become a hate charm, and there was no getting away from it: what he'd done in the first place had to do with what had happened in the second. Sad, sad Antera sobbed tearlessly into his spadelike hands and thought of how things could have been – should have been. Time deepened the melancholy wound. Atonement was impossible. Devotion was all that was left to give. So that was what he gave, fully and silently. Not a word did he say. He'd meant to speak to her one day, to tell her things, but now that day was out of reach. He'd never spoken to her and he never would. He could not tell her how he felt, so he showed her instead.

Devotion became an obsession. He would not have called it an obsession, he would have called it 'a wedding of spirits'. His to hers; 'til death do us part . . . Oh yes, death came into it in a big way. Though she was doomed, and he too, the blossom of his courage was still fully formed, bright and beautiful and desirous of a bright and beautiful ending. That noble, terminal deed, the hero's death.

At night, when the house was sodden with sleep, he would awake and crawl slowly up the stairs, slowly and quietly, like a dog. And like a dog he'd lay himself down at the threshold of her bedroom door, curled up there, with one ear pressed to the floor boards, listening, even as he slept. Listening for an enemy. Longing for an enemy.

A legend in the making.

Twenty-nine

The whipping tree was as Jenny had suspected, the middle one of the trio of tamarinds. This recognition was brought about, not by physical but by mental determination – a technique of vision acquirement as practised by none other than Carl Jung, who'd called it 'Active Imagination'. Jenny, who was adept at it, called it 'Total Recall', for that was certainly what it was: a lifting of the psychic curtain that separates present from past. It's there, then it's gone. Brief but total recall. In the event it nearly killed her.

A cyclone had struck.

As Antera would have put it: Father Sky was not pleased with Mother Earth. A lashing was being administered to the 'wife', who was writhing. Mighty trees were bending and howling, waving their thick trunks as though made of wheat not of wood, while cables of vines groaned and thrummed and strained against the wind, and sometimes snapped with the sound of a rifle shot. And the rain was not rain, but something berzerkly hurled to earth in order to crush and rip and flatten every herb, leaf and blossom.

It was ignorance of its power and danger that set Jenny off into the gale. She wanted to be unhindered by the presence of any other human, and thought this was the time. It should have been, but it wasn't. Antera saw her go, and could hardly believe his eyes. She had on a raincoat and a rainproof hat; he, just a loin cloth. She waddled down the path, now part river, that led to Peter's church, somewhat scared of the force she was facing, and quite unaware that she was not alone.

At the island of Peter's church she paused. Noah would have liked what he saw here; he would have been out collecting animals, marching them two-by-two into this fragile wooden

245

shell. A lamp was burning behind the panes of the rectory window. The glass was opaque with rain, but even so she was careful not to be seen. He would herd her into his ark if he saw her in this rain. He would think her mad.

She was beginning to wonder herself as to whether this course of action was quite sane. Her body was being pounded: her ears were full of howling; her specs would not stay true on her nose and she could hardly see. She was a stubborn woman, however, and she went stubbornly on.

The digging and Theo's grave had become a mire. She skirted the black water and looked about for the trio of tamarinds. The centre tree beckoned, and she came to it. It was wailing in the storm, bending and convulsing. She stood close to it for a while, running her fingertips over the rough, wet braille of its bark, asking, 'Is this the place where it began? Are you the whipping tree?'

The question, of course, was not as concisely framed as that. It was put out wordlessly, in images; intensely generated images, hurtling outwards. Enormous volumes of energy were applied. All the energy that would normally flow into outer life, she committed to this task; compressed and concentrated from every fibre of her being into a single potent outrush, like blood from an arterial wound, the artery of her spirit. There were risks. The expenditure could be too high. The citadel of consciousness could be so weakened that possession by psychic enemies was a danger. Still, she tried for all she was worth, and failed.

There was no response: not a whisper. She stood back for a moment, trembling from the exertion, and unbuttoned her raincoat, shrugging it off her shoulders. It fell like a dead person. Then she unpeeled her blouse and brassiere. Her skirt joined the pile of wilted fabric. She rid herself of every possible impediment, then went to the second tamarind, close to it. She hugged into it like a lover and willed herself into its ancient sap, demanding all secrets. Through the conglomerate roar of thunder and wind and lash of rain on her skull came the sound of a distant bell – a summoning bell in the depths of her mind.

The tamarind took her coarsely.

This was it.

This was *it*.

Her mind glowed, then went out like a stubbed cigarette. This was helplessness, and fear. A great force was above her, but she could not sense whether it was good or evil. She was small, in huge hands; huge insensible hands. Extinguished. Dead. Not quite. Almost dead. The barest of glimmerings remained. And she was answered.

The tree was thinner; thinner by a hundred years. She was trussed up, stretched to the limit, strung by her wrists to a branch of the tamarind, and in agony. A celebration of pain was playing over her back ribs. An inrush of unbelievable pain. No single living person, no dead person, not even the Devil himself could be so devoted to agony, as to cause this, surely. It had to be God. It had to be God who was wielding the searing whip as if on Satan's back. It was fire, it was ice; burning and melting, scorching, flooding, rupturing through layers of sanity. She writhed. The whole jungle writhed. She screamed. She wrenched back her head and snarled, cried, moaned and whimpered. On went the punishment of God – on and on. It was more than her body could take. Death's mercy was close, and closing, and escape was critical. She groped towards the speck of consciousness she still owned: her ember of life. It was almost obliterated. It was at its limit; anaesthetised in time. She willed herself towards it; willed herself to get there with the tenacity of the desperate. She grasped the spark, and held on. And was rewarded with insight: a tamarind tree and her naked self; jungle and pouring rain . . . *And* Theo.

Yes, Theo, too, had traversed the mortal divide. He'd ridden over it on the power of pain. But only just. There he stood for an instant: God's passionate agent and avenger. His eyes and his whip-hand were the last parts to vanish.

'I will remember you,' said the fading eyes.

She slid to the ground and lay there scarcely breathing. Her thighs and belly were marked by the bark of the tamarind; bits of foliage were stuck to her skin. Her back burned with memorised pain. 'Theo,' she shouted. 'You bastard. I'll remember you too.'

Then for a while memory departed, or at least hid itself so effectively that she had no recollection of having walked through the gale back to her room. Yet that is what she must have done during that period of vanished time, because that is

247

where she discovered herself to be, warmly wrapped and dry. And yet doubted that she'd possessed the strength at the time of the whipping to have taken a single step.

She got up and went to her window, and gazed into a sky that was fragilely poised between clarity and cloud. She saw Antera sitting on a tree stump, looking down dismally at his huge, ugly feet, and felt ashamed of her disgust for him; then disgusted with her shame. Why should she feel anything? There was nothing she could do to alter his state.

And then, as people sometimes do when being secretly watched, he looked towards the source of curiosity, and their eyes met. She waved, and he grinned and emerged from his gloom. It was as though he'd been suddenly freed from mortal care. Antera's joy spoke, and all doubt was instantaneously dispelled as to who had borne her home.

'Heavens, Jenny! Where've you been?'

She turned towards this chiding enquiry. James Tremayne strode fully into her room, unladening his anxieties: 'You didn't go out in the storm, did you? Are you crazy?'

She lied mildly: 'It wasn't so bad when I went out. It got worse.'

'It's been bad all day.'

She shrugged.

'Don't do that sort of thing,' he pleaded.

'I went to the tamarind trees . . . I hardly noticed the storm. I found the whipping tree . . .'

'My God.'

'Rory didn't lie about the whipping preacher. I saw him. I saw Theo, and I felt his whip. From heaven or from hell, wherever he came from, he crossed the divide of more than a century, and came to his tree . . .'

'There's no more left to prove.'

'Isn't there?'

They lapsed into silence, each within the realm of amazing thoughts.

Jenny could still feel the pain put there by Theo. Her wrists ached. Her back felt numbly raw. She had done what she had set out to do; what she had promised herself she would do in this sodden green immensity. She'd wrung out its reeking secrets. Rory Tremayne's integrity was beyond doubt. She had thoroughly examined both story and storyteller, and had discovered nothing but bruising truth. An ordinary man thrown down by extraordinary forces; forces so powerful that even their residue was lethal. So many of Rory's claims were authentic that it was inconceivable that he'd fabricated a single line.

How stunning an acquittal . . . and how contritely unsatisfying. She had achieved incredible success. She had achieved enough to guarantee acclaim. Her voice would be heard and her opinions quoted, and this was what she'd craved, strived and been hurt for. And now it seemed so pallidly irrelevant. This was no enigma. She knew why. She knew the exact reason why she was feeling so drastically unfulfilled. It was because she had but scratched the surface. The true riches lay deeper, and there was not enough time left to go deeper.

As one providing comfort, James said, 'The *Darling* will be back in a day or two.'

There it was. The *Darling* was due back. She wished the river boat ill. She threw obstructions in its path.

'Tell me about your encounter with Theo.'

'He whipped me.'

'Jesus.'

'I had to find out. It was an obligation: my absolute anchor of belief in Rory. Now I reject nothing that he wrote.'

He kissed her forehead with placid tenderness, and then her hand. 'It's all right now,' he said, making her sit on the edge of the bed. 'It's all over now.'

'It is?' she said without enthusiasm. If it were, then she had lost. If she went away now, then she would have failed. Mammy Yellowbelly's house of secrets was down on its knees, and ready to give her anything she wanted. And in delivering its mysteries the jungle had promised more, so much more. If only she could stay. It would empower her, enrich her with pagan knowledge: the doctrines of the gods; the very secrets of life. Bodiless intelligences were poised to offer these marvels. 'Stay,' they'd breathed into her ear. 'Be with us and we will be with you.'

'You don't look well,' said James Tremayne. 'The sooner we clear out the better.'

'I've had bloody awful headaches.'

249

'I can see it.' He plumped her pillow. 'Lie down. You've done fantastically, but thank God it's all over . . . This Creek Town is the arsehole of the world. When I was down at the river looking for you, I saw a human corpse float by – just float by – just like that. No one gave it a second glance. Just imagine if I'd been strolling on the Thames Embankment, and – '

'But you weren't. And Creek Town is not London. It's a thousand miles from London.'

'It's still part of our world, is it not?'

'The point is that such comparisons are meaningless. I couldn't have achieved what I have while strolling along the Thames Embankment. I agree, it's ugly. It stinks . . .'

'It gives you headaches.'

'And that. But in mitigation, it's potently charged with magic. You've experienced it too. You were awed by it . . . Now the difference between you and me, is that you see the supernatural as a natural enemy, and I don't. You shouldn't be so implacably opposed to something you don't understand. You should rather attempt to improve your understanding. You could, you know. You have the aptitude. I could help you. I would love to help you.'

'No thanks. No magic.'

'Then don't call it that. Don't call it magic. It's a misnomer, anyway. Call it esoteric power. Call it mystic knowledge, or the ability to change things according to your will.'

'Call it what you like, Jen. I don't want anything to do with it. I want that to be absolutely clear.'

'But, James, my darling. You already are *so* deeply involved. Yes, you are. You enlisted me to help you search for the truth, and I've enlisted you for the same purpose . . . I'm in your dreams, James. I'm with you every night in an altered state. I synchronise my dreams with yours. I am your mulatto lover, the provider of your wants.'

'I don't believe you,' he said flatly.

'What don't you believe? That I'm the mulatto? Or that I know what goes on in your night mind?'

'Jenny, cut it out!'

'Do you believe I love you, James? Because I do. I really do. If I didn't, I couldn't have done what I've done. I love you, and that's the truth. I am your dream lover, and that's also the truth.

What's more, *you* made me into this passionate whore: your subconscious did. It's only what you wanted, James: a ghost of your own making. So don't tell me you haven't the aptitude. Hell, you've got aptitude enough for both of us. I've been there with you, and it was beautiful.'

'Tell me one instance,' he said sharply. 'Prove it.'

'I can. I intended to. I've written it down. It's all documented . . . You've no idea of the conflict that I've gone through to arrive at this point: the point where I could admit that I love you and care for you. Please don't be angry. Anger would just spoil everything.'

'Jesus, Jenny . . . I'm not angry. Okay?'

She held him; found a place for her cheek in the muscle of his neck, and kissed words onto his skin: 'I love you.'

'I love you, too. But this is so strange. The mulatto? Where will it end?'

'Does it matter? If it was eternal would it matter? If this was death I'd open my arms to it. Don't question it; take it.'

'It's the crazy-seed, Jen. Twice as crazy as before . . . And yet it *is* beautiful.'

'Lovers in flesh and spirit,' she whispered. 'United night and day. A magnificent obsession. And it's ours.' She kissed him on the mouth. She watched him intently, her eyes inches from his. 'Do you want it or not?' she questioned, drawing away.

'Prove to me that you and the mulatto are one. I need that proof.'

'Of course you do.' She gestured empathetically with wrist and fingers towards a sheaf of papers. 'There it is.'

He gathered the typed pages, glancing at them tentatively. 'Are you sure this is what you want?'

'God, I want it so much. You and I, James, uniquely together, awake and asleep. I'll teach you the Names of Power. We'll be invincible. We'll capture thunder. Read it, my love.'

'I want no more than the truth.'

'And you'll have it. You'll have what no religion has been able to reveal. The Truth.'

Thirty

James's entry into Jenny Oxenham's field of expertise was not, as promised, a glide into the Land of All Possibilities, but rather a series of hard shocks. A bumpy, uncompromising ride that led to several truths, none of which he liked.

Back in his room he had availed himself of his only armchair, a chronically mistreated and deformed article that he suspected of harbouring many bugs; fewer bugs, however, than were camped in his bed. He was pimpled with the evidence of massed bedbug attack. He gave himself the pleasure of a cigarette, then read *Sensualistic Realities in Cross-Dreaming*, and the introductory paragraph: 'Faced as we are with the pervasive religio-cultural taboos of Christian society, it is unsurprising that the field of the erotic dream has been so inadequately researched. However . . .'

A good opener. Assertive. Appealingly rebellious. He flipped a few pages, dipping randomly into the text, mainly to discover where and how he fitted into the picture: 'Masturbation . . . Clitoral orgasm . . .' He recoiled as though caught with his eye to the bathroom keyhole, then doubled back to the beginning: '*However*, the erotic dream is arguably the most potent of all parapsychological vehicles available to the researcher of ESP. Its frequency of occurrence and stimulative potential (ejaculation, female orgasm) on the central nervous system are demonstrable. An advantage that no other dream form can provide.'

True – when you thought of it like that. A deeply buried comment caught his eye: 'A category of telepathic dream coherence between two (or more) participants is, therefore, feasible. Dreamer "A" (masculine) . . .'

It was at that point that disillusionment began. Dreamer 'A'!

He felt as though he had been methodically insulted. He skipped a few paragraphs, then read on: 'That thought trans-ference (ESP) and dream transference are one and the same thing, and require no alteration in techinque, is a fact that the African witch doctor has been aware of since the dawn of time. The psychodynamic elements that they have used for centuries in clairvoyant dream manipulation we know hardly anything about. In this respect they are the master; we are the primitives. They have the science, the catalysts, the dream stealers . . .'

Was this then love and devotion? Dreamer 'A' and dreamer 'O', provoked by psychodynamic elements – in other words, chivvied by the Dream Stealer into pornographic exercise. A breathless coming together of A and O, subsequently combined in erudite dissertation. How very sad.

He continued his study of this scholarly smut. A basic knowledge of Latin was required thereafter: *Mox se totum retraxit et aliquantum pulveris rubri in summo posuit . . . Subito semen album effunditur, quasi argentum vivum . . .* My God. Had they really done that? And: *Quem cum rursus urgebat cannus mulieris adeo titillabatur ut vix pati posset . . .Penis erat valde durus . . .*

It didn't get much more affectionate than that. He read about her symbolic uteral metamorphosis; the psychological death of her body; and its rebirth as the mulatto. There was a reference to dreamer 'A's' powers of penile tumescence which in dream mode were markedly more formidable than in conscious mode. He'd noticed that wonderful occurrence, too.

The rest was very dry, very tutorial. He couldn't rid himself of the feeling that love, to Jenny, was comprehended in a strange, unloving way, and that her affection was more a state of breathless fraternity than warmth. What on earth had come over her? What was going on? Was this incubus, this wooden manufacturer of dreams, so potent that it was remaking her conscious mind? There was no doubt in his mind that he'd been manipulated and that it would happen again if he let it.

He was also still absolutely convinced that he loved Jenny and that he would be able to change her in due course. In the meantime, that grand and elusive secret of life would have to remain just that. They had done what they had set out to do, and he didn't give a damn about the realities of cross-dreaming. He was going home. And so was she. This was reality.

A shaft of sunlight, the first in days, struck goldenly into his room. Sunlight! Like a miner from a coal pit he blinked at it, then wrenched himself from the chair. The whole sky was one big, blue, gaping smile.

James took time off. He walked in no particular direction, and with no particular destination in mind, and presently found himself in the village at the bend in the river. He was coming to know this place now; its ugly, clay fetishes and tatty huts. Chickens scratched the earth in his path; one white rooster was hanging upside down from a doorway, as it had been since yesterday. Amazingly, it was still giving twitches of life. The sun did not reach here. It hadn't visited for a hundred years. It hadn't ever shone on this part of Creek Town. It never would.

A drum was throbbing from far off.

The eyes of the people – the lesser people – felt him out. Retractable eyes. A colony of snails. They touched him then withdrew; fear inbred into them. What had Antera said about these slum people? That they were half human, half slave. Leftovers of a low-down race . . . Strangeways would have had them clapped in irons and off to Jamaica in no time, poor buggers.

The water of the lake had risen. Small, toothless waves were joking with the shore, ceaselessly chuckling in the reed beds. The jetty, where it had sagged, was swamped and as he walked along it, it gave precarious signals to his feet. Where it was dry, it was by the barest of margins, and the heads of wavelets were bobbing noisily through the gaps in the planks. A rare, stenchless breeze drew into his lungs. Then he saw a smudge of black, an upriver sky stain that developed, as he watched it, into smoke billowing from the funnel of the river ferry, the *Darling*.

Yes, there she was, crawling out of the neck of the river on her flailing elbows, laden as usual to the gunnels.

Now he could also see Captain Crow, hunched at his wheel, still clothed, apparently, in the same forlorn suit of pyjamas. A blast of steam shot from the funnel, followed by a series of traumatising whistle-shrieks. Inevitably, the bird population of Creek Town took to the air. The *Darling* raved and shoved.

Was Logan on board? It would be nice to speak to Logan – to get drunk with a white man on Scotch whisky. James raised his sun helmet, and saw one doffed in return. Logan's great moustache was beneath it.

Onwards came the geriatric river boat, kicking up the waters, filthying the air, fast growing in dimension and detail. A shade too fast, James imagined. A short while later he became convinced of this. He had seen enough of docking ships to know that this particular one was going to have to do something drastic, and soon, or run smack into the rickety, plank structure on which he currently stood. James made a rapid decision to get off the jetty. But no one else seemed even slightly concerned. No one but he had set off towards the shore. Stevedores had assembled at the head of the jetty, where they were matter-of-factly uncoiling ropes, or just lounging about, convinced of Crow's seamanship.

James's decision, however, turned out to be the wiser one. For, though at the last minute Crow could be seen doing everything possible to the wheel, and though the paddles went frantically into reverse, the *Darling* struck the jetty with a blunt and savage blow. Planks were dislodged, as were stevedores, as were passengers who had inadvisably been standing upright as she hit.

The water at the head of the jetty thrashed with human arms, buttocks and legs: a mess of panicked limbs. The culprit, however, had come to rest. Its steam whistle gave another demented screech. Again, birds were expelled from the reed beds like dust from a beaten carpet. A lot of yelling was coming from the water, a lot of screeching, and very little effective swimming. Fortunately, the water was not deep. Unfortunately, it contained a large crocodile.

James didn't even see the beast until it had a woman in its jaws; until what had been not an altogether unhumorous uproar had become a stunning tragedy. And this in the blink of an eye. She had almost reached safety when it took her. She was quite beautiful. Her face was gamine; her breasts barely nubile. She was waist deep in the muddy reeds, wading forward with the peculiar lack of agility of the upright animal in water. Her eyes met James's and seemed to smile. He couldn't really read them, but they seemed to enjoy his concern. Then inexplicably she sank, then rose, thrashing about in a skirt of red. A gun fired. A cone of whitened water rose near her shoulder.

Then James saw the dark shape; the white rows of impaling teeth. Another bang – another useless splash. The eyes of the girl found James again, roped him to her. He stood shouting, railing with clenched fists, while she held to the invisible connection. But what could he do but stare and shout. The jaws widened, as though to release her, then clamped deeper. The beast writhed, bit, turned her, and wagged her like a plaything in its snout. *Bang* went the mordant gun. There was no worthwhile target, just a mess of tawny churned water, blossoming redly; and something human now and then – an arm, a faintly kicking leg – then nothing. Not a ripple.

There was a sky-change; a scudding of squat clouds; grey moody dwarfs that gracelessly dumped their loads, then passed. He was wet again. And incomprehensibly angry.

Captain Crow's voice was the dominant sound in the following minutes. He was winding down, but slowly. Percussive exhalations of disappointment pervaded: 'Shit! Blast! Bloody hell!' Amazing volumes of noise for one so dramatically emaciated.

He observed James's arrival on his bridge. 'Damn it, Tremayne.' His eyes were jaundiced, his nostrils veined and flared. His bottom teeth were arrayed, suggesting determination: 'Damn it, Tremayne. Shot to the right. Should have corrected. Heat of the moment. Blast. Still, that's the way of it. Here today . . .' Evidently Crow still remembered the last conversation that he'd had with James, for he squinted critically at him. 'Where was your four-seventy, double, Tremayne? Where was your bloody gun?'

'I didn't think . . .'

'Didn't think it was necessary, did you? Well, let this be a lesson. Always, *always* carry your gun with you. Rule number one.'

Logan appeared, stroking his whiskers. *He* was armed. Crow enlisted him: 'I say, Logan. Tell Tremayne here what rule number one is.'

In answer Logan patted the butt of his heavy automatic pistol. 'And rule number two is not to shoot to the right.'

'Rule number three,' said James, 'might be to avoid colliding flat out with the jetty when docking. Thus keeping the passengers dry. I've never seen such a pathetic display of seamanship in my life . . .'

'Now wait a minute.' Crow wagged his finger at James. 'You don't know . . .'

'I should report you, Crow. Are you blind drunk, man, or merely insane?'

Crow sprang to his own defence. 'Damn your impudence, sir. You'll leave my ship at once.' He advanced as though to support his order bodily. His face filled James's vision. 'At *once*, sir. And do not return.'

Thank God for Logan; for the voice of reason. 'Hold on, boys. Hold on. This is no good at all.' He came between them, pressing a hand against each breast. 'We're *Englishmen*,' he said admonishingly. 'Now, James, you don't know the facts . . .'

'Damn right, he doesn't.'

'You should know the facts.'

The fact that James was ignorant of was that on the previous day, the *Darling* had lost the major part of her rudder. A submerged tree trunk had carried it away; had sheared it clean off its shaft, leaving the paddle steamer practically at the mercy of the flood current, which had been merciful. It had carried them downstream from Ikonetu Landing to Creek Town, where, by a feat of unsurpassed seamanship, Captain Crow had brought them in. An apology was due.

James gave it, and more. 'It was crass of me to act as I did, sir.'

Crow was just as big; 'We were overwrought, Tremayne. Think nothing of it. We could all do with a drink.'

'A drink,' said Logan, 'is exactly what *I* need.'

They went to Crow's cabin and uncorked a bottle of Vat 69. Three serious-sized tots were poured into a trio of variously shaped, unwashed tumblers, and drunk almost at once. Crow then set the bottle on a table and invited them to sit. He did not do so himself, but took the stub of a cigarette from the breast pocket of his pyjamas and stuck it between his lips. 'Finish it,' he said of the bottle, then left.

'Is he quite all right?' James enquired of the departed man. 'I mean, his facial expression, and those pyjamas . . . Isn't he a bit out of touch? He was trying to dump his guilt on me. I wasn't going to have it . . . I honestly think he's a bit batty.'

'As mad as a hatter,' Logan said. 'Too long out here, I'm afraid. An overheated brain, but first-rate at his job, Tremayne. You had it all wrong there, I'm afraid. He wouldn't have stopped here if it wasn't for you two. You really did him an injustice, old man. Cheers! Now tell me how you've been getting on.'

'I've been better.'

'Are you ready to leave?'

'Just about, I'd say.'

'How is the fair Jenny?'

'Fine.'

'Antera behaving?'

'As far as I know, yes.'

'Yes. Well, that's interesting . . . Interesting in the sense that, depending on your point of view, the opposite is true. He killed someone just the other day, not far from here. A young girl I'm told . . .'

James set his glass down with a clatter.

'A young witch. Chased her. Caught her. Strung her up and butchered her. Just like that.'

'I don't believe it.'

'Quite so. I found the same difficulty.'

'That's terrible – terrible . . . You're not pulling my leg, are you? No, I can see that you aren't. But why should he do such a barbaric thing? And how the hell did you get to know about it? I've heard nothing.'

'Ah, but surely you've heard the throb of the drums, my friend. All day and half the night. Gossip. Gossip. Gossip. They talk. They never stop. And I, my friend, have informants – translators of the sound who, for a fee . . .' He made a talking puppet face of his hand. 'One has to know what's going on. For instance, I know that you've dug up an old metal cross. Remarkable. Is that what you came to Creek Town to look for?'

James's tumbler was at his lips. He gave it a good tilt. 'Yes.' Another tilt. 'Partly . . . I shall confront Antera. I'll have the truth out of him.'

'I wouldn't, if I were you.'

'But I can't have a murderer – '

'Tremayne. Killing a witch, even an undersized one, is no crime here. It's a virtuous act. It's a cause for celebration. It happens so frequently that it doesn't even make the papers, and no one's ever brought to book. Take my advice: leave it alone. It's none of your business.'

'But I employ the bloody man.'

'Not to kill witches you don't.'

'Something should be done.'

'But not by you. What you do is to ignore it. If the authorities want to make something out of it – which they won't – then that's up to them.'

'Why did he kill her?'

Logan shrugged. 'There is a word here, Tremayne, a single word; an accusation "ifot". It means "witch". It's deadly. It will convert your average dozy villager into a raving homicidal maniac in an instant. Antera used it to advantage. He had reason. There's always a reason.'

'Good God! This is hard to believe.'

'Believe it. And as for the gods, Tremayne. It's also worth remembering that ours – our merciful God, He of Sunday – is small potatoes in this neck of the woods. Now, as to reason, I have to tell you this. There's talk; rumours, no more than that; whispers on the wind as it were, that Jenny . . . that there's more to Jenny than meets the eye. This is not good. This is dangerous. Do you understand?'

'What sort of rumours? What sort of danger?'

'In the light of what I've just told you; ugly rumours. Life-threatening dangers. Do you get my drift?'

'Not really.'

'You don't?' The bottle gurgled in disbelief, half filling Logan's glass. 'I don't know how better to put it to you. There was the severed hand incident at Calbar – now *this*. Antera, so the story goes, caught the little witch redhanded casting a particularly nasty spell on – guess who?'

'Jenny?'

'That's right, on your Jenny. This probably sounds awfully fanciful to you, Tremayne.'

'Macabre is a better description.'

'And there's more; another rumour that you really ought to know about. It is that Jenny has attained some sort of magical hold over Antera.'

James swigged fiercely. 'Well, *that's* absolute bloody tosh.'

'Of course it is,' Logan said. 'You know it. I know it. But do *they*?' He widened his eyes earnestly and rambled on for a while in patriotic vein; as one Englishman to another in savage, distant lands. He saw it as his duty to advise James to leave: 'Finished or not, old man. Pack up and get out. For the memsahib's sake.'

'I want to go. I've got a feeling she doesn't. In fact, I know she doesn't. It's a problem.'

'Not good enough, old man. Tell her what I've told you. Warn her of the implications. Take a firm line.'

Crow came back then, grinning with a bottom-tooth smile, or a grimace of consternation. It was impossible to tell which. However, he showed evidence of a more relaxed frame of mind. He made his Martini Henry comfortable on his bunk, maternally plumping the pillow for it, then emptied what was left of the whisky (not an inconsiderable tot) into his tumbler.

'Down the hatch!'

'Chin-chin,' said Logan.

'Cheers,' said James, who felt he had reached his limit, but was prepared to exceed it.

A flea or a nit, or in any case something small and carnivorous, was travelling over Crow's blemished skin en route towards his awful moustache, and presumably, home. Crow clicked his teeth in a pacified way; he was a pacified man. Why? Because, after having thoroughly investigated the stern end of his paddle steamer, he'd discovered that things were not as bad as they could have been, as he had first thought them to be. His beloved *Darling* was not damaged beyond repair. Hurt but not mortally so. The brass steering gudgeon (made in England, thank God) was holding on by its teeth. A jury rudder could be rigged. It would take a few days. He said, 'Sorry about that, Tremayne.'

'Sorry?'

'Can't be helped.'

'Why are you sorry?'

'Standard procedure.'

They were missing each other. Never mind. James took another swig. No one spoke for a while. The ship's machinery had stopped. Several large flies backed up by a squadron of mosquitoes had James under attack. His armpits itched. His crotch was crying to be scratched.

Creek Town: it crawled over him. He hated it. He hated it ardently and painfully. He had the feeling that it hated him, too.

'Look here,' he said to Logan. 'Just in case . . . Just in case there is a problem with Jenny; that is to say, between Jenny and the local wogs, I want you to give me an undertaking, old man.'

'Name it, old man.'

'Look, say she was in trouble, and for some reason or other I wasn't able to help her . . .'

'Say no more,' said Logan, squaring his shoulders.

'We all hate it, James,' said Jenny evenly. 'But that doesn't mean we have to run from it.'

'It wouldn't be running. And in any case what's so terrible about running when the odds are stacked so menacingly against you. As they are here.'

'But my study isn't complete, James. The job isn't done. Don't you understand?' She decelerated her voice, adding a tinge of sad inevitability, 'You go. I'll stay.'

That was out of the question. He said so emphatically. Then in a more consolatory tone, 'Look, the *Darling* has had its rudder torn off. Crow's trying to rig a jury rudder . . .'

'The rudder torn off?' she questioned brightly. 'When?'

'I don't know. Yesterday I suppose.'

'Go on – '

'Well, he's banded the local canoe-makers guild into a repair team. But it could take a few days to get the job done. That would give you time . . .'

'A few days?'

'Yes,' he said. 'Perhaps a week.'

'Not enough time.'

'How long do you need?'

'James.' She smiled sadly without opening her mouth, then renewed the rejected offer. 'I don't mind staying on my own.'

He shook his head, then placed it exhaustedly in his hands. He was done. He loved her. He hated the river. He loved her more than he hated the river. A long drawn-out sign of frustration proved even to himself that his argument wasn't working. She went to him, kneeled in front of him, took his hands from his cheeks and replaced them with hers.

'I love you,' she said.

'Oh, Jen, I love you so much. And that's the problem. I'm worried about you, Jen. I'm bloody worried . . .'

'Hush. There's nothing to fear.'

He had been on the point of telling her of Logan's disclosures of the awful rumours that were permeating the river. But with her lips so close to his, in the puff of her tingling, sweet breath, other opportunities opened. He found himself kissing her. And truthfully, at that moment, Logan's warnings paled.

They made slow love right there on the chair; slow, unctuous love that did not entail the removal of many garments. Slow, lucent-eyed love on the dirty, bashed-up, flea-ridden, horsehair chair.

Then she went to her room. He heard the tentative tick-tick of her typewriter as she warmed to her task. Then the keyboard was thrashed into action, volley after volley.

How much more was there to tell? How many more nights to be spent in miraculous copulation with his transformed lover, before she was satisfied that dreamer 'A' and dreamer 'O' had done all they could to advance the cause of hyper-reality; before they'd screwed themselves into telepathic exhaustion; before the whole episode was typed up and squared away. He didn't know. And if *she* did, she wasn't saying.

He also had things to do: a bit of unpacking. John Wilkes was to see the light of day. John Wilkes, handcrafted and gold inlaid double-barrelled rifle, came out of its velvet-lined case, offering masculine pleasure; a tingling way down to his testicles that bespoke genetic knowledge; savage stuff on the horizons of his mind; protection by any means of what was his. He felt he could bring this weapon to its ultimate use, and kill. He would hate to do that. But if Logan were right, if the Devil were riding out . . . *If Jenny were seriously threatened.* Then: he lifted the heavy rifle to his shoulder and aimed it randomly: *click. Click.*

He took half a dozen of the long, brass cartridges and pressed them, one by one, into the loops stitched onto the breast of his shirt, until the extra weight of gun and bullets was something in excess of sixteen pounds. An exceedingly authoritive weight. He practised loading and unloading, thumbing the puissant brass into the deep, black, side-by-side chambers. They homed with emphatic crispness: metallic clicks that could be felt right up to the elbow on closing the breech.

To get off on the right foot. To make the bond between rifle and rifleman, he took the John Wilkes with him for a walk, slung over his shoulder. The dwarf clouds had summoned their masters. Great, black-buttocked monsters had overtaken the sky and squeezed the horizons inwards. As yet it was not raining, but it would do so soon; it grumblingly promised this.

James Tremayne walked rather aimlessly with his head cast down, reflecting more on what had happened than what might still happen. He was planless, yet somehow aware that plans were unfolding; unsure of what he was looking for, yet looking for something – some sequestered yet significant thing that might or might not be revealed. Not expectant of revelation. That was his frame of mind. He was aware that he was following a similar path of discovery to that of Rory's. But whether this was by pure fluke, or by esoteric design, was impossible to tell. And because of this uncertainty he was incapable of working out whether this was good or bad, or merely inconsequential.

So he walked with his untried gun, just as his ancestor had done with his, and with no more noteworthy intention than to bang off a few shots at some or other target. And he found the ideal spot at the open end of a tunnel of dripping undergrowth, on the shore of the lake.

What presented itself to James was a dozing crocodile, a huge one. He didn't see it at first. Well, it's wrong to say that he didn't see it. He saw the shape and size and texture of the beast, and took it to be – part of the sand bank? A drift-line of mud? A log? Nothing at all? Its million-year camouflage was so perfect that his mind simply did not assimilate it. Nor did the giant croc give itself away by movement. It had dined amply, there was no reason for it to move. And James was almost as quiet. The frogs creaked and groaned. A fleet of white pelicans sailed by on their own reflections, all quite untroubled by human presence. The crocodile slumbered, unseen.

What James *had* seen – his target – lay on a narrow mudbank a little further out. A large, green, washed-up Chianti bottle, with its heel stuck in the crook of a mangrove root. Humming quietly to himself he thumbed the breech lever to the right, an all but silent manoeuvre amid the screech of frogs. He inserted two cartridges, then closed the breech. Click. This was louder. Audible news of this action reached out. The frogs fell silent. James twined the rifle-sling around his left wrist and took aim at the bottle.

A bird; a sandpiper of nervous disposition gave a squawk of dismay and thrashed into the air. The croc gave a start. Its tail, which alone weighed twice as much as James and which was ridged with rock-hard scales, gave a vicious sideways flail, knocking the man onto his rump. He did not know what had hit him; something dark and awful that had sprung from the earth. James scrambled to his knees. Now he saw it. *Now* he saw the monster – eight times larger than he. He saw its pink epiglottis as it turned and roared. The cold green eyes.

Shoot it. Shoot the bloody thing.

Having given this instruction to himself he proceeded to carry it out, but far too slowly. His reaction, braked by hideous shock, was delayed. This was a nightmare of the sort where creeping lethargy replaces the cry for speed. There was no combustion in him, no killing rage, just the paralysis of horror. He still held the rifle. Despite his tumble, it was still in his grip and pointed in the right direction, right up the throat of the advancing beast. He pulled the trigger; crooked his finger on it and yanked. It didn't budge. It didn't fire. The expected mighty explosion failed to arrive. The safety catch was on. It wasn't designed to fire with safety on. He'd forgotten that fact; nor did his mind come to it at that point. The croc lunged forward. James lunged backwards. He, too, was now roaring.

Now the stimulant fear of death was speeding him and making him harder to kill. He defended himself with the unfired gun by jabbing at the snapping jaw and saw a red gash open on its snout.

Then things went badly. The weight of the reptile, its sheer rapacity and keenness to destroy, inevitably gave it the upper hand. It lunged, James parried with the gun barrel while leaping back. Jagged teeth snapped, and now it held the gun barrel while James held the butt. It tugged. James toppled with his finger still crooked around the unmoving trigger in a spasm of desperation. But the safety catch was on – and forgotten. He would have let the weapon go if he could have, for now the rifle was a perilous liability, but his left wrist, as it had been all along, was lassoed by the rifle-sling, and so, at a rapid pace, he was being dragged by it down the bank into the muddy reeds.

The croc, with another lunge forward, improved its grip. If it did that again it would surely sever James's wrist.

It did it, but before it touched his skin, it also knocked the safety catch with one of its fine teeth; clicked it off and in so doing set up its own instantaneous death. The trigger was released; both triggers in fact. There was a throat-muffled double detonation as two large bullets impacted into the beast; tore through the base of its primitive brain and pulped several vertebrae, then deflected variously upwards and downwards, tearing two massive passageways through vital organs. Many tons of energy made soup out of its innards. Its cold, green eyes popped out of their sockets, as though comically boggled by the event. Its jaw unhinged, and smoke drifted from an aperture at the base of its skull. It was over. He'd killed it.

Any pragmatist would agree: he'd killed it. On the other hand, one could argue that the old croc had killed itself, by accident. One could look at it like that. Or, like the villagers who came running (the very fishermen who had killed off the little witch, Tuesday) one might find either theory to be too casual, too coincidental. Especially in view of what happened thereafter.

The villagers were quickly on the scene. So quickly, in fact, did they arrive that the slayer of the croc had not yet got to his feet. Shaken to his core, James was lying in a sprawled heap, several yards from the jaws of the beast and quite unable to explain to himself how this shift had come about. Nor had he yet determined why the rifle, which he still held, and which was still intact (but for its severed sling), had apparently malfunctioned. But that it had ultimately fired and that he was unscathed, was really all that mattered. Many hands reached out to help him to his feet; many more wished to pat his back. Heroically, he stood.

It took eighteen strong men to carry the dead beast back to the village. The commotion was great. James, though thoroughly invited by gesture to go with them, declined to do so. Thus he did not see them slash open the belly of their old enemy to get at the medicinal parts. He was not on hand to observe the aborted celebration; the sudden change from avid joy to horrible dismay. But he was told about it. He was told about the find. Inside the stomach of the beast was discovered some bones, very slim, small bones; a child's bones. There was one small putrefied arm, with one small amulet still attached.

There was ululating and moaning. These were the remains of little Tuesday. There was no doubt about it. Her unique little amulet was recognised by everyone.

That very afternoon, deluged by rain, the fisher folk tore their own village down; pulled out the centre pole of every hut. Killed every hut. Then, taking all that they owned, they trekked upriver to a new, clean site. Of course, they didn't take the dead crocodile or anything that had come from it; the witch-child's bones, the arm and the twisted copper amulet. These dangerous pollutions were left where they'd fallen on the ground, never to be spoken of again by a member of that cursed tribe. They would never prosper again, they knew it. Everyone knew it.

A scavenging leopard came that night and took away the remains of the girl. It was heard, but not seen. Only its spoor was to be seen. Pug marks in the mud.

The drums. They told the whole story, over and over, every detail; everything that had happened, and some things that hadn't yet, but would. The matter was not at an end, the wheel was still turning . . . Ah, the drums. If only the white folk could have heard what they were saying. If only. But, needless to say, these things, these dire predictions were kept secret. Even Logan's most faithful informants would not have dared to have breathed a word of this. Not for any sum of money. But even had he found out what awful predictions were riding the air, and even had he told Jenny, would she have heeded the warnings? Would she have accepted that the game had changed, and dangerously so? Would she have cut short the experiment in depth, and left that place at once? It's doubtful.

She had come so far; so very far. She was beating at the very Gates of Knowledge. She wanted the lot: the dream and the reality. A release from the crush and mud of ignorance on Earth. She wanted to know more than it was humanly reasonable to know. It was all there. Behind the gates. In the out-world. And a visit had been promised. The Dream Stealer had vowed to take her there if certain conditions were met: Antera was to be part of it. She agreed. He was not to be told in advance that his dream spirit would be included in the party. She agreed.

Of course she did. How could she resist the offer?

Thirty-one

'She was born to die,' said the magician Run Run to his apprentice. 'Therefore I give her the name Abiku.'

'Abiku?' Monday said through a chewy mouthful of yam. 'But how will that help her?'

'Stupid. It's not intended to *help* her, merely to *name* her. Jen? What does that tell you about her? Nothing. A person should have a name that suits their ambition.'

It was night. The mottled glint of old coals lay between them, giving each face a veneer of orange. Run Run, Monday thought, looked discontented and out of sorts. A man whose problems outweighed his joys. He said to his teacher, 'But why should she wish to die?'

'Now there's a question that only she can answer. She's perilously ambitious. She wants, while in this world, to gain knowledge that doesn't belong to this world; knowledge that would be a danger to this world.'

'What knowledge is this, Teacher?'

'The Secret.'

'What secret?'

'That which belongs to the Owner of the Sky.'

'What's that?'

'If I told you,' Run Run said acidly, 'then it wouldn't be a secret.'

They ate for a while, the sound of chewing their only communication. Then as a resentful sigh Run Run said, 'It's immortality.'

'That's the secret she's after?'

'That's it. To find it you must go through the doorway of the grave.'

'So you have to be dead in order to know how to survive

death? No wonder I've hardly met anyone who knows it. Why shouldn't she have it then?'

'She wants fame. She'd spread the word. The Secret would be out.'

'But she'd be *dead*. So how?'

'She knows the way back.'

'Ah,' said Monday. 'So she doesn't have a decent fear of death. I can see how that could be bad. Like a thief, she knows how to get in and how to get out. But does she have the guts to try?'

'That's the thing. She may not have. But she's got enemies who'd love to put her in the grave. She may not even have to try.'

'Who would kill her?'

'Sassabonsum, for one. He and his little wooden juju. Their plans are well advanced.'

'I could easily get hold of the wooden man, Teacher. It's on Jen's . . . I mean Abiku's table, in her room in Mammy Yellowbelly's house. If you want me to, I'll steal it.'

'You're a good boy, Monday . . . But no. Leave it there. That juju is Yoruba's only hope. And though that leopard has saddened me, and hurt me, and though I wouldn't help her now, I also wouldn't do anything to injure her. No, leave the juju where it is.'

'How will Sassabonsum kill Abiku?'

'Oh, in the nastiest and most degrading way that he can think of.'

'Why don't we help her? Warn her, at least.'

'How would that help? She was born to die and die again. She might welcome Sassabonsum's help in the matter. I don't know. I don't know . . .'

'But what if she brings back the Secret?'

'I don't see how I can stop her.'

Thirty-two

Rain strummed the corrugations of the roof of Mammy Yellowbelly's while boulders of thunder rumbled over the bare boards, skittling the furniture and shaking the walls. Everything trembled. Everything creaked. How much more of this could the old house take?

Antera slept like a dog; a guard dog at the door of Jenny's bedroom, listening for the footfall of the enemy. Needless to say, he didn't hear it. It came, but he didn't hear it. Had the night been perfectly still, he wouldn't have detected it. It was weightless and it was soundless. It was colour, form and depth. It was an entire world marvellously condensed into one woolly head. Yes, a dream. It said to him, 'Antera, rise up, there's things to do.' And he obeyed.

He stood and left his post, and went downstairs to Mammy Yellowbelly's dining room, where a noisy party was in progress. People; some spectacularly dressed whites and more of his own skin colour were seated at the long table, all of them feasting and drinking gin and mimbo. At the head of the table, with her back towards him, sat a woman of such massive proportions that her buttocks were fortified by not one, but two chairs set side by side. Her arms were so ponderous and decked with gold that the added muscle of several slaves was needed to operate her arms. She was tented in a dress of silver damask.

Antera came further into the room. Slaves were coming and going, bearing plates and jars. He walked close to the wall in order to give them space, observing as he advanced all that was going on in this room which he knew so well, yet didn't know at all.

Ah, but here was someone whose features looked familiar; a

white man. He was outlandishly dressed in loose cotton garments, and heavily armed. At his waist a sash was tied from which protruded the handle of a pistol, and a naval cutlass hung from a strap. His eyebrows were pinched with curiosity, and the eyes beneath them fixed on Antera as though seeing him at a great distance; or as something yet hidden, but slowly emerging from a mist.

'Don't you know who it is?' said a voice at Antera's side. 'Look again.'

'It's an olden-days sailor.'

'Anyone can see that,' said the wooden man rudely. 'Which sailor?'

'I've seen him before.'

'Of course you have. Well, if you're *so* stupid that you can't recognise him, that's your look-out. Have you seen me before?'

'I'm not sure.'

'Then stop staring. It's rude to stare.'

'I'm sorry. It's just that . . .'

'You're a sorry animal in every way, Antera. Never mind. How's you head? How are the pains?'

'They come. They go. Who are you?'

'I'm part of you. In every man there is a little man.'

'Oh!'

'I, too, come and go.'

'Oh!'

'I've arranged a very nice death for you, Antera. It was the least I could do.'

'Oh!'

'Shit, you're a monotonous creature. I've had better conversations with trees. Look, there's no escaping the Fangaree charm, you know that, don't you? Yoruba's little helper did a good job on you before you killed her. That was a bad move, by the way. Killing the child complicated things for Yoruba in a big way, and she doesn't like you at all. No chance of the Fangaree being lifted, but I'm doing all I can to hurry things along for you. As a favour . . . But it's your fault. If you hadn't fallen in love with the white woman, and gone and had that stupid, *stupid* love juju made, you wouldn't have been hit by the Fangaree. It was never intended for you. Did you know that?'

'I couldn't help it. I couldn't help loving her. She's so . . .
so . . .'

'Delicious? Juicy?'

'Yes. And . . .'

'Fuckable?'

'That too.'

'Well, Antera, I've got good news, and I've got bad news.
You already know the bad news.'

'Yes, I do. I saw the Fangaree. I saw the gecko with its head
crushed in. I know that nothing can be changed, and that I'm
going to die. But, tell me, what's the *good* news?'

'You're going to die doing what you'd love to do most. And I
mean *most* . . . Well, what a nice surprise! Look who's just
walked in.'

'Oh, I know *her*.'

'Your lady love. The woman of your dreams. The woman
who you would most like to *shag*.'

'Keep your voice down.'

'Antera, where you are now, deception is quite purposeless.
If you don't speak your mind you don't get what you want.
Look, I've been doing this sort of thing for a few hundred years,
so I know what I'm talking about. Everything is possible. *If*
you ask. Go ahead. Ask her.'

'I couldn't. She's so pure.'

'Pure! You're talking through your arse flap, son. No one is
that pure under the skin. I ought to know. I see them all in the
raw. Royalty and commoners; rich and poor; cowards and
warriors; they've all got one thing in common between the
knees and the navel: a little patch of joy. And everyone wants to
dig their neighbour's patch. It's nice. It's the kindly thing to
do.'

Antera thought about that. It did seem as though his little
wooden pal had it all worked out. The subject was worth
pursuing. '*How* do I get under the skin?' he said eagerly. 'How
do I get to the little patch of joy?'

'You're there already. I thought I'd made that plain enough.
This is the place. *Now* is the time . . . give or take a hundred
years. But let's not confuse the issue. The point is that I'm in
charge here. What I say goes. If you want to shag her then go
ahead and do so. It's perfectly all right . . .Well, *do* you?'

'More and more.' The absolute truth. A lopsided shoving at the fabric of his trousers testified to this.

'All right,' said the Dream Stealer. 'I can see that you need some help. That's what I like doing most – helping people. I'm going to make things easier for you, easier for *all* of us.'

'How?'

'You just stand here, and leave the rest to me.'

Antera did as he was bade. His fear of slow disintegration, of grindingly slow separation from life, had been removed. A warm and comfortable feeling of confidence was beginning to seep into him. He felt as one who has come to terms with existence, and *non*existence. Earth and sky.

Death was there; invisible, but *there*, just the same. Waiting to perform its cruelties. Waiting for a signal; Antera knew not what. That was someone else's responsibility, not his. As had been the signal for life. Admission and ejection – here then gone – at someone else's bidding – turning on unseen hinges. 'Why worry?' Antera said to himself. 'Why struggle?'

Though nourished and sustained by this state of submission, it didn't apply to all things. For instance, Antera's keenness to (as the Dream Stealer put it) *shag* the beautiful white woman was undiminished, and perhaps even strengthened. His male department was sending up messages of powerful readiness. As instructed, he was watching the Dream Stealer make things easier for him; for all of them.

Nevertheless, he didn't see the change take place – the transformation from white woman to half-caste. Perhaps no change had occurred. Perhaps they were one and the same, and always had been. Just a hybrid state of mind. But there she suddenly was, a ravishing mulatto. The Dream Stealer had kept his word. He'd made things easier, by far.

The transport from one room to another was just as effortless. They were in the crowded dining room, then they were not, but were in a bedroom, her bedroom, alone. Lightning was whitening the square of the window and the kick of thunder was on all sides.

Death was here too; at the end. There was a tunnel . . . no, it was more like a tubular extension of vision, wall-less, but confining. He, Antera, was at the one end, Death at the other, advancing. The mulatto, his most beautiful lover-to-be, stood somewhere in between. And to reach her Antera would have to advance, too. That was obvious.

'I'm sorry,' she whispered in his direction. 'I'm so sorry. You shouldn't be here. It's my fault.'

He made no conscious decision to walk. He just did it. He loved her. He loved the Dream Stealer for what he had done. He loved his killer-to-be for what he would do. It was a tunnel of high emotion through which he walked. He felt joyous, and tremendously excited.

'I'm *so* sorry.'

Her regret was well meant, but unnecessary. He wished she knew that. He didn't mind. He wasn't perturbed by the fact that in coming closer to her he was also advancng his moment of death. He said, 'It doesn't matter. It's all right.'

She beckoned compellingly, urging him onwards with both arms, gathering to her the empty space as though frustrated by its very substanceless. She was closer.

Death was closer.

She looked over her shoulder and saw this too, and turned back to Antera, distressed. And for one awful moment he thought that he might not reach her in time, that he would die before he'd reached her and love her. But on judging the distances again, he perceived this to be unlikely.

Death was recognised. It was the sailor. The white man in the white shirt, with pistol and sword. Antera knew him now. He knew exactly who his killer was to be. And he loved him. It was perfect. It rhymed like poetry; rang like a song. He wanted this end, this excellent termination. He smiled so that the killer might see his joy. But the smile was warded off. Hard eyes the killer had. They polished Antera with a cold stare that took away the smile, but not the joy or the sense of harmony.

He reached her then. She held her ovate breasts out to him; the fruit of her. She gave him whole ownership of her body, and he possessed it.

He felt the pistol muzzle. It came like a dog's cold snout, sniffing tentatively at the space of his forehead. Then it hardened into steel.

Then it flashed.

MAGIC

Thirty-three

'Murder' is a cold-fingered word. It tickles beneath the heart, feeling for any number of states of emotion. Fury, cruelty, cowardice, insanity, hate. The hidden iniquities. The worms of the soul, there but for the grace of God . . .

That isn't to say that James believed he'd killed Antera Duke. Such thoughts as those he did not entertain. Why? Because he was incapable of such brutality. Earlier, there had been moments of doubt. But, thank God, he'd pulled himself together; lifted his prostrated faculties and stood them in line. He was no murderer. Moreover, his reaction to the bloody state of affairs was not that of the dyed-in-the-wool blackguard. He wanted to confess to his part in it. He did confess to Jenny: 'I knew I was going to do it; that I was Rory, and that I had no option but to kill him. Right from the beginning – the beginning of the dream that is.'

'The dream. You dreamed you killed him?'

'Yes. It was inevitable. I knew I was going to do it from the moment he came into the room, the dining room, downstairs. That's where it began. We were all there: Mammy Yellowbelly, Jemmy Honesty . . .'

'Excuse me, James. Having dreamed that you, as Rory, killed him, and having actually done so, are two different things. I know about your dream. You realise that, don't you. I had access to it. Our dream scenarios were identical. But by now I shouldn't have to tell you that. The point is that I saw you there, in your dream state. And so we can conclude that you were asleep at the time when Antera was murdered and, thus, couldn't have done it.'

'I know. I'm not saying . . . what I'm saying is that it's *bizarre*. It was my pistol, and – '

'I hate to cut in again, but that statement, too, is not entirely correct. It was Rory's pistol. You inherited it. But symbolically, and in an esoteric sense . . .'

'That is splitting hairs.'

'It was Rory's. Some hairs need to be split, and split again.'

'There's a murderer on the loose.'

'And in the morning we will report that fact. In the meantime, James, let's examine your statement. Firstly the pistol. If I remembered correctly, the last time you showed it to me, it was not loaded. How did it become loaded?'

'I don't know.'

'Did you, at any stage, load it?'

'It would have been impossible for me to do so. You see, the firearms of that era were primed with percussion caps. I haven't got such an article – nor have I ever had one – nor so much as seen one. And where did the powder come from, and the ball? And yet I dreamed that I held it, pressed the barrel against his forehead, and shot him. And there he lies, fallen, just as I saw him fall. It's . . . it's insanity. I didn't do it. I know it. You know it. But what the hell are *they* going to believe?'

'Hold on a sec. You did tell me that you thought it was possible to load that pistol with the bits and pieces from a rifle cartridge. You said there were some brass caps in the gun case.'

'I said that *theoretically* it was possible.' He growled, 'Christ, you don't think for a moment . . . ?'

'Of course I don't think *that*. Don't lose your cool. It's not like you to lose your cool.'

'What *is* like me? I've forgotten what it's like to be me. I recommend that you think about that. Everything has altered. Even you've altered. What the hell is going on? *Murder*. With Rory's pistol. Murder dreamed, as done. Jen, it's unbelievable. What next will be dreamed, *as done*. Call a stop, Jen. No more. *No* more.'

'Yes, of course. It's terrible. I quite agree . . . So you didn't load the pistol?'

'No, I bloody well didn't. Leave that one alone, will you? Let's look at your involvement in this thing for a moment. Jenny, you ought to know this. The local gossip is that Antera recently killed someone, a girl, who's suspected of having cast a spell on you.'

'Good heavens. Are you serious?'

'Logan told me. He was dead serious. He also said that the locals believed that you had some sort of hold over Antera. Absolute rubbish of course. But that's the sort of superstitious nonsense being circulated. Those are the sort of people who we are going to have to rely on to believe that I didn't kill Antera Duke. General sympathy will not be on our side.'

'So, whoever loaded the pistol . . .'

'Jen, you're not listening.'

'I've heard everything you've said. I know what you're driving at.'

'What?'

'That we should leave. Run out. Vamoose.'

'You *must* agree.'

If she did, she didn't say so. In the trembling candlelight she watched him in a serene sort of way; not the sort of way he would have considered appropriate; not the sort of expression that he'd expected; for example, consternation. In the next room, at its entrance, lay a corpse, minus fully a quarter of its head. The missing quarter was distributed over much of the adjacent wall and door. *This* was worthy of consternation.

'They won't believe us, Jen.'

'They certainly won't if you do a bunk.'

'I don't care what they believe when I'm in England with my lawyer at my side. We've got to get out of this place, and now.'

'We can't do that.' Her pink tongue did a circuit of her lips. She closed her eyes and when she opened them again was looking elsewhere. 'We simply can*not* do that.'

She didn't get it. She didn't know what was going on outside there; out there, where the jungle drums broadcast the news of the day; out there where dead witchlets rebirthed themselves via crocodiles *he had shot* . . . Jenny was out of touch and, as is the nature of this condition, was oblivious of the fact. He thought that the time had arrived for him to tell her that, and a few other painful truths. A re-evaluation. 'Jen, this experiment, this depth experiment of yours is a disaster. More than that; a tragedy. I don't think you're in control, in fact I doubt if you ever were. This cannot go on. I won't allow it. We're packing up – *now*. Get your things.'

'Are you blaming me?'

'No. But it's as though you've totally forgotten why we came . . .'

'Why are you blaming me?'

'I'm not *blaming* you,' he said. 'It wasn't intentional.'

'I don't like your tone. Of course I regret what happened to Antera.'

'It was murder.'

'I know that.'

'I draw the line at murder, absolutely draw the line. Antera, my darling, is *dead*. And it had to do with your experiment.'

'In a round-about way,' she said placidly.

'But then don't you see . . . ?'

'You must realise, James, that such work as mine is fraught with danger. I told you that before we came to Africa. Yes, things went out of control. We – you, I and Antera – were manipulated. I admit it. But now I'm better prepared.'

'Prepared for what? Do you know what King Sam's people would do to you if they thought you were a witch. Why am I saying "if"? They *do* think you're a witch. They kill witches here. As an act of godliness they exterminate witches, and no one gives a damn.'

'Yes. That's not a factor. We were manipulated in our dream state, subjugated. All three of us. If poor Antera were alive and able to give an account of his experience, it would match yours and mine in every detail. Tragic but conclusive proof of Jung's theory of synchronicity. Think of it.'

He thought. He watched her and thought to himself, This woman is not doing well. She looks ill. She looks very ill. And that is not surprising. He placed his extended arm on her shoulder and with mild authority said, 'It's got to end, Jen. Now. Give me the fetish doll and I'll get rid of it.'

'Ah, the dream fetish . . . the stealer of dream souls. You think it was that little incubus that manipulated us. No, you're quite wrong. It wasn't that fetish, but something much greater; some generic force of this locality which I have, as yet, not been able to identify. An aberrant nature spirit. It's huge. It straddles the jungle and steps on us as we step on the scorpions in our path. It's there. The master of all fetishes. I know of it, and it knows of us . . . Rory felt it. It overpowered him. Theo knew of it. He railed against it; held up his cross and hurtled prayers at

280

it and it overpowered him too. We were manipulated, I believe, to make us submit. We were arrogantly treated by it, crushed. Antera didn't survive it . . . But I'm totally prepared now. I know what I'm dealing with now.'

He watched. He listened. She thinks, he said to himself, that survival is synonymous with 'being prepared'. Whereas the opposite is true. This thing that straddles the jungle kills for the joy of it: kills both those prepared and those not, crushing its victim underfoot, into the mud. And those that it doesn't kill it subjugates by making them insane. He watched her closely. He listened.

'But we can't give up, not just because of *that*. Not just because of such arrogance. We must deal with it. Face up to it. We must carry on. There's so much to be gained.'

She was not doing well.

A silver, sluglike trail of light was evolving into dawn. It crept upon them unhealthily. It was still raining, but hissing, not roaring. He could see her better in this light. Her eyes were ringed and her mouth pinched at the corners. He quietly insisted, 'Give me the Dream Stealer.'

'No.' She massaged her temples at the point where the swelling pain was threatening to crack her bones. Emphatically she said, 'I *won't*.'

He stood. 'I'm going down to the jetty,' he said. 'I'm going to find Logan and tell him what's happened. He'll know what to do.'

'Take your raincoat,' she advised his departing figure.

She was grateful that he'd gone. The pain was severe and the argument – the ridiculous argument – had made it worse. How could he expect her to stop now, give up, go home. She had arrived at a crucial point in her research – that magically seminal moment that forms the divide between speculation and conclusion; between birth and abortion. She would go on. She thought of typing; there was so much to be said about the death dream. The ultimate proof of dream synchronicity that had eluded even Jung in his lifetime, and his Valkyries after his death. She strung a few sentences together in her head, but even these minor vibrations were unsupportable. Her body slid sideways, toppling with no expenditure of energy onto the mattress.

'Well,' said the Dream Stealer, 'I suppose I should thank you. But I can't find it in me to do so. You diminished my role.'

'Go away,' she pleaded. 'You lied to me.'

'What was all that shit about huge nature spirits that straddle the jungle?'

'I believe it to be true. You're small fry. You make out that you're bigger and more powerful than you are.'

'Hold on!' he screeched. 'That's not fair. I've shown you marvels.'

'You've shown me very little I couldn't have found by myself.'

'You expected more?'

'You promised secrets, great truths, not a minor assassination.'

'You can't expect to get there in one hop. That was an excursion; a glimpse. You must drink of the stream before drinking of the source. Keep following. Keep moving on. You're getting there.'

'Go away. I'm in too much pain to argue.'

'It's the Fangaree. I had my doubts about its effectiveness against a witch like you. Why don't you dream up a counter spell.'

'Because I haven't the knowledge.'

'Cut the crap. I know all about you. You're potent. You could stop it if you wanted to. You could make a deal with Yoruba and reverse its course. But no. You prefer to suffer; to test it to its limits. Well, that's your choice.'

'Yes it is.'

'But I'd be sorry to see you dead. I've a lot of respect for you.'

She opened one eye. 'Have you?'

'You know I have.'

'No, I don't. Tell me why.'

'Why? I've spent time on you. I see you as part of me now. A bodily extension. We've grown together. That's why.'

'Those are poor reasons for respect.'

'I'll ignore the insult. I respect you because you're so much like me: you can see the beauty of wickedness. And because you have absorbed the lesson.'

'What is the lesson?'

'That's it. The question is the answer.'

'What came before the answer, then?'

'Look at it this way. What came before was me, and what came later was you. And the one has absorbed the other, and you have become so fully changed in the process that you are now what you were not before, and there is no residue of what was before. That is the answer.'

'Have I become so changed that I'm hidden, even from myself?'

'Be happy. The old is dead. Eliminated. Expunged. What was fake is broken and discarded. What is new is pure, and I respect it. I'm reconciled to you. I love you.'

'You give me hope.'

'I am your hope: your new intelligence, your direction in the dark. Respect me too.'

'I do . . . I have a question.'

'I expected a question.'

'Who did kill Antera Duke?'

'The sailor.'

'But who was the sailor?'

'The Ancestor is the imitator of the Living Man.'

Though couched in different terms, and in a different locality, that question was being framed by Logan, too: 'Can you think of anyone who would have wanted Antera dead?'

James said, 'What about the witch whose apprentice Antera murdered?'

Logan swung his feet off his bunk, one, then the other. Then his torso became deliberately upright. He was a hairy man. A bundle of black, curly stuff forested his chest. He stretched the layered flab of his upper body, showing lumps of muscle as he did, then yawned. He looked different. 'Could be.' He yawned again. 'That's just the sort of trick one might expect from a witch. How was he killed? Head bludgeoned in? Spear through the chest? Poison? Is there evidence as to how it was done?'

'A pistol was used. Blew his head off, practically. Horrible mess.'

'Good heavens!' Logan retrieved his teeth from a glass where they'd spent the night, inserted them with the flat of his hand, smacked his jowls a few times, then said, 'How odd.' He no longer looked different now that his teeth were home. 'How very bizarre.'

'Why odd? Why bizarre?'

'Well,' said the trader, standing, then performing several deep knee bends. 'Odd in the sense that no witch doctor worth her salt would kill in such a way. It's just *not* how it's done out here, you follow.' Logan farted mightily on his final exertion. Satisfied that all of him was working as it should, he got into his jodhpurs and shirt, then strapped on his heavy automatic. James was glad to have this sterling fellow at his side. On reaching the deck Logan paused to light a Turkish cigarette, then said, 'You didn't shoot him, did you, old man? Be honest with me.'

'I say, Logan, that's no joke.'

'It wasn't meant to be.' He exhaled, coughed, regarded the cigarette as one might a tiresome but beloved mistress, then said, 'It's a damn serious matter, killing the nephew of a chief. *Damn* serious.'

'Now why would I want to do a thing like that?'

'Why indeed,' said Logan, taking to the gang plank.

They walked together, not saying much more about the murder, but discussing instead the progress of the repairs to the aft end of the *Darling*. It was taking longer than anticipated to install a jury rudder on account of a lack of craftsmen and tools. A few more days of sawing and hammering might see the emergence of a suitable article. In the meantime the sun struggled up from a thick bed of clouds, sank in again, then finally rose with ungracious resolve. The walkers became wrapped in intolerable vapour. Every leaf glistened. Every bird had something to say. Brown, earthy grubs split their backs and the air became mortal with butterflies. James crushed a roving scorpion into the mud, then viciously rode it with his boot heel. It survived. It extricated itself, limb by limb, from its intended grave, then limped away. What on earth did it think had just occurred in its life? There was a lesson to be learned here, but James doubted if it had learned it.

A body of sullen, spear-bearing tribesmen had come to stand in uncharacteristic silence before the mansion of Mammy Yellowbelly. The music of J. S. Bach was reaching out scratchily from the open windows and being converted into pop by the additional thump of tom-toms. Grandy King Sam was at home.

He was upstairs. The gramophone's automatic winder told

284

Logan this. So they went upstairs: Logan with bold, wide strides, James to the rear. Both men slowed their ascent on being confronted by the querulous voice of the monarch: 'Look dis man gone dead, one time.'

They could not see Sam yet, but the tone of the statement conveyed a rather disconcerted frown. As did this question: 'Which pusson done such damn ting suppose?'

'Whoever loaded the pistol,' the calm voice of Jenny Oxenham suggested.

'Who did dat?'

At this point, preceded by Logan, James arrived on the landing. King Sam swivelled suddenly towards them, turned his white eyeballs into orbs of suspicion, and repeated the question: 'Who did dat ting?'

James offered up his waterproof alibi: 'I heard a bang. It woke me up. I practically fell over him when I went to investigate. He was lying there, just where he is now. There was a smell of gunpowder.'

'By God, someone him shoot dis good man from de head . . . Where dat gun?' King Sam made a quick visual search of the floor as if expecting to find the weapon lying there. It wasn't.

It wasn't lying there because James had previously removed it. He admitted to this: 'I took it to my room, you see.'

'Why you do dat? You get dat gun. You bring dat gun here, now. Why you do dat?' The king, it seemed, knew a bit about forensic procedures.

James fetched the weapon from his room. The king took it gingerly, looking meaningfully at James as he sniffed the barrel snout. He then drew back the hammer and peered into the percussion lock. The flattened percussion cap, the little brass pill that James had earlier described to Jenny, was scratched out of its socket. This, too, was subjected to the sniff test, then rolled about between thumb and fingertip while King Sam ruminated deeply. He asked one pertinent question: 'Which pusson belong dis?'

'The pistol is mine,' said James. 'The ammunition is not.'

This statement was considered by the great man. In the music department, Handel took over from J.S.B. The first few bars from 'Concerto Grosso' limped up the stairs. That was how long it took to wrap up the investigation.

Arrest followed swiftly. James saw the king's big fist come up, draw back, then discharge towards his face. He had more than enough time to evade it. It was sheer dumbfoundedness that froze him in its path. He simply could not believe the evidence of his eyes. There was the big, black, bunched-up fist; big, black, bunched-up *royal* fist in accelerated flight with nowhere to go but straight into James's undefended jaw, and still he couldn't believe it. It was just inconceivable. It wasn't going to happen. It would pull up short.

Nothing of the sort. Bang!

James heard Jenny's trembling scream; then the sound of breaking wood, or bones (or both). He judged himself to be airborne, in headlong descent of the staircase, quite out of control. His neck wrenched sickeningly. Inside his skull a gate slammed shut.

Thirty-four

Where the small patch of sunlight went, there James Tremayne went too, crawling like a begger along the floor. Its point of admission was a funnel, a cobwebbed duct that passed through the breadth of the thick, cell wall. It was wide at its closest point, wide enough to have enabled James to plug his upper body into it with reasonable hope of being able to fit the rest of him into it, and along it, and of course, out of it. It was long. He found that it accepted him entirely; swallowed him whole before squeezing off his escape attempt. It was tapered, cunningly and gradually, so that no matter how driven by desperation, no one could possibly traverse its entire length before becoming stuck fast like a cork in a bottle. That was clearly its purpose: to deceive, to mock, to increase the prisoner's sense of failure. In this it succeeded.

Yet on sunny afternoons it admitted a single, moving tile of light. And this was hope; unfounded, unintelligible hope. The setting sun. And it showed him many things. The east wall of his cell. Grey, slatey stone and pitted shackles. Old coiled links of metal, disarranged like fossilised vertebrae of prehistory. It showed the studded door through which he had been admitted several days previously, and through which, he hoped, ultimately to exit . . .

Scoffing at such optimism was his cell-mate. He was dead – drastically so; he was an anatomically perfect skeleton. His skull was propped against the north wall in a posture that suggested repose. The rest of him lay stretched out fairly lengthily, as though he'd known that there would be a wait. A patient, philosophical fellow. A fine example for those not yet dead.

There were colonies of insects that came and went,

287

congregated, then dispersed, that made the most of James – his pockets, his hair, the alpine challenge of the wall at his back. The solar spotlight played over them too, picked them out from the gloom like principal players in a pantomime.

But it was the exterior view that, despite its tubular limitations and its ugliness, James sought most of all. It was as a postcard from the outside: a snipped-off view of the thatched and corrugated iron rooftops of Creek Town as well as some riverine trees and a section of the reed beds and the jetty. Not all of the jetty could be observed, just a tiny portion. What James could see was that section of planking that the *Darling* had bumped into. What he could deduce was that the paddle steamer was still there. He could see the bollard and the hawsers to which the vessel was attached and a segment of the gang plank along which he'd so recently walked. The *Darling* was still there . . .

She had been there, according to his reckoning, for four days. It might have been five. There was a portion of memory that seemed to have more or less vanished, or at least to have become so watered down and lacking in incident as to be unrecognisable as an element of time. Another period was decorated by a series of photographically brilliant pictures. One was of fat King Sam sitting on him, plumped squarely on his chest, wagging his finger under his nose, saying something ominously unintelligible. Another was of fat King Sam, this time on a chair (a throne?), the backrest of which was decorated with a pair of human skulls, saying even less intelligible and even more ominous things. He had a vivid flash, a recollection of Jenny showing lots of fortitude . . . That was it. That was all there was to fit into the dead space. It was as if he had been knocked off his feet and straight into prison. Tried, convicted and sentenced en route. Concussion had whacked the rest away. But of one thing he was dead sure: he had not killed Antera Duke.

He could not have done such a thing. No. Never. Nor could he believe that Jenny was capable of such an act . . . Though what remarkable motivation she'd had: unassailable evidence in support of dream synchronicity. He had dreamed he'd killed. She'd dreamed she'd seen him kill. Antera had been killed. Confirmation in triplicate. What more perfect measurement of unconscious ability could the researcher of this subject want?

Nevertheless he was convinced she'd had nothing to do with it. In which case, who had shot Antera Duke?

A scurrying rat drew his attention away from this critical question. The rats knew things. They knew when it was feeding time for the convict in their midst. When they judged this time to be near they came out for the occasion. They assembled gradually in the corners and nether regions of the prison cell, chattering and squeaking anonymously until their numbers were great enough. Then, emboldened by their head count, they came forth. Not all at once. First came the scouts, such as the fellow he'd just spotted, who dashed out, established that the enemy was as puny as ever, then gave the go-ahead for the massed advance. They were well organised. He'd heard them marshalling their forces for some time now. And sure enough there came then the scrape of metal on stone as his food pan came whizzing through the gap beneath the door, quickly losing inertia, immediately under attack. By the time the yam chop missile had halted, half a hundred squirming rats were riding it. He had no idea what would happen if he tried to oppose them. They looked tough. They regarded him viciously as they ate. He didn't want the disgusting food in any case.

The sun was vacating the sky. The gate to night fears was squeaking open. He went to the tunnel, to his picture postcard view. Before light had vanished he'd checked half a dozen times on the hawser and the gang plank, and had seen that both were still in place, and had, on the sixth occasion also seen smoke – a thick black smear of smoke such as the *Darling* would make when getting up steam. And he throbbed with the wound of desertion. They were going. They had fixed the rudder, and were going without him. The redoubtable Logan was running out, leaving his fellow Englishman to rot. How the hell could he do that and live with his conscience? James spotted the flaw in the argument at once. Logan's conscience had probably not been exposed to the facts. Logan might well think he *had* done it. He should have told the man, straight, that he hadn't killed Antera. But at the time he'd found Logan's line of questioning absolutely outrageous; unworthy of so much as a denial. A crushing blow to his confidence.

A tin mug containing water was the next gift from the outside. This he grabbed, and held into his chest. This was precious. This he craved. He took a gulp then put the mug on the floor within his perimeter of defence. The rats watched. Their sharp little eyes watched the man. They formed into groups; sat on their rumps, elongated their bodies and avidly discussed the circumstances. They knew things, those rats. Was it his death they were contemplating? He thought it might be. He laughed briefly and the sound made a circuit of the bare stone walls and came back as though from the mouth of an idiot. 'Idiot,' he said into the closing gloom. 'Idiot.' The rats agreed. A foot-long centipede with nippers like canine teeth, crawled under the door in time to agree.

He was an idiot for having allowed himself in the first place to become an accessory in the experiment in depth. He should have been much stronger. He should have heeded the brilliant warning he'd received on first entering Mammy Yellowbelly's dream factory. Jemmy Honesty's fair warning that one more step would be one too many. He'd taken the irreversible, foolhardy step; then compounded his foolishness night after night, while the insatiable typewriter put it into print; every fumble, every fabulous, idiot, record-breaking erection, every slurp and grunt. Sexual hallucinations. All scholastically described in didactic Latin. Proof of dream synchronicity. How crazy and demeaning it all seemed now.

Darkness slid in. What could be seen now? Black. Whether he held his eyes open or closed: black. A terrible thing is this visual mono-diet of utter darkness, because it is the perfect nutrition for fear. Little specks of fear like germ-plasm or RNA floating free in this primordial soup – tiny, improbable proto-plasmic globules – urged by means of some mystical evolu-tionary urge to grow, begin to grow, and to grow molars and incisors and hair on their backs, and hooded eyes. It doesn't take long for them to put on weight and come looking for a better meal.

James was consumed by a monstrous fear, not for himself, but for Jenny. It took him, bit by bit. He saw her in a hundred situations of awful danger; progressively worsening situations growing out of the blackness with such unwholesome reality that he beat his fists against the heavy door, raging.

But the blackness was as merciless as his keepers. After fear had killed him, and anger buried him, he sank into night's incorporeal swamp like a decomposing corpse, absorbed, asleep, dreaming dreams of hopelessness.

Jenny came to him, but with no proximal warmth. She hovered untouchably like the chill small face of a winter moon. She had nothing to say, but he sensed that she needed help. In fact, her face implored him to help. But he didn't know what to do. He struggled slowly and dumbly to devise a scheme of assistance. But he had forgotten how to assist, if he had ever known. Indeed, the very world he was in had forgotten how to assist. It was a mess; a laborious, unsolvable mess in which no one knew their role. He was bewildered. She was lost. Wayward King Sam knew a few things, but he had taken a vow of silence.

A large and furry rat, with claws that gripped like tacks, had taken advantage of James's sleep. It was perched in his face, seated with its anus on his open mouth and its long, lusty worm-length of tail rooted in his gullet. James swiped at it in a reflex of horror; grabbed it and hurtled it against the wall. He gagged and growled with bile, and bolted upright, yelling and flailing. 'Jenny,' he shouted, then realised that she was nowhere near, and that his bed was stone and his only companion a skeleton. He was awake. He was shivering as though lying on ice. His name, or something resembling it, was being called.

'Jems. Jems. Wake it up. Jems.'

'Who is it?' he whispered through a gullet clogged with bile.

'Dis is de friend.'

That was a relief. He needed a friend, desperately. 'Which friend? Where are you?'

'I knew de man, Rory one time. He be'd good man. We friend. Dat's right.'

'You knew him?' It was an effort to keep the tremble out of his voice. 'How can I believe that?'

'You ain got no other way, see. You better believe dat.'

Evidence that this was so was on every side. James rubbed his eyes and wrenched himself stiffly from the floor. There was a deep chill in his gut; a cold so possessive that it had taken hold of his entire length. He felt horribly dizzy, and not ready for this. Not ready for midnight contemporaries of Great-great-grandfather, friendly or not.

'Sorry bout de rat tail.'

'*You* did that? Shit.'

'It was dat or de centipede bite. You sleep like de dead man here.'

'Where are you?' And, 'Who are you?'

'I'm Run Run. I'm here by de windah. Come over here. I dont wan no shout.'

James did as instructed. He could see a faint and milky flow of moon towards which he advanced. He came to the hole in the wall, and peered down it and sure enough, saw a man's face at the other end. The moonlight was brilliant, silver on black. Glinting at the end of the tunnel was great age, great sagacity.

'Run Run?'

'Dat's me, sah.'

Of course, it was inevitable. There could be no conclusion without such mediation as Run Run the magician could provide. Disbelief slunk away. 'I've read about you.' James said. 'Rory was my great-great-grandfather. He wrote about you.'

'He was de good man, for sure.'

'Yes. I think so too.'

'Did he write down all de truth? Did he tell de whole story to de end?'

'He tried but he wasn't believed. He was imprisoned.'

'Sad for him. But dats water down de river. Now *you* isn't believed, and *you* must finish de story.'

'I didn't kill Antera.'

Run Run cackled. 'Well, I sabe dat, so why tell me? You and me, we sabe dat aint your fash to done kill dat good man. But den what? Jems, we got get you out dis place or you die here fo sure. Den what? Den wrong is de winner. Dat's no good. Where is de leopard dat can't live and can't die? Where is de father's father dat dead but not gone to rest? All de spirits dat got lost and never found de way home? You hab need fix all dis mess up. Dat's why you come back dis place, Jems. To finish de story. To make de end right. You is de one. Dat's your job.'

'*My* job?' James reflected negatively on this. 'Hold on. I gave no such undertaking. I made no such promise to myself or any one else for that matter. I can't take on such a job. I'm not qualified. And in any case, I'm in prison, as you can see, and I'm sick so nothing can be expected from me.'

The silvered features at the end of the tunnel didn't alter in expression, yet James sensed disappointment. He couldn't help that. It wasn't his fault. He made his views absolutely clear: 'I want no part of it. I've been through hell. I've had enough.'

'Enough?' said Run Run querulously.

'Yes. Look, it's nothing personal, but I've had my fill of ghosts and spirits, and of dreams. Okay? Especially of dreams that somehow convert into realities. Run Run, help me to get out of here, if you can. But don't expect anything from me in return.'

'*You* is de one we waited for.'

It was said in such a way that James felt that his friend hadn't read him yet. Perhaps his usage of English had been too complicated. He simplified his refusal: 'Run Run. You are a friend, I know it. And I would like to help you, but I can't, I haven't got power. No power, *sabe*?'

'Power?'

Run Run's inability to grasp the situation was beginning to irritate: 'Yes,' said James. 'Look at me. I'm a prisoner behind six-fucking-foot-thick walls and a door that never opens. Okay? I'm not your man.'

'I will give you dat power stuff.'

James's intention had been to explain what he lacked, not to request what he wanted. But if power was to be delegated he couldn't see the harm in some coming his way. He accepted; 'Thanks a million.'

'Hold out de hand.'

James's hands and arms had been cross-bound over his freezing abdomen. He did as instructed, staring at the pale shape of his palms.

'Close de hand.'

He closed on something about the size of a pebble; something warm. More than warm. A whole arena of noonday heat condensed into one tiny article. Yes – *power*. It sped into the veins and sinews of his forearm; into the shoulder, into the chest. Heat imparted as if by a shot of raw alcohol in the gut. All weakness vanished. All fear, cold and hunger drained away. He could hear the words of battle hymns. He knew he could do things that he could not have done before. That was Run Run's gift of power. He opened his fist and looked at his acquisition. It glowed with a little tongue of flame: 'The cowrie spirit?'

'Yes,' said Run Run. 'Wear him. Him is de over-spirit; de *ori*. Him is guide and warrior and friend. Be easy in de mind. Trust de cowrie spirit wid de big mind.'

'De big mind . . . Okay. I will. Jesus, this is incredible, and confusing. I feel like I'm still dreaming, but I know I'm not. I feel great. How do I use it?'

'Him will lead, if you say "lead". Him will help, if you say "help". Dis juju carry de big load.'

'I still don't really understand: don't *sabe*.'

'You *will* sabe,' Run Run said authoritatively. 'Now I should go another place.'

Run Run withdrew. Moonlight radiated fully into the tunnel.

'Wait . . .'

'What then now?' This said impatiently. The silvered features returned but seemed less coherent; less defined.

James hurried to say, 'But there's so much to ask you. Why must you go so quickly? You haven't told me how to use the cowrie juju properly. We haven't spoken about Jenny. She needs my help, but how can I help her now? I love her, Run Run.'

'She tricked you.'

'Yes, I know. It wasn't her fault. Something's gone wrong with her that she can't fix. Something big. She wouldn't do anything bad on purpose; she's not like that. She's really a very nice person, Run Run – when you know her like I do. She just somehow got the wrong idea, that's all.'

'Can't see no hope for dat woman. Better you leave dat woman, sah. She got de bad friend. She and dat dream soul stealer. Dat juju is de damn rocky thing. She and dat juju got de same strife.'

'Help her, Run Run, for God's sake.'

'Can't do dat.'

'She'll die here, if you don't.'

'She dead maybe already. She mess wid de soul, dat's right. De goodness all sucked out. She walk alright, and talk, yes, but de soul gone missing. You better believe dis speak.'

'If you don't help her, I won't help you.'

As to whether this declaration was heard by anyone other than himself, James did not know. He saw now that what he'd taken to be the face of Run Run was no more than reflections of

294

the accumulated cobwebs at the tunnel's end. Was that all he had ever been? He shouted into the space, 'And how the hell am I supposed to get out of here?'

Forced by the magician's absence into his previous condition of self-dependence, James grappled with that question. No answer came. After a while he lay down again and listened to the scuffle of the rats. In his hand, tightly held, was the cowrie. It seemed to have lost its vigour for the moment, and was as cool as a river pebble. Still, he felt stronger. He didn't sleep again, but stared distrustfully at the hole in the wall until it palely signalled dawn; a rainy dawn. Thunder groaned and groped its way into the depths of his cell. He drank the last of his water then threw the mug into the gap beneath the door.

Thirty-five

For the occasion of the tribunal Grandy King Sam had called out his guard. They lined the walls of Mammy Yellowbelly's dining room as though carved in postures of diminished optimism, epitomising gloom. In Jenny they engendered no good feeling. She had never seen one of these sarong-clad spear men before. King Sam had put on his admiral's uniform. He bumped his fat tummy into Jenny's abdomen in a friendly way, probably to convey to her that he wished her to be seated. So she sat. And he sat. He'd had his special chair brought into the dining room to accommodate him. It was higher by far than the mean height of the rest of the furniture, and finely made with spiral upright pieces culminating in carved human skulls. Somewhere, someone began rubbing a drum. Thunder quaked. Rain rattled on tin. Subservience deeply permeated the room. Expressing kindly indifference by means of the occasional cavernous yawn, fat Sam surveyed the assembly.

That there was to be a period of suffering was clear to Jenny. She'd had morbid expectations since the dawn. She'd awakened early, feeling fearful and oppressed – sure tidings of a crisis. The enemy was at hand and ready to take her on. She'd gathered her energies to do combat with it. She'd added a pinch of salt to the shower bucket before she stood beneath it and thoroughly doused herself. She had dressed in clean, defiant white, and had then gone down to the church, where she had prayed and meditated, quite alone, and called upon the guidance of Christ. And the Watchers – her angelic police – where close too. Then she had calmly walked back to the house: to Mammy Yellowbelly's psychic factory. The summons to appear before the king had come soon thereafter. Now things were crystallising; the bad was getting worse, and giving an accurate idea of its intentions.

She looked expressionlessly at fat King Sam. Some nasty event that pertained to her (or possibly James) would soon occur.

Logan was responsible for the delay. It was he whom they were waiting for. He arrived in a clatter of shoe leather on plank and he came into the room shaking off his raincoat. He slicked the moisture from his hair then offered a springy bow in the direction of the monarch. At this signal everyone made obeisance: all the king's soldiers; all the king's men. They kneeled on their right knees, touching the floor with their right hands, muttering solemn litanies. Even Jenny made a brief bend at the waist. She noticed in her peripheral vision Logan's glance towards her of acute concern.

Conversation in a vowel-rich language was bowled down the length of the table that separated trader from the king; conversation that went on for some time, and which included nods and significant gestures, all more or less in Jenny's direction. She noted that a certain uncomplimentary word, the meaning of which she'd learned, was being vehemently inserted into the dialogue. It was 'ifot'. Logan was becoming agitated. He'd hooked his thumb into the cross-strap of his belt where it was dragging the buckle discomfortedly about. Finally, in a gesture of ultimate exasperation, he threw up his hands.

'Jenny,' he said apologetically. 'You must be wondering what all this is about. I'm going to tell you, but I want you to keep calm and let me handle things. And whatever you do, don't address the king directly. Protocol forbids that, do you understand? That's taboo. I'm here to talk for you. Which is not a bad thing. The king has instructed me to tell you certain things, and so I will. He is very much in charge here, as you can see. It's a bad situation, lass, but I can't quite see how to get out of it for the moment. The Law, like the tide, influences life in the delta, but doesn't reach this far upriver. It never really has. We take our chances this far up the river, as I warned you.'

'Logan,' she said evenly, 'what is it that King Sam has on his mind? He's kept me waiting long enough. Has he accused me of witchcraft?'

'How did you know? Yes, that's precisely what this is all about. He claims, amongst other things, that you had a hand in Antera Duke's murder. Of course, I told him in no uncertain terms that that was utter rubbish. But I couldn't budge him.'

'That's all right, Logan. Let him think anything he wants. And in any case, in a very indirect way, I do blame myself. Perhaps I did have something to do with it.'

Logan said loudly, 'Of course you didn't.' Then in an undertone, 'You can't understand the seriousness of the matter. Our man's English is limited, but don't underestimate him, I beg you. And please don't say *anything* like that again. Here witches are killed. It's diabolical. King Sam's accusation is that serious.'

'*That* serious?'

'I'm sorry to have put it so bluntly.'

'It's a time for bluntness, Mr Logan.'

'I agree.' Logan cast a glance towards the king. 'It must appear to him as though I am merely translating, as instructed, you gather, and not evolving an escape plan, so . . .'

'But, Mr Logan, why should we be evolving an escape plan?'

'That must be plain to you. The man intends to try you for witchcraft.'

His Majesty, as predicted, aimed some loud abuse at Logan, who made a conciliatory response, then hissed at Jenny, 'Look here, I'm sticking my neck out for you. At least try to look a bit troubled.'

'If you feel that it would help my case.'

'It would look more authentic, don't you think?'

'Very well.' She gnawed at the edge of her mouth and frowned. 'Will that do?'

'You are an amazing woman. Well, the king has specifically asked that you respond to the charge. Are you a witch or not?'

'No, I'm not. Tell the buffoon that.'

Logan translated, approximately. The king looked unconvinced.

Jenny said, 'Now what?'

'Now I'll explain to you how I intend to get you off the hook. No interruptions, please. Thank you. Now, the *Darling* is standing by. Her rudder is fixed, more or less. Crow thinks she can be navigated, anyway, and we have got up steam. Now, on some pretext or other, we must get you down to the jetty. As part of your rebuttal, as it were . . . Yes, that might work. Well, once you're there, Crow and I can hold these buggers off with gunfire.'

298

'And we'll make a run for it?'

'Precisely.'

'No, thank you.'

'But, my dear – '

'Mr Logan, you are a very brave man, as is Captain Crow.'

'We're Englishmen. Our duty is clear.'

'Let me finish. There is no need for such heroics, no matter what. Such a blotting of your copybook would have a serious impact on your business. I won't have that. As I said, there isn't any need for such a massive deed of bravery. This beastly man won't kill me. He might try to but the attempt would be futile.'

Another belch of anger came from the direction of the throne.

'He wants to know what you're saying.'

'Tell him then.'

'You can't mean that.'

'I do.'

'I won't.' He didn't. That was clear. King Sam became joyful again, or at least less scowl-ridden. What he said to Logan, however, turned the trader pale. 'It's worse than I thought, lass. I think the bugger's gone off his head. God! If he does that I'll have him hanged . . .'

'If he does what, Logan?'

'No, I'll personally shoot the swine. I've half a mind to . . .' Logan's hand fleetingly brushed his pistol holster. 'No. We must keep calm.'

'I am calm.'

'He wants to subject you to an ordeal. That's what he's got in mind. I've warned him not to, but he's determined to go through with it. I always thought there was madness in the man. But *this* is incredible.' Logan inhaled several deep breaths that did nothing for his colour, then emphatically re-addressed the king.

Fat Sam reflected, then ponderously shook his head. Logan spoke passionately. The big head shook ponderously.

'Jesus!' said Logan in an appeal to the roof.

'What sort of ordeal?' Jenny enquired.

'Poison, Jen . . . God, I never thought he'd stoop to that. Despicable bastard. Poison from the ordeal tree. Its seed is made into a concoction that the accused must drink. The

299

innocent are supposed to survive it. But I've never heard of anyone surrviving it. It's barbaric. It's murder, pure and simple. And I'm not about to allow it.'

'And how would you prevent it, Mr Logan?'

'I have my Luger.'

'And how many bullets does it contain?'

'Ten rounds.'

'And more than six times that number surround us.'

'It is better to die . . .'

'No, it is not, Mr Logan. It is better to live; as I was saying to you before we were interrupted. This horrible man has no hope of killing me. I'm not a witch; not of the baby's fat and bat's blood variety, at any rate, but I don't deny that I have psychic powers. I know when things are going to happen, and especially when they are going to happen to me. Bits of futurity are available to me, and the more relevant they are, the more accessible they become. This death, this poisoned death, is not my destiny. King Sam won't manage it. Nor will I die in Africa. This I can say with absolute certainty.'

Logan set to tugging his mighty moustache as one who is too perplexed to trust his mouth with words. He barely nodded to signal that he'd heard what he had heard, and was neither willing nor prepared to believe or disbelieve, or to argue further.

'So,' said Jenny with the right degree of concern. 'Let our king do his worst. Tell him I'm ready for the ordeal.'

Logan launched into his translation. He spoke from behind his hand, as liars speak, to the king. He had a lot to say.

King Sam slapped his thigh with a report like a pistol shot. The rows of ebony knights became animated in a small way. A leaning together took place. As though touched by some obscure but elevating sentiment, they momentarily conversed. Then silence gathered again; a wait of some twenty minutes on Jenny's wristwatch, during which time she began to prepare herself to survive. With eyes shut and in silent potent prayer, she called upon the Name above all other names to hear her; to bring into this room the spell of His omnipotent force of angels. She built up in her hand the weight of a mighty sword; a flame-tipped, crusader's sword with which to scorch a defensive circle. Then she named Raphael, Gabriel, Michael and Uriel as her protectors, one at each corner of the room, and, to further empower this mighty team, said the powerful words of exorcism: *Ec-ominum Sanctorum ordini. Ex-gestis Domini Nostri Jesu Christi.*

But whereas abundant strength should have been the reward by now, she felt nothing. Nothing beyond the drip of a drop of water on her forehead, an escapee from the puddled room above. She closed her eyes and repeated the procedure.

No strength arrived; no overwhelming authority over evil. In fact, if anything, she felt weaker than she had. She became worried, then alarmed. On the third attempt to associate with the forces of light she was mocked by a voice that she recognised at once.

'Will you please shut up, woman. Where do you think all that crap is going to get you?'

'So it's you,' she said. '*You're* doing this to me.'

'I'm just small fry – remember?'

'Don't mock me.'

'It's illogical to think you're being mocked. You're being exalted. You've worked towards this day. Well, now it's here! Your initiation day. You deserve the distinction. You're going to have to face up to your examiners all on your own though, so please stop wailing for help. Your god doesn't hang out around here, and the ones who do aren't interested in your opinion.'

'I'll survive the ordeal.'

'Well, I think you've got the wrong idea. Survival is not what you asked for. You asked for secret knowledge. And seeing that you already own quite a bit more of that than the average person does, it follows that to give you more requires quite a spectacular effort. I've gone to a lot of trouble to lay this on. This is a celebration. Today your body becomes spirit and your spirit becomes *family*! A magic of astonishing complexity, laid on at no cost. Are you getting the picture? It's all waiting for you there at the table; at Mammy Yellowbelly's table.'

'You can't mean that. That wouldn't be knowledge. That would be injury. No, I won't accept that, you can't expect that.'

'I'm disappointed in you,' said the Dream Stealer. 'Injury is knowledge. Melancholy is knowledge. Hopelessness is knowledge. Suffering is knowledge. How else can one find one's self? And besides, it's not all doom and gloom. There are compensations. Antera's there. He'll love you strenuously. And the feasting never stops.'

'This is utterly sordid.'

'Sordid?' came the reply. 'What is sordid is to attribute to me what you've brought about yourself. I'm merely your willing collaborator. You enrolled in my syllabus, woman; this is what I teach. Stop objecting.'

'I don't object to death,' she said. 'I object to premature death. Let me go.'

'I think it's too late. King Sam's become involved. But don't take it so hard. Peace comes with understanding, and you don't yet understand. You're still so wrapped up in the grand myth of superiority of Life that you can't see the merit of Death. It's just a passing phase. You'll change . . . Need I say that you'll *have* to?'

'I know the rules,' she interrupted. 'The innocent survive.'

'There! You've brought your argument round in a circle. I'm not saying that it's a bad thing to repeat yourself, mind you. It's just that there isn't enough time. Don't be so inflexible. It's getting you nowhere. Sam has found you guilty. And Sam is the Law. It's really quite unreasonable of you to contest the very Law. It would be more heroic to confess. Spit it out. Right now they see you as a coward. Confess. Stand tall and confess, and they'll see you as a martyr. You have to ask yourself: which is the grander way to die?'

'I won't confess to something – '

'You haven't heard me,' said the incubus irritably. 'Oh well, when you have deaf ears, then deafness isn't a fault. I understand. I wish you great knowledge.'

'But I'm *not* guilty,' she protested. 'You *know* that. If you could see into my mind you'd know that. You'd find no guilt.'

'I thought I'd made that clear. I am in your mind. All of us at the table are in your mind. And we're *all as guilty as hell* . . . That's it. Time's up.'

A giant bird – or what at first glance appeared to be so, but was no doubt a human completely dressed in feathers, had come into the room. Its head was a wooden mask with carved, ovate eye holes outlined with white, and a ferocious curved beak. It squawked and cavorted. It pecked the table, once, twice, three times, as a bird in search of grain. King Sam smacked his thigh.

The bird-man danced, or flapped around the room. And, as Jenny knew it would, came to a stop at her chair.

She had forgotten the presence of Logan until his hand clamped on her shoulder: 'Steady, girl. Say the word and I'll shoot the damned thing here and now, and have done with it.'

'Logan,' she said. 'I'm scared.'

'I'm here, girl. I'm at your command. My God, you're trembling.'

'I've been a bit of a fool.'

'No need to die because of it.'

'Don't let them harm James.'

'You're my only concern right now. You're – '

Logan's words were obliterated, smothered in a mush of damp feathers. The intrepid hand grip was also forcibly detached. The thing had shoved itself between Logan and herself, and drawn its wing over her head. Her nostrils flared on the gunpowder stink of raw armpit. She'd become a struggling prisoner; a hopelessly pinioned, squirming, asphyxiating prisoner. The draught was administered. It was expertly done. Her mouth, gasping for air, took in a shock of fluid. She choked. She gagged. She swallowed. Then she was released. Not much of the draught had been taken in, a spoonful perhaps. It tasted like coffee – Turkish coffee; not unpleasant, not deadly. But within seconds it had dried her mouth; dried it like a desert; like a corpse. Yes, like death. She thought about death then: about its visionary magnificence; its inflood of creative power and realms of ineffable purity. Or was it a place at the riotous table of Mammy Yellowbelly, quaffing mimbo, forever and ever. Was death in Creek Town something unique? Something quite beyond the European equivalent?

'Well,' said the Dream Stealer. 'I expect you're glad that doctor's over and done with.'

'Am I dying?'

'Look upon it as living again. New life as one of us.'

'What will happen to James?'

'Stupid question. His place at the table has never been in doubt. Which you knew from the outset, and warned him about. He is the incarnation of the first Cursed, so naturally his time is up, too.'

The bird-thing, the poisoner, Doctor Death, had made a few

more curcuits of the room, cackling and pecking and waggling its rooster-like rump. Its feathers hissed. It was pleased with itself. King Sam rewarded it with a punch to the throat, and it exited, squawking.

Suddenly her saliva was back. She was swamped with it. It filled the cavity of mouth; she couldn't swallow it quickly enough. It foamed over her chin, then revoltingly spilled onto the white cloth of her dress. Logan's face, concentrated with desperate indecision, came into view.

'Logan.' Her tongue had sluggardly expanded, and was still growing; fully filling her gullet as a snail fills its shell. 'Logan . . . get me water.'

'Water makes it worse,' warned the Dream Stealer.

Unbelievable thirst possessed her. She placed her hand on Logan's, or thought that was what she had done. There was no confirming feeling of touch. 'Water.'

Logan shouted an instruction.

'Logan,' she said, 'do something else for me?'

'Anything, Jen.'

'There is a brass cross upstairs . . . God, it's hard . . . talk . . . Getting harder to breathe, Logan.'

'Do you want the cross?'

She nodded. Saliva swilled out.

'I'll get it, lass.'

'It's in the . . .'

'Shush. I'll find it.'

Thirty-six

A thunder-beaten dawn, diluted with rain. Its aspirations were low. It crept like a miser through the hole in the wall and limped across the floor. James didn't care to greet it, but, as there was nothing better to do, he went towards the tragic light. What could it tell him, this wetted, dismal air? Nothing. Bugger all. He peered into it anyway; down the tunnel and over the roofs. He was surprised that he could see as far as that; as far as the roofs of Creek Town. The rain could be all-obliterating, and usually was so. The desperate chill had relinquished its hold, and he felt better than he had for days. He stretched, massaged his aching neck, scratched more or less his entire body, made a comb of his fingertips and ran them through this hair, all the while maintaining his watch. He also came across the cowrie shell. It was dangling from his neck by its leather thong, just as Rory had worn it a century before. *Him will help if you say help.* He fervently said, 'Help.' He took it off and regarded it pessimistically; turned it onto its spotted rump and blew into its mouth. It made an ooo-sound from his breath but otherwise showed no awareness of his presence or inclination to co-operate. So he hung it back in place.

In order to do these things he'd had to transfer his attention from exterior to interior for a while, perhaps for five or ten seconds. No more time than that could have passed before he took up his old position. But in that interval there had come about a marvellous transition from saturation to sunshine. That was how eccentric the weather was here. He gained clear vision all the way to the jetty. And lo! The *Darling* was still there, tied to her bollard, belching filthy smoke.

Faith returned. Possibilities blossomed. Large quests seemed smaller. James felt the need for reckless action. He micturated angrily against the wall, as though trying to drill a hole in the stone, then set off to pace the cell. It was almost breakfast-time and the rats were gathering; their scouts were out and about, crisscrossing the floor, making a terminal of the gap beneath the door.

The *gap* beneath the door.

He crouched and studied it. He lay on his shoulder with his temple pressed hard to the stone and gazed into the slot, and beyond it; and saw more stone – a bare platform of stone upon which his warder would have to stand when delivering the food dish, and whose ankles and feet would be frustratingly visible while so doing.

Frustration ended. A practical plan hatched from its broken shell. What he would have to do in order to get out of there became absolutely clear to him at that moment. The tools he would require were at hand. His friend, the skeleton, possessed them – a set of leg irons.

It wasn't in James's nature willingly to cause damage to anything; it just wasn't in him. So he went about the task of taking off the riveted cuffs gingerly, and with kindness. It caused him anguish therefore when an entire foot disintegrated; simply came apart and dropped off. He apologised. He explained his desperate position, then went for the opposite cuff. A slightly different, but equally disquieting result: the leg; the tibia and fibula disengaged from the knee with a clatter. God, he felt awful. With one cuff free but the other still entangled in leg bones he inadvertently stood on a hand, quite crushing it, and worse still, causing disequilibrium amongst the structures of the neck and thorax. A clavicle drooped disconcertingly. And was he imagining it, or did the lower jaw also look more dispirited than before? Anyway, the cuff was almost free. James couldn't bear the thought of breaking the remaining foot, so he worked it in the opposite direction, towards the pelvis. Disaster. Ligaments as yet unsevered caused strain to progress from hip to spine to cranium. It was awful to watch.

By the time James had finished looting his erstwhile companion, the job of demolition was substantial. However, he had in his possession the heavy piece of chain upon which his hopes rested. It was about a yard long and stiff with rust. He lashed it against the wall a few times to make it flexible and get its feel. But there wasn't much time for practice. The rats advised him of that. They'd formed into talkative ranks near the door. Excitement plucked his innards. He lowered himself to the floor and gained the appropriate, one-eyed view, laid out the leg irons to his rear, then waited.

The wait was short.

A naked pair to feet and ankles made their appearance. James lashed at them with the chain. The object was encircle-ment and entrapment of that part of the warder's extremities. The plan, as conceived, was that the free end of the chain would, having captured the man's feet, swing on this axis and return into the cell, there to be grasped and tightly pulled. A trap, and painful one, too. He would have held on until a deal had been struck. In theory, that was it. A desperate but multi-flawed plan.

One of its flaws was instantly exposed. The throw was poorly angled. Instead of winding itself around the man's foot and returning to its sender, the chain with its heavy cuff hit a naked row of toes full on, and stopped dead. There was a yelp of surprise and pain from that side of the door. The tray was dropped. James retrieved the leg irons, wondering what would be the result of his attack. Retribution seemed inevitable.

James stood, breathing heavily, awaiting the inevitable. He was not afraid. He assumed he would be beaten up again. This seemed unavoidable. He drew back in order to put space between himself and the expected assailants, then changed his mind and took up position at the edge of the door. How many of them would there be? Two at least, probably more. He would fight them. No matter how many of them came for him, he would not go down without a fight. There was the chain, the yard-long series of links with its heavy terminal cuffs that had failed him the first time round, but might still come in handy. He tested it, swinging it viciously. He could do damage with this thing, he thought, then stood lightly, crouched, ready.

There were four of them. They came in a bunch, moving quickly with concerted aggression as though they'd planned it so. They would find him and fall on him *en masse*, and wallop the shit out of him with the clubs in their hands. They did not

307

find him where they expected him to be: cringing against the furthest wall. They didn't find him at all until he'd swung the chain and cracked open the nearest skull. He didn't have any luck with the other skulls. They were ducking and weaving in avoidance of his weapon now, though he did make contact with someone's forearm with good effect. As he'd expected it would, the business became one-sided after that. Their blows began to tell; to thud into his body and hurt deeply. They grunted with effort. Sticks rose and fell, swished and thudded. His neck was struck and jagged pain impaled him to his hips. A voice from his interior cried out: 'They're going to kill you, fight on.' He lashed out again, at no particular target and by chance the blow was deadly. One of them gasped and reeled back, clutching the meat of his face. His attackers, reduced to two, came forward warily, feinting with their sticks, herding him into a corner. He was struck again. A rib high in his chest gave way; gave entry to sudden numbness. An arm ceased to work and this was more serious still. He fought on, the lower part of his face making noises of defiance. He did not recognise the voice as his own, but let it continue. It would soon be over. Soon he and his voice would be shut out from the present. One more small victory: a left-handed swing with his fist that overbalanced James but also achieved the impossible and met with the enemy. Then something awful happened inside his head.

Thoughts scurried like crabs on a rock, stopping and starting for no apparent reason. Planless, random, jerky fits of small thoughts doing this and that. Waves swelling, rolling in, breaking. Big and little thoughts surging and scrabbling sequentially over dark rocks that seemed to have no purpose but to represent hard pain. Sharp pain. He could not feel pain but sensed that he was surrounded by it; overwhelmed by it. It had put him where he was. It was dominant. Amid it, thoughts came and went.

Run Run flowed into this crisis in face and voice: 'It was de good fight.'

'I'm hurt.'

'You done good.'

'Help me.'

'Help yourself. You got de power.'

A leopard snarled softly: pink mouthed; sharp toothed. The wooden man danced jerkily, creaking with laughter.

'Finish de story,' said Run Run. 'Dat's why you become to dis place. Finish de story. Make de end right.'

'I don't know how.'

'No one other pusson can do it. You is de one.'

Grinning fat Sam slapped his thigh. Jenny, as pale as death, pleaded, 'James, help me. James, I love you. I love you.'

Mind pictures that came and went, flowed then died, their space instantly re-occupied. What was real, and becoming more so, was his relationship with pain. The hard rock on which he lay had mutated into his body, which was becoming recognisable by degrees. His neck, his limbs, his head; all dubiously attached and giving massive offence. He became the James Tremayne he knew, with a groan, and sat up. A grating noise in his chest produced sensational agony. Nevertheless it was *his* chest and it was up to him to cope with it and all the other bits and pieces attached to it. He made groping efforts with his arms and legs and raised himself.

Now here was something to be seriously observed and with wonderment, fear and awe. The cell door was fully open. Light had access; such light as had been locked out while he had been imprisoned. The entire cell was disclosed. He bent again to examine the floor more closely and saw that what he'd imaginatively supposed to be a column of ants on the move, was just that. It was a swathe; a glistening black swathe that began at the hole in the wall and broadened as it advanced. It bisected the cell and exited at the door. An empire of insect warriors on the march. Of the warders there remained but one, and he, lying fully in the path of the driver ants, was not the man he used to be. The intolerant invaders had taken out one eye, and God knows what else was going on beneath the writhing black carpet. Even as James watched they snipped the other eye loose and carried off the trophy towards the door. They were not silent, their tweezered bodies and billions of feet were hissing with triumphant movement. They were incontestable and they knew it.

James knew it. He drew back hard against the wall. He'd never seen or heard of anything like this, but common sense told him that at some stage the last of them would arrive. And that if he could remain undetected for that long, he would survive.

It took almost an hour for this assumption to be proved true. The tail end of the grand army passed by, leaving their meal half eaten. James stepped over the semi-skeleton of his former jailer as the last half-inch warrior scurried off. Ahead lay a descending flight of stone stairs; a passage, a series of doors, then freedom. He took it at speed and found himself in the ruins of the old fort. No one was in sight. No one to hear the clap of his escapee boot-heels but a group of agile monkeys.

Everything, every part of him, did its best to slow and disorganise him. Mauled nerves screamed. There was crisis in his legs. He gave them no favours as he scrambled through the jungle, slithered, fell, and occasionally ran in the direction of Mammy Yellowbelly's noxious house. By simple measurement the distance was not great. In terms of pain the route was formidable. A squall of rain deluged the track and beat him into the mud, but was advantageous to him, too. It absorbed him, bleaching him into its fabric. It permitted him to arrive unnoticed by the sentry at the door, then covered the creak of his footsteps on the old wooden floor, and saw him safely all the way to Jenny's room.

Logan was there, digging into the drawers of her cabin trunk. The two men saw each other simultaneously.

'My God,' said Logan. 'It's you.'

James came fully into the room. His comment was equally as inept: 'I escaped.'

'I think Jenny's dying.'

A passion for violence was still on the boil. James flew at Logan and in that instant realised just how weak he'd become. Logan caught his wrists and pinioned them with ease, then spoke bitterly into James's face. 'Look, it wasn't my fault.'

'You *promised*.'

'I know. But there was nothing I could do. What the hell do you want to fight *me* for? I tried. I failed. She insisted. I couldn't get through to her, couldn't sway her. She's simply the most stubborn woman I've ever known. Damn it, we're wasting time.'

'Let me go, you fool.'

Logan opened his fingers. He said, 'She sent me to her room to fetch a cross. A brass cross. I can't find it.'

'That because it's in *my* room.'

Logan stared at him furiously. 'Then get it, man, before it's too late.'

Both men rushed to the door. In the passage James asked: 'Why is she dying?'

The very question that lay unanswered in Logan's mind. He shook his head. But, as James deserved a reply, he focused on events rather than causes. 'Because she made a drastic mistake. And because King Sam ordained it . . . By the way, old man, you've got leeches all over your face and arms. Did you know that?'

'No.' Nor did he care.

The cross was where he had left it. In fact, everything in James's room was as he'd left it. His sun helmet, his change of clothes. The hands of his portable alarm clock pointed incorrectly to noon, and a spider's web trailed from the barrel of his rifle. These were the only indications of his absence. He snatched up the cross and gave it to Logan, who at once turned to leave.

'Logan,' said James, 'I'm going to kill the fucker.'

'King Sam? Are you up to it? You look totally knackered. Mind you, he is exactly due for death.'

'I'm going to do it now.'

That would make the ending right. Run Run would approve. Yes. That was unquestionably how things should be settled.

A small boy bearing a calabash on his head stepped warily into the room. Water. He came on with the serenely balanced cargo, letting his eyes glide over the assembled elders. Eyewhites that were moons of enquiry came finally to settle on Jenny.

Logan was next to arrive. He had the cross. He was holding it before him as in a scriptural illustration. His strides were wide. He overtook the water bearer. 'There,' he said to Jenny, manoeuvring her hand; closing her fingers on the artefact. 'There.' He raised her forearm. Theo's brass cross lay imbedded in her grip.

A massive belly cramp kicked her forward.

'Steady,' said Logan. The cross had spilled from her grasp. He retrieved it and again locked her fist around it. There was amazing empathy in his touch.

The twin moons were nearer, much nearer. She was in their sphere of knowledge. The little boy shone with knowledge. Where had he come from, this little provider? This was no mere carrier of water, yet it was by means of the little one's hand that she drank. A gourd appeared and, held steady, was rested on the pad of her lower lip. Cool. Cool. Magically cool, its contents fell upon the terrors and dismay. 'Thank you.' She spoke with the mind, and the shining eyes blinked in a signal of recognition. 'Thank you.' she said to the Lords of Light. 'Thank you for my little black saviour.'

Ineffable calm. This was the ingredient of the gourd. This was the gift of Run Run. She drank more. The calm deepened; rippled outwards, cleansing as it went.

'Well,' said the Dream Stealer scathingly. 'That's just like Run Run: always meddling in affairs that have nothing to do with him. Yoruba was the same, and look where it got her . . . Mind you, you've got to admire his cheek: sending his minion into the very lion's den. The boy's got guts, too.'

'I'm stronger now.'

'No. You just *feel* stronger. Temporary magic. It won't change things. Sam's poison is rough stuff.'

'I have the cross.'

'A chunk of brass. A contemptible cult, and of no use when you're in a fix. Did He of Sunday help poor old Theo when he called on him? Not a bit. Get it into your head: He's not at all reliable. I haven't seen Him around here for a long, long time, and as for archangels and flaming swords – what can I say? It's been tried before . . . Look, be sensible. It's all arranged. Everyone expects you to die, even Run Run. It's time you came along.'

And in confirmation of this her respiratory distress increased. Her lungs were willing to take air; no blame could be attached to her lungs. Nor were her chest muscles at fault. They were labouring. They were trying. But cast-iron fingers had a good grip on her ribs, had her in an immovable hug.

More of Run Run's potion; his temporary magic. Panic fled.

Hope came pallidly to take its place; temporary hope. The cast-iron suffocation persevered; and had, in fact, expanded its action. Now it was killing her head. But she was still inquisitive. Why had her spirit guides – the Watchers – let her down? Why had she not been forewarned of this toxic trial? Had she inadvertently entered the blind spot of their vision, or were they merely fallible?

The Dream Stealer said encouragingly, 'Don't ask now. Wait.'

'I have to know why King Sam is so determined to kill me.'

'You can't blame him. Sam's afraid of you. You've been interfering with the past, and in a clumsy way. You're a dangerous woman. He's scared to offend you, so he wants to put you comfortably out of the way: at the table with Jemmy Honesty and Mammy Yellowbelly, and poor old Antera. It's getting crowded, but who cares. There's plenty for everyone.'

'You tricked me.'

'Not at all.'

'You said you respected me; that you were my new direction. You said you'd be sorry to see me dead.'

'I do. I am . . . And as for "sorry", like any other word it comes in different sizes. My sorrow was greater while you were alive. And remember, I promised you knowledge, not life. And I intend to keep my word. The hurt is temporary, but knowledge is the privilege of eternity. Now you see the beauty of the idea.'

'I am *not* going to die.'

She hardly believed that, however. Run Run's marvellous sedative was doing little to inhibit the advance of destruction, and she was aware of the onset of something less than life. And Sam, himself, had come down from his throne to find out personally how things were progressing. His face, roundly distorted, with a speculative finger up one nostril, loomed into view. Jenny stabbed the cross in that direction with all the strength she could command, or thought that was what she had done.

The hand that held the crucifix did move, but not with the perceived velocity. Its course was wobbly, but more or less as intended, so that King Sam was ultimately confronted by the upheld Christian symbol. He saw the joke. An uproarious wind of mirth broke from him, and the sound fell on Jenny with force. She held her position, her hand upheld: the doubted and mocked symbol of faith. And between alternating surges of clear vision and blindness, she perceived a startling result.

It was as though a meteorite had struck King Sam. There was a clap of thunder; a stunning, sudden concussion of Godlike magnitude that hurtled the huge man backwards over the breadth of the table. Then a series of lesser reports that had nothing to do with God, but with Logan, emptying his pistol this way and that, cursing triumphantly as he did. She was hauled about. Her view became that of the floor, upon which lay sprawled several men, contorted and groaning amid gouache patterns of red, much red. Then nothing.

The voice of the Dream Stealer entered this void: 'King Sam's dead. Oh, he won't like that. He's not the sort. He's really not the sort.'

'A miracle. Dear God, a miracle.'

'An unexpected event, I agree. And just as you hit him with the cross. I'm impressed.'

'Jenny . . . Jenny . . .'

James's voice. 'Jenny . . . *Jenny*.' As though from the opposite cliff of a canyon; as though warped by ground and sky, dropped into abysses, salvaged by breezes, uncannily surviving despite impossible odds, came the voice of James: 'You . . . will . . . not die . . . Hear me . . . You will *not* die.'

'I love you, James.' No strength to emit the words. She sped them from her mind: 'I love you.'

'I love *you*,' came the echo.

'You're really hanging on,' said the Dream Stealer, 'which is *so* silly. Come on over. I love you, too. Let go. Come on in. There's no place like this place.'

James's voice-link was weakening perceptibly; fading, as a shadow fades at dusk when all is shadow, and all is lost: 'We're going to get to the *Darling*. We're going to get there somehow, and then to Calbar.'

'A deliberate lie,' snapped the Dream Stealer. 'You're staying here. I've made promises.'

'Then home,' said James.

'Home is at the table,' said the Dream Stealer. 'With Mammy Y, and Jemmy and Antera, and now, thanks to you, fat Sam. I see you're close. Come on.'

'I think she's had it,' said Logan gravely. He took his hand from her pulse. 'I'm sorry, old man.' He fired a shot at something hidden from James, then said, 'Damn it. Missed the blighter.'

James broke the action of the John Wilkes, threw out the used brass and reloaded with two new shells. He had the hang of it now. A measure of care was needed when firing, for both left and right triggers could be pulled at once, resulting in simultaneous discharge of both barrels; as had occurred when he'd shot King Sam. He said, 'She's not dead, Logan. I know it. Can you manage her?'

'Easily.' Truthfully, Logan did not consider the load across his shoulder to be beyond him. He felt marvellously strong: a Hercules, a Lysander.

'Have you more ammunition, Logan?'

'A few rounds.'

'Conserve them. I'll go out first and knock down anyone who gets in the way. I've a pocket full of bullets.'

'All right, old man. It's been good knowing you.'

'Don't talk like that, Logan.'

'Quite so. Defeatist.'

'It's barely half a mile to the jetty.'

'An absolute jaunt.'

'Are you ready?'

'As ready as I'll ever be . . . *There's that boy again.*'

It was Monday, the calabash bearer, who had discarded his vessel, and now held under his arm a wooden carving; a small and inimically ugly little man.

'Oi! That's mine,' said James accusingly. 'You took that from Jenny's case, didn't you?'

What else Monday was holding was a large, spike-headed battle-axe. He looked willing to defend his acquisition with it. Squaring his small shoulders, tightening his grip on both weapon and carving, he came on down the stairs.

James's objection to the theft of the Dream Stealer wasn't solid. A momentary principle; a fragment of distaste for what was actually a most meritorious act. 'Keep the bloody thing,' he said. 'Logan, tell the lad he's welcome to it. It's good riddance.'

Logan caused the boy's cheeks to crease into a grin. Monday returned the favour.

'What a stroke of luck,' Logan said. 'He's offered to show us a hidden short cut to the landing.'

Not so much luck as sheer impetuousness. Just the sort of rash decision one might expect from a smallish boy with a largish battle axe, obsessed with legends of heroism. Just the sort of obtuse mentality that Run Run had been trying, unsuccessfully, to knuckle out of that young cranium for years.

If only the white men could have heard the cries, threats and anguished protestations that were at that moment filling the air; the warnings and profanities. They would have been shaken to the core. But they didn't; they couldn't. And so the abduction of the little wooden fetish doll proceeded, un-checked. Monday, of course, could hear every word, and was so delighted by the Dream Stealer's dismay, that he giggled out loud. This caused the two foreigners to pause and regard the boy with shared concern. It was not a time for flippancy. The dangers were huge and obvious, and they might have sent Monday packing had the prospect of being shown a short cut to the *Darling* not been so thoroughly appealing. In any event, they went on, as one.

They came onto the balcony. A spear hurtled by an unseen arm embedded itself in the door frame, twanging. A drum was beating; kicking up a fervid rhythm – *boom-boom-boom* – stirring the air with warlike shocks. The jungle was wailing with fear and sadness, and though there was no doubt that the sound was of human origin, it had to be thought that something beyond human ken was purging those tormented throats. A tyrant had fallen. How many lives would be sacrificed to accompany his soul? Did they imagine that worse was to follow? Had all hope fled the earth?

James fired at nothing; at the trees, at the sound arising from the totality of green. A warning, he hoped, to those hidden there, of the potency of his weapon. The pop of a bubble might have achieved more. The ululation formed into human shapes, here then gone; darting transparently from shadow to shadow, leaping, bounding, raising their awful sound. Ephemera, impossible to shoot at, but shooting at him. Arrows, as thin as straws, flew, chirping like sparrows. 'Poisoned,' was Logan's only comment.

'I forgot the manuscript.' James was aiming the .470 when that precise thought caused him to halt his action, turn and dash back into the house. He took the stairs three at a stride, and kept up that pace until he'd reached his room and gathered Rory's precious document. Then he turned to leave.

Jemmy Honesty was barring the door. What could pass as a grin was moving an unscarred portion of cheek, and in his good hand he was holding a long pistol. He spoke. 'Jenny's with us,' he said in his laconic way. 'She's at the table now. I came to tell you that.' And for as long as it took to say those words he remained visible.

James ran through the vacated space; ran until he'd regained his friends on the balcony. The boy was laughing again, chuckling as if privy to some amazing source of humour. He tweaked the cowrie shell hanging in the V of James's open shirt, then made off.

They followed Monday out into the open, where by all the laws of warfare they should have died before they'd taken ten paces. Logan, with Jenny cast over his shoulders like a sack, was incapable of speed. He jogged a few steps, then walked, then jogged again, grunting at each pace. They should have died there and then, but didn't, because something wonderful occurred. The air became translucent around them. An opalescent screen composed of avidly fluttering wings billowed out of the tree line and came over the fugitives, immersing them in bronze, soaking the entire jungle in that single shimmering colour: butterflies. Butterflies choking the air. Butterflies in the eyes and in the nostrils, in front and behind and under and above. Butterflies, shutting out the sky and obscuring the land. The great migration of painted ladies. A natural biological event. Oh, but how glorious, how welcome. How divinely coincidental.

Monday gave a yell, threw the Dream Stealer up high and caught it, then turned and beckoned. Logan galloped on like an old draught-horse after the boy. The heat of the cowrie juju had become perceptible again. Yes, here was magic. Here was a whole skyful of magic.

*

Yoruba, in her detested leopard body, did not lose the fleeing trio. The butterflies were irrelevant. The human scent was rich on the ground; a trail of messages along which she loped on silent feet. Her eyes glowed yellow. Her tail tip was upwards bent. If opposed in her task she would kill. In fact, killing was on her mind. The thing to do was to get ahead of the abductors of the dream soul stealer, then lie in ambush. Then kill.

Thirty-seven

From his high post on the bridge of the *Darling*, Captain Crow saw the thick, bronze ribbon of butterflies and cursed. He hated this pointless annual clogging of the air. He hated all fervid insects and animals; anything, in fact, that acted with hidden purpose. Lolling animals he could tolerate; hippos, for example, he shot at but without hate. Snakes provided unsatisfactory targets. Bats, monkeys, bushbuck, and certain forms of river fish that made *ng-ng* noises on dark nights, he detested. Parrots drove him to distraction. He took up his telescope and rammed it to his eye. 'Bloody butterflies,' he confirmed, then snapped the instrument shut. He passed the next few minutes musing on the practicability of torching the entire riverine margin in an effort to eliminate its various pestilences. The butterflies, he noted, seemed set on a confrontational flight path. The smoke the *Darling* was emitting would, at least, account for a couple of million of the foe.

He called for a gin and tonic, and also spoke gruffly into the brass-mouthed voice-pipe that would shoot his ire deep into the engine room. He enquired as to the pressure of the boiler, and was given this information after a short delay. He swore into the mouthpiece, then swore towards the shore. Logan was taking too long. He was supposed to have returned hours ago with the woman – whatever her name was . . . It was a bad thing to remember women's names. Inevitably it led to attempts to remember other things about them – how they walked; how they held themselves; the tone and size of their breasts; the width of hip; the depth of hip; the general lovability of hip, and so on . . . The net result of such imaginings was more likely than not to result in disturbed siestas and wearying semi-erections. There were better things to do than remember women's names.

319

The G and T arrived concurrently with the advance aviators, several of which immediately assembled on the rim of the tumbler and uncoiled their long tongues. Crow observed the painted ladies with vaguely scientific intent. What if the path finders could be alcoholically induced into taking a wrong direction? Would mass extermination ensue? This line of thought was aborted, for at that moment, his attention was drawn to the shore. Not just drawn, but riveted to it. For there amongst the low scrub, he felt sure he'd glimpsed the stalking figure of a leopard . . . By Jove! Yes. Absolutely. Shoulders low and hunched – bellied into the ground in between the ferns and the streaks of low mist. Gone. No. There it was again. A full-grown, magnificent beast.

He could hardly believe his luck.

The bronze-winged screen was thinning. As they approached the lake the collective instinct of this species was to gain height. And so they did. They formed a living bridge from bank to bank, which at its apogee caressed the mast tip of the *Darling*.

James noticed the desertion of his allies moments before he saw the glint of water. Then he saw the superstructure of the paddle steamer, and upon it, the head and shoulders of its captain. Crow was crouched over the rail of the bridge as though aiming his trusty Martini Henry; aiming it, moreover, exactly in their direction. Logan must have seen the danger too, for he gave a low shout: 'Look out, James.' Then, with their little guide still leading them, they burst through the tree line and entered the area of marsh-reeds and ferns that formed the soft lip of the lake. Logan was shambling along. He was all in. His breath was rasping, and so badly were his legs trembling that James thought he would buckle and fall. But, no, he would not give up his load. He grimaced determinedly and staggered on, a credit to his race. Still, they had all done well. They could all look back on this day with pride; even the boy . . . *especially* the boy. James would reward the lad when they reached the *Darling*. A hundred paces to the *Darling*; that was his estimate of the distance still to be traversed. Ninety paces . . . Eighty-nine – eighty-eight – eighty-seven paces to safety.

It was at that distance, or thereabouts, that Crow fired his rifle. A puff of smoke; a sound like a stock whip being cracked overhead. James's immediate thought was that Crow had gone bonkers, and shot the boy. Logan was obscuring James's view – but he'd heard the lad scream piercingly and jerk backwards as if struck, then go down, still screaming with terror. Then Logan toppled over too, granting James a view of the track ahead, of a snarling, spotted blur of violence, and of the thin black limbs of Monday flailing hopelessly beneath fangs and raking claws. He saw the the sabre teeth sink into the young, black neck, and tear it, the leopard's face turning red. Jets of red. James saw all this. He saw the death of Monday to its end, before he had so much as lifted the rifle in anger. So quickly, so stunningly quickly had death revealed its intention that he'd had no chance to fire. Now he would fire.

Yellow eyes held James with concentrated hate. He brought up the rifle. He aimed. He drew the weapon into his shoulder and set his sights on the beast, on the snarling, bloody head. He would have killed Logan had he fired, for suddenly it was Logan's khaki shirt that was the object of his aim. Up staggered Logan, quite cutting off his view again. James raged loudly and incoherently, which did nothing to cause Logan to subside.

Crow's Martini Henry cracked again. Logan jumped and threw up his arms, roaring with triumph.

When they reached the leopard it was barely alive. But it was Monday who looked the nearer to death of the pair. They lay facing each other those two; their lustrous eyes as close as lovers. Then the cat lifted its head and sniffed at the white men. It took the wooden fetish in its teeth, not biting, but retaining it with teeth-tips in as precious a grip as it would have held its own cub. It dropped the doll, then retrieved it. Then the light went out of its eyes. It shuddered, and lay still. Little Monday reached out his hand and stroked the dead cat's head. He ran his fingers tenderly, wistfully, into the spotted fur. And, united to his killer in this loving way, he died.

Logan, his chest still straining, bent down and retrieved the wooden man. It was wet with saliva and blood to which some segments of grass were stuck. He gazed at the fetish carving in a bewildered way, then blew a long, dismayed sigh. 'Crazy,' he whispered in the same breath. 'Madness. Total madness.' All and everything was included in this assessment. Logan held up the fetish by its leg, looking at it curiously. 'It was almost as if this was the cause of the attack; as if it killed the boy to dispossess him of this.'

'It wanted the fetish?'

'That's how it seemed. I've heard of such a legend.'

James declined Logan's hip flask as they went to Jenny. She lay where she had fallen, looking small; small and inanimate like a doll discarded after a session of play. A ring of butterflies was circling her forehead.

James noticed that there were tears in the corners of Logan's eyes. No need for tears. With emphasis on each word, James told him, 'She's not dead.'

'Help me lift her,' Logan said. 'I'm all in.'

Relief, however, in the form of the captain of the *Darling* and a knot of Negro firemen armed with axes, was fast on the way.

Thirty-eight

Out of the darkness: a pinprick of light. It expanded. It grew in size and brightened in colour. It rushed to meet Jenny; dilating and distending and coming on with such speed and intent that collision was inevitable. It met her. It absorbed and encapsulated her. It was as promised: the Table. It was set for twenty, but twice that number of guzzling, shoving gluttons were besieging it.

There was a fervid throb of drums. Antera Duke rose when he saw her come in, and wept. He provided her with a place, a chair on which to sit, then, when she was seated, he kneeled, took her hand and kissed it. He revered her with his sorrowful, disbelieving eyes, then curled up like a dog on the floor at her feet.

Captain Strangeways was watching her too; dividing his gaze between her and the heavy pistol before him on the table top. He shook his head. He passed his tongue over his lips uncetainly, then strained his head towards her and said something inaudible. But the effort of speech was too great to be sustained so he drank instead, mechanically raising and lowering his tumbler which, despite what was being absorbed from it, did not empty.

Jemmy Honesty was leering and winking, crouched over a wristful of snuff.

Mammy Yellowbelly was shrieking, spraying food and guffawing, paying not the slightest bit of attention to her guests.

That was the most striking aspect of all. The self-absorbtion. The endemic lack of interest in adjacent events. It wasn't just Mammy Yellowbelly who was infected by it. It was all of them. Everyone at that compulsory feast. It was to be expected, of course. The very merit of the event was its curse. Like Zeno's paradoxical tortoise they were without the concept of time; caught up in a race that was distanceless and impossible and could not be ended by anything less than the absolute destruction of all who were in it. And she, too, was a particle of this formula; altered, converted, doomed.

Antera was licking her toes. After a hundred years had passed he would still be licking her toes; still lethargically ignored. Even now she could feel herself slipping inevitably into this Cenozoic marsh. She could feel the onset of never-ending satiety; of the moribund principle of the table.

Mammy's whole, huge, jellylike body rippled with unshared mirth. Strangeways tried to pass on his indecipherable message, then drank, rolling yellowed eyes. Honesty was mining something out of his nose.

Then – a *revolution*. A thunderbolt in the form of King Sam.

She was shocked by the arrival of the monarch: Grandy King Sam, in spirit and in a wicked temper. There was blood all over the front of his uniform. He'd had no time to repair. He stormed in, looked around, saw the white woman who he believed had been responsible for his awful demise, and gave a wounded bellow. A chair was given to him: a chair at the opposite end of the table. He glared at her.

She cringed. Then didn't cringe, but sat forward in her chair and brazenly sneered at the new arrival, and went on sneering to the point where such blatant contempt was bound to cause an extreme reaction. Disintegrative reaction. Sam got to his feet and leaned his knuckles on the table top, and radiated hate: a livid spew of hate; an insane and disordered energy so laden with loathing that it staggered her. She rapidly calculated her course of action. The intoxicating strength that she'd prayed for before, she prayed for again. *And it came*. Holy guardian angels were near, and their rapture was upon her. She knew what she had to do, and did it. She converted to her cause the very force that was thundering at her from the monarch's end of the table – an inarticulate rage that might shatter the time-trap of Parmenidian logic – she withstood it, turned it and hurtled it back towards the tormented monarch, sweeping him back, bewildering him, further increasing the velocity of malice. So awful was the exchange becoming, so fervid the spasms of shock, that both contestants were in danger of being hurtled head over heels, out and away. The table was beginning to gyrate and the guests, screaming and whooping in the ecstasy of terror, were holding on to it as to wreckage in a violent sea.

'Do not fear,' called angelic voices.

The Watchers were back.

Hell groaned.

'Stand firm!' she was ordered.

The threshold of cohesion was reached; then exceeded. Still she might not have broken loose but for a further miracle: a battle-axe – a big, bright, spike-headed battle-axe, hurtled from a hidden hand into the vortex of the storm; into the belly of the beast, into its agony. Then all and everything ruptured, shattered, exploded and disintegrated before her eyes.

Hell opened its gullet wide and disgorged her whole.

The *Darling* had more wrong with her than had been first diagnosed. One could feel in the soles of one's feet the organic suffering; vibrations and weird, repetitive thumps. One could see it written on the face of her captain. Crow, when he was not at the wheel, could be found below, with bald head cocked in attentive observance of these various indications of decrepitude. He didn't let Logan into the secret of these ailments, but held whispered conversations with his Negro helmsman, conversations from which he broke away frowning, his jaw jutting, as though dreadfully let down by a lifelong compatriot.

Logan, acting under the captain's instructions, was keeping an eye on the only other paying passenger on that downriver voyage. He caught Crow on his way to the bridge, and had this to report of the situation: 'He's taking it badly. He hasn't come out of her cabin all day. Just won't accept that she's dead. Sits there holding her hand as though expecting her to sit up at any minute and ask for tea and toast.'

'Unhealthy state of affairs.'

'Mind you, she doesn't look dead, if you know what I mean . . .'

'Is she breathing?'

'No.'

'If she was she'd be alive.'

'No, she's not breathing.'

'Then she's dead – tragic.'

'Absolutely.'

'Dreadful blow,' Crow said distractedly. 'Beautiful girl. Dies in his arms . . . A man could go off his head.'

'I almost think he has.'

'Got to make him accept it, Logan.' He prepared to climb the ladder to the bridge. 'Tomorrow we'll reach Calbar. Give her a decent burial there . . . Tell him that. Be firm with the man. Fill his belly with whisky, then break it to him – straight to the point – "Look, old fella, she's a gonner." Just like that. Shock treatment.' As though this was his everyday experience, Crow said, 'Works every time.'

From ensnarement to freedom: from malignant depths to euphoric summits. From dark insanity to brilliant reason: from the hell of the table to the astral splendid lights. That was the route of the material of her spirit, the replica of her physical body that was now all that she owned. An extended and new conception of life, yet interpretable by old ideas. There was above, where she was going, and there was below, from where she had come; a past and a future, joined by a chord of inevitability. She rejected this experience. She felt defiant. There was a growing dissatisfaction (this, despite its glories and amazements) with her current etheric state and direction. She wanted to go back. She wanted to be alive and possessed of a body that was affected by terrestrial laws, and particularly, gravity. This release and splendid radiance was wonderful; bewilderingly beautiful, and greatly undesired. She knew, however, that her will was of secondary influence here and now. There *was* a route back and it lay through qualities that, though presently obscured by the abstraction of grandeur, would, in due course, become clear. There were rites of passage that would be of advantage to her in this quest. There was a pathway, perfectly illuminated and downwards deflected that was in itself an ignition of Life.

But, to descend she would need, firstly, to find this seminal route, and, secondly, stay on it. There was a system, and she knew it. And she also knew that there was a firmament of wrong turns and false advice, which if foolishly followed would lead into insoluble eternity. She would have to beware.

And coinciding with that thought, that recognition of the awesome problems associated with this amazing voyage, she was suddenly dazzled by a light; a magnificent light, so bright that it was lost within its own topazlike radiance. She had reached the first signpost: the sphere of Sol. The essential encounter of every ascending spirit, and a place mistaken as Heaven by most. But this was not the capital of God, not Heaven, not the true Crown of All Knowledge, which lay onwards and upwards, and which had to be attained in the pursuit of life, or even to discover the truth of death. But at least she had arrived at a point that was known to her; an azimuth by which to navigate.

Now she knew where to go, and this keen sense of direction propelled her from the brilliance of that sphere towards the looming ruby red glow of the knowledge of Strength, the light of Mars. But she only stopped for as long as it took to draw a single gasp of admiration, then she turned sharply and acquisitively like a jackdaw, fleet and sleek, attracted to the loose-lying amethyst gem glow that was the knowledge of Mercy. Nor did she stop there for longer than the beat of a wing, before switching direction once more, this time towards the deep black light that could be mistaken for no more than a hole, a vacant, staring aperture in the fabric of the sky, but which in reality was a more vital signpost than any so far passed: a celestial sea. It was the knowledge of Understanding.

She didn't arrive at this vital source of intelligence. And didn't know why. It was as if what had seemed so visible and easily attainable had vanished at the instant of reception. It had been there – in sight – an onyx lake, an Athena – protector of the brave. And what was she if not brave? Yet it had vanished, to be replaced by what seemed at first to have been caused by such a dire fall that she was stunned by it.

She found herself in a moonlit landscape of blurred but breathtaking beauty, which, once the shock of reacquaintance had worn off, yielded details of plants, of flowers and trees, such as could only be found on Earth, and the weighty scent of jasmine. The place resembled, more than anything, a jungle clearing. She was hemmed in on all sides by exquisite blooms, indigo, orange, white, red, like daubs of bright paint on a canvas of dappled black.

She was desolated by an overpowering solitude, so thoroughly pervasive that she began to weep; and in weeping she further diminished her vision and added to her confusion, though in her mind hope was growing that this awful change of circumstances might yet result in something good. And the hope grew further when on looking down she saw that where her tears had fallen, as though manufactured by the very substance of her sorrow, some crystals lay glinting in the milky light.

There were three of them; three bright reflections describing the points of a perfectly symmetrical triangle. An astrological trine as in the uranography of the Ancients? The seal of the Illuminati? Or as in the triquetrous planes of mental, astral, physical? Or as some other trimorphic truth: the father; the Son; the Holy Ghost? What imperative instruction lay concealed in this pattern of three? And what had to be done in order to apprehend this major gift? She kneeled near the ownerless objects, examining them more closely, picking them up, holding them individually in the cuddle of her palm, then replacing them. They were, she observed, very close in size and raw appearance, yet different in detail. Each piece of quartz had its own distinctive micro-character. Each was an oracle of pits and craters, crenels, flaws and seams. It was while she was thus closely engaged that something large and dark came into the corner of her vision . . . She raised her eyes.

An impressive yet previously unnoticed boulder greeted her solemnly. Its face was craggy with age, blemished with lichen. Its brow jutted sagely, and was randomly fissured by the roots of a large tree. A majestic rock. A significant rock. In three places on its face were three geometrically spaced apertures. Obvious receptacles for the crystals! That fact was immediately conveyed; as was the information that it was up to her to place each crystal in its natural home before any further advancement would be considered. The task seemed fairly straightforward, and she began to do it. And then to undo it. She sensed a rejection of her effort. It came to her that permutational complexities were involved. Not only was it required of her that she should get the right fit, but that she should do it in the right sequence. Perfect correspondence had to be achieved. She began to experiment. The task was very complex. The possibility of error was far greater than that of accuracy. She would have to be very systematic in her approach.

Advancement was essential, and there could be no advancement, no movement away from this duplicate of existence, until she'd worked through the problem. That was the Law. There was no sidestepping the Law.

She felt ignorant and in great awe. She knew, without being told, that she was involved in a process of learning. Like a thirteenth-century stargazer, she did not know what she was learning, but only that some immutable truth would ultimately take her hand. A simpleton in the service of knowledge, she felt ill-fitted to the task, but determined . . .

It was her very doggedness that caused the first disclosure: that she was a prisoner of what she had caused to exist; and she had caused nothing to exist but a series of fantastic errors. She was, therefore, less than her mistakes; less that her chimeric fallacies. Less than vacuity. Merely a thought, independent of matter. It was a disappointing revelation.

She had to find out more without delay. She continued to divine for knowledge with the crystals and the rock. Probing. Probing. Seeking the connection between rock and persona and quartz – longing to adapt to this mysterious trio of potentials, looking for the Secret, the Meaning, finding only incoherence and disorder. Frustrated by her state, resentful of her deficit, she worked, picking up and putting down; picking up and putting down . . .

It was this mood of dissent that brought out the Second Disclosure. It came as if by voice: 'Your purpose in nature is accomplished.'

How could it have been? She had, truthfully, accomplished nothing. She could not accept that life's plan for her had been so abstract and incorporeal.

'Your legacy is in spirit,' said the voice. It had come from the rock.

She answered it. 'It was a valueless life.'

'It intensified your love as nothing else could have done. Therefore it had value.'

'Is love so vital a concept?'

'It is the absolute standard; the epitomy of standards.'

'That's well known. That's no secret.'

329

'Well known, but not well received.'

True, but there had to be more to it than that. How could such superficial knowledge be at the heart of the formula? She argued: 'I was striving to achieve; to discover. I need more time.'

'There will be another time: a future time. Rebirth into a ceaseless tide.'

'I must go back.'

'You've had a second chance.'

'I want a third.'

'As it is above; so it is below. You hold it in your hand.'

'The Earth is the duplicate of Heaven, is that it? Is that the reconciliatory bond between man and his God? And does the opposite hold: as is below, so it is above? Do I hold in my hand a chance to alter the sky?'

'You do.'

Stunning! In two words, confusion was reduced to order and consistency. The Law was of action and reaction, silently and inexorably at work – shaping destiny. That was it. That was the wisdom of the ages; available to all who had eyes to see with and ears to hear with. The secret, therefore, was that there was no secret; no secret beyond that which each man had held in his own hand since the days of Adam: to love is to align with God.

'*Choose!*' said the voice commandingly.

Emotions descended on her sorely. Only by death could she remake the consequences of what, in life, she had thought and done. No evasion was possible. And only in life could she do what she had not yet done. Love was all that she had to gain by life. There was no more to it than that. To go, or to stay. It was up to her. From deep within her soul came the answer:

'I choose to go back.'

'So be it.'

The crystals were in place. And she was thrust under by the penalty of pain. Life-giving pain. The pain of Earth.

Thirty-nine

And so the story was running to an end. Not as James would have had it do so; or as the venerable Run Run had beseeched that it should though Run Run had never been forthright as to the conclusion he aspired to. But if anyone deserved to be lauded as Champion of the day, Sassabonsum did. The half-god, half-mortal Sassabonsum. For his constant challenger and single rival was dead. Dead, skinned, salted and destined to be a rug on the otherwise naked floor of Captain Crow's stateroom. An epic revenge if ever there was one, and never mind the price: the loss of his most wonderful stealer of souls.

His faithful servant, the Dream Stealer, had become, as it were, a prisoner of war. Logan still had in his possession the wooden manikin. It was, in his experienced opinion, a valuable example of antique fetish art, and quite unique. Well worth keeping. Though some might be put off by its malignant visage, he was not. In fact, in its very grimness he'd found a measure of paradoxical fellowship. This aspect wasn't available to everyone. James Tremayne, for instance, couldn't see it. He'd informed Logan that he could do whatever he liked with the damned thing, just as long as he never laid eyes on it again. Mind you, Tremayne wasn't rational, and hadn't been so since the murder of Jenny Oxenham. The poor fellow was suffocated with guilt.

Logan was pleased to hear the steam whistle blast – the *Darling*'s shrill warning to the dreamy port of Calbar that she was coming in.

It was at that precise moment that Tremayne knocked on his cabin door, and without waiting for permission to do so, came in . . . smiling from ear to ear. Came in and embraced Logan in a muscular hug of joy.